KING OF CAVANON

To Mike,
Thanks for all your support.
I greatly appreciate everything.
Best wishes in the future,
and enjoy the Story!

Your friend, the Author
Edward C. Sala

King of Cavanon

BLOOD OF HEROES

Edward C. Baker

iUniverse, Inc.
New York Lincoln Shanghai

King of Cavanon
BLOOD OF HEROES

Copyright © 2006 by Edward C. Baker

All rights reserved. No part of this book may be used or reproduced by any means, graphic, electronic, or mechanical, including photocopying, recording, taping or by any information storage retrieval system without the written permission of the publisher except in the case of brief quotations embodied in critical articles and reviews.

iUniverse books may be ordered through booksellers or by contacting:

iUniverse
2021 Pine Lake Road, Suite 100
Lincoln, NE 68512
www.iuniverse.com
1-800-Authors (1-800-288-4677)

ISBN-13: 978-0-595-39958-1 (pbk)
ISBN-13: 978-0-595-84346-6 (ebk)
ISBN-10: 0-595-39958-4 (pbk)
ISBN-10: 0-595-84346-8 (ebk)

Printed in the United States of America

Prologue

▼

Throughout his life, John Rykus never dreamed of a world beyond his grasp of vision and imagination. Content with the way things were going, he pressed on through the day-to-day activities each new day brought to him. However, one day he and his family realized the harsh truth and discovered, tragically, that what they had believed in amounted to nothing more than a fleeting moment in time, easily distorted and redirected at the mercy of whatever forces existed in the universe.

Since the nightmare began in the year 2005, the life Rykus once lived on Earth of that era changed to an entirely new perspective of the unreal. Tragedy struck the moment he and his family were taken out of the human race and thrust forward in time to a dimension laced with chaos and conflict. Forced to live a completely new life on a fierce and dangerous planet, Rykus adapted to this strange environment and sought to overcome unbelievable odds and survive in a world never known before, hell, never even *thought* of in all his previous years of life. During a perilous escape from the black fortress of the Dominion, John lost his wife, Kayla, while dodging the maze of desolation that enclosed them. Evading the enemy and escaping the fortress gave John and his surviving daughter, Sarah, the renewed ability of determination, a direction of hope, and restored fleeting, inept dreams of finding their way back to the old world.

Their course of survival forced them to interact with strange creatures and, in time, come to rely on some of them, heavily. Taken in and provided shelter from the first of his friends, Tanazakh and his family (Anadonians), they were again sheltered and protected as the Queen of the Cavanonian Empire, Xashsa, insisted they remain with them for the purposes of safety and security, and a hidden agenda she later revealed to Rykus. To be human was to be limited; Rykus discovered. However, through sanctimonious teachings, and a mind filled with fantasy and intrigue, he possessed the will to enable a subtle change in his *human* attributes and become Cavanonian, temporarily. As he lived amongst the Queen and her servants, he developed into the life force missing from their leadership and his stature elevated amongst their heavenly Ancestors as he proved not only to himself but also to those who now served him, that he was capable of defending their lives as well as his own.

The discovery and rescue of a large group of brutally molested humans instinctively triggered Adoné to provide the necessities of life to those who were of irregular instinct. The reanimation of fear came from the discovery of other humans that existed as sexual toys of play at the hands of a gruesome and unforgiving enemy. Anger, which had been dormant in John's body for decades, finally emerged and displayed itself to this enemy force, vigorously. Resistance, it seems, was a new entity to an insurmountable adversary and its agents of wickedness.

With an ever-growing community of creatures living in a undersized location, Rykus, the Cavanonians, the humans, and others in their community were forced to relocate to an area rich with abundant resources. The increase in distance from the progressively more despondent enemy fortress and their new location meant that they could live on with the hopes and dreams of a peaceful life once again…or so they thought.

Trials and tribulations affected each of the different tribes that made up the new lakeside community and tested their will to live and die. With the belief of triumph over adversity, their shredded lives regained strength despite the fact that the odds were against them. By locating to the new lakeside community, each of the creatures with Rykus and Xashsa slowly rebuilt their lives and came to enjoy the peace of the surrounding area. Lakeside offered them tranquility, peace, and a place to release their fears and tension. Many things happened in this serene environment.

Rykus further underwent change from his old self, forever shedding his outer human characteristics by transforming into a formidable Cavanonian warrior. His transformation filled the Cavanonian Ancestors with pride and contentment of his acceptance into the new race and marriage to the Queen. Friends and allies were on the rise and all in lakeside thought they were untouchable now that there was a new king amongst them. However, that dream shattered the moment Rykus learned the horrifying plan devised by the Nogzakh Forces to send him back to the past. The enemy crushed his perception and reality with the reanimation of his dead wife, Kayla. The purpose being, no more would this incessant renegade be a potential threat to the Nogzakh existence and their sole method of procuring food, simply send him back in time and be done with it. The Nogzakhs sent Rykus through the same hellish time machine by using a dagger with technology connected to the time machine protocol.

Through his disappearance, the house of Cavanon had to cope with devastating losses of the heart and regain their lives amidst the dust and sadness, and recount their blessings as the community of followers aided each other in the desperate times of need. After a period of ten years, all rejoiced as Rykus found a way to return. From that time on, he formally changed his name to "*Adoné*" and established himself back in their lives. Their determination and fortitude was stronger than ever, elevated to the status of near invincibility as they carried out unconventional attacks and ambushes on the confused enemy.

The moment in time when all seemed lost forever came when Gadnoc forces kidnapped the Queen and obliterated their community in a massive blast from an unlikely bomb. Destitute and beaten down into the ground, Adoné had to not only save this community which now depended on him for everything, but simultaneously strip his mind and heart of what actions might be happening to his beloved Queen in the clutches of a brutally unconscionable enemy.

Unlikely alliances proved a blessing in disguise as he found out that even below the surface of the planet; the very same enemy used other strange and bizarre creatures as puppets. By freeing the enslaved Srotaderp from their captivity and giving them their lives back, Adoné discovered another possible way of rescuing the Queen, one that took the work of every manner of creature that lived amongst them. By using a mined out tunnel system Adoné headed straight up and into the heart of the enemy complex.

Inside the fortress did not prove so trying a task as Adoné had experienced twice before, and this time the enemy was in for a surprise, but unknown to Adoné, so was he. His friends launched attacks on the east and west sides of the fortress to distract the enemy forces secluded inside in order to allow him, and his servants, the time needed to find his love. Once rescued, Adoné received a revelation of a shocking magnitude. He learned that all of the pain he, Xashsa, and all of his community of followers suffered was the result of an evil banished from the Cavanonian Kingdom that attempted to destroy the Crown and eliminate their race from existence. Adoné dealt with this traitor, Federoth, by subjecting him to the very same treatment suffered by the once miserable humans of Noleon. This Adoné did by subjecting Federoth to the sick vices of the Gadnoc thugs, concluding with the total annihilation of the Black Fortress itself.

The Lakeside community thought they won the day with the destruction of the enemy and the birth of the new prince. In a surprise twist of fate, Federoth escaped the destruction and threw a wayward dagger once again at the King and sent him into the netherworld, trapped and locked away, with only one way out: through the capture of his old *human* self of the past.

With the aid of the Cavanonian Crystals, Xashsa maintained constant communication with her love while he remained trapped on the other side, but efforts were already underway by the Nogzakhs to reclaim the life of John Rykus a second time and prevent this reemergence from happening. They succeeded in bringing him, singularly; to the future, which went against any programming protocol the time machine was limited too, but…successful. All instances of time travel from a desired past to the present future was limited to only three of any kind, singular snatchings were committed only by its creator. To the rest of the Dominion, time travel was widely regarded as one way.

After the death of Aurora, Ariel, the new most trusted and highly respected head servant to the Crown, interceded and rescued the *human* Rykus before the enemy had the chance to carry out their plans and prevent the Cavanonian King from returning. Once the King returned, all sensed an unknown danger that dwelt amongst them as the ungrateful Rykus rejected this new life forced upon him and vanished from their newly reformed world of Cavanon to a place filled with uncertainty and strangeness. They were unaware of the forces that took place in his mind and body, forces that none would know until later on. The main reason for the change in his character remained hidden and would be revealed later on through mysterious revelation.

Federoth had been given a second chance to carry on his command of forces, despite his failure on Earth by losing a very sizeable force of troops and equipment, and a valuable fortress stronghold that was to be an ultimate authority in that region of space. Nevertheless, the evil commander's luck was to change in a way he could not foresee: when the human Rykus inevitably fell into his clutches so soon after his emergence and escape from Cavanon. The sinister thoughts in the mind of Federoth raced a mile a minute as he succeeded in tricking the human Rykus into becoming the agent of destruction he had long desired to create through the black arts for the glory of Ellononis, the ultimate nemesis of the Crown itself.

A dreadful feeling came over the inhabitants of the house of Cavanon the same time Rykus underwent the transformation to the unhallowed creature that now breathed life. Adoné (with the aid of Tanazakh and a host of other volunteers) sought to discover the whereabouts of the human Rykus and bring him back to safety. Unfortunately, while the King stowed away inside the enemy vessel searching for his old self, the enemy ship departed from its location on Nomaseri to a planet of command and control. While inside, Adoné learned of Federoth's sinister plan to seek the total destruction of the old Dominion and its ultimate ruler, Othragon.

Unbeknownst to the King and during his infiltration of the enemy planetary stronghold, the evil Rykus had discovered the whereabouts of the location of Cavanon behind its secretly dormant curtain, hidden away from all view in space. While Adoné inadvertently helped Federoth to seek the destruction of the enemy, the evil Rykus had brought the forces of Nomaseri to Cavanon and laid waste to the inhabitants thereof, while desecrating the royal family with unspeakable acts of molestation and torture, the end result: death.

Federoth came face to face with the ruler, Othragon, and then learned that the Cavanonian King had followed him there to Dominion soil. Adoné's body instantly froze stiff since he was unaware of Othragon's inherent powers of indomitability and telekinesis. While Adoné remained in preparation of becoming dinner, Federoth sought to instill the final piece of the trigger that would set the scene of destruction on a planetary scale, which would annihilate the Dominion planet in one swift moment. Adoné, frozen to the ceiling of the cavernous hell, had relieved his spirit from his encapsulated body in time before witnessing its savage disembowelment by Othragon. Now, stuck in spirituous form, Adoné sought to repay the Dominion leader by destroying the ruler inside his own chambers. Othragon narrowly escaped his own death through a method of teleportation only moments before the planet exploded.

Upon returning to Cavanon, the spirituous Adoné discovered the devastation to his homeland and the murder of his family. Those who remained alive were shaken and desolate, no longer containing the will to carry on. Below the surface, one who had saved the prince from death had come up from underground to remain with the King, her father, and help to set things right. Laura vowed to aid her father in any way possible to fulfill a prophecy that all were unaware of, except one.

Federoth now had the ability to assume the new leadership role of the Cavanonians, but now he needed the crown. During the battle, he forgot about this one little important item and knew soon after that he would have to find it...*but where is it now?*

CHAPTER 1

▼

UNDER NEW MANAGEMENT

In a remote area of the universe, tucked away to what seemed to be the very edge of deep space, the once frozen system of Muidiri exists now only as fragments of rock and debris. The total destruction of the planet gave proof to legendary belief of the 'Big bang' theory as remnants of the system spread outward through space and traveled for great distances, unobstructed. Planetary destruction was not unheard of in this day in age, but the destruction of a Nogzakh/Dominion owned system was. It was also widely surmised by all of the Dominion species that they were untouchable, their forces formidable, and their systems impenetrable and inaccessible, oblivious to any thought of attack or campaign of destruction directed at their forces. These ideas/beliefs would now undergo change and reconstruction in order to prevent the possibility of such action from happening again.

Of the two Dominion systems that remained, Samajap is the more sizeable and strategically important. Primarily because of the bulk of the *"Fleet of Dread"* housed on this system, and because it was a secondary base for the Dominion hierarchy in what was thought to be an unlikely event of a Dominion system suffering destruction. Obviously, they had made a wise choice in its past construction. Tiracus, the lesser system, was badly in need of semi-major repairs. Once

Muidiri exploded, immense fragments of the planet flew in the direction of Tiracus and collided with the planet, creating major structural damage to the systems defenses but not actually destroying the planet itself. The outer surface consisted primarily of dried up dirt, powdery, with a subsurface composition of mostly iron ferrite and granite, mixed with a heavy-laden film of gold for the illuminating brilliance visible from space.

The nexus of the systems facilities did not exist underground as constructed on Muidiri. The hubs themselves were located above ground with troop housings and ground force equipment located in great maintenance hangars underground several hundred feet below the surface. An equally impressive underground tunnel system provided the main arteries for subsurface transportation to and from the different areas and also allowed for the outside surface hubs to be maintained by workers without having to venture out into the zero gravity surface environment. It would take some time to repair the outside structural damage to the hubs in need, but that would not detract the battle ready gun emplacements from operating along with the planetary defense system, which remained intact.

Samajap, the more formidable of the two remaining Dominion systems, suffered no damage from the explosion despite the two hundred thousand mile distance from Muidiri. Now, Samajap would be the main central base of the remaining Dominion forces, which bragged of a composition of three-fourths of the fearsome 'Fleet of Dread'. This fleet possessed a show of force that was unheard of and unmatched by anything that existed in space, at least that they were aware of anyway. Disposition of the fleet revealed more than one thousand short range fighters, two hundred destroyers and fifty main fortress cruisers, all in a state of battle readiness for anything that might come about to pose as an insignificant threat.

As in the past, the Dominion had the fleet and its arsenal of destruction within its commanding grasp, but the Nogzakhs were the key to its survival and attributed much, if not all, to its success. The Nogzakhs were small but they compensated for this limitation in the design, implementation, construction, and operation of the war machines in the Dominion arsenal.

The physical features of a typical Nogzakh creature were dissimilar to the other Dominion beings. Their boney arms extended from their tiny shoulders down to well below the knees and were able to rotate a full three hundred and sixty degrees, without such obstructions as an elbow. The body mass contained barely enough to fill the stomach of any creature that would even care to eat it. Legs that could barely be conceived as strong were lanky and possessed only the slightest amount of bioluminescent skin covering, and had larger than proportionally correct feet below them. The head was the most peculiar of all. The eyes sat in two huge sockets of blackness containing bite-sized eyeballs that were black in color and absent of cornea. There as no nose to speak of and the mouth was uppermost to their faces just below the eyes, which slightly protruded outward from an oval shaped cranium that did not contain a shred of hair. Outside of their sleep chambers, they paraded around in their normal routine wearing a brilliantly luminous bio-suit that circulated crude like substances, which comprised their systems version of blood. With their program instituted, the slimy blue Nogzakhs were pretty much left alone to follow the regular routine they had established long ago and they reacted to orders whenever received. As long as they had food, they were content.

The one characteristic of the Dominion (that would always be their ace card), was that of the undeniable existence of the time travel machines. The hellish apparatus ran continuously to provide sustenance to the Nogzakhs and other forms of life that served under Dominion rule. Not a single creature in existence, in any past time or space, was safe from randomized capture. The unwilling victims unwittingly and unknowingly played an important role in the Nogzakh survival.

With the remaining forces continually focused on improving and hardening the structural facilities with armor upgrades, heads of the *New* Dominion counsel met together to discuss the previous happenings and what the future would hold for them. There was plenty on the agenda for this meeting, and many questions answered as well. This Federoth was ready for and would provide them with the answers they would need, plus a few more just to keep the edge above their heads and their wits in check.

Twelve division commanders entered into the meeting hall. Each one with a personal security escort/duty officer present in the event an action item was important enough for consideration at any given moment. Communication requirements were of no concern at this stage, there were plenty to go around but it was not necessary to broadcast this meeting out to the masses; others outside the meeting would receive information as it passed down from superiors to subordinate commanders, etc. Still, there was much talk and conjecture throughout that had every one of them wanting answers. The Commander of the Ellis Fighter Regiment was the first to burst out his comments.

"Well, I for one have no knowledge of any type of attack launched against us," he commented forcefully. "If there had been any type of force, significant or otherwise, we would have been alerted and the fighters would have launched automatically according to reactionary programming protocol."

"It did not appear to be any kind of attack, Segnach," said the Division Fortress Cruiser Commander, Dehllia. "The planet appeared to have exploded from the inside. Even if an attack were proven, there is nothing in the universe with the amount of firepower that could have completely destroyed Muidiri, except one of our own Fortress Cruisers."

The Commander of the ERMS (Epoch Retrieval and Management System), Rachaz, had to add his findings into the mix of conjecture.

"There has been a serious disruption in the deep space reclamation process at precisely the same period of time the explosion occurred."

Gazing at the other officers who surrounded the table, it was apparent that Rachaz would have to explain his answer down to the level of understanding of the others. Not because of their obvious inability to comprehend, but because the technical nature of the findings revealed was clearly above their grasp.

"Obviously, the Absolute, the supreme ruler Othragon himself, must have been destroyed in the process," Segnach commented. "Therefore, whatever initiated the explosion would have had to come from the inside—exactly where Othragon subsisted."

"You must further elucidate this cause you've dreamed up," Segnach said for all, "or we'll all be staring into oblivion by the time you are finished."

"Fine," Rachaz sighed. "Othragon was, as we all know, a creature of *pure energy* and a massive coagulation of powers beyond our sphere of knowledge. It could be that the initiator or igniter set off the explosion inside his quarters, which amplified his energy further enhanced by the thermal generation system within the nexus of the core power cells. To put it in terms even you can understand…something inside set off the explosion in the cavern that started a chain reaction."

There was a slight upheaval of sighs around the table. "Then why didn't you just say that before, instead of taking pleasure in hearing yourself talk? Calculated procrastination does not sit well in this environment."

"Segnach," said Rachaz, "you of all officers should take pride in meaningful conversation instead of simple truths; it would detract from our inherent superior attributes further enhanced by virtue of rank."

The Commander of the Rhineous Destroyer Division whispered to a colleague seated to his left, "I am convinced that in Rachaz' mind he is a self-propagating species." The comment received a nod of acknowledgement.

Outside in the hall the inflated, malevolent Federoth monitored the conversations taking place in the conference room through a monitor, viewing the reactions to the proposed reasons of why the planet exploded in the first place. If they all knew what he knew, they would surely have him strung up by his entrails and subjected him to a bath in boiling acid. When the conversations inside seemed to take pause, Federoth and his 1st Officer Slagis at last made their entrance.

Federoth heightened his posture as he entered in and for various reasons, namely to show that he did not have to report to anyone. He was in charge of himself, but now to instill the belief that he was in charge of all forces. The meeting continued with a stern look to all of the department representatives. A glaring look of seriousness and conviction covered Federoth's face while hiding both his contentment and excitement of finally being in total achievement of his goals. Resentment towards this self-centered Commander was evident within the ranks. Each division head became uneasy and apprehensive of his character, mainly due to the widespread hearsay and rumors of his unquestionably forceful techniques of information extraction, mixed with the unjustified reports of his activities concerning the Black Arts of his extinct heritage.

"If you only knew what I knew," Federoth began, "you would very quickly disregard your previous suppositions."

"Federoth," Dehllia interjected boldly, "why have you called this meeting and then plague us with your presence?" This commented only entertained the controlled look of aggression blatant in Federoth's expression. "Why, it is as if you assume you are in charge of us!"

The officer sat back relishing his open criticism, approval signified by all who sat around the table. Vacant expressions gave way into snickers and contemptuous laughter, which only enraged Federoth's already heightened anger even further. With controlled movement and forcibly controlled anger, Federoth positioned himself close to Dehllia and swiftly thrust a jagged, double-edged dagger into the base of his skull. The sudden trauma caused uncontrollable spasms and putrid green slime to erupt violently from his mouth and eye sockets, splattering with a gelatinous texture all over the luxurious conference table. The security personnel of the dead commander did not possess a hint of concern or motion to intercede. All of the other commanders jumped from their seats in shock.

"*Federoth!*" exclaimed Segnach. "What is the meaning of this? What rights have you to kill one of our own?"

"*BE SILENT!*" the Commander shouted in return. "Before Othragon died, he placed *ME* in charge of these forces. Primarily because of my leadership abilities and secondly because I've also knowledge of the one who is responsible for the destruction of Muidiri and our Supreme Ruler."

Stunned with the sudden revelation of this news, the counsel of officers remained motionless for a minute or two, then. As the security personnel carried off the remains of the dead commander, they all one by one sat down in their chairs and waited for the rest of the explanation.

"I was summoned to his cavernous lair by his personal order," Federoth explained, "and once inside he revealed a hard truth to believe. It was his determination that out of all the ranks of officers contained in his massive forces, I alone was the one to lead them as demonstrated by capturing the one evil Cavanonian being that could ultimately destroy him."

"I find that a hard truth to believe as well," commented Segnach, who by now was straining desperately to keep from striking out at the arrogant bastard.

"But it was a truth that he did not deny, and an order he gave without hesitation." Federoth circled around the table slowly, viewing all with a sinister red glow of his eyes. The look alone was enough to make the hairs on the backs of their necks stand up and cause shivers to run down their weak spines.

"Unfortunately for Othragon, the captured Cavanonian King had a bomb strapped to him," Federoth lied, "and pulled the timer after it was revealed. I attempted to disarm the bomb, but Othragon threw me out of the room issuing his orders that I was to get out and take control of his forces before it was too late. Then, as I made it to my ship, I felt a great rumbling below the surface. Afterwards, I witnessed first hand the devastation caused by the insurgent which killed our ruler."

Everyone pondered his explanation for a few moments thereafter, struggling to rationalize and verify if this was in fact the truth of the matter at all. A vague haze of doubt loomed over the hall and drenched the occupants with even more questions of uncertainty and reservation. At the end of the table sat Delushan, the Commander of the C2 facility within the main hub system on Samajap, and the one who monitored the destruction from his own office. "If what you say is true," he said, "than in essence, you *did* deliver the one who would ultimately destroy our ruler…didn't you?"

Federoth had perceived the notion of doubt would raise its ugly head, and prepared for it. "I received a communication from Othragon stating that I was being followed from within the complex of the planet. He instructed me to come to his chambers and, indirectly, deliver the enemy into our rulers' hands. I was following Othragon's order without question as you, no doubt, would have done had you been in my position."

"But," Delushan continued, "didn't you at least question how the Cavanonian even came to be in our planets structure to begin with? I am confused about how this intruder could have slipped past our security in the first place. Mind you, our ruler knew such things as none would ever possess the power to do ourselves. But, if he did do as you say and gave you both orders to take control of the forces of his command *and* save your life before his untimely death, then surely he must have had a better reason."

"One thing is obvious," said Segnach, "whatever the reason, it has traveled to the great beyond with him. It seems that you get the benefit of the doubt, Federoth. But that does not make you the wisest choice by far."

"We shall see Segnach," Federoth replied. "For now, we have much to do in preparing our defenses on Tiracus; return to your posts!"

Immediately the room vacated as if some odd smell entered and wreaked its vileness on its contents. Federoth salivated over his conduct and initial contact with the heads of subordinate departments. Despite the lack of respect shown to him, he would have his little ways to yet instill fear and dread in their insignificant lives, and right now was not the time to apply undue pressure. In time, they would see his way…or suffer.

One by one, the other subordinate commanders caught the transport to their own place of control, to catch up on other briefings and status of systems. Work was always common and to keep up with the condition of critical systems and not be caught with a surprise outage. Higher HQ would never stop hounding the culprits when they discovered glitches in the signal matrix.

Before they split up into separate transports, Delushan and Segnach had a few more things to say.

"Personally," said Segnach, "I don't see how he can even live with himself; all puffed up with pride and swelling from the stench of his own hot air."

"I, for one, have never been able to stand for his demeanor," replied Delushan. "To even think of bastardizing our rulers name with his wretched lies turns my stomach to rot! We should take him out while we yet have the opportunity," Segnach suggested.

"Be on your guard, Segnach," Delushan warned, "one thing I have learned in all my years of dealing with Federoth is that he has moles in nearly every department of our forces. Although I detest his incredulous attitude, its best to keep such ideas locked away for your own sake, lest a dagger find its way secretly into your head as well."

"So, you're saying we should go along with what he said?" his comrade in arms questioned with a staggering look about his face, doubled with erratic breathing which signified his stirring outrage.

"No," answered Delushan calmly, "but I am stating a mere fact. Let him think he has won the day and is in charge after all; that will give us all the time we need to deduce for ourselves whether or not he is telling the truth. For I have seen things of Othragon with my own eyes and heard with my own ears of the magnitude of power inherent in his being. He would not have perished as easily as was stated. Exercise patience my friend, in time you will come to see my reasoning."

"I hope you are correct!"

In another part of Samajap, away from the busy activities associated with the base operations, Federoth stood in his very spacious and austere office area listening in on the conversation between Delushan and Segnach. Federoth had learned of the locations of hidden audio devices secretly placed throughout the entirety of Dominion property. One could listen in on just about anyone, anywhere, and at any given time…so much for information being 'close hold.' As he listened, discontent surfaced with respect to the nature of the dialogue, which clearly indicated that these disbelieving subordinates were going to provide no end of trouble for him.

"Seems to me that you weren't as effective as you thought you were."

This comment came from a darkened area of the office with barely enough light to indicate there was even an area empty to begin with. The occupant of the space had made his own way into the luxurious office suite prior to anyone's arrival. The mere fact that he gained entrance at all without detection revealed a weakness in security. Here was another security issue without a solution, but one that would not be made known to others and not require spontaneous resolution.

Federoth paced the floor in a more controlled manner with thoughts of how best to deal with these malcontents. A more forceful technique would be required and one not as permanent as killing Dehllia. He would eventually run out of commanders at that rate. Whatever his decision, it must be convincing in a way that would leave no further doubt in anyone's mind as to who would be giving the orders.

"Eventually, they will see my way of thinking and come to recognize the truth," Federoth stated, "even though I lied about a majority of the main issues, per se. But, that is for me to know and for them to never find out, *Rykus*."

The evil agent of Federoth's creation sat slightly puzzled as he leaned back in his chair facing the desk, propping his feet on top and enjoying a pleasant concoction of something potent enough to have smoke billowing over the brim. "Correction Federoth, it's not '*Rykus*' to any further extent. That name no longer holds any meaning with me. From now on, refer to me as '*Nosrévis*'."

"Nosrévis?" asked Federoth, as he stared out the window at the vast expanse of the interconnected Dominion fortress tunnel systems half below the surface. "Where did you get that name?"

"Check the Book of the Zalestole which you read from when you created me," Nosrévis replied. "You will see that the meaning of Nosrévis is synonymous with first of my kind created centuries ago, which received the title of 'Scourge of Cavanon'; I am the Firebrand. It was passed on long ago to one who brought pestilence and death to many a star system long before they attempted to destroy the father of the now dead Queen Xashsa."

"It seems I am in need of a history lesson then," replied Federoth, while making his way to the salon filled with a wide variety of rustic bottles. The only choice here was which poison to fancy his fetch. After a few choice tastes from a tarnished old chalice, his mind entertained other thoughts that would slightly change the subject.

"It seems your methods of dealing with the Cavanonian monarchy were more effective than even I had dreamed," Federoth commented. "I wasn't sure if you were up to the level of malevolence needed in so short a time."

A blindingly wicked smile came across the face of the created killer, a smile that showed more pride in his actions than Federoth knew in his heart. To see the shrewdness of his being, coupled with the manipulatively evil mind, proved more than Federoth knew.

"That was just the beginning," Nosrévis said. "I must graciously thank you for bringing my character fully into being and allowing me the opportunity to be all that I can."

"And what of your old human nature, the compassionate being you once were...surely you miss your old self?" Federoth asked him inquisitively. He remembered how well his trickery had played into the hands of the Rykus he had captured and converted on his ship, the thought had crossed his mind of whether or not the fully developed Nosrévis harbored some ill-will against his maker. No matter if there was or was not, it would be prudent for Federoth to be on his guard anyhow, just in case.

"Ha," Federoth's evil creation laughed, "I was never really happy with my past life anyway. What transpired after my materialization into this time did elevate my animosity toward whatever caused it. However, further humiliation by those bastards back on Cavanon only fueled the fire and caused me to forgive my initial captors. It was a good thing you found me when you did, otherwise I would probably end up dead without knowing what I could become."

"But, it was the fault of the time machine of the Nogzakhs who brought you into this era; certainly you are angered at them for setting the scene that placed this enactment in motion."

"On the contrary," Nosrévis answered, "I *should* be thanking them as well. If they did not bring me here, then I could never be what I am now, nor would I ever know the power in which I have become."

"Then shall we toast to your new found glory!" Both of them smacked their chalices together and drank of the substance. A feeling of calmness fell over the room and on their chairs, causing them to relax and sit back a bit. "So," Federoth spoke up, "what shall we do now that Cavanon is no more, Hmm?"

"I do regret that I was not able to seek out that Adoné fellow," his evil friend said. "I would have so loved to show him a thing or two that I have learned so far, I suppose now I'll never get the chance at a good rival."

Federoth himself was not at all happy with the way things transpired; he himself robbed of the chance as well had he known that the enemy was in his midst the whole time while on Muidiri.

"The moment I saw him appear in the chambers of Othragon, I knew I wouldn't get the chance at *my* revenge. Standing in his presence instinctively told me that. But to see the ruling monarch materialize there, in the cave, right in front of me left me feeling more vulnerable and exposed then ever I had been."

"So, he caught you with your pants down; don't you think he would have done a lot more if things hadn't transpired the way they did?"

"I suppose your right, but nevertheless I should eventually get back to the practices of the black arts. I have seen my weakness and I must rectify my ignorance. My main goal is still the matter of the Fire Sword of Solisynas, I must find it."

Nosrévis glanced up at his friend with a look of curiosity, wondering what importance a simple sword could have. "And what's so great about a fire sword? Not that I've had the pleasure of viewing such a rarity, but my interest is peaked."

"The Fire Sword of Solisynas," he went on to explain, "was the original sword of the very first Cavanonian monarch ever to rule the empire; it was created by the Ancient Gods. The Sword was seldom used or seen and remained so elusive and mysterious that all of the ancestors dating back to the beginning of our time had never known the nature of its true identity."

"So you're saying that omnipotent beings created a sword of fire and gave it to the first created Cavanon? Is that correct?" asked Nosrévis.

"Precisely, the sword is the key to the crown. The fire that surrounds the sword burns perpetually, signifying the everlasting authority to whoever possesses it." Federoth spoke solemnly as he glided over to pour himself another drink, as well as attending to his guest's desire for a refill.

"So why not just search for the crown itself?" Nosrévis asked. "Shouldn't it be back on Cavanon somewhere, or is it much more *mysterious* as well?"

Federoth laughed, "There is no *real* crown per se. That is because the sword *is* the crown!"

"And have you ever seen such a thing in you life?"

Federoth cast a sigh of regret from his face and a slight blemish of dismay appeared in his eyes. "The last time I saw that sword was in the hands of my very own enemy, Adoné, and he is no more. So, the problem then becomes; if he is dead, where is it?"

"Maybe you should check the history books, assuming that you *have* any," Nosrévis suggested. "They might provide some more insight on some situation such as what you've described. I mean, if it is that important then it cannot simply vanish for all time without showing up somewhere else. After all, there are still Cavanon such as us alive and if we were to find it…?"

"Then one of us would be the ruling authority," Federoth stood firm, "which by right is mine!"

"Yeah, okay, you are the *ruling authority* then," Nosrévis laughed. "I've no such appetites for elevating my status to an authoritative parliamentary figure, and I've much more to do with my own time." He adjusted his position in the chair. "Why do you want the sword so much if you do not wish to represent Cavanon anymore?"

"Simple," Federoth smiled, "I will taunt the Ancients who forbid me to have it, plus I would use it to create a race for the glory of Ellononis, whose descendants gave me another chance at life, and revenge."

A break in the dialogue came as the monitor brought on an image of the Nogzakh officer on duty. "Commander Federoth," the voice broke in sounding rather monotonous and uninterested.

"Yes what is it?"

"The Nogzakh leader requests counsel with you."

"Fine, tell him I will meet with him after the next shift change."

"Yes, Sir."

"Well," Nosrévis said, "I guess you have more important matters to attend to."

Federoth nodded and slightly waved, "I'm sure it is nothing more than administrative responsibility and nothing to really enhance excitement."

"Then I will leave you to your tasks, administrative duties do not concern me nor peak my interest. Besides, I have other matters of relocation to attend to."

"Where will you go?" asked Federoth, "I need to be able to reach you should the need arise."

"Once I've established myself, I will send word," Nosrévis replied. "Who knows, with the aid of the Nogzakhs, maybe a hub system on another planet would ease the travel?"

"Understood and approved, keep me informed."

"As you wish," replied Nosrévis, and he departed the office.

Federoth wandered the huge, almost vacant halls of the darkened structure while remnants of the previous conversation still raced through his mind. The facts stated earlier only heightened his curiosity of the possible disposition of the sword in question, and gave rise to the thought of its current location. The possibilities seemed limitless and they were almost futile to ponder, yet still he could not help but lose his place in contemplation and supposition. Others, aware of his passing, felt that distance was best as the new Commander of Forces wandered the hall preoccupied in his mind-set. Perhaps his mind engaged in other activities related to duty, but it was better to avoid the deranged officer and any unwarranted interruptions.

The long journey between halls, stations, and hubs took a considerable amount of time before he arrived at a completely isolated and secluded hallway with only one entrance; located down a smoky, yet bitterly cold passageway. An eerie mist, cloud like in nature, rolled gently against the dark blue and grey spackled floor, colliding in slow motion with the ancient stone cased walls on both sides. This would be quite the chilling view for one who was not wise as to the very nature of the Nogzakhs themselves. The hallway seemed endless as torch lit lights hung from the ceiling every twenty feet or so and extended off into the barely lit horizon some one thousand feet ahead. As Federoth moved forward, each step caused him to remember the first time he met the ones who would be more dependable then any other creature he had ever known.

The mind of Federoth drifted back to the day when King Solisynas sentenced him to banishment from his homeland of Cavanon. Federoth's persecution for the crime of treason against the crown was swift and furious, and so was the judgment handed down. The banishment to the frozen wasteland served a fitting sentence for a traitor such as him. Bound by chains and manacles, security couriers transported the prisoner on a waiting ship from a nearby system headed in the direction intended. Once in the atmosphere of the frozen planet, the guards threw him out of the ship onto the ice and snow below, and left Federoth to fend for himself, or die trying. One thing Federoth did note in this bone chilling tundra of desolation, King Solisynas was so outraged and wrathful that he overlooked one important step.

Usually, the banished being was de-spirited (a process of removing the soul). The extracted soul remained in a sacred steel container and dispatched to the other side of the galaxy, leaving the body as a walking automaton for eternity, never to see the light of day. This did not happen to Federoth; perhaps the King was forgetful and hasty in his decision. What a lucky break for the condemned Federoth. The entire ordeal had been a rush job.

Federoth wandered about the frozen surface finding no shelter from the blisteringly icy winds that whipped his face and hands, legs and torso, gripping his skin in its penetrating teeth. Unrelenting and unforgiving, the tundraic covering produced nothing of empathy for this condemned insignificant, and would not stand for a blemish on its stain free skin to remain above ground. A few steps in either direction did not matter at all, as the view through the icicles in Federoth's blood red hair gave the same picture in all directions. Stumbling feverously back and forth did nothing but topple his body from its already weakened and frozen knees.

A fall to the snow seemed to be a blessing in disguise as the thin coat of white gave way into a series of ice caves miraculously located beneath his location. His body took a hell of a beating as it fell against numerous ledges and underground glaciers, hurling him further down at an angle into depths unknown until all at once the limp twisted body of Federoth crashed against a wall of steel.

When his eyes did open again, they did not see the shivering attributes of the barren arctic wasteland. Instead, he viewed a room billowing with soft smoke and mist, with a glow of bluish illuminations in the air. The temperature was considerably chilling to the touch of the steel rails of his bed, but not nearly as punishing as the outside air. Blankets covered his bed and body, providing him some warmth and protection to put him at ease and comfort his already painfully shaken limbs and bones. An ever-brighter light positioned behind him and well back from view covered the immediate area where he remained. Federoth's eyes could barely make out any other revealing features of the room other than what the smoke allowed.

Gentle footsteps echoed through what he perceived to be a hallway, but the acoustics did not reveal the direction from which way they emanated. As he slowly moved his ache-ridden head left, there he could see the weirdest creature possible. The slimy bluish thing standing before him did not make any sounds or emissions to acknowledge his presence, but instead immediately pressed a button that was out of the patient's sight. This action produced a machine that lowered from above and covered his body from head to toe with a flickering blue light that changed intermittently to red at certain stages of its program. Federoth noticed the pulsating light changed to red whenever it passed over a damaged area within him and he instantly felt the slightest tingle of pain, and then felt it disappear as fast as it began. No longer able to remain conscious, his head lolled to his left as far as it would fall and he remained unconscious for as long as his body needed to repair itself.

After an undetermined period, he awakened and felt safe and alive once again. The pain that he felt inside, however long ago, was gone, vanished from within as though it had never been. A small group of maybe three or four of what he perceived as doctors entered the room and stood before him. Their features were the same as the one seen earlier during the observation. At once, he noticed heads of oval proportions absent of hair, eyes without pupils and black as night itself, lanky bones for arms, legs, and overly proportional feet at its base. All of which covered a thin blue film of a bio-illuminant matter, under which thin lines of brilliantly lighted cogitative matter visibly displayed blood circulation.

They motioned for Federoth to rise up and stand. This would take some doing, as there was no telling how long he had been incapacitated. Trying as it was, he stood up with some degree of difficulty but not without help by the four, each positioned to a side of him for balance. After slowly parading down a short hallway, they brought him into a room with rudimentary tables and chairs on one side and three or four modern standard metal closets on the other. Three of the doctors positioned Federoth by a table as another retrieved fresh new clothes in which to dress him. In no time, he was a brand new being, freshly clothed and very hungry.

The next room contained a large dining area with a multitude of other creatures choking down on whatever was available from a feeding line loaded to the gills with different variations of meat and other assorted body parts. Questions of finding such food surfaced immediately as he recalled nothing visible on the surface. Nothing could survive the intense bitter cold and live. So where did they get this? Those and other questions left his mind as soon as he sank his teeth into what used to be an arm of some creature. The seared flesh wept of some red substance out of a vessel or possibly an artery, but no matter, the taste pleased him and felt good churning in his stomach. Other creatures took a few seconds to glance over this new arrival and there Federoth noticed hideous creatures he would later befriend as his trusted Gadnoc thugs on Earth in a future time.

When Federoth finished the meal, the Nogzakhs led him through a maze of hallways and tunnel systems that eventually emptied out into a vast meeting hall with many of the same Nogzakh creatures tending to various duties on their interconnected system of monitors and TV screens. The main operations area, it seems, was well in working order. Unnoticed by the busy workers on the operations floor, Federoth glided along a path to the outer walls in order to keep out of the way of the workers. From here, he reported directly into the chambers of the Nogzakh leader, where Federoth would not only meet the principle director of his forces, but also would receive introductions to the other various Dominion commanders and learn then of what his new role in life would be.

A door to his front opened gradually and interrupted his daydream. Through the doorway, the bellowing mists outside slowly penetrated the exposed atmosphere of the area, distorting the view directly to his front and dancing hazily in the light. The room was simple in construction; an ancient wall of stone, which encircled the room, allowed for a center area of approximately one hundred feet in diameter. No windows were visible; torches lined the walls about ten feet up and spread out in an orderly fashion all the way around the room. A two-foot wide grating circled around an immense stone shrine in the very center of the room. Under the grating, a small canal of boiling water emitted large amounts of steam into the air, giving a mystical impression all around the shrine. This was Irol's rumination chambers, and his own private space for contemplation and meditation of Nogzakh religious mysticism. Federoth knew he was not here for a sermon, but understood that this was a comforting place for the mystic to hold a tranquil and peaceful discussion.

Irol's nature was the very same as the other Nogzakh beings in that much of the same physical features was evident, with a slight modification to his attire of course. Dressed in galactic antediluvian garb, the composition of the coverings boasted of an intricate woven system of luminous lights throughout the edges of the extraterrestrial material. The texture of the inner material itself consisted of a crude covering of leather from head to toe, with scaly plates feathered one above the other. Upon his brow sat a pontificate sort of headdress one would see in such pious figures of exemplary status.

"It seems that many decades have passed since I last saw you, Federoth," said Irol. His voice was clear and concise, a bit on the high side and slightly below the level of ominous, yet comforting to the commander. "The recent events of destruction have weighed heavily in my mind and psyche; perhaps you can enlighten me as to the nature of its source?"

Federoth sat upon a simple stone block in front of Irol, elevated so that the two were of equal height. "I assure you, first and foremost, that what has transpired will never happen again."

"And how can you make such a claim of assurance unless, of course, you have good reason?" Irol asked.

"I am aware of what has caused this destruction, yes." Replied Federoth calmly. "There were multiple factors involved which set off a chain reaction that destroyed the system. Othragon, along with his enemy and mine, had set the stage for their demise."

"Unfortunate this is," Irol sighed, "and strange how the ominous ruler of the Dominion realm could be erased so easily. I must contemplate this thoroughly, for my feelings tell me otherwise unless my sadness consumes my rationality."

"I wouldn't trouble yourself too much, you're Excellency," said Federoth, "I'm sure that whatever the true reason is for this unfortunate accident, in time it will manifest itself and become understood."

"It is sad that an occurrence such as this was required for us to have this little visit, my friend. I remember the day we found you as if it were only hours in the past."

"It was a sad day in my lineage," Federoth lowered his head, "one of regret for the things I had not the chance to accomplish, and the unjustified reasons for expulsion from my own homeland."

"But as I recall," Irol added, "you did finally wreak havoc against those who were responsible for your unwarranted exile, by utterly erasing all life of their kind in one swift stroke."

"That is true," Federoth replied, "and a great day it was indeed for the untold acts of terror and fear that brought forth their cries and at once, silenced! However, I am sure you remember the situation reports sent back to you regarding a race of creatures that plagued us for much of our time-spent dwelling and colonizing the Earth system. There, we discovered some remnants of the Cavanonian Empire that had escaped my wrath and started all over again with the emergence of a new male species within its ranks. That same enemy who had destroyed my fortress base was also the one who initiated the destruction done to our ruler and planet."

"You know, Federoth," Irol, leaned forward, "everything in the universe that happens is done so for a specific purpose. Whether or not we are aware of that purpose is inconsequential, but rather how we guide our actions to meet with *our* specific purpose is what should be upper most in your thoughts. It seems to me, that something else as guided this purpose and unleashed actions, which affected more than just your forces on another planet. Perhaps, with this incident, another purpose has been initiated on a much greater frame of reference?"

"I apologize you're Excellency," he said in a confused state, "but could you elaborate a bit more on your explanation?"

"To put it mildly, as to not insult your intelligence Federoth, I was guiding my thoughts to a point of fact that maybe what has transpired has done so according to a higher arrangement."

"But that is ridiculous," he replied, "no one controls or guides us."

"No," Irol replied, "not openly and with no amount of direct control or involvement. But on a much grander scale, universally there are forces at work in the netherworld which affect more than one may know about."

"Now you have me thoroughly confused, Sir."

"My Friend," Irol explained, "you control the forces of our command and their functions and actions. The smaller and lesser creatures, which make up our mutual Dominion, have their own actions and functions that they themselves control and coordinate. In the netherworld, spiritualities in the constant are at work themselves continually influencing our inevitable purposes to meet a desired outcome for us all. There are prophecies which have yet to be fulfilled and destiny awaits them."

"Then, this was destined to happen?" asked Federoth, "but to what end and purpose?"

"Destined, yes, but to know its purpose would be to travel to the end of its term to find out, and discover its meaning when the precise moment arrives. I speak specifically of the return of Ellononis."

"Ellononis!" exclaimed Federoth, "you know this to be true?"

"Yes," Irol answered. "It is written in his holy words left to us long ago, but only those of us graced by his blessings can understand its meaning and decipher it clearly."

"When is this to happen then?" asked Federoth, "and what events will lead up to this, can you tell me?"

"This can only come about through significant events. Unfortunately for you, you must hear this and be disturbed by revelation." Irol readjusted his bearing and continued. "Othragon cannot be dead as he will play an integral part in the rebirth of his Lord. Othragon is the Son of Zalestole, who is the son of Ellononis. He has the power of reincarnation and cannot die. However, of all the created beings, only one can undo the rebirth and if this elusive being were not alive, the prophecy could not come to pass."

"I'm almost afraid to ask who this elusive being is," said Federoth.

"It is your nemesis, the Cavanonian King."

"He's alive?" Federoth scoured, "how can that be? He was destroyed in the blast that annihilated Muidiri."

"Unbeknownst to you, the King of Cavanon has unlimited power and split himself from the physical realm and now exists in the ethereal. The sword you seek resides with him as well. But there is hope for you still to acquire this sword since it is the one item that is needed for the return of our beloved, Ellononis."

"So if my enemy is alive, then that must mean that Othragon is alive, too, but where?"

"I've no concrete thoughts as to where he could be, but he will return when the time is right. You must be on your guard, search out this enemy King, and obtain the sword of fire. Without it, the reemergence of Ellononis will be brief."

"I must do it through the best manner of trickery and disguise that I have ever used," said Federoth, who was already running circles in his mind to come up with the ultimate plan. "There is no way he would give it to me freely, I tried that. I shall have to use alternative method."

"Then you have your tasks and should be at them," replied his Excellency.

"Don't you ever become bored in this place?" Federoth hinted at the particular state of apparent dilapidation of the room.

"Never," replied Irol, "for what seems uninteresting to you, does not necessarily mean so to me."

At the end of his statement, the room took on a very different viewpoint. With a whirling momentum of wavelike energy, the walls and ceiling vanished from their apparent position of permanence revealing the magnificent view of a very different planet. Immense wide-open plains filled of green and yellow grasses caressed the gently rolling hills with its touch. Off in the distance, the granite sentinels of might stood in the way of anything that would attempt passage into the great forests of the other side. Thick rolling clouds glistened from the brilliant nearby starlight that barely penetrated its outer covering. A heavenly view painted in front of Federoth and was a remarkable sight. Federoth cold only stare at its marvel, its grandeur, and magnificence. For the first time in his life, he understood beauty and the effects it would have if one were appreciative of such sights.

"Now," said Irol, "if you will forgive me, my friend, I must return to my meditations. The Ancients of Ellononis must be appeased. Please do not hesitate to stop by more often."

"That I will do, you're Excellency," bowed Federoth.

As the darkness brought on the inevitable daily signs of fatigue, one by one each creature of the day shift filtered their way into their sleep chambers for the night. As with all creatures, rest was a necessity and virtually nothing could survive without it, unless you were a machine of the Nogzakhs.

The machines or Zeka's themselves, were not a form of Artificial Intelligence. They were more of an intelligent armed conveyance programmed to do certain functions if unmanned. This was the case of their creation when they had ultimately destroyed their creators due to a huge programming error. A glitch in the system unknown until the Nogzakhs had come upon their system sometime afterwards. The Nogzakh creatures could understand the language of the machines easily and quickly rectified the problem, which in turn made the machines subservient to their new friends. By understanding the nature of the machines, they formed an alliance with these creatures of metal, wires, computers, and steel. Maintenance was necessary and as long as the Nogzakhs kept up the routine repairs and preservation, together they would be unstoppable.

Once the Zeka's and the Nogzakhs came together, they joined with the dreaded Dominion hierarchy for an extra shield of protection when news of the Dominion had spread throughout the galaxy as a terror without remorse or fear. Since then, they have enjoyed a uniqueness of kinship and protection. With the Dominion time machine, the difficulty of continually seeking sustenance no longer posed a problem, and it only encouraged them to work harder and more diligently toward Dominion goals and struggles. The enemy achieved total power and stability.

Later that evening, as Federoth slept, visions of some unforeseen event plagued his thoughts and permeated his dreams. Sweat began to drip off his forehead as he tossed and turned from a restless spirit struggling to cope with the visions. All at once, he jolted and sat up—a nightmare? Possibly, but one that would cause him to shudder in fear of the possibilities of what could come about if, in fact, his visions were true.

Simultaneous with Federoth's frightening vision, Nosrévis sat upon a large chair in his own private suite aboard a Dominion Destroyer headed for a set course. He had heard about possible systems that could support life forms such as his and now he was out to search for whichever one would catch his fancy. While lost in sleep himself, he suddenly jerked up and forward to catch himself from totally falling out of his chair. "What the hell was that?" he murmured to himself while straining his eyesight as if to peer inside his own mind. He was unaware of the nature of the nightmare. However, he would no doubt come to know in time.

Chapter 2

Strange New Worlds

On a damp, musty floor covered with dirt and grime stood a menacing creature with a purposeful vision. This vision would shake the ethereal world with a jolt and ultimately send shock waves through the galaxy. And what of the intended victim in the vision? He would never know what importance his character held in the mind of this soon to be captor. Coordinates had been set and the program instituted, beginning its phase one sequence without the worry of malfunction. Malfunction wasn't even a concern. Even if it did breakdown from the raw energy of wrapping the time dimension, the target would be well on the way after the sequenced keyed a lock. As the creature stood on shaky ground inside a huge underground expanse, a lock engaged and the target summoned; everything was going according to programming. Now it would be just a matter of time before his prize catch would be in his possession once again and the state or possibility of worry forever removed from thought.

Back on Earth of 2004, a year earlier than the previous dates of initial time travel, John Rykus and his family sat on a porch swing in front of their home. Sarah sat in the yard playing with the two Shih-Tzu dogs and enjoyed the school free time of summer. The summertime breeze gave them a warm feeling of a carefree attitude that usually went hand in hand with laziness. The long hot days moved out of the way of the evening and allowed a tranquil peace to linger in the air.

It had been some time since John had the weird dreams that somewhat haunted him. He had bad dreams before, as did everyone else, but these were different. Sequential dreams, which continued every night for weeks. The types of creatures and circumstances he dreamt about appeared disturbing and relentless. John Rykus laughed about it often and knew that the chances of his dreams actually coming true were remote, much like visits from aliens. It took him awhile, but he was able to shake himself of the plaguing dreams and get on with life. Every now and then, a fleeting glimpse of the dreams came back. Flashes of scenes horribly familiar yet never known before popped into his brain and vanished just as quick. Medication seemed to be the key that kept his sanity from escaping him.

Today, as they sat swinging, John and Kayla reviewed Sarah's school report card that had just arrived in the mail. Sarah did not look up or appear worried at all. She was a straight 'A' student and excelled in all areas of education. Her parents were overjoyed at her grades and aptitude and often wondered where she got her smarts. John and Kayla knew that she appeared as a typical teenager and often tested the waters, as teenagers are prone to do. However, in school, Sarah was just the opposite; her attention focused to the instruction, unwavering in determination to be the best. She was a model student and had very impressive abilities in the eyes of her teachers. Why they could not have more students like her was a mystery. This day would change the face of what they knew was real. A change was coming, and it was coming for them.

The wind picked up a bit and blew the freshly cut grass around the yard. Sarah moved up on the porch with the dogs, not wanting to get dirty as she was a clean freak, prepped for any occasion that might warrant a visit from friends. Before their eyes, the lawn furniture instantly flew out of the yard as if an unseen force had purposefully thrown it out of the way. The trees bent outward toward the edges of the yard and snapped like twigs between fingers. The roof above the Rykus family flew off above them and soared behind the house, leaving them exposed to the sky above.

All three of them instantly stood close together and nervously wondered what the cause could be. Rykus tried to walk forward but a film in front of him prevented from doing so. The film displayed a distortion of the view like ripples in a pond spreading outward and swirling around them. The air inside began to whip around their bodies with such velocity and speed forcing them to cover their faces and close their eyes. John had a scary feeling come over him; this was in one of the dreams he had long ago. He shuddered to think that a dream, a damn stinking dream from his mind erupted right in front of him.

Tiny streaks of light flashed before their eyes and gave illumination to the sphere that surrounded them, slowly but surely getting smaller and smaller. The distortion they saw buzzed and blurred like static on a TV screen, but a growing white light emerged and blinded further visions. John felt he should quickly warn his family of what he thought was about to happen, if his dreams were in fact, true.

"Sarah, Kayla, can you hear me?" John screamed.

"Dad, what's happening?" Sarah screamed loudly.

"Remember the story I told you about a long time ago? Well I've got a bad feeling this is it!" he shouted back.

Their thoughts raced and fought against the current of the void, unnatural and unrelenting, encouraging panic and instilling the deepest feeling of horror in their minds as they remembered fleeting glimpses of the story he had told them back in the hospital many years ago.

"This isn't possible," screamed Kayla, "you said it was just a dream, it wasn't real!"

"Apparently," he quickly answered, "it's not just a dream after all!"

"What do we do now Dad, where are we going?" Sarah screamed again with an even higher pitch in her voice, trying to raise her voice above the whirling sounds of wind and pressure.

"We're going to be alright, we just can't get separated. Can you grab my hand?" Try as they might and with all the strength in their muscles, they could not get closer, hell they could not even see each other. Limbs reached out in the direction of each other's voices. Kayla felt something, someone and grabbed with all her might to find that she had secured her daughter, but as she reached for her husband their voices began to drift away. John screamed for them in fright, *"Kayla, Sarrraaahhhhhh!"* His voice fell into oblivion, gone in one swift instant and without any echoes or reverb.

"Sarah, hold on to me!" Kayla screamed. As they struggled to focus their eyesight, flashing lights grew brighter and brighter as the current time/space dynamic forcefully shot them through another dimension with a powerful blast of energy, illuminating to a brilliant base of solid white and then…gone.

Like a feather trapped in a hot air pocket, the two bodies frozen in time floated, weightless and immovable in the atmosphere of the void. Caught between time and space, they were neither dead nor alive but trapped in a suspended state of animation. No thoughts raced through their heads, not a single atom altered from its state of protection and pause. The two human bodies began to move forward through no help of their own and no will of force, but the spirituous hands that clenched them gave motion to advance towards a place Sarah and Kayla would come to know for security and safety. Hesitantly that is, for these were humans and not the same ones who would have the knowledge of Rykus' dreams.

Passing celestial bodies, planets, and brilliant star systems, they might think of this as breathtaking if they had been awake. Their suspended, stiff bodies glided with purpose to a system that had regained much of its brilliance and luster lost to war and chaos long ago. Although the countryside had suffered greatly, the natural vegetation had once again flourished and renewed itself over the once battle ravaged planet.

Unconsciously, Sarah and Kayla touched ground and with a little ancestral help and aid, they were unlocked from their suspended animation and limply rolled onto their backs underneath a thundercloud sky. Drops of precipitation fell softly from the heavens onto their delicate faces and gave a fresh new scent of air into their lungs; reaction caused by the subtle coldness of the rain. Their breathing returned and within a few minutes, they both opened up their eyes to a world they could not have imagined or would ever believe true to begin with.

Impossibility embraced them from the sudden act of time travel that brought them to the unknown, filling them with chilling doubt, uncertainty. Slowly, Kayla and Sarah focused their attention to the area around them. Raising their glances up extended their vision to the horizon at the magnificence of the majestic mountains off in the distance. The wide-open plains filled with grasses and flowers unlike any they had ever seen in their lifetime on Earth. Rolling hills that seemed to accentuate the landscape sensuously kissed the foothills beneath the mountains where glorious trees boasted of their grand heights and bragged of their dominance.

They were greeted—Sarah and Kayla—by some unlikely visitors who made their way towards them in a welcoming fashion. A female—one who used to be very little—had reached the age of early adolescence, thirteen, came to them gently and with arms slightly open. The girl crept forward with controlled excitement and reserved thoughts, anticipating nervousness in the new arrivals.

"Do not fear me," the young woman said softly to them in a voice that seemed to waver slightly as if an apparition or dream. "You are safe now, be not afraid."

Sarah and Kayla became alarmed despite the plea for the opposite.

"Who are you?" asked Sarah.

The young woman knelt down in front of her and replied, "My name is Laura, you are Sarah, and this," looking at the other, "must be your mother, Kayla."

Stunned from this sight, the puzzling look of Kayla's face told the others around her that she truly did not have any knowledge of where they were.

"What has happened to us, why are we here?" Kayla spouted uncontrollably.

"You were the victims, once again, of the dreaded enemy time machine," Laura calmly answered. "Whether or not it was the Nogzakhs who did this to you is a question to be answered later on."

"What are you going to do to us?" Sarah answered fearfully and with tears running down her frightened cheeks.

"As I said before, be not afraid for you are in no danger here."

"Where is my father?" Sarah questioned while she looked around but did not find him. "He was with us in the darkness and the wind; why isn't he here?"

"I know not where he is," Laura replied, "but I assure you that attempts to locate him are being carried out as we speak." Laura stood up and offered her hand to them. "Come, we must get you inside where it is safe, we are vulnerable out in the open."

"Where," Kayla asked, "where are we going?"

"You will see, please follow." Laura turned around and began walking toward the mountain that used to be there home. The badly damaged balcony loomed high above, still with the ropes of agony hanging from the stone ledge, blowing and swaying in the wind as grim reminders of the tragedy that befell them years past. Sarah and her mother followed reluctantly, looking all around at the other strange creatures that were bringing up the rear.

The column of alien creatures came to a stone face that showed no passageway at all, until Laura waved her hand in front of her revealing stairs that lead downward into a dark and dreary tunnel. On both sides of the carved out walls hung torches every so often, producing enough light to show the way before another torch illuminated the path. Oversized steps proceeded downward into the abyss and appeared to have no end in sight.

For at least half an hour they walked, cautiously and carefully not wishing to suffer a nasty fall from ill footing. Soon after, the stairway emptied into a very large room containing crude stone furniture with some animal skin coverings. The ceiling was approximately fifteen feet high with torches that lighted the area around four more hallways to various other locations. In the center of the room, there was a huge hole with a crank and some buckets, presumably to fetch water. Laura motioned for them to sit on a very spacious, makeshift couch, and as they did, the others who were following close behind filtered themselves around the room and stood silently against the walls as Laura continued to speak to them.

"There is much that I have to tell you," she said, "although I sense you are not ready to hear, but you must listen to me."

"Why should we," answered Kayla, "we don't know what the hell happened to us or where we are, or where my husband is, and yet you say we are safe?"

"If you had been taken by the Nogzakhs, you would have suffered already and would die suffering. Be thankful we found you first."

"Who are the...Nogzakhs?" Sarah asked.

"I must tell you the story and then you will understand the nature of what has happened to you."

Laura began to tell the tale of how they first came to know John Rykus many years ago. She relayed those whom he had met first and those who remained alive in turn stepped forward as Laura called out their names. Tanazakh was the first up and as before when he met Rykus, he received the same type of reaction. They cringed in their seats and became horrified at the sight of the type of creature he was, not understanding how this could be his first and most trusted friend.

This strange alien had very broad shoulders; his estimated height must have been seven to eight feet high. His skin was like something seen on a lizard or a Komodo dragon, perhaps. He had long fingers that came to a point, fingernails that were cylindrical, and twice the size on his feet. The facial features were hideous; teeth in rows like human, but all sharp and three times their size. His eyes were difficult to imagine, one solid eye from one side of his face to the other, but two pupils about in the same spot as humans. His face was long and wide at its base and his head was absent of hair, but in its place was what appeared to be a lanky boned tail coming out the back of his head.

Lokcha was second as Tejrasel was third in line, with them there are an even more strange reaction to their features and composition. Lokcha appeared to be no more than two feet tall, kind of bony, as if he had not eaten in awhile. His color was gray with a tint of brown on him, a flat face with two eyes, a pencil thin mouth, no nose or hair. In fact, he did not have any hair at all. A horn jutted out from his forehead that curved upward slightly and behind him, a long tail maybe three feet long seemed to move on its own. Tejrasel had the same features but a few more inches in height made the distinction between the two.

The strange and grotesque digger men were the Srotaderps. They naturally lived underground and had done so before, during, and after the war. A big difference from their existence on Earth was the discovery of changes in their physical form from prolonged periods of time underground on Cavanon. It seems that natural essence of the planet core mixed with the chemical composition of deep rock layers transformed their bodies into larger creatures than before. Now, the

Srotaderps were twice their size with feral eyes and grungy long hair, muscular bodies and an enhanced natural forward hunch. These creatures scared the hell out of Kayla and Sarah, worse than Tanazakh's appearance had.

With the others identified as being Cavanon, surreal images of their spirits entered into their midst and floated dreamlike in the air above and in front of them. This caused immediate fear and shock, as they did not know how to react to seeing apparitions or ghosts. Sarah and Kayla's eyes almost bulged out from their sockets as they both tried to take in all they were seeing while still trying to follow the story. This was all excessively much for them to digest so soon after falling out of the sky. Sarah had to speak up, displaying her disbelief.

"My dad," Sarah said, "is a King?"

"The father he once was had changed to become one of us—a Cavanon—and married the Queen," Laura explained. "He is not the father you once knew."

"So where is he now...?" Sarah asked, "my *real* father; the human guy who was taken with us?"

"We do not know for sure," said the spirit of Xashsa, but *"Adoné is out looking for him this very moment."*

Sarah and Kayla were fed up and frustrated beyond the point of further discussion.

"You all are nuts!" shouted Kayla, "And this is only a bad frickin dream. Who the hell are you to play around with our lives and bring us to this place where we—" the ghostly spirit instantly stopped her.

Xashsa knew that in her heart Kayla was nowhere near the point of believing, and needed a reminder of her surroundings. Xashsa summoned her energy, which sent a forceful blast of air throughout the cave area, enough of a force to knock down those not prepared for Xashsa's method of convincing.

"Be silent!" The exalted spirit exclaimed. Her ethereal voice echoed and filled up the large room, causing all others who were wise to hide their ears. *"Who are you to inject disbelief and conjecture and direct your insolence toward those who saved you from certain death? Are you not thankful in the least that we are not ripping your bodies apart? Are you not mindful of the fact that if we were such barbarians you would be dead already?"* The mere fact alone of the tone in Xashsa's voice was enough for the disbelieving humans to think twice, but then Laura further instilled a fact to the Queen that her point was getting across to them.

"Ungratefulness is not her pet pea," Laura added with confidence. "The Queen can be very forceful when her anger is aroused, so it would be wise to not incite her fury again, lest you see what she is *really* capable of."

The two humans appeared to have seen a ghost, hell they *did* but not in the generally wide spread belief of the state of ghosts back in the 20th century. This appearance was very different from any story they might have heard in the past. It took several minutes before they came out of the anger-induced trance forced upon them. Sarah finally summoned up the courage to calm down and ask more information of their new hosts.

"My Dad, or this guy you say *was* my dad long ago, how did he react to all of this?"

"I can answer that," said Tanazakh, as he stepped closer and sat down on a medium sized block of stone. "I was the first creature to befriend your father one day's time after the enemy brought him into this era. You," he pointed to Sarah, "do not look a day older than you did then; let us not forget that you accompanied him on this journey."

"For if not," Laura added, "the spirit of your future self would not be in the netherworld as you see." As Sarah glanced over Laura's right shoulder, she could see the spiritual image of her future self in focus. Sarah was beside herself with a menagerie of feelings; curious, scared, surprised, bewildered, inquisitive, and impressed that this creature could actually be she of the future. However, since the Queen was murdered, then it was the past/future…very complicated for the confused human.

"That's me of the future?" Sarah asked.

"It was you up until the moment you changed over to our species," Laura answered. "At that time you ceased to be human, hence the reason you are able to be here."

"I don't understand," replied Sarah.

"Same matter cannot occupy the same space," Laura answered. "If you of the future were here with you of the past, opposites would attract and a tragic condensing of mind, body, and soul would take place within an instant. You'd go from your present state to the size of an atom in less time than it would take for me to blink once."

"So what happened to *me* during that time?" Kayla asked.

"Oh!" replied Laura, hesitantly, "you did not survive the escape. Why do you think he remarried?"

Kayla just sat shaking her head.

"We'll have another lesson of that nature later," Tanazakh said. "You're father came here as scared and nervous as you are now. Since he was your father, and the typical figurehead fathers can be, he would not let you see just how scared he was. He put on a face for you and took everything at face value, giving off the impression that he was fearless. Well, even though he did an excellent job for through all the events of the past, there was plenty to have him worried. He took a temporary change over to the Cavanonian species and performed much better than anyone could have anticipated. The mind matured rapidly in his new form and took to his new senses and lifestyle very well. Once his body completely transformed, your father ceased to be human from that day forward; I am willing to believe *that* is when his human counterpart started to receive…visions?"

"The dreams," Kayla spoke up, "that's what he was talking about. Back on Earth he woke up one morning and told us this ridiculous story about the future that had people in it just like you."

"He was actually speaking of us," Laura replied, "as if he had lived out the dreams for himself. That is how he could have such intricate details. The mind of Adoné was still in tune with his old self of the past."

"So what will happen to us here, what will we do now that we can't get back?"

"There is no going back, unfortunately," Laura said, sadly, "but you can adapt and overcome as John did. You have to accept the fact that you are in another world and in another time. Open up your mind and accept your surroundings. It will make your acclimation that much easier if you begin to believe the unbelievable, because that is all you will see from now on."

After Laura had finished her explanation, the next phases of their "in-processing" was to show the new humans to the other dwellings and introduce them to the other tribal leaders. Of what tenements did remain, a majority of them housed humans. The old "newcomers" had changed their reference to that of the Helena's, in honor of their old friend Helen who was saved by the Nylantians decades ago and taken to a place on Earth, far away from the Labyrinth. Sadly, she ultimately perished during the invasion of the Nomaseri.

Sarah and Kayla entered into a new dwelling that would be their home for as long as they wished to remain there. It was not clear if they would begin to accept their surroundings as easily as others already had. However, surrounded by other humans might help to ease their forced transition from their old beliefs to new ones.

Food was another matter for them to consider; what new things would they have to eat, would it be safe, would they get sick, etcetera. These questions surfaced the moment food ushered in. After witnessing the consumption of different types of food by the other humans, they felt a little better in their minds. If *other* humans were eating it, then it must be safe.

Provisions were not as plentiful as they had been in the past. These new arrivals faced all sorts of new ways to deal with food procurement, preservation, preparation; the theory of evolution seemed to have come full circle again. What a challenge this would be to those influenced by 21st century technology. In their mindset, they were well educated and knowledgeable on how to manage their lives with all sorts of gadgets and widgets that made life so much easier. Now, they would consider themselves primitively challenged. As much as it seemed to be barbaric for hunting and killing animals, things they were in opposition to in the past needed consideration. It was a way of life they would have to learn and succumb to if they were to survive at all.

Clothing would be a challenge, too. Not that they were against wearing clothes, but their previous choices of apparel were no more and now items that were not too totally primitive in design would have to suffice. Instead of whirled away in time with nothing, they did retain the original clothing they wore prior to the time incident, but more in need of repair from the whipping nature of travel through time itself. Ann and the others who lived in domiciles around theirs provided them with the necessities and afforded every comfort available in order to ease their transition, until they fully accepted and adapted to this new life. Laura would be a useful and helpful hand to them, seeing to their comfort and providing education of the era. She would provide them with answers to whatever questions they would have, and they would have plenty to ask.

Between taking care of them, the prince, and her self, Laura would have a full schedule of tasks to keep her busy. She remembered how much Adoné, Xashsa, and the entire house of Cavanon had done to see to the needs of those rescued from the gripping, relentless clutches of the Gadnoc at Noleon. Those days were abhorrent to recollect and brought nothing but pain whenever the memory resurfaced. Remembering how they were saved and taken care of erased the nightmare and gave them peace of mind knowing that was the last of that type of torture they would suffer while under Adoné's careful watch and guardianship. For now, Laura sighed and smiled knowing it would take Sarah and Kayla time to adjust and begin their new lives, but now all they had was time, more so now than they even realized.

Because of the Nomaseri invasion, the annihilation had taken its toll on the once luscious and beautiful Cavanonian planet. During the attack, the Nomaseri and Nogzakh forces destroyed and damaged everything, and also pillaged and sacked, or burned and buried any hint of their existence. The enemy left traces of what once was a city to begin with lying in utter ruins. The invading enemy rested on the premise that they had destroyed everything, permanently, thus no further missions to the devastated planet were necessary. However, those who did escape the persecution considered themselves lucky, despite the sadness and tragedy of so many loved and cherished ones who had died at the hands of a brutal and vile opponent. With the near entire house of Cavanon gone, murdered and raped, molested, and finally hanged, the tragedy was more than anyone could stand to bear. The sentence heaped upon them was much more permanent than any other series of events they have lived through. Laura and the others who survived had no choice but to go on living, as stated when the spirituous Adoné visited them just before he set out to find the cause.

Since living underground was the best choice of cover and concealment, many of those who survived, aided by the useful digging techniques of the Srotaderp, had carved out domiciles underground. The process was trying and very hard work for the small force of maybe three hundred left alive. Nevertheless, Laura had developed her Cavanonian skills to a great degree during the time she dwelled underground in the house of Cavanon. Her refined skills almost matched those of the Queen, but more years behind her would perfect her skills to attain Xashsa's standards. Still, she mastered the cave-carving ability greatly and assisted those who needed help in constructing homes.

A few days later, aside from considering the daily needs of the baby prince, she went to visit Sarah and Kayla to see how they were progressing. They sat with the other humans and learned much about how to insure their survival by listening to all of the stories of the past told by nearly everyone. Sarah and Kayla did not understand much. This was due to their ignorance of the era and the extraordinary abilities inherent in different alien characters amongst them and in the stories told.

Laura entered in through the cleanly cut stairwell and chose a side route around the outer perimeter of the room in order to keep the viewing path open and clear for all who were attentive. She sat close to Kayla; Sarah did not sit far away at all, but it was close enough to be within hearing distance. They both noticed how cute and cuddly the baby was and they were surprised at his quietness. Usually, a baby that small would be finicky and struggling either for food or attention, but he was not. His mannerisms were much different then they expected.

Kayla did notice that Laura had pulled out a small bowl and poured in some sort of yellowish pasty mix that appeared very unappetizing. Using a spoon carved out of wood, she began to feed the baby prince. He took delight in every bite and emitted those cute little baby sounds that usually signified content.

"What is that stuff you are feeding him?" Kayla inquisitively asked her.

"This is a ground up food from the Agemoi," she answered.

"Oh, is that a plant that grows around here?"

"No," Laura chuckled. "It is a combination of ground liver and intestines. He doesn't particularly like plant life, and I can tell he is a meat eater and will probably take after his mother more than his father." Kayla was unaware that her stomach contents did not especially care for the entrée given to the little one; she really thought this was not the type of food to feed babies.

"Oh don't worry," Laura spoke up, "it seems to be the only thing he will eat, aside from gnawing on a raw piece of seared joojoo flesh."

"I didn't say anything?" Kayla said, with a very surprised look on her face. *"How did she know what I thought?"*

"We Cavanon have an inherent ability to read minds…all sorts of minds."

"So, you can read my mind all the time then?" asked Kayla, "that's not fair to us."

"We do not read the thoughts of others all the time," Laura tried to assure her. "We have the ability to do so, but I shall refrain from reading your thoughts. You have expressed a desire for me not to do so, and I shall honor your wish."

"How can you do this," the astonished Kayla said, "I mean, we can't do that and I've no idea how even if I wanted to."

"I remember the very first time I wanted to try it," Laura said, remembering back at the time when she lived on Lakeside. She stared into nothing and recalled the tale. "My father, Adoné, was returning from an underwater excursion where some really nasty bad guys wanted to hurt him. Instead, he showed them no mercy and gave them a taste of their own medicine. Anyway, on his way back he called to me with his thoughts—a mind communiqué if you will—instructing me on how to communicate. Concentration was the key and I was so overwhelmed from missing him that I nearly failed the task. But, I blocked out all other thoughts, noises, and disturbances and then, as if my thoughts had caught a whispering wind blowing in his direction, I was able to get a clear thought to him as though I spoke in my head without moving my lips."

"That must have been difficult to do?" Kayla commented while having a hard time herself envisioning how it was possible in the first place.

"That was nothing," Laura smiled. "Afterwards he rose up through the middle of the lake in a most glorious fashion and stood on the water some distance in front of me."

"He stood on water, real water?" Kayla blinked and stared.

"Yes, but then he thought to me and told me to concentrate even harder and walk out to him. Well you can imagine how that must have felt, knowing I could never do that myself, or so I thought. However, seeing him performing the feat he was asking of me, I knew then that it was not impossible. Therefore, after a few tries and getting my feet wet, he told me to try one more time for him, and I did. My feet touched the water as if I was on dry land, so I kept going and nearly cried my eyes out when I reached him. I will never forget that day, ever. He has meant so much that I've no idea what I would do without him."

"This man used to be my husband?" Kayla thought strangely. *"That does not sound like John at all."*

"Be mindful," Laura warned her, a serious note in her eyes, "I get really offended with thoughts against my father. True, he *used* to be your husband, but that was before he accepted the transformation and became Cavanon. Since then, he has become *my* father. From that moment on, he ceased to be the human you once knew."

"I thought you said you wouldn't read my mind?"

"For that, I apologize. In the future, know that if at anytime a thought about my father comes to your mind, I am paying attention."

Kayla took her words seriously and would make double sure to check her thoughts before actually thinking about them.

The notion of dinnertime was evident as others were bringing in food from another room in the back of the huge carved out enclosure. One section of hallway led to a kitchen area for cooking and preparing meals for whomever was in the house at the time. There were no hints of animosity to anyone, they were all a part of each other, and that meant each one helped their neighbors.

"Is this the same thing that happens every day?" asked Kayla. "Over and over again everyone just sits underground and tells stories or eats? This doesn't seem like much of a life to me."

"We are waiting for my father to return," Laura answered.

"That's it?" Kayla asked, impatiently. "We do nothing else but sit here?"

"Presently," Laura stated, "we are not a large enough population to protect ourselves if we venture outside for long periods of time. We go out in darkness to hunt for the next day's food and remain underground where it is safe. Since the war, we have no defenses large enough to fend off any would be attackers who might discover us. If someone does visit the planet, which is not of us, we know straight away. We escape detection by remaining hidden until a suitable situation presents itself and relieves us from our subterranean life."

It was clear to Laura that Kayla was getting restless and fidgety; she would have to calm her anxiety somehow.

"Patience Kayla," she said calmly, "we can walk around outside if you wish, but only for short periods of time. That is the best thing for us right now. I'm sure that when my father returns there will be changes."

"I hope you are right," Kayla said, pessimistically, "I don't think I could survive in this world living in a hole in the ground."

CHAPTER 3

▼

UNEXPLAINED PHENOMENON

In a remote part of the galaxy amidst a swirling gaseous nebula, clouded with cosmic dust and in the dulled light of stars existed a black void, a dark perimeter of nothingness, which surrounded the mysterious and depressing planet of Cinodas. Beneath the near impenetrable atmosphere of ash and volcanic vapors lay a lifeless planet, void of hope, and containing nothing that would suggest even the remotest of possibilities for existence. Yet, on this particular world, there was life. Impossible as time might suggest, one being had decided to lay claim to this abandoned barren wasteland. It was a perfect place to live undisturbed and undetected, the ideal setting for plotting and planning…revenge.

On the northern most tip of the planet lay an ice layer that encompassed approximately one quarter of the planets surface. Huge sentinels of volcanic rock stood firm in the near darkness surrounded by steam and smoke, which emitted through fissures on the outer crust. Deep inside one of these hideous mountains sat an enormous machine with a command center, alone and uninhabited, except for one. All the necessities of power generation existed that would provide the energy needed to operate mechanisms of this sort. A time machine breathed, powered up, shiny, new, perfectly fashioned, and operational. A programmed situation was running its course with a specific target in mind and well on its way to the doom that waited.

In another room, a creature filled its belly with the innards of another life form, which had perished, horribly. Hundreds of bones of its previous kills littered the ground everywhere, revealing that the creature occupied this place for some time. An alarm suddenly sounded, indicating that at any moment the target would be imported and reintegrate on a platform off to the left side of the humming machine. The expectant one stood impatiently waiting, watching, and growling.

John Rykus had no idea what was about to happen to him. He knew from his dreams of the bright light and the increase of energy in the park of what was to come. That was what he experienced in his dreams in the past, but this would definitely be different in many respects. Blinking lights began to illuminate the ceiling, as alarms grew increasingly louder still. With the sudden sound of a damp thud around a spiral of smoke, there laid Rykus on the floor all curled up and shaking.

The ominous being shook the floor with its massive body, vibrating everything in its near vicinity as it walked proudly towards the victim on the floor. No remorse afforded him, not even this quickly brought forth in time. A huge hand snatched John Rykus off the floor and held him by his throat. The hideous creature appeared as his victim's eyesight began to restore. Coughing and gurgling to keep from choking, shock entered into his system as the dark image in front of him grew larger and larger with its grotesque and threatening mouth full of teeth, more sinister and damaging than on any animal John had ever seen before. The intimidating height of Othragon stood twenty feet high from head to toe. His body was that of a lizard with eight legs like a spider, and a head of a dragon with four horns, two up, and two down.

"The first time I summoned you was only a test to see if in fact you would do the impossible," said Othragon, *"but to actually discover that you had accomplished the feat and were without your inherent faculties suggested I let you carry on and see what you would become. I was no longer amused when I sensed you were about to go far enough and become much more of a threat than even I had realized. However, you did something I did not expect and could not foresee. You separated yourself from the material dimension before I had time to devour your soul. From that moment when you attacked me and attempted to destroy me, I escaped and quickly realized that to prevent you from coming back again you would have to be recaptured in your significant form and I should encase you in solid matter."*

The once menacing ruler of the Dominion gripped his catch tightly, treating the human like a rag doll while walking around the various areas within his personal, yet isolated, command center. *"Without your powers you could never free yourself, so in essence, your ultimate choice doomed you to death. Now that I have you, finally, I will show you to your prison, one that you will remain in…forever."* With that said, he happily staggered over to a gloomy steel chamber with the doors already opened for him. Othragon thrust John's body into the chamber and upon crashing to the floor, the solid steel doors swiftly shut, sealing him off from the outside or any type of escape. John managed to stand up, only after a few clumsy falls into the wall.

The inside of the chamber was dark and damp, misty, and ice cold. Without knowing what was to come, John tried to surmise how large the interior of the chamber was by feeling his way around in the darkness. The chamber was only about fifteen feet in diameter from his rough estimation. He positioned himself in the middle of the enclosure as a bright light emitted from the center of the ceiling, which boasted a height of about twenty feet. A heavy volume of steam rose up like a mystical curtain from the vibrating floor, turning to frost on his skin. Sounds of metallic clanking, motors whirling into motion echoed throughout the chamber, and rang out loudly in his ears. With a profuse amount of gooey solution dripping from the ceiling, John began to wonder what was to come and felt whatever was coming could not be good. With a powerful force, the ceiling spouts released their massive tension in the drainage systems and dumped an enormous amount of ice-cold solution into the room, filling up the room within seconds. John's feet became frozen in place the moment the solution splattered on the floor and surrounded his feet and legs. It only took a few minutes for the entire area to fill with the freezing slushy liquid solution that would harden into an ice cube the size of a small room. Once the motors shut off and the drainage sequence disengaged, the steel walls that surrounded the room parted revealing a massive ice cube for Othragons viewing pleasure. The hideous monster let out an enormously gyrating laugh that bounced off the walls and ran its course throughout his underground lair, signifying his intense happiness, and overwhelming contentment. *"Welcome to your new infinity, my one time nemesis!"*

The encased John Rykus lowered into the pits of the planet to a depth near that of the planets' solid ice core. The subzero temperatures would ensure the catch never thawed or melted away, and guaranteed that there was no possible hope of escape…this time. The elated and satisfied Othragon went back to his private lair to contemplate the events and savor the moment of triumph. He had finally achieved a significant level of gratification.

When Johns frozen body stopped at a permanent depth, a force unseen and undetected by Othragon worked quickly to thwart the plans of the malevolent creature responsible. A magical and auspicious act was in the works for John, but one he would never know. His body had lost consciousness the moment the freezing cold solution totally engulfed his being and solidified with him in it. The mind only had a few minutes afterwards before it would fully shutdown and die. The unseen force worked feverously to disintegrate the body and reintegrate it again on the planet surface. As the body thawed, the empty space occupied by John's body began to fill up with dirt and grime of the planets darkened soil from above ground. The powers of the unseen force held themselves at bay and kept out of the detection of Othragon—who would know if some sentient life was above ground. Knowledge or detection of anything in the ethereal was his constraint.

The solidified body of John Rykus lay on the ground thawing out, emitting steam off the melted ice and pressure heaped upon it for only a few minutes, but it was enough to do its dirty work. An analysis of his body revealed that only few cells remained alive in the torso, but not the brain…it was dead and very empty of any surviving atoms of energy to sustain it.

"*I am truly sorry,*" said a spirituous voice to the corpse, "*I did not save you in time.*" A simple hug of his old form showed that even Adoné suffered the loss of life of such an innocent at the hands of a devilish creature. Knowing there was only a few fleeting moments left, he began warming preparations for reintegration of his spirit.

"*Perhaps then, as to not let you totally go to waste and die in vain, I shall use you and regain my strength, regenerate my being. In so doing, I shall reclaim the lives of those who were lost in my kingdom.*"

The spirit of Adoné stepped into the body of John Rykus and reengaged the life force that had departed the human. Since the old John Rykus was gone, again, transformation reestablished and the human body reshaped into the Cavanonian Monarch. Without giving the enemy below the chance to discover what had transpired, Adoné quickly left the planet through a portal to another nearby system to put the final changes on his newly formed carcass.

Of course, other individuals in the universe were wise to the sensations of such limited acts of transference. Othragon was oblivious to this, only because it was his assumption that the human struggling to maintain his life died and crossed over to the ethereal, the cause of the slight disturbance. There were others who knew this not, but *did* know that something traveled the opposite way of the normal. Federoth felt it when he awakened from sleep due to a bad dream, and so had Nosrévis as he napped aboard his ship. However, others felt it too, Laura to be exact.

A few days after the sensation, the prince began to giggle and laugh, smiling much more than a baby normally would. This roused Laura from her erratic sleep and she began to wonder what the cause of the weird feeling was that had overcome her dreams, and she went to see to the prince's excitement. The wraithlike Spirits of the Ancestors knew it for what it was; the King had reemerged. A whole new turn of events was to come that would change the Cavanonian race once more, which started with the passing of the King from the spirituous realm into the physical world, and back into the dimension of time he had narrowly escaped.

The baby Solisynas had fallen back to sleep, drifting off in the dream world peacefully after being touched by a heavenly sensation. Laura herself felt this unseen event and went outside to gaze up at the stars as if to see the cause of her awakening. Gases in the atmosphere shimmered and glistened with brilliant illuminations of white and blue, and flew energetically through the night sky, creating a magnificent spectacle of creativity and radiance. This astounded and amazed Laura; the atmospheric phenomenon completely mesmerized her with its hypnotic visions and illusions painted throughout the heavens above. Her essence received an overwhelming delight and excitation enhanced her aura. All that she needed now was the encore that would put her senses over the edge of exhilaration and anchor them within her soul.

"That is quite a light show, is it not?" said a familiar voice rising up over the hill to her front. The approaching image was not menacing or overbearing at all, but rather tranquil and serene in nature, enlightening and soothing…hopeful. The peaceful security of old returned to the area and its inhabitants, although they knew it not, yet.

"Father!" she gasped as his full features came into view. Her mind now understood the reason for the light show, as it was the skies way of ushering back the Cavanonian King to his rightful place. She also knew this as the reason for the restlessness she experienced and the waking of her conscience from sleep. Laura raced up the hill to meet him, and jumped up high in the air into his arms. The enormous hug she gave him left no doubt in his mind as to whether or not she missed him. He knew she missed him and she always showed this no matter what took place or who was around.

There was a difference in him, a change she immediately noticed after her excitement withdrew, slightly. He was physical now, not in the spirituous form as when he departed to find the cause for the disturbance in the space-time field. She had questions, and as always, he would provide answers to her.

"Father, I'm so glad your back," she cried as she continued to hold him.

"I regret that I was not able to return sooner," he replied. "Things have transpired that delayed me—important items that had to be taken care of—but turned out unfortunate."

"But your physical again," she asked, as she eased the tension in her arms to look over him. "Where did you get this body? It is you but there are changes to your form."

"Yes, it is me. I located my old self, John Rykus, in the hands of a great enemy that still exists." He put her down gently and stood back a pace to look over himself as well. "Rykus was killed by the Nogzakh ruler that tried to kill *me* back on the Dominion planet. I rescued John's body, but I was not able to save him from the damage already done to his system. Rather than let him die in vain, my spirit entered into his body and took over. Even though he was dead, there was a little life left in a few cells that remained, and it was enough to cause reanimation of the dead tissue by transforming his remains into my being. In essence, I was born all over again and as you can see, there are still some changes taking place within the new me."

"It is unfortunate indeed, but a blessing nonetheless." She answered happily. It was not that she felt no sorrow for the demise of John Rykus—she never knew *him* at all, in any fashion. The one she knew was right in front of her and had been with her since he found her in the Gadnoc hell. Formerly known only as Rykus prior to his transfiguration, Adoné, as she came to know him, was the one who took care of her religiously and looked after her constantly the way a loving father does.

"I did not see his wife or daughter," he said, "only John, so I have no idea where they could have gone or if they had been taken at all."

"They are here, and safe." She quickly answered.

"They are, how?" he said, with a staggering look in his face.

"The spirituous Queen felt the disturbance as well and guided them here through the ethereal portal. There was no danger to them and they appear to be well, but very confused and equally strange."

"So your mother has not ascended to the Ancestors then?"

"No," Laura stated. "She refuses to rest for a minute until she has completed tasks she has set for herself."

"And what tasks would those be?"

"Those things she will inform you of directly," Laura answered, happily, "and when she sees that you have returned in physical form, she might have other plans as well. I wouldn't put it past her to have an idea from the moment she sees the new you!"

"That," he said, "is a vision I have also already foreseen. There is only one thing that troubles me," he said, staring into the heavens. "If she felt the disturbance in the ethereal as I have, then maybe a few others did as well."

"But who else would know?" she asked. A dire look of concern came over her, slightly. She was not overly concerned if someone else also sensed what had taken place, but rather worried that if whoever it was would know where to look or come back searching for answers.

"There are two others," he said. "The evil Rykus who desecrated the planet and murdered our family might have felt it, since he knows the wicked ways of the Dominion. I sense he would feel it, but not know exactly what the nature is."

"Him?" she asked, worriedly. "If there is a possibility that he knows, then we've much to do to keep our alert up and be on our guard."

"And then there is Federoth himself."

"By the stars," she gasped, "do you really think he knows, too?"

"It is a possibility as well," Adoné said, "since he is the one who started our downfall to begin with. That—and the fact that he is Cavanon as well—leads me to believe he does know something, but not the actual fact."

"When everyone wakes up there will be news to tell them," she said, but then smiled and gave him another hug, "—and also to tell them that our worries are over."

The morning sun came up over the southern horizon, as did the northeastern sun. The two suns did not excessively heat the planets surface more than what was comfortable according to the global position of the planet. One sun provided heat and light, the other provided a lesser light but stronger than the amount of light reflected off a nearby planet. From the rotational cycle of the suns, daylight on Cavanon accounted for almost fifteen hours; the night lasted for almost twenty-four. It was the ideal planet and location as well, for the night was the calling of the Cavanon and what a brilliant location indeed to start up another generation.

The other inhabitants began to stir and wake up in their subterranean dwellings, preparing themselves to welcome the morning. Each creature ran through the morning rituals of cleanliness and washing, dressing, and a quick tidy up of the beds. All below ground prepared substances for the breakfast meal and started the day as they had done since the ravages of war swept across the surface.

Sarah and Kayla started the rhythm of the morning by watching the others in their tasks that seemed meaningless, but ones that kept their routine organized and complacent. Things had drastically changed from their old ways of the 20th century. Electricity, for one, was a luxury that did not exist; did neither running water nor refrigeration for that matter. They would have to learn the habits that Laura and others had accepted since their introduction to the Cavanonian ways, and the ways of the other tribes. Although they did the tasks, reluctantly, they did them anyway; it gave them something to do. Boredom mixed with missing their own era set in much quicker with them, and the others could not relate to that way of life. Exercising patience and constancy fit their program and was necessary for each living creature. Today, they all would get a break from the new normal lifestyle and some excitement.

Laura hurried downstairs and began to tell the occupants in each of their houses that they were to go outdoors. There was no question in their minds; if Laura said it was important, then they had no choice but to see the reason for all the excitement. Everyone emerged from a single exit point and instructed to go to the hill just above the entrance and wait until all the others were outside as well. Once they were outside, she began to tell them the news.

"Everyone," she shouted, "I have great news to tell you, the greatest news of all that will bring happiness back to our devastated little community."

Each one looked at each other as questions rose in their minds, but she would continue before anyone could ask them.

"I have seen the King, Adoné has returned to us once again."

Tanazakh stepped forward a few steps and spoke up to her. "He has been here, in the night while we were sleeping?"

"Yes," she answered with a smile bigger than life, "and his intention is to stay this time, to help us recover from our losses, regain our lives, and build up on what we have left."

The big Anadon was leery of this news since the last time he saw his friend was in his spirituous form. "Surely there isn't much he can do in his present state; the spirits are limited to their abilities, even in the ethereal world."

"Ah, but not anymore," Laura said, happily. "He is not *in* the ethereal world any longer, for look!" Her voice rose in fervor and pitch as she pointed to the mountain where the royal family used to live. On the old balcony of his once beautiful home, Adoné stood poised on the edge of it, waving to all down below.

"That—" Tanazakh said in disbelief, "—cannot be him."

"Ah! But it is!"

Sensing his disagreement with what his eyes were seeing, she knew the only way for him to believe was to see him first hand. She waved for her father to come closer. All watched as he made the enormously long jump from the balcony to a spot a few feet shy of their present position. As he crept closer to them, he spoke happily to clear the air of any misconceptions.

"It's good to see you my friend," he said. "What's the matter? You look as if you've seen a ghost!"

"Is it really you, come back from the ethereal world?" Tanazakh said, holding out his hand to him.

"Absolutely, and in the flesh I might add." He shook his friends hand and arm, and held on with the mighty grip that Tanazakh knew was truly his.

"It is, it is you!" he said, touching his friends hands, arms, face and back, finally giving an enormous bear hug to him, while simultaneously letting out a yell that seemed to echo throughout the valley floor. "It's him, hoa by the stars it *is* you my friend, my friend, I am so happy you've returned!"

"I am just as happy to see you, too. You've no idea how much I've missed you, or how much I've missed you all." This he said as he looked out over the small multitude of gatherers that now made their way to him to greet him and welcome him back as well.

Everyone became happy and convinced that it was him as they all either shook his hand or held him close to themselves. Laura—smiling from ear to ear—was the happiest of all to see that life was returning to their people once again. Her father was the key to unlocking the door to their happiness and hope, and with him back, they would not only be less afraid of the day, but they could finally get on with their lives in a more normal fashion rather than secluded underground.

Laura had brought the prince for Adoné to see, and as he held him gently, the baby Solisynas smiled and giggled with delight and content. Even the little one knew it was he and not a fake or apparition.

Out of all of the creatures gathered outside, only two were somewhat miffed, as they had no idea what was transpiring or who he was, let alone know of his importance or what role he played in the lives of the small community. All they saw was a freakish being of some seven feet in height, covered with skin that appeared black and blue, having white hair and eyes, and a muscularly build for his size. Simple black clothes were his adornment and larger than normal wristbands. For what purpose, they had no idea.

Adoné caught sight of them standing by themselves and segregated from the rest of the gathering. He hated to give orders but asked Laura to bring some food out, or rather for everyone to bring what breakfast they had left outdoors to eat in the warmth of the suns light and breathe the freshness of the air. As they hastened to his request, he walked over to the edge of a rather large group of rocks and pick out one to sit on that would allow the gathering to see him as he told the tale of how things happened. He motioned for Sarah and Kayla to come over and sit closer to him; he directed a majority of his explanation towards them and in a manner that they would understand. Hesitantly, they came forward and sat on a nearby rock. They only did this not out of the respect due him, but because of being intimidated from his sheer size and appearance. Laura came and relieved him of the baby; to feed him as her father began to speak.

"I am happy and yet sad to see you both," he said, as he sighed shortly. "You've no idea who I am, do you?"

"No," they both spoke in unison with Kayla finishing the sentence. "We don't have any idea who you are, would you mind telling us?"

He snickered a bit from her comment and commenced again, "spoken as only you could, Kayla." His comment caught her off guard right away. She began wondering in her mind of how he knew her name. "I know much about you Kayla, and Sarah; I know both of you very, very well."

"You can read minds too," she grunted. "Is there no such thing as privacy here?"

"First," he said calmly, "let me tell you a few things up front that will cause you some degree of worry, but you will need to know in order to get your thoughts in the right frame of mind, if you are going to survive this place." He took a chalice offered to him from his friend and took a few drinks to quench his thirst; he was going to need it for explanation he would give them. "The place you are now is in no way, shape, or form, Earth of the past, present, or future. The Earth you knew is gone, its inhabitants wiped out, and the surface destroyed."

"How do you know that?" Sarah asked.

"Because I've seen it," Adoné replied. "I've lived there many centuries after its destruction and I know for a fact that it is a planet of nothingness, lifeless in the Milky Way Galaxy. Everything you used to know about it is gone, all of it. Not even a shred of proof that life even existed there is to be seen anywhere."

Those comments did give them something to be sad about and worry over. His comments were direct and to the point, no use in sugarcoating them; he would continue to be direct with them.

"So if this is not Earth, then where are we?" Kayla asked.

"We are on a planet that is many light years away from Earth. This—" he said, while slowly waving his hands across the sky, "—is the planet of Cavanon, a once beautiful and luscious planet that used to be filled with life and a great multitude of beings all living together for peace and prosperity. But, a war here finished that and ended what we all came to love and cherish."

"Can you tell us how we got here and where my husband John is?"

"Prepare yourselves; this will not be easy for you." He prepped himself and knew that, despite his gut feeling, he had to tell them the truth of what had happened and would have to give all of it, no sense in hiding anything from them, what good would that do here?

"I assume that John did not tell you about the visions, the dreams he had?"

"Oh sure he did," Kayla spouted, "If you want to *call* them dreams. He was almost a raving lunatic, telling us about how he escaped a huge black building, married a vampire looking woman, and killed some ugly bad guys that had friends in big white machines. It was crazy! The places he spoke of were too much to understand, some place where the planet was four times the size of Earth and located on the other side of the galaxy." Fed up with her own speech, she stopped when frustrated beyond the point of continuing.

"Kayla, where do you think you are?" he said, as he looked around at the others and then regained contact with their eyes. "This is that planet; these people are the ones who followed us. The white machines are the Nogzakhs, the very same ones who destroyed Earth and forced us to relocate here. The 'vampire' woman he told you about is my wife, my Queen, who rests in the ethereal world as we speak. She was a victim of the white machine commanders who came here and murdered her in cold blood. What John told you was the truth and you should believe it."

"Why, why should I believe it, tell me why! And why did you say she was *your* wife when he told us that *he* was married to her?"

"Because Kayla, I *was* John Rykus, your former husband in the past."

Stunned and silenced, she sat there just staring at him, blankly, and Sarah repeated the same look. That was too much information for her now, and that was evident to Adoné. Feelings were going to be hurt, he knew that, but there was no use hiding what needed to be said, even though it would probably send them into seclusion or isolation, much like the evil Rykus had done prior to running away from the sanctity of their world.

"This can't be true, you're a liar!" Kayla shouted back.

"I can prove it to you, ask me something that only John would remember or know…something personal. Don't worry; no one here cares about anything that could be embarrassing. After all, they don't know anything of the past."

"Okay," she said thinking she was going to win this match of wits, "on what day is my birthday?"

"January 25th," he replied.

"When were we married?"

"April 9th, 1990."

She was getting a little worried now, two for two and those were considered open source information, but not to this particular public audience. "What kind of present did you give Sarah when she was five years old? And what kind of car did I buy in the year 2004?"

"It was a talking teddy bear that scared her when it talked to her. The car you bought was a dark green SUV."

"No," she staggered as she tried to get up and fell. "No, no, this can't be real, this can't be, you can't be him, you can't," and the flood of tears raced down her face as she wailed and cried knowing full well he gave all the right answers. "This…this can't be real, it just can't!" her crying was out of control.

Adoné understood the pain she was feeling, all too well, and he knew that more was to come, eventually.

"Kayla," he said calmly as he went over and kneeled down to her, "there is much more that I could tell you, but in your present state I know that you are not ready to hear it. However, I will tell you this. The bad guys have a time machine and they used it to bring you here into this time of the future. There is no huge black building because we destroyed it on Earth. Xashsa saved you and guided you here after I disrupted the time machine's dimensional phases. Unfortunately, the enemy captured and killed John. If you had gone with him, you would have been killed, too, by an evil being without remorse or thought of forgiveness."

Kayla could not speak, she could not move. She just stared into his eyes in disbelief and cried more as she fell towards him. He held her close and shook her ever so gently while feeling the pain inside her through his arms.

"I am so sorry for what happened to you."

Now that Sarah, too, understood what befell her father, she cried as well and attempted to comfort her mother. Adoné knew this was painful as well as the pain of bearing the news in the first place. Still, he had to, eventually. Together, mother and daughter went inside to grieve in private, the new arrivals were not ready for strangers to be around, and all afforded them the personal time they required.

Laura felt compelled to ask her father of a concern she had. "Do you think they know whose body you have?"

"No," he said, quietly, "and we should bury that knowledge as well. We will leave them with the memory, which is all they will be able to understand. It's too soon to suggest revealing news of that sort."

Laura looked about at the gathering seated outside, all waiting their turn to speak with them as well. Adoné did not intentionally forget them, he gave the new humans their time first as it should be.

"What of King Gahnepoc and his Nylantians, and the Kostejaanians…where are they?"

"Oh," Laura replied, "they departed. The attack was a little more than they could bear and set off for their home planet."

"It was probably in their best interests," he answered. "I'm sure this place would bring them nothing but pain, anyway."

"But," she spoke up, "they did say they would send word to us of their progress, and to check on us as well. I just don't know when."

Chapter 4

Setting up shop

The Nylantians had suffered some losses during the war on Cavanon and mourned the loss of not only some of their own, but the Cavanonian Royal family as well. With the looming possibility of future attacks or the threat of constant danger, King Gahnepoc felt it wiser to seek refuge on another system rather than suffer any more losses to his creatures. The Nylantian King knew the remaining friends on Cavanon would survive and make do with what they had left; there was no need to be more of a burden to their already decimated numbers.

On a system not far from the Kostejaanians, the Nylantians discovered a planet filled with water and rich with undersea life. Mountain peaks rose to grand heights and ranges that would dwarf any found on Earth, ran throughout the enormous oceans that covered the surface of the planet. These ancient rock formations of granite stood poised and firm amidst the rumbling waters below, actively engaged in eroding the rock away.

A nearby star system provided the light, which illuminated the underwater area beautifully, enhancing the algae green and aqua colors by piercing deep into the depths some five hundred feet. The above surface heat burned slightly hotter than what would seem bearable to them, but it elevated the temperature of the circulating current that provided warm water throughout the planet. The excessive heat was the reason for the barren granite sentinels above with barely any life. A few strangely small aerial creatures, adapted to this environment, and survived by diving into the depths to retrieve food and water, returning to small caves and fissures in the rock.

The entire surface of the planet, named Nylantia, comprised of mostly fresh water. Enormous underwater valleys, ranges, and depressions made it possible for many areas of habitation for the Nylantian submariners and their families. The depth of the waters reached deep into the core of the planet composed of rock itself and branched out into huge granite arms that interconnected with the mid-level rock above. It then further connected to the mountains and ranges above the waters. An aerial view showed nothing more than liquid and rock and revealed no clue as to the state of creation that existed below the surface.

The underwater creatures that existed before the Nylantian occupation consisted of many strange and wondrous species of mutated mammals, fishes, and other waterborne creatures ranging in sizes from the miniscule plankton to the massive dragon creatures resembling Earths prehistoric period. To the Nylantians, accommodating themselves to the existing ecosystem did not pose a problem. In addition, from their abilities to understand underwater life, they were able to discern which creatures were friendly from those that were ill tempered. The latter received warning of possible retaliation should they impress their ill-tempered mannerisms onto any Nylantian.

Gahnepoc and his people were able to construct their sub-aquatic city in record time, a little over three months. The entire area of the newly constructed city of Sirrahsew was busy with labor and the excitement of a new beginning, away from the savageness of the old enemy they came to hate with a passion. The Nylantians did pose a formidable resistance to any enemy that made their presence known to them. However, that was only effective if displayed in their natural underwater environment. They were vulnerable above ground. With teeming swarms of food at their disposal and a great area in which to live, the Nylantians faired very well, indeed.

Several systems away, the Kostejaanians had been busy restoring their own lives on their own home planet of Kostejaan. They reunited with old friends, family, and loved ones thought to have suffered annihilation at the hands of the warring Nomaseri and Dolumek systems located several hundred thousand miles away. Kostejaan remained untouched and for reasons unknown, the system escaped the war as its atmosphere and natural planetary defenses did not offer much in the way of attractiveness and resources. However, to the Kostejaanians, what the planet did offer remained a secret known only by them.

Since Kostejaan faintly hid from any nearby sun, the outer atmosphere was cold and bitter in its natural elements. The polar caps on its east and west covered much of the surface with its blanket of white and ice. Jagged mountains and staggered ranges littered the remaining uncovered territories and kept the snows from ever reaching each other. In the middle of the planet, separated by the mountains, forests of trees similar to pine and other odd variations of vegetation existed in abundance. A huge covering of gray/green color ran north and south over the surface of the planet. The forests existed and thrived in the nocturnal nature, requiring not sunlight, but starlight instead. These forests provided rich nutrition and sustenance to the Kostejaanians with its abundance of bitter tastes prevalent in the flora and fauna. There was hardly any water to speak of, at least above surface. However, the grand total of its natural resources would not be above ground anyway.

Miles below, layers of granite and limestone separated impressive oceans of water from equally impressive oceans of molten lava. The core consisted of a compromised system of elemental balance unknown to any in the universe, except its creator. Separated by impenetrable rock, on one side of the internal western hemisphere the volume of water that existed would cover the Earth twice over. The other side contained the enormous amount of molten lava, which boasted a size to that of three Earths. Separately, they flowed from their locations throughout thousands of natural tunnel systems that circulated throughout the subterranean world. A magnetic field from the center of the planet pushed and pulled liquefied elements through their locations into the tunnels, creating the pumping effect of circulation. The last layer of water, which situated throughout the middle portion of the planet, boiled its vapors through the planets mantle, and fed the vegetation with life sustaining fluids.

The Kostejaanians were happy with their planet and their life spent in vast underground caves and caverns. The environment remained independent and continued without the need for outside influence or unnecessary socializing. The Kostejaanians had learned to remove themselves from the role of mediators and ultimately decided to let other warring systems fend for themselves. The Nogzakhs on Earth cured them of this.

A different kind of planetary system existed deep within a red glaring nebulous cloud of gases and cosmic dust. A diffuse mass of interstellar dust and gas surrounded a minute solar system, making it visible as a luminous patch or area of darkness thought to be void of life, ignored, and untouched. One look at this system from afar instilled an eerie sense of dread and provided the fear needed to remain disregarded by the minds of any would be prospectors. This did not deter Nosrévis from looking. To him, the celestial red beauty was intriguing and inviting. It seemed to be the perfect example of what he wished for in a galaxy such as this.

Passing by asteroid fields and planets with grand rings of cosmic debris and rock, Nosrévis marveled at the sights of such a collection of interstellar jewels hidden away by the immense nebula. At the center of this area sat a glowing planet of crimson and black emanations. Six other planets revolved around the crimson globe and Nosrévis sought to inhabit the nucleus of this solar system.

As the Dominion ship descended to the planets surface, Nosrévis discovered the reason for the planets patched bright red and dark colors. This world revealed a dark damp surface covered with ash and soot from volcanic eruptions. Furious winds assisted the continual spreading of the ash that shot forth from immense fissures in the ground.

In his eyes, marvelous towers of hardened magna stood poised as gargantuan teeth from the surface high into the heavens. The sheer size alone of these stone towers dwarfed the memory of Mt. Everest on Earth. For miles upon miles, he saw magnificent eruptions of molten rock soar high into the sky and drench the already perilous wasteland below. Steam and gases underneath the crust shrieked out of cracks and crevices with enormous force and pressure. Nosrévis knew that the ship would have to land away from any concentration of pressure, if it were to remain intact.

A suitable landing zone at the foothills of a great mountain would suffice for now, until a better, stronger landing pad could be constructed. The dark Cavanon fully intended to occupy and inhabit this desolation of hell in order to give rise to his malevolence and establish his name along those serving descendants of Ellononis. As he stood on the face of the planet, he gazed at the sights and beheld his visions of possible immortality. What a grand location to establish himself and launch his own reign of terror and chaos; from an ideal position in the universe that would be regarded as treacherous and dangerous if visited.

At the base of the mountain, Nosrévis gave instructions to the Nogzakhs and the machines to analyze the mass and excavate a grand area for habitation. At no time at all did they question his motives or orders. This particular crew was under the direct control of Nosrévis, given to him by his creator, Federoth, as a gift to start his new life. Federoth retained a hidden agenda of counting on his evil creation's morbid paradise as another staging base or point of control in a new region of space. The commander of the Dominion forces knew that Nosrévis would be a formidable ally in whatever region his fancy held sway. However, his creation would be more formidable than he thought.

It took several weeks to carve and excavate a suitable area out of the mountain. Work went on round the clock and kept its pace as dictated by the near impatient commander. Tons of rock fell into a gulley beside a long five-mile ramp that led to an entrance situated approximately two miles above the base of the mountain.

Once the inside area became completely vacant, Nosrévis supervised the emplacement of various systems with which to command and control his future forces. The communications section was the first installed. Temporary power stations provided power to all systems until the Nogzakhs could engineer a solution for harnessing the energetic powers of the immense force below ground. Dwellings existed on the lowest of the five levels contained within the mountain.

Nosrévis himself chose a level mid-level of the mountain for his chambers. He would take a great deal of time in its construction and manifestation. He did not build a stair or walkway from his chambers to the lower levels. Instead, he emplaced a teleport platform inside the command center and the other half in his chambers for his own personal use, as well as to remain secluded when he wanted silence. The teleporter also provided direct communications in case command required his presence.

The last item installed was a piece of equipment to connect him with the past. An enhanced version of the time machine, which guaranteed their continued survival through endless sustenance, stood ready to import whenever the sequence initiated. Instead of the trapped pens on the Labyrinth, a great rectangular hole carved out of the flooring would be the holding place for imported food. In no time at all, the Nogzakhs enthusiastically setup shop and began to prepare meals from the screaming victims brought in from all past time dimensions.

They had learned early on that some creatures were more dangerous than others were, and had a unique way of dealing with them. As others wrestled the enraged victim, a mind probe attached to its head ingested powerful magnetism, making the victim suffer from constriction of brain tissue and impulses that are more susceptible to hypnotic suggestion. Afterwards, depending on the strength and size of the creature, they would either suffer the same fate as the others, which only seemed like a waste, or become slaves injected with a mixture of Nogzakh blood to cease all inherent thoughts. This made for an extremely docile, yet programmable servant of the Nogzakhs.

The Nogzakhs sent probes to the other six nearby planets to observe and report any activity found. Outside the atmosphere of each planet, the probe launched another smaller probe into orbit for use of viewing the planet at any given time. Nosrévis ordered the Dominion destroyer to orbit the upper atmosphere and provide relay of probe signals, and to remain out of possible danger of the raging planet.

After Nosrévis sat in his command chair, he made communications with Federoth through use of his own wide screen monitor. The rumbling from below ground gave off an ominous presentation when viewed by Federoth on the other side of his screen. Nosrévis occupied the middle of the screen and the view of the outside planet shown on both sides. Even Federoth himself shuddered upon seeing this sight, as if he sensed a slight hint of what he truly created finally appeared.

"It appears as though you are doing well at your new location," said Federoth. "I have the coordinates of your system and I see that you have been guided close to your calling."

Nosrévis smiled, inquisitively. "What do you mean by that?"

"The system you have taken control of," explained Federoth, "is very near the planet of the forth Son of Ellononis, his name is Elaveshan." Nosrévis lowered his glance and thought as his commander continued. "It appears as if you were guided to this spot by his very spirit. If I were you, I would search the surrounding systems and see what you can find. Who knows what treasures and secrets you will discover."

"Federoth," he replied, "probes have already been dispatched to the outlying areas and I should know very soon if I can practice my arts or search for the system you mentioned."

He thought for a moment and smiled, devilishly. "Since this system is without a name, I shall honor the fourth Son of Ellononis by naming my planet after him."

"The system of Elaveshan sounds very befitting," Federoth smiled proudly. "Take heed in his wise teachings and wisdom. Now I sense you have work to do, so I will leave you to it. We can make weekly progress reports unless a situation dictates otherwise."

"So be it, Elaveshan, out."

Nosrévis switched off the communication and sat quietly, contemplating what his commander had told him. If the planet of the fourth son were close by, as Federoth said, then he must seek out this place and investigate, thoroughly.

For nearly two months, the probes sent back information of the six surrounding planets containing composition, location, resources, and distances. Each of the planets named Sornoc, Emad, Erton, Gendis, Dnadiz, and Khaz were unique

Setting up shop 59

in their design and planetary composition. However, Nosrévis noted that the farthest planet, Khaz, revealed a hidden planet on the other side of it. Dark, blue, and distant, he decided to send a probe to that location and discover its contents as well.

While that went on, smaller destroyer ships had arrived, courtesy of Federoth, and colonization of the other six planets commenced. If Nosrévis were to create his own grand army to serve Dominion purposes, he would need various bases to avoid becoming wiped out, as were the Cavanonians. Nosrévis learned from their mistakes and did not wish to repeat the same.

Nosrévis was stunned to see the visual images of the frozen planets surface sent back from the probe to the distant planet beyond. There were signs of previous life there evident from ancient stone towers and buildings of immense proportions surrounding a dead volcano that appeared to have blown its top and extinguished itself.

A large cavernous tunnel drove deep into the volcano to a depth unknown and not shown by the probe. Nosrévis wondered if this was the planet of Elaveshan's existence. The only way to know for sure would be to investigate it, personally. Without patience, he immediately set out for this system by one of the smaller destroyer ships.

As his ship drew closer, the planet boasted of an intemperate climate, frozen and obscured through fierce winds and violent storms. Turbulence shook the ship upon its descent to the surface. The temperature inside the ship dropped suddenly, indicating that the chill could pierce through solid steel in a matter of minutes. Nosrévis quickly exited the ship and ran into the entrance to the gigantic tunnel the led downward. Once inside a safe distance, he signaled the ship to orbit the planet and await his orders. No sense in leaving the ship subjected to the whim of the elements.

Through the dark musty stench of decades past he walked. The immense tunnel ceiling arched overhead and possessed age and despair prevalent with its dusty hanging webs and frozen fungus. Through miles of descent he walked, taking in the scenic drawings and carvings of war that lined both sides of the passageway. The farther he descended, the cleaner the area appeared as if tended to by an unknown creature.

Up ahead, he could see an opened area empty into a large room with a glowing light coming from a center shrine of some sort. The twenty-foot tall cylindrical tower anchored itself in the middle of the room. Fungus and dust covered the tower and prevented the engravings from clear view, until a swipe of Nosrévis' hand removed it. The badly scratched engravings contained ancient incantations that spiraled from the top of the tower to its base below. He could make out a majority of the words such as *vengeance, no remorse, destroyer of worlds,* and *divine right.* Even though he could only make out a few because of the obvious scaring, he stopped suddenly and dropped to his knees when he read the phrase at the bottom of the tower.

'*Seek vengeance against the Cavanon for their blasphemous treachery against our Father, Ellononis. The might of Cavanon must fall and the sword of fire captured, into our hands, whose descendants hail from Ellononis. So decrees Elaveshan!*'

Nosrévis shivered, his hands quaked from the revelation contained in the writings. His eyes stared at the floor and his thoughts contemplated the meaning. He stood up and looked about the chamber to find three hallways, left, right, and center.

The left hallway led to a room with a vast library of books, ancient, and forgotten. Huge tapestries lined the wall from one side to the other with images of past descendants.

The right hallway led to an area containing a huge stone slab in the middle of a forty-foot circular room. A dagger lodge in the stone at one-end and dark depressions on the top of the stone indicated that this must have been a sacrificial chamber. Who did they sacrifice and why? With no other clues about, or evidence of other uses, he ventured down the third center hallway. The passage was dark and musty, with the aura of sadness thrown about. Nosrévis could hear faint screams, agonizing screams from creatures unknown, and they rose in tone and fervor. The size of the room was almost as great as the length of the last hallway traveled. A vast expanse opened up before him as far as the eyes could see, containing stone shelves, hundred of stone shelves filled with ancient vases and fragile steel containers. The screams he heard were louder now, and growing as he slowly walked through the maze of shelves. In the center he stood, gazing all around and in the middle of the expanse, he spotted a slanted stone tablet set in its base on top a metal rack of giant, rust covered pipes. Nosrévis brushed the decayed webbing, dusted the tablet, and began to read the inscription carved in the ancient language of Cavanon.

'*In this chamber rests the spirits of treachery, damned and forever forgotten, never again to see the light of the heavens. The wretched souls that lie within these sacred jars are the accursed of Cavanon, doomed to an eternity of despair for deceitfulness against the Crown. Whosoever shall open of these jars shall inherit the wrath of Cavanon himself and shall never enter the ancient heavens.*'

"What?" he exclaimed, quietly. Not only did the towers inscription confuse him, but also did this; what meaning could *this* hold?

"The inscription on the tower says that Cavanonians committed blasphemy against Ellononis, and yet this says the souls of the accursed of Cavanon are to blame for deceit against the crown." He slowly walked to a nearby shelf and gently picked up a jar. While gazing at the outside, the jar revealed a vague face on it and fear moved him as the face spoke.

"Slave," said the spirit within, "you must release me at once!"

"Slave?" replied Nosrévis, "Slave my ass! Who the hell are you and why should I release you?"

The spirit answered, "I apologize. I am Esnemia, the seventh son of Cavanon himself."

"And that means what to me?" Nosrévis said, cynically. His hands shook a bit from the cold and he steadied himself before he accidentally released his grip on the jar.

"Why are you in here if you are a descendant of Cavanon?"

"Because," the spirit continued, "I was banished from my homeland and from my people for practicing arts which my ancient father decreed blasphemous against our race. I chose not the admirable ways as he, for I learned of a greater power through Ellononis. I sought to discover the one secret that Ellononis kept hidden away from Cavanon himself."

"And what is this secret?" Nosrévis calmly asked.

"Why, the secret to immortality!" said the ethereal spirit.

The whirling motors inside the brain of Nosrévis spun drastically out of control upon hearing this. The key to immortality was considered nothing more than a myth, a delusion that some crazed souls dreamed up since the beginning of time. Now, after hearing this news, it actually seemed a possibility, and this accursed soul inside a jar knew it for truth.

"So how do I free you?" Nosrévis asked.

"Simple," the soul replied. "Drop the jar and break it to pieces, then I shall inherit your body and be free at least."

"Whoa there, friend," Nosrévis answered, holding the jar with a firm grip. "No one is taking over my body, not ever!"

"I must have a host to reside in; otherwise I will die forever if the jar is broken without a host for my spirit to consume."

"Fine, then we shall make a deal, you and I," said Nosrévis.

"Anything!" shouted the soul, "I shall be your right hand and you will have my services forever, just free me!"

"Agreed," Nosrévis smiled in delight. "I must depart to fetch fresh hosts. In the meantime, your first duty is to secure the same promise from all of the other souls in here. If you fail, I will break your jar into pieces and you will never have the chance to fulfill your promise to me, agreed?"

"So be it!" the soul of the face said, bowing his head before the image on the jar faded.

At the mountain cave entrance, Nosrévis gave commands to the ship that waited. "Bring me a hundred bodies, live ones, and they must be of the biggest *human* male imports. Go now, you have your orders!" the ship acknowledged the order and departed.

"While I'm waiting," he said to himself, "I shall see who else we have down here."

Chapter 5

Secret Allies

As time progressed, life slowly returned to the planet and for those on Cavanon as well. With the King back on his home soil, the surface shined with joy and exuberance apparent in the abundant life that regained its status on the plains. The planet also sensed his return and immediately showed its happiness, evident in the new greenness of the pastures and the forests of trees. Carpets of grass and moss replaced the littered remnants of the old war, and erased its signs as best it could.

Adoné returned to inhabit the once peaceful home he and his Queen had created together. Painfully, he thoroughly removed the presence of any wrong doings or signs of the torture his family had received. The *first* things he removed were the hanging ropes of death that swayed in the outside breezes. The memory of his loved ones would not plague his thoughts or heart, as they were with him there in spirit, constantly over watching their future savior.

One day, Adoné was entertaining questions from Sarah and Kayla after explaining to them, in detail, how it all began. Kayla would be persistent in her questioning, as always; there were a lot of things she wanted to know, and with no one else around here to ask, she might as well start with him.

"You still haven't told us why my husband is so important," said Kayla. She asked.

"That, I'm afraid, is a question which even I do not know the answer," he replied. "I have wondered that many times in the past and tossed and turned because of wandering thoughts or ideas of why this happened to me, specifically. Why did they want me? But I never found the answer."

"There has to be some reason," Sarah spoke up, "why else would they go after the same guy three times?"

"I have thought of that as well," replied Adoné, "and if there is some significance to this human, then why not capture him as a baby, before he could have a chance to grow up? Why did they not do that instead and save themselves the trouble they went through?"

"But you are human," said Kayla, "how come you deny it?"

"*Was* human," he corrected her. "When I accepted the change to become Cavanonian, not only did my body change, but my spirit as well. The body underwent a transformation from the old human body of cells, tissue, organs, and bones, and reemerged into this being on a cellular level. I ceased to be human from that point on, fully encapsulated in this reformed body, and I became this new being to preside over a dying race."

"It sounds like you made a bad decision to me," said Kayla, "you have no race now."

"I'm still working on it," he replied. "Things were going great for awhile, and then it all went downhill."

"Adoné!" exclaimed Laura outside, "you better come see this!"

Adoné and all of the others watched as five huge winged creatures soared through the heavens high above the plains, effortlessly. From this distance, the clouds and the moisture within blurred the images that appeared to glide like great pterodactyls or some similar creature, sailing through the sky they flew until out of sight.

"I wonder what those were?" asked Laura.

"And why are they here," said Tanazakh, coming up the front steps. "It seems we are not alone anymore. We should seek shelter."

"Too late for that," replied Adoné, "for their size, they are much swifter than I judged."

The winged creatures descended to ground level and returned, landing in front of the mountain below the steps.

"I'd better see what we're up against," Adoné said.

As he descended to meet them, their size and features astounded him. Their massive bodies possessed wings of membranous bones and material, and overly proportional legs and arms. Claws adorned their hands and feet with razor sharp nails that glistened against the light. Their heads were evil in appearance because of their arched, pointy ears and protruding sharp teeth. The cycloptic eyesight occupied much of the forehead and nose area, barely leaving any room for the nostril holes. Each creature pulled out a sword of its own to their new opponent as he reached the bottom set of steps.

Tanazakh took several of his Srotaderp friends and circled round the strange intruders hoping to catch them off guard. Adoné mentally signaled his friend to initiate the surprise ambush and draw their attention away, but to no avail. It seems the strange winged warriors were anticipating this and all five spread out in a star formation, initiating the attack themselves.

With effortless flight, their oversized blades struck down at the wooden mallets, shattering them to pieces turning them into kindling. Their facial features revealed no emotion or worry, or fear. They were here for a purpose, regardless of whether the inhabitants of Cavanon wished it or not.

Tanazakh did not fair any bettering his defensive maneuvers; his battle-ax took a blow to one end when he hastily swung at the nearest opponent. The ax lost one end as the winged warriors blade neatly clipped off the end as if it were just wood. Staggering back from his position, he armed himself with the remaining segment of his wounded ax. Adoné had seen enough and initiated his own attack by launching himself into the air and swinging his black blade at the winged warrior to his front, but a blocking move met with the King's sternum, propelling him back to his starting position. Separated from his black blade, he revealed the blade of fire and stood firm waiting for them to approach. As he prepared to use his powers to freeze the lot of them, he withheld his energy because of the creatures' next move.

Together, they menacingly stepped toward the King and raised their swords high above their heads, and let them fall to the ground. All five creatures suddenly dropped to their knees and knelt before him. Adoné looked at the groveling creatures and stood extremely puzzled by this response. A glance up to Tanazakh and the others received shrugs of ignorance as well. Not knowing what to do, he ordered them, "You can get up now."

"My lord," replied the center most creature, respectively, "we must kneel in honor before you as we have done so in the past." His voice was low with deep intonation, yet clear and concise. He spoke eloquently and with purpose, something Adoné did not think he would hear from a creature of this size.

"I'm sorry?" the King replied, noticing the docile change in these massive creatures. "I don't know who you are. Why are you here and why did you attack us?"

"Because you attacked us first and because *you* did not know." All five creatures stood up, positioned themselves at the foot of the steps, and sat before him with smiles on their faces. "My Lord, I am Maillewvan of the Tnemucodas," he replied. "It has been ages since we served you, and we are here to serve you again."

"Served me?" the bewildered king replied. "What are you talking about? I know nothing of you."

"We served King Cavanon ages ago during his time of need," answered Maillewvan. "He created us from a slithering wretch that served no purpose and gave us bodies, life, and the will to exist. He gave us the strength to be his protectors in time of crisis, and now we are here to serve our creator."

"Whoa there, Maillewvan," laughed Adoné, "I think you have the wrong guy here."

"But you are the ruling Cavanon, signified by the Sword of Fire, the Crown!" the cycloptic giant replied.

"True, but I did not create you."

"It is true then," said Maillewvan, puzzled, "the ancient prophecy has not yet come to pass!"

"What are you talking about?" asked Adoné.

"I shall enlighten your mind as you have instructed me ages in the past," he said, and went on to explain. Adoné sat down on the bottom row of steps; all the others gathered round as well to not only hear this, but to see these new creatures. Even Tanazakh picked himself up and joined his friend. The manner of Maillewvan's speech gave peace of mind to all within earshot. The mysterious calmness fell over them as if subliminally telling all there was nothing to fear.

"Since the creation of King Cavanon," the Tnemucodan spokesman said, "many Kings assumed his role. Cavanon watched from the heavens as his species thrived throughout the centuries, bringing peace and security to those in need. However, Ellononis despised his brother, Cavanon, and pursued their destruction and extinction. Determined to end the jealous hatred of his brother and ensure the continuation of his race, in the ancestral world, Cavanon threw himself at the mercy of the Ancient Gods and begged them to give him another chance at life by hurling his spirit, essence, and attributes into another form. By doing so, he would give up his place in the Ancients and be given a *new* life. This was not without consequence though. It has been said that his request was granted, but none could say for sure. Determined to find the truth of the matter, the descendants of Ellononis possessed the knowledge to create time machines to import from whatever life existed in the universe in hopes of capturing this secretive host and Cavanon along with him. Unfortunate for Ellononis' line, when one of the creators bragged of this information, another followed suit, and thus the prophecy of Cavanon's return was born."

All outside listened intently and received the same shock as Adoné upon hearing this revelation. "Come on," replied Adoné, "there is nothing written in the Cavanonian Holy Book that speaks about this…I would have read it."

Maillewvan continued, "Ah, this is true, as I stated earlier, it is but a rumor, a tale from the ancients. The search for Cavanon is the reason why all creatures must suffer at the hands of Ellononis' descendants. In addition, one remaining member of the Ellononis line created this race of the Dominion and its forces of the Nogzakhs. Even now, he is still at large."

"So you're saying that I am he, Cavanon himself, come back in another form?"

"That is a possibility," replied Maillewvan. "This is why the Nogzakhs have pursued you and brought you forward in time."

"And this is why Othragon believes he still has John Rykus imprisoned, because he believes *him* to possess the reincarnated spirit of Cavanon." Adoné sat down and thought about his explanation for a while. "That would explain why they brought John Rykus into the future in the first place," he said as he looked up at Kayla and Sarah. "But, isn't it true that the same could be said for the second Rykus that was brought to this time period."

"I know nothing of this other one you speak of," the Tnemucodan answered truthfully. "Our senses led us here, and the prophecy spoke of the ruling authority of Cavanon, no other."

"Let's just hope that is the case. So how do you know this, I mean, where do *you* fit into all of this?" he asked.

"Secretly," Maillewvan said, "when we served King Cavanon, we were told of the treachery to come and the constant threat Ellononis kept against his brother and his heritage. Our race has sworn to protect the King at all costs and to emerge when the time was right. When King Cavanon's life extinguished from natural causes, we slept deep in our planet, frozen in time, locked away from the elements of the universe by the spirit of Cavanon himself. However, we became confused after we arrived and found his home planet void of life. Not knowing the truth of the matter, we discovered the line of Ellononis had spread chaos and destruction through this new line of terror, the Nogzakhs. We surmised that in time, we would find a surviving member of Cavanon, and we have at long last."

"I mean no disrespect to you and your kind, Maillewvan," Adoné said, "but this is too much for me to comprehend right now. I mean, I *know* I am not the real Cavanon. I'm just the same person I always was."

"Be that as it may, we have come to guard and serve you. If there were no truth to the tale, then we would not have awakened."

"Well," Adoné replied, "I wish you would have woke up while we were having all of this trouble to begin with. That would have saved us a lot of pain and suffering."

"As the King repeatedly told us, time and time again, everything happens for a specific reason. Whether or not we understand that reason remains to be seen, but we must realize that whatever the reason is, the path of our destiny is still there before us."

Adoné thought much about his eloquent elucidation and explanation, calm and soothing, graceful, not overbearing or dominant. He could see why Cavanon himself had chosen them to be his secret protectors. Not only were they intelligent, but very intimidating from their size and features. The Tnemucodas gave off the impression they were gentle giants, but one wrong move of an enemy would bring about the worst in their demeanor; something Adoné and his friends had already seen, but only a small sampling.

"I can see why Cavanon chose you," Adoné said. "I do not require you to be my personal protectors, but everyone here could really use your protection."

"We must then relocate our forces here," Maillewvan replied, "it would be a welcome change from the wasteland we currently occupy, not that we are ungrateful, Lord—?"

"Adoné," he replied. "By the way, exactly how many of your kind are there on your planet?"

"Our numbers are one thousand, Lord."

"One thousand?" asked Adoné, shaking his head. He slightly pressed his fingers into his eyes and stroked his hair back over his head, out of his face.

Maillewvan took a step back, "Lord, I spoke wrongfully?"

"Oh! No, my friend," he answered, stepping closer to the huge giant. "I only wished you would have been here much earlier than now, perhaps we would have been spared the pain of losing so many lives to the enemy."

Maillewvan placed his hand on the King's shoulder and said, "Everything happens for a reason, Lord." He received a smile in return. "We shall leave at once and ready our forces for departure. In five days time we shall arrive, you have the word of the Tnemucodas!"

"Make haste my friend," Adoné replied, shaking his new friends' huge hand. "We will all feel better with you here."

After that, the Tnemucodas departed.

Dusk brought about a welcome change to the area and the inhabitants as they dined, for once, outside. Sitting around grand fires, eating hardy servings of Agemoi meat, a sort of oversized deer with six legs and a longer than normal neck. From the staircase, leading up to the Cavanonian chambers, Adoné, Laura, and the baby could see many fires spread out over the plains, brightening up the area with a medieval glow. The nearby forests provided an endless supply of wood to keep the fires burning brightly, and very warm.

To the surviving Royal family, all the other creatures seemed to be enjoying the difference that came with Adoné's return, that and the promise of coming security. The instilled belief that help was here and more on the way gave them peace of mind once again, alleviating the fear that resided in their minds for far too long. Change was welcome in this stage of their lives, and they embraced it, completely.

As Adoné sat on the steps, Laura handed him some food and then sat to feed the baby prince, who cooed and giggled; he knew what was coming. It was evident in his acts that any time food was well in his reach; he forgot everything until his belly was full. Once he finished, the baby began to drift away into dreamland, peacefully, but faster than normal; Adoné was about to find out why. The sudden calmness in the air fell even on Laura, as well as he. Laura took her leave from her father, kissing him on the cheek and heading up the steps to their home. Adoné watched as they entered inside and as he resumed his normal sitting stance, he saw the reason for their sudden departure.

His spirituous Queen hovered in front of him, shimmering with the firelight in the background gave him an eerie image of her to behold. Even in death, her beauty was undeniable, captivating, and enticing. Despite the frosty covering of the viewable image, she held all the qualities he had long since held near and dear to his heart, superseding all prior standards of loveliness and fascination. Perfection was the word he thought to describe his Queen, and in all of her attributes and characteristics, there was not a single flaw whatsoever. Even if he were to *find* a flaw, everything else about her would instantly shadow it, keeping it well hidden; the flaw would not stand a chance of exposing itself to him, she would not allow it. She came to her husband and slowly knelt down in front of him.

"My Love," Xashsa said, floating in the air in front of him, "did you miss me?"

He chuckled, "You know better than to ask me that. I am thankful that all these creatures are here, but in all the worlds there is only one I wish to hold at this moment."

Her ethereal touch caressed his face and her lips gave love to his, passing her feelings and emotion into his very spirit.

"Even in death," she whispered to him, canting her head to the left, "I still love you more than life itself, more than there are stars in the heavens, and it transcends all bounds of time and space; nothing in any form could possess my heart, save you."

"Xashsa," he said, with a tear forming, "I am so very sorry for not being here when I should have been." He shook his head and wiped his tears away from his face, knowing she knew he did not like her to see him this way. "I failed you when you needed me the most. On one hand, I destroyed much of the enemy, or so I thought. But, on the other hand, I lost you and those with you. The pain you suffered is unimaginable and I dare not think about it, lest my own anger consume me and drive me to rage."

"But, Love, as Maillewvan stated earlier, everything happens for a reason." She tried to comfort him with her words and her embrace, feeling the madness rising in him. "The promise of hope is here, and it will reveal itself, very soon. What you must consider is this: if you are, indeed, Cavanon himself, then you must realize that when you fully awaken, you will be unstoppable. Not you, not even I could have known whom you really were, or would come to be. Do you remember when Father deliberately did not tell you about the legions of Cavanonian Warriors that helped you destroy the Dominion fortress on Earth? Well, if everything were revealed to us at the beginning, it would make the journey less meaningful and not as significant as if we discovered it for ourselves. I can tell you, from existing in the ethereal plain, that there is no prouder parent in the universe, save my father. He exists, boasting of his pride and contentment in you to all in the heavens. Once again, you have transcended even his greatest expectations. And, since your life began in another form, he now has a grand love for humans, something he never had before for any other creature outside of our own race."

"Sometimes I think he speaks too highly of me," Adoné spoke up, "but then again, since he never had a son of his own, I can understand why. So, when is this *hope* going to show its face to us?"

"It appears it already has with the Tnemucodas, but not to mention the fact that you have a new body, even if it is the old *human* Rykus. Which means that soon, we should find a likeness for me?"

"Yes," he answered. "I have thought about that. Does it matter what size or features?"

"No," she giggled, "in death I will transform the body to match my characteristics and attributes. Do not worry, Love, I shall be myself for you, again. Remember, Cavanonians regenerate life from death, so death is a blessing for us both!"

"So, are there any others who wish to come back as well?"

"Only myself, and Sarah, your former daughter; the rest have entered into their heavenly paradise to abide with the rest of the family, and watch as we change the face of our race once again."

"All I have to do now is find some bodies," he said, shaking his head, "I didn't mean it like that. What I meant is, hopefully a way presents itself soon."

"It is coming," she whispered, "trust me!" She hugged his spirit in her ethereal arms and held on tightly, causing them both to lose track of their surroundings, everything else, oblivious.

Chapter 6

▼

Twin twists of fate!

On the planet of forgotten souls, the Nogzakhs brought in the human specimens requested by Nosrévis to the chambers deep at the end of the third sacred hallway, in the chamber of lost souls. One hundred of the largest imports of various builds and sizes—exactly what Nosrévis asked for—were stationed all about the large room. Each of the specimens wore a magnetic restraint on their heads, controlling their actions and restricting their thoughts to absolute nothingness. Nosrévis placed a sacred container in the hands of each one of the intended victims and then stood back in the entranceway to initiate the mind control device. Simultaneously, each one of the victims smashed the container at their feet and stood motionless. What transpired next was this:

A great howling and wailing of voices filled the area and echoed with an ominous volume that permeated the room with its presence. A glow of immense proportions lit up the room with colors of red and white light, signifying the release of the imprisoned souls. One by one, each of the freed souls entered into the body of their host, immediately seizing all control and functions. With staggered metallic echoes, the mind control devices fell to the floor, as did the victims. The bodies of the victims began to transform and change their characteristics to match those of their new host; the banished souls began the other important phase.

Inside each victim, a fight for the right to claim the body began. The souls of the victims were no match for the overpowering forces of the imprisoned souls, and they were defeated, easily. Transformation at the cellular level began the moment the body lost the battle to the new soul. The horrifying sounds of alteration accepted by the winds of change whipping around the room, furiously in bright red and white streaks of light and smoke. Cracking bones, bubbling skins, and reconstruction of the tissue showed a presence of will unlike anything Nosrévis had ever seen before. Nails broke through fingertips, teeth reshaped and reformed and became sharpened fangs ready to rip and lacerate through flesh or bone. Newly opened eyes gleamed red throughout the cavern, viewing the doomed confines of their captivity for the first time. Nosrévis' visions of power heightened as he witnessed the spectacle at work before him. Soon, his army of hellions would be ready, and he would use their powers, and will, to his advantage.

Once the assumption was complete, one by one they stood to their new height and gathered into a rectangular formation in the center of the room, with one at the forefront of their ranks. Rows upon rows of howling damned Cavanonians stood firm, shaking their fists to the heavens and laughing at their previous judges.

"We are ready to do thy will, Nosrévis," said Esnemia, proudly. "You have freed us from ages of torture and stagnation and by doing this we shall serve you until the end of our days."

Nosrévis stood proud at the sight of his new army of hellions. With the knowledge they possessed from ages past, his perceived invincibility rose to a new height and implanted ominous thoughts in his mind. He would use their knowledge—all of their knowledge—to serve his purpose and seat himself upon his own throne of domination in the universe. Why settle for a second-hand mercenary when he could be a grand power in his own right?

"How long before your new form is ready for battle?" Nosrévis asked.

"It will take weeks to heal fully," replied Esnemia. "These body compositions are new to us and will require extra time to acclimate ourselves. Until then, we have much to do."

"Yes," his new boss replied. "We must bring you up to speed on what has transpired during your imprisonment. Also, there is much you have to tell me as well, and that will take some time."

"Then let us get started," Esnemia hastily replied, "I wish to rid myself at once of this cavernous hell."

"Come," Nosrévis motioned to the passageway, "let us begin your new life with a trip to our new planet of Elaveshan."

Maillewvan was as good as his word. Five days later, he and the rest of the Tnemucodas entered into the Cavanonian atmosphere. Soaring through the heavens above, a thousand winged warriors blanketed the skies in a great covering so large that the suns could barely penetrate through to the surface. As far as the eyes could see, the winged warriors flew with organization and arrangement. Formations traveled through the skies and broke off at various points to descend down to the planet surface.

Adoné stood on his balcony with his family and friends witnessing the spectacular aerial display in progress. He noticed after the formations broke off that the majority of the new aerial forces took to the mountainous region, spreading themselves out along the ridges and mountain peaks. Despite the ten miles to the mountain range, their giant sized bodies and great wingspans were plainly visible to all. The worry of security left the area now that their new arrivals were here. All began to calm their fears and savor the moment; with the return of their King and these new arrivals, they could resume their normal lives once again.

At the base of Royal Mountain, Maillewvan greeted Adoné and revealed startling information to the Cavanonian King, such that would surprise his new sovereign greatly.

"You are as good as your word, Maillewvan," the King said, "and what a grand force you have brought with you."

"They are eager to serve you, my Lord," the Tnemucodan replied. "They will need some time to establish homes in the mountains and ranges, and set up launching platforms in the mountain sides."

"Do they require assistance?" asked the King.

"Oh! No, my Lord, they are tenacious in their own right and will be done in no time. There is one other item I must disclose to you, Lord," the Tnemucodan stated. "It brings many questions, yet troubles me as well."

"What is it?" Adoné asked.

"We have a machine that we found buried deep within the secret chambers of our planet, and we've no idea as to its function or reason. We are not knowledgeable in such devices and we became very perplexed when we saw it."

"Where is it now?"

"We've brought it here with us, to the new caves," Maillewvan answered.

"Well, lets take a look," Adoné said, excitedly. "Let me bring Tanazakh, my Anadonian friend along, he might know what it is."

Quite a crowd had gathered outside of the Royal house, there were many more creatures that insisted on visiting the mountains as well, even if it were only ten miles away. They never had reason to venture very far away from their own dwellings or the old city when it stood in its beginning stages. Cavanonians and the other creatures that lived amongst them had everything they required within the vicinity of their own homes. The only one to ever venture outside the area was Laura, who in her subterranean abode viewed the entire surface in one form or another.

Now everything must be reestablished—security and defenses—in order to maintain readiness. Even though the inhabitants of Cavanon were in no shape to fight another war, with the arrival of the Tnemucodas, they could at least resume the defensive role. The winged warriors would alleviate the rest of the detail of security and reconnaissance; the Tnemucodas were fit for both.

Although they possessed only on eye each, the level of eyesight was ten times greater than all the rest of the inhabitants of the planet. The eyeball itself did not have an iris layer; overstrained blood veins in the sclera surrounded the blackish-grey pupil. Viewing the surroundings from the mountain ranges to the lone mountain of the King was no great task to perform, everything in between was clearly visible and tracked.

Inside the newly established Tnemucodan sanctuary, large platforms or launching bays were constructed for the ease of takeoff and landing. Individual quarters were split-level, above and below the platforms, which ran lengthwise through the mountainsides. This allowed for immediate departure for all creatures rather than become bottlenecked in a few areas. Once alerted to danger, the winged warriors could be airborne and within minutes the skies could he filled with a formidable deterrent against any outside aggression.

Maillewvan guided the King and his gathering throughout their mountain dwellings to an enormous area that contained a huge construction of metal, wires, and cables. A space of maybe twenty feet by twenty feet contained a six-inch layer of solid steel, imbedded with electrical filaments, spread out in a circular pattern. At four corners of the base sat four steel pillars, six feet high, and had a collection of six, two-inch steel rods, protruding outward from each of the blocks. The head of each block angled inward to a center point within the middle of the base. Off to the rear of the steel apparatus, stood a console of some sort, with large electrical type cabling emerging outward and connecting all four end blocks.

All in the room gathered around the machine and studied its construction, gazing at each piece and wondering what the whole thing could be. None of them had ever seen a machine of this nature, and frankly, they really did not know what to make of it. Actually, it had been some time since anyone had viewed any kind of contraption that needed electrical power. Since they did not use any types of machines or electrical devices, why worry about power, at least why worry about *that* type of power.

"We found this when we awakened from our long sleep," said Maillewvan, "but we've no idea what it is. We are not knowledgeable on contraptions of this sort and we thought maybe you—or someone with you—might be."

"Interesting," replied Adoné. He studied its construction and dimensions, passed the steel console, and gazed into the center of the platform. The buttons on the console did not work, as it had no power. Adoné placed his hand on the console. As he did this, a raw force of energy shot into him from the metal casing. He instantly saw visions race through his eyes and heard screams of terror in his ears. The others saw and heard nothing. His hand retracted quickly from the console and his white sclera filled eyes opened wide as he stood back from the machine. He knew what it was, but could not believe it existed only ten feet away.

"I don't believe it!" he exclaimed, loudly.

"What, what don't you believe?" Tanazakh asked him, glancing between his friend and the machine.

"It's…it's a Time Machine!" he said in disbelief.

"This? Surely you must be joking?" the Anadonian asked.

"It is…I know it!" Adoné replied, and approached the console and placed both of his hands on it. Again, he felt the sensations run through the mysterious current of the machine into his mind. It felt as if the machine had a mind of its own with no one to talk to; all of the memories visually appeared to Adoné as he stood there watching, staring into thin air.

"Father, what do you see?" asked Laura, whose curiosity was peaked just as much as everyone else's in the room. She knew he saw visions; this was evident in his blank stare into the air and twitches he made every so often.

"It's the lives of all those who have passed through this machine," he replied. "It is showing me all those scared, innocent victims from the very beginning of its operation, to its eventual shut down. I never thought I would ever see one of these machines up close."

"So, you are glad then that we brought it to you?" asked Maillewvan.

"Absolutely, my friend," the King scratched his head for a moment. "The only question now is how do we turn it on?"

"But why would you want to do that?" asked Kayla. "Why would you want to bring more innocent victims from their peaceful lives into this forsaken wasteland?"

"Maybe," he said, controlling his anger, "we might be able to find a way to send you back?"

Kayla shut up at once. The direct answer was exactly what she needed to hear in order to refocus her mind and calm her rising antagonism. It was obvious to Adoné that Kayla would not be as understanding as he had initially become when he first became subject to time travel. But then again, there were other forces at work here and maybe they had a hand in his destiny.

"One thing is obvious," said Tanazakh, after inspecting the machine, "we need a power source for it to work. I may not know much about time travel, but I do know that without power, it's pretty much useless for now."

"Where are we going to get a power source?" Adoné asked.

"How about the Kostejaanians," Laura suggested. "They have ships again, ever since they returned to their home planet."

"When are they due to return?" Adoné asked. "Didn't you say they make periodic stops here to check on us?"

"They aren't due for awhile yet," she replied, "not for another month or so. Shouldn't we wait until then, just to be safe?"

"Probably," her father answered. "It would be best to wait until then, no sense in jumping the gun with this thing. Besides, who knows what will happen when we turn this thing on!"

Xashsa could not wait that long. She had ideas, plans, everything prepared and ready in her mind to find a replacement body as he did, in hopes of returning soon to the physical realm. There were many reasons for her impatience at this point.

Firstly, she detested the fact that she had lost control of all of her functions the moment the evil Nosrévis came amongst them and subjected them to the worst possible humiliation and torture. Not only did her anger and hatred rouse at the mere thought of these acts done to her, but also soared even higher as the thoughts reminded her of the same abhorrent acts placed on *all* those in the Royal house.

Secondly, she hated herself for letting her guard down as much as she had in the past. Prior to ever meeting her love, she had been at the pinnacle of her power in all matters of defense, enlightenment, and secrecy. She had been foremost in preventing anything from ever coming within a considerable distance of her house, and she protected it against anything she did not like. Her current husband and his daughter were the only exceptions to date. Since then, her guard lowered drastically. All because of resting her thoughts on his being there, always, and taking care of things for her, instead of her getting involved. She learned the hard way.

Lastly, she missed being in the arms of her King. Not being able to lose herself deep in the comfort of his loving embrace left her emotions untouched and stagnant, begging to be quenched and satiated. This time away from him caused her to remember everything, every moment from initial contact until she was ruthlessly murdered. Her memories were more alive in the ethereal than ever before, and they spoke to her constantly. Not only did her thoughts remind her of what she lost, but also they instilled the instinctive need to protect herself and her King, if she made it back.

In the ethereal realm, the spirituous Queen could move freely and quickly, unobstructed. The journey to the planet Kostejaan did not take long for her. She remembered the course from following their ships back to the Kostejaanian home planet, as well as witnessing the unloading of the Nylantians on their new planet. Traveling there now was a lot easier than providing directions to anyone else that may get lost, disoriented, or simply not able to make the journey without much help. Besides, taking initiative on her part proved quicker.

The Kostejaanian planet seemed barren and absent of life or activity as it sat amidst its smaller moons and asteroid fields. She knew from their relocation they did not dwell above ground anyway. Any would be adversary would think the planet uninhabited, which was the goal of the Kostejaanians to begin with.

Below the surface, the activity and livelihood of the Kostejaanians flourished and thrived. Left alone with no enemies to bother them gave them peace of mind, and they relished it, daily. Every now and then, they thought about life in the past and wondered what ever became of their friends on Cavanon. Naturally, they would check on them, but the schedule called for one more month before they would venture there.

Nyfletoné sat in his own private chambers with others of his race discussing items of importance saved for weekly meetings such as this. He received an updated status on food storages, social organization, and maintenance of ships and equipment secured underground. Status of the planets condition was also a topic of importance, but that usually came up if there were an incident of a large nature that warranted immediate attention. Today the Kostejaanian ruler and his council received a greeting much dissimilar to any of the past.

Xashsa appeared at one end of the room, floating like a ghost in a gentle breeze. Some of the Kostejaanians jumped away from the apparition and began to shout sporadically in their own language, discernable to her. With her apparent telekinetic abilities intact, she conjured up a globe of Cavanon out of the thin air. Nyfletoné paid strict attention as she pointed to a spot on the planet he knew very well. After which she manipulated a like fixture on a nearby table and summoned it to hover in the air before her. While it did, she pointed to the power source slowly and repeatedly, in hopes of getting her point across. After a few choice words between Nyfletoné and his comrades, he motioned for her to follow. Venturing through many passageways, underground gorges, beneath subterranean waterfalls and over lava flows, they reached a passageway to a large, reinforced structure. Midway through the next passage, the structure changed from the natural stone to hardened steel.

Inside the structure sat their massive maintenance bays and hangars. The expanse ran for miles throughout the subterranean area, giving Xashsa a clear indication of just how advanced the Kostejaanians were, technologically anyway. After guiding themselves through work bays, current construction, and rebuilding projectsand workers getting their hands dirtythey came upon a field of equipment that caused Xashsa to become very happy, indeed.

Nyfletoné instructed one of his comrades to summon a power generation specialist to the scene and within minutes, he stood ready for further commands. Xashsa stood amidst the field of power generators all working very well, providing the necessary generation required for the hangars and bays. Nyfletoné stood next to a generator and motioned to it, as if asking if this one would suffice. Xashsa pointed to the generator two systems over, which was double the size of his choice. He motioned his head towards the generation specialist and off he went. Xashsa had no idea whether or not it would provide the amount of power her King needed, but why take the chance on a smaller system only to find out it wasn't enough.

The Kostejaanian gave more orders to his comrades, and then each one departed for another area to carry out his instructions. He turned to the ghostly Queen and found her nodding her head to him, smiling profusely. It seems she was successful in her task of getting her point across, despite the lack of insufficient vocal communications. Once the workers loaded a similar generator onto a ship, Xashsa headed home.

Back on Cavanon, everyone prepared for dinner in his or her own homes. Tanazakh and his family had chosen to dine with his friend and their family, as did Kayla and Sarah. With the amount of excitement that came with this day, there would be more talk and conjecture around the table than ever before.

Many questions came up that required answers, but without a knowledgeable individual around to confidently instruct them, everything would be trial and error. Adoné did not like to think about the error part. Too many variables existed that would, or could, ultimately end the life of whatever came or went through the ancient machine. Would it or would not work? What would they bring in? From where, what coordinates, and how is it programmed? If someone tried to go back in time, where would he or she go? Would they end up in space, on a safe planet, or end up in the middle of a supernova? Clearly, this was a subject above the level of their understanding. They would receive the answers in due time but right now help was on the way.

High above the plains, halfway between Royal Mountain and the newly occupied northern mountain ranges, a ship descended from the upper atmosphere and hovered some two thousand feet above the ground. Tanazakh new it to be the Kostejaanians, but Adoné had never seen them with ships before, shaped in the form of a giant cylinder with enormous spikes protruding off each end. Six massive fixed legs with stabilizers attached, angled down from the lower sections of the main body. Grayish in color, the ships moved with incredible agility and grace, clearly something different that what Adoné thought possible.

"Who is it?" he asked.

"It's the Kostejaanians," his friend replied.

"Laura, I thought you said they were not due to check in for another month?" her father asked. However, all she could do was give a shrug of her shoulders in return. By the time they all rose up to go and meet with them, the ship had moved towards the mountains and landed.

When Adoné and company had arrived, the Kostejaanians had carried equipment and parts into the Tnemucodan room containing the time machine. Once Adoné entered into the room, he saw the Kostejaanians setting up a power generator in the back of the room, laying cables to connect the generator to the strange apparatus.

"How did they know we needed a generator?" asked Adoné, bewildered.

"Who knows," Tanazakh replied, as Nyfletoné approached and extended his arm in greeting. After several minutes of conversation, Tanazakh laughingly turned to his friend and answered his earlier question.

"My friend, it seems that a ghostly apparition, described much like your Xashsa, paid them a visit, recently."

"Ah," he said, smiling, eventually laughing himself. "I guess she couldn't wait."

As soon as he said that, her ethereal arms wrapped around him and enveloped his spirit, signifying her presence.

She whispered into his ear, *"do you really think I would sit and wait for another month to pass before finding out if I were that much closer to being in your arms, physically?"*

"No," he replied, "but I did not think the possibility would happen this soon either. Of course, we still have to figure out if it works, and then we face the problem of how to work it."

"Regardless," she firmly said, "I don't want to wait another second, and your heart tells me it shares my thoughts, exactly."

The Kostejaanian mechanics finished the cabling and hook up, and were now ready for power-up procedures to initialize. Dialogue went back and forth between the operator and Nyfletoné, who then turned to Tanazakh for translation.

"He says we should all back up," Tanazakh spoke loudly over the generator humming. "They aren't sure what will happen, so we also need to be prepared for anything that does come through, dangerous or otherwise."

"Right," acknowledged Adoné. "Maillewvan, spread out a few of your warriors to the other side and have them ready themselves."

"Yes, my Lord," he quickly answered.

Tanazakh moved the others back well out of the way not only to protect them against anything dangerous, but also to keep them out of the way of whatever forces might be at work in this monstrosity. This was a maiden voyage of untold years of abandonment and neglect in the machine, and it was a first time operation of a machine of this type, so they were taking no chances. All eyes stared into the center portion of the machine, waiting, wondering, and watching.

The machine hissed and sputtered at first, spinning a whirlpool of energy between the six-foot metal pillars. Swirling energetic beams of lightening danced around a globe of darkness held in place by the force of the energy, the space existed ten feet in diameter and remained motionless. The initial power up procedures had finished.

After the energy dissipated, a white sphere of light no bigger than a few inches in diameter shined brightly from the center of the platform. The brilliance of the light captured everyone's attention in a hypnotic fashion, flickering every few seconds with distortion. Soon after, faint echoes of sounds, screams, and the roars of something on the other side chanted throughout the area. Screeches and howls of something, beast or otherwise were growing in loudness and volume.

In a brief flash of light, a small amphibious mutation of a crustacean plopped on the steel floor out of the light. All witnessing this event jerked back, slightly overreacting from a greater expectation. Surely, this little thing did not make those sounds, and they were right. In the next instant, another creature, much larger and more deadly plopped out of the light and grabbed the crustacean, savagely ripping it to pieces in its jaws. Before the Gadnoc realized where he was, they gave him no time to react.

"SHIT!" screamed Adoné, "*Gadnoc*—KILL IT!"

No sooner had he screamed and the Tnemucodas, without question, fulfilled his order. One of Maillewvan's counterparts, Kélon, grabbed the Gadnoc thug and wrenched the head clean off its body, tossing the blood spurting carcass aside as if it a mere paperweight.

Astonished, Kayla and Sarah both stood shocked at this order and sentence, unable to understand the meaning for this unjustified murder.

"Why did you do that?" screamed Kayla, "what did that creature ever do to you?"

Adoné gave her a look of coldness and controllably he guided Laura to her. "Where do you think I found her? In their *clutches*, that's where!"

Laura even became slightly agitated from her remarks, "I suggest you keep quiet until you have some idea of what you are talking about. I will tell you the tale when we have more time."

"*You know, Love,*" Xashsa whispered into his mind, "*if you continue to treat her like that, she might yet turn out the same way the second Rykus did—evil and distorted.*"

"*I am sorry,*" he thought back, "*the heat of the moment controlled me, you know the anger I hold against the Gadnoc and the reasons for it.*"

"*Then allow me to explain it to her while we wait,*" Xashsa replied, and went to Kayla.

Kayla was unaware that she talked to herself as she gazed even more intently into the lighted energy, center of the platform. The words of warning given to her occupied her mind and caused her some degree of grief.

"*He is sorry for his outburst, Kayla,*" said the voice of Xashsa in the human's mind, "*but he has good reason to hate the species that emerged a moment ago.*"

"But, I don't understand why?" she replied. "I thought he was trying to bring creatures here?"

Xashsa continued her explanation: "*The one he ordered put to death was from a race responsible for the molestation and killing of many innocent humans. He discovered this before he became Cavanonian. Ever since then, they have sought us out and continually plagued us with dread. We thought we had destroyed them, but now it seems that there are more. Although, there is no telling where they could be now or even where they come from, we must be on our guard in the future.*"

"Thank you," Kayla answered, "at least I have some answers."

The next thing that came through the machine dropped one greenish, froth-covered leg through the lighted energy. The distortion flickered, cutting the leg off from its owner, falling to the platform with a half cut scream that followed.

"Eww," coughed Sarah, "I think I'm going to be sick!"

"Ha! That's nothing," laughed Tanazakh, "imagine what the owner thinks and feels right now?"

"What caused that?" asked Adoné.

After a few seconds of Tanazakh asking the Kostejaanian operator, his friend told Adoné the reason.

"Something in the time disruption pulled the remaining part into another realm."

"You mean another time machine?" asked Adoné, even more anxious for an answer.

"Exactly," Tanazakh replied. "Whatever it was, another time machine claimed the rest. They are probably wondering where the leg is."

"Shit!" exclaimed the King, "we can't risk being detected with this machine. If the enemy finds out we have one, they'll come for us again, and we aren't ready for another attack."

"Then we'd better shut it down, now!" shouted Tanazakh.

Before he could issue instructions to do so, roars emanated from the energetic time sphere, and onto the platform fell one, two, three…ten *humans* of various shapes and sizes, all screaming and wiggling in a conglomeration of pretzel shapes forms. Quickly, Adoné and the others pulled them off the platform and placed them up against the wall. Two males, four girls, and four women all total. One medium aged woman had wide eyes of shock in her face and she was not breathing. The time travel had scared the life out of her, literally. Adoné tried CPR on the woman for several minutes but received no response. Knowing her fate, he screamed, "XASHSA, *Here!*"

Instantly, the woman's body began to show signs of forced life, evident of her puppet movements and gyrations. Adoné carried her off to another part of the room, not wishing for the human Sarah or Kayla to see this; they might not understand the meaning at this very moment.

Tanazakh and the others saw to the others, except one girl who had fallen out cold. One other entity in the room that did not make her presence known dove into the body of the unconscious girl and the same type of action began in her as well.

"By the Gods, this is strange," Tanazakh said, wondering what that cause was. "Adoné, what do you make of this?" he said as he pointed to the collapse, spastic girl. "Is she sick?"

"Oh no!" he said, with a slight idea of the cause, "please say she didn't do this!" he quickly took her away to join Xashsa, still transforming with in the dead body.

"Shut off the machine!" Tanazakh shouted to the operator.

Shut down procedures commenced and the sequence immediately terminated before anything else could come through. All at once, the energy dissipated from the platform and the noise of the generator died out to a solid thin whistle remaining in all ears. Nothing remained from the time travel test except for the cries of the fresh new arrivals seated on one side of the room. Adoné new this was no place for them to be, but with no other alternative available to them, they might as well begin the indoctrination to their new lives.

Adoné segregated one male human and brought him away from the others, seating him against the wall. The man appeared to be unharmed, but severely shaken as anyone would be from the traumatic experience; the Cavanonian King hoped it was not his fault.

"What is your name?" he asked him, directly.

"Please don't hurt me," the man screamed and squirmed, "god, what *are* you?"

"Relax, you're safe, I asked you what your name is, *answer*!" Adoné demanded.

"Stan, my name's Stan," he replied, "what are you going to do with me?"

"Nothing, I told you, you are safe. What do you remember prior to this happening?"

The human, Stan, looked about the place at the other creatures tending to those who had come through with him. It was clear to him then that this creature was telling the truth that they were safe; otherwise, they would be treated differently.

"We were in a dark room," Stan said, horridly, "a place with lots of others like us, and some other weird creatures, too, but much uglier creatures I've never seen before."

"Go on," Adoné replied.

"It was a big room, and these ugly wolfen creatures beat us badly and killed most of us. Then some bluish things took out the bodies and began to chop them up, eating them at the same time."

"And this room you were in, was there many rooms like that, or was that the only room?" Adoné was curious at this point; his questions led up to a point unknown to the terrified human.

"I think there were more. I could hear louder screams outside the room, but I could not see outside the door. Soon after, they moved us somewhere different, I don't know how or where to, but we ended up in a cave. What were those things?"

"Believe me when I tell you that we saved you from a fate worse than death," Adoné said, happily. "It will take longer to explain it. Right now, join the others and do not worry, no harm will come to you."

Stan did as the strange creature instructed and went to the others.

"What about them?" Stan asked, pointed to the two segregated bodies, still squirming on the floor.

"They are passing, do not fear for them. It will be explained to you in due time."

"My friend," Tanazakh said, coming closer to him, "the Kostejaanian has some good news to reveal." His friend listened intently as he watched Xashsa and the other at work within the dying women. "It seems they have a lock on the last coordinates engaged by the time machine. It is apparent there are more humans there, do you know what this means?"

"Yes, my good friend," Adoné replied, still looking at the bodies. "If my guess is right, we've locked onto a storage room somewhere within one of the Dominion importation centers. But, if they came from a cave, it could mean somewhere else."

"That was my guess, too." Tanazakh scratched his head and contemplated further. "That means we can save more humans and other creatures, and at the same time reduce the food supply of the enemy."

"If we do that now," Adoné said, looking at his friend, "then the enemy might detect this and be able to lock onto *us*. It is too soon to implement a plan like that, but it is a plan, no doubt. Please, thank the Kostejaanians for this; they are invaluable to us, more so now than ever before. Make it so to them."

"Right you are," he pointed to the new human arrivals, "but what about them?"

"We need to take them to the Helena's; they will know what to do with them. Sarah and Kayla will help," he said as he looked at both Sarah and Kayla. "These two others I will see to…personally."

After thanking the Kostejaanians and the Tnemucodas, Tanazakh and the others escorted the frightened new arrivals to the Helena's, while Adoné and Laura carried the other two to Royal Mountain. The new arrivals needed immediate assistance of assimilation with those who were already accustomed to the era and environment, and it would be some time before they became a productive part of *this* society.

Inside the Royal home, the returning party placed the transforming bodies in a closed room to finish gestating. Adoné and Laura would patiently wait and keep themselves occupied, gainfully, until the process was completed. During this time, Adoné would be impatient but appear to be in control. He knew who was coming, and his heart and soul could not wait one minute longer for her to emerge. He would also become happy with the emergence of Sarah. He knew she dove impatiently into the body of the other, she simply followed suit of her Queen. Still, her father would have to counsel her severely for taking over the body of another, forcefully. This was the first time ever that his daughter had taken a life before, and he must remind her of her unscrupulous deed. However, that would come later and well after the initial happiness had settled.

Chapter 7

Unexpected Sights

Federoth felt trapped in his solitude on Samajap. Administration duties did not sit well with him and flared against his inherent traits of plaguing others with dread and fear. Somehow, the management of his forces in the form of organization, logistics, personnel issues, acquisition, and procurement of additional equipment and food shrouded his overall plan of dominance. He might have thought differently had this been pointed out to him sooner. The new commander now had to face facts and come to the realization that being in charge of everything did have drawbacks; the idea of being taken out of the fight simply went against his will.

Bound for Nomaseri, Federoth placed his second in command in charge for a while and decided to pay his friend in crime a little visit to see what mischief they had recently come into. He had not seen his friend since the annihilation of Cavanon and felt it was time to make up for his absence.

As his ship descended on the face of Nomaseri, a greeting party already waited below, the same as they had on previous occasions. A full compliment of Nomaseri warriors stood formed and ready to receive the Dominion commander. And as soon as the ship landed, the warriors immediately escorted the commander and his entourage off to the city.

Federoth visited this planet in the past only a few times, but during those visits he did not notice what a jewel the planet Nomaseri actually was. Giant red trees lined the edges of the golden moss covered ground on the plains to the dominant mountains afar off. Immense rivers ran through plains and valleys, carrying green algae colored waters everywhere on the planets surface, gathering in seas statically located throughout the region. Mountains of grayish brown possessing age and decay stood quite solid and firmly fixed. In this area, no cities or civilization were evident, only the strange indigenous creatures that roamed wild and fierce, hence the reason for the warriors.

Some of the creatures viewed were violent in nature and equally abhorrent in size and features. Dragons of various sizes and shapes dominated the lower life forms such as deformed boars, spidery shaped Ghegnas (similar to bears, but with eight legs with claws), herds of Boradus resembling a warped shade of Antelope or Elk, and the myriad of winged Khasdan that roamed the skies without fear.

Federoth took in the sights with pleasure, as creatures such as these did not inhabit the desolate zero gravity planet of Samajap. Nothing could survive on the surface of his planet without some type of assistance from a bio-suit or thermal pressurized environment, much like the Nogzakhs had invented. The flickering idea of relocating Samajap and Tiracus forces to a different planet entered his mind, but the immense task of relocating such numerous forces would take ages to complete erased that idea, quickly.

After moving through a huge rusty gorge, for what seemed like hours, the city of Edoratis came into view. Spread out through the vast valley floor, the city invested a beauty that appeared to contradict the Nomaseri characteristics.

Towering pylons of security existed and encircled the entire area around the city. Based in solid stone, these pylons towered up five hundred feet in the shape of a huge candlestick. Bluish paths of light connected the tops of the pylon towers one to another, boasting a conveyance carried by the light to each tower. Some one thousand feet behind the perimeter of the pylons, a two hundred foot steel wall encircled the city that provided extra protection from unwarranted intrusion. Additionally, it kept out the myriad of surface wildlife, which could pose a serious threat if unchecked.

The city itself spread out inside the walls and proved a marvelous aptitude of engineering. Steel buildings built in the shapes of pyramids lined the city for as far as the eyes could see. All buildings were the same shape except for the five dead center of the city, which doubled in height of the five hundred foot pylon towers. Four other pyramids of equal size sat on the four corners of the main pyramid. As the precession drew closer, the tops of the four cornered pyramids opened up and allowed the Nomaseri fighters to exit, taking flight.

"Not a bad place to house fighters," thought Federoth, *"right where no one would look."*

Federoth's attention was elsewhere as they glided over grand floors composed of titan marble, shielded with a substance stronger than glass, and unbreakable. When his glance lowered, his breath escaped him as the magnificence of the ground stunned him. As he walked over the unblemished surface, he did notice that in certain diamond shapes areas, bodies of their dead enemies laid under the glass with the horrid shape of death evident on its face. Some two hundred feet he walked, gazing at the fear and stagnation in those slain ages ago. Of all the different dead creatures beneath his feet, none made him smile more than seeing a *Cavanonian* under his feet. *"How long has this one been here?"* He wondered.

"That one," a familiar voice said, "was slain many eons ago in the wars against the Dolumek."

"Rudecor, my old friend," replied Federoth, "pardon my hesitation, but the ground has caught my attention, most enjoyably."

Their hands met with a firm shake and compliments as the explanation of the dead continued. Glancing back at the ground, Federoth knelt down to get a better look at the expressionless face of the encased warrior.

"This Cavanonian," explained Rudecor, "singularly tried to infiltrate the Nomaseri ranks while our attention was elsewhere. He did manage to kill a significant number of our troops, but the overwhelming numbers captured him, ripped out his heart, and ate it in front of his eyes, hence the reason for his apparent lack of expression."

"As he was no doubt stunned from such action opposite of his beliefs," replied Federoth. "I'm sure your warriors wished to disembowel him right then and there, no?"

"On the contrary, it was all our fathers could do to prevent it. But, the body was secured and ordered to this place to serve as a reminder that even *we* can kill Cavanonians…no offense meant."

"None taken," Federoth replied with smile. "Need I remind you that I am so far removed from Cavanon that the Gods themselves have disavowed me?"

"Actually, I never considered you Cavanonian to begin with, my friend. Surely you did not come here to marvel at our collection of the dead?"

"Not quite, but I do have other matters I wish to discuss with you, privately, if you don't mind?"

"Then come with me," Rudecor led the way. "While we walk, I shall show you of the creatures most recently placed in the flooring, you simply *must* see them!"

The top most level of the main pyramid housed the private chambers of the Nomaseri ruler. Here, he had the most luxurious of accommodations at his disposal. The level had many rooms such as his own grand meeting room, a dining area enough to sit an entire platoon of troops, sleeping quarters of equal size, and his own library of literature, acquired from all over the galaxy.

The chambers on this private level were constructed much the same. Walls and pylons of precise angles and measurements gave genius to the motif designed by their ancestor's eons ago. Windows were non-existent; instead, the walls of a particular area gently disintegrated and allowed the natural light in; a controlled motion by the degree of light required. Sheer walls of untouchable matter took the place of the steel allowing objects out, but nothing coming in. The unnatural engineering kept the rains and winds at bay, which gave the Nomaseri something to sulk in, controlling the elements.

While Federoth and his friend roamed the chambers, lesser Nomaseri women brought grand dishes of seared Ghegnas meat and flesh into the dining area and placed them on a solid marble table. Special drinks of the well-known Zalestolian blood wine were served to both the ruler and his guest. Nomaseri women were something of a dish themselves, opposite of Cavanonian belief.

Greenish yellow hair adorned their heads in a row from the forehead to the base of its skull, flowing down to mid waist. Slightly bulbous light green eyes protruded faintly from their sockets, giving a strained yet piercing glance. Overly membranous ears shaped as batwings flapping effortlessly on both sides of the head, and held up sharply when items of importance found their way inside their minds. Slender light green figures and shapely bosoms found their way through sheer makeshift clothing absent over areas of privacy. Delicate hands possessed a thumb and three fingers, with extended nails capable of slicing the meat from a carcass with ease. Federoth could not help his glance as his friend carried on his conversation, fully aware of Federoth's attention span. All the servants left the room, except one.

"She is a sight is she not?" Rudecor said, smiling.

"I apologize, Rudecor," he replied, embarrassed, "but I did not expect to see such a beautiful creature."

"Then permit me to introduce you." Rudecor motioned for the woman to come closer to him and she knelt as she came within arms reach. "Rise, Eñala," commanded Rudecor, "meet our guest and please him."

The servant came to Federoth and gave him a seemingly innocent hug. Suddenly, and without warning, she kissed him in her own passionate, yet violent way, causing Federoth to think twice about their method of pleasure. She was strong, much stronger than he perceived her to be, and forceful as she held her mouth to his, swallowing his fluids, while simultaneously running her other hand in through his clothing, down to the throbbing pylon of his own. Once she grasped him, firmly, he pulled back away from her and stood gasping for air. Too late, the amount of eroticism she dished out caused his emissions to weep.

"By the Gods!" he exclaimed, "how did she do that?"

"Ha!" laughed Rudecor, "did she not please you as so ordered?"

Federoth quickly glanced between the two, noticing a very big smile on the servants face mixed with an expression of slyness.

"Yes, she did, but you ordered her to do that?"

"My friend, in what way do you think our women give pleasure? She knows the arts of sexual gratification very well and she practices them very efficiently."

"Well," he said, still gasping for air, "I can see why the enemy would fall so easily to her. A Cavanonian could not hold a candle to your women."

"Thank you, my friend; she is yours for the duration your stay here. Do not worry about being gentle with her, and I won't mind the screaming."

Federoth glanced at Rudecor who stood smiling from ear to ear, as did Eñala. *"Screaming?"* He thought to himself, *"I've no idea what he means by that, but I'm sure I will definitely enjoy the experience!"*

After dinner, the scraps of remaining flesh and meat were carted off to the lower forms of waste management, namely the wild dogs kept in pens underground that ate just about anything thrown to them. Leftovers never posed a problem; every strip of uneaten flesh would fill the packs stomachs.

Rudecor relaxed on his spacious pillow cushioned couch while Federoth lost his gaze to the outside view of the city. The ruling Nomaseri wondered if the cause of his friend's attention really was the view, or was it the servant?

"Yes," Federoth answered his friends thought. "My mind does dwell on the woman. It seems she has awakened a dead spot in me I thought long departed."

"She has a way of doing that, unexpectedly," Rudecor chuckled. "Supposing she does bring lost life back into you, you know what she will do if you intend to love her and leave, don't you?"

"Why would I do that?"

"Here is a friendly warning, before you get yourself too far in trouble," his friend said, cautiously. "Nomaseri women can become possessive when their feelings have picked a mate for life. If she, Eñala, should feel that way, know then that she will never leave your side, or allow you to leave without her. Once her inner being senses she is appreciated, she will then turn to become yours for eternity."

"Oh! Come now, my friend, what makes you think for one minute that she would latch onto me in that manner? I just met her and you said she could be mine for the duration of my stay here."

"Your thoughts cannot keep your feelings at bay; this is evident in your erratic breathing and glance into the unknown. She can sense emotions and feelings within you, and I did not expect you to react this way."

"Well," replied Federoth, "we'll just have to wait and see. Surely, you don't think I came here to discuss matters of carnal knowledge, do you?"

"Of course not; please enlighten me as to the purpose of your visit, aside from the long absence." Rudecor rose, went to the table, and poured two drinks, giving one to his friend.

"During the time you were on Cavanon, did you once see a sword of fire anywhere?" Federoth asked.

"No," he replied, "I saw nothing of that nature. If I had, I surely would have taken it. Something of that nature seems very valuable to you."

"It does. It means a great deal to me and I would give any amount of wealth to have it in my grasp just once."

"So what is it, exactly?"

Federoth turned to his friend and sat opposite of him. "It is the ruling Crown of Cavanon, and I would give anything to have it."

"So, why do you come here seeking it?"

"Because," Federoth lowered his head, "the last time I saw it was on Muidiri. It was there, so close to me and yet Othragon ruined my chance to get it. The whole time I was there, it secretly followed me around inside the station. Unfortunately, once I learned the Cavanonian King was amongst us, it was too late. Othragon made it abundantly clear that this King would die and at that moment I knew that if he were to have the crown then my chances of getting it were futile."

"So then he took it with him?"

"Not necessarily, no. A crown of that nature cannot simply disappear. I do not believe it can exist in the ethereal realm, only the physical, unless possessed by a ruling Cavanon."

"So that means that it quite possibly has returned to its home planet?"

"That is why I asked if you had seen it at all on the surface." Federoth stood up and looked again outside the chamber walls. "It has to be somewhere, some place elusive, hidden from view, and I must find it. Perhaps we should dispatch a patrol to the planet Cavanon and search it, thoroughly, just to be sure."

"Federoth," Rudecor rose up and joined his friend, placing a hand on his shoulder, "there is nothing there, nothing. We destroyed everything, murdered all those who supported the royal family, to include the family itself. Our warriors were very thorough in their tasks. Even I, standing inside the house of Cavanon, felt no such emanations of such a crown. If I had, I think you would have read it in my mind already."

"I suppose your right. I must re-read the ancient books to include the Book of Zalestole; perhaps I have overlooked some key evidence hidden within its secret meanings."

"That you should," his friend agreed, "but that can wait for later." Rudecor turned his glance towards the door, Federoth followed suit and his eyes met with the servant, Eñala. "Perhaps something else to take your mind away for awhile?" hinted the Nomaseri ruler. "Be gentle, yes?"

"Its not her I'm worried about, my friend!"

Eñala's eyes locked onto Federoth, even as she descended the stairway to his own quarter's levels below. She knew he was on his way and he read it in her mind.

Nosrévis finished the indoctrination process for his one hundred new hellions brought back from ages past. There was much to tell them of the time they had lost locked away in that isolated chamber of horrors. What madness drove through their minds relentlessly, savagely, picking away at their sanity along the way? Nosrévis knew the rage in his hellions would make them a horrifying sight to behold in mortal combat. Their fighting skills with swords, clubs, and weapons of just about anything, gave them the feeling of power that had long escaped their grasp.

In secret battle chambers constructed specifically with them in mind, Nosrévis watched the sparring between each one. Skillfully, they dueled amongst themselves, whisking their weapons in the air and subjecting themselves to within mere inches of death with each swing of the opponent. They were neither afraid of death nor afraid of dying, not at this point. Dying would be a favorable outcome opposed to the prison of steel that once held them captive. Subjecting themselves to the whims of fate pleased them very much, tempting fate worse than they ever had in the past.

Esnemia told his new lord all the names of those freed. Many once held stature and semi-prominent status in the once luxurious Cavanonian realm eons before their untimely destruction. Amongst those freed—aside from Esnemia—the brothers Komachis, Zhaseek, Kelesor, and Eteledos received punishment in a purgatory of steel simply for practicing the worship of Cavanon's long time enemy, his own brother. That was enough to have the brothers imprisoned in regular dungeons, but the fact that they were princes at one time mattered greatly to the Royal Cavanonian family at the time. Their sentence was to be a final lesson in life.

The others freed consisted of many members of the guards, elite warrior forces of the King, and guardians of the crown itself. Generations of Cavanonian soldiers from the time of Cavanon until the reign of Solisynas gained imprisonment for just about the same crime, treason against the race, their religion, and their King. The various reasons for their imprisonment did not matter to them. Their conduct and belief in the aspect of immortality meant more to them and seemed an attainable possibility, if it were truly feasible.

While Nosrévis observed his hellions in practice of their combative skills, Esnemia came to him and joined him. Both watched the hellions with pride as their Cavanonian skills displayed their knowledge of hand-to-hand combat, and it became abundantly clear to their new boss that these were not mere guards or slaves of any sort, but rather swift killing machines designed and trained in the arts of desecration.

"They are impressive, yes?" Esnemia asked.

"More than I envisioned," Nosrévis replied. "No wonder you were all locked away for life. If you had been left unchecked, you would have proved to be very formidable to anyone who would have opposed you."

"Singularly, no, but combined we would have easily defeated the reigning king and then everything would have changed. Unfortunately, we did not live during the same lifetime. Each one, or two, lived one generation after the other, so combining was impossible. But now, you have made it a reality and I guarantee you nothing will oppose us this time, save you, of course."

"And let it remain that way," Nosrévis said, cautiously. "I did not come to power simply because of my good looks."

Esnemia smiled at his remarks and questioned him a bit further. "Exactly how did you come into power, if you don't mind my asking?"

Nosrévis turned his red-eyed glance to him and proudly said the reason. "I annihilated all those who lived on Cavanon."

"You single handedly removed the reigning monarch from his throne?"

"The monarch was not home. Othragon vanquished him in his chamber of horrors on Muidiri, while I vengefully raped, tortured, and killed the entire royal family, quite easily. My forces, aided by Federoth and his new Dominion, destroyed the remaining alien inhabitants of the planet."

"Very impressive I must say," Esnemia replied while clapping. "So where is the crown then, if the King is no more?"

"I'm not sure. Federoth wanted it badly and vowed to his end to get it. Maybe he has it already?"

"I remember hearing about Federoth from the others who were around in his generation. The warrior, Raftan, who was there with him, seduced the queen's daughter Xashsa and used her for his own displeasure. Apparently, he was the sixth husband to her before his treasonous acts found their way into the King's ears. It seems that his crime of performing sacrilegious rituals, coupled with his ill-tempered treatment of the princess, doomed him to his fate. Nevertheless, he enjoyed every minute of having her, knowing the king despised him greatly and was looking for a reason to rid him from sight. He told the stories constantly while in that damn room."

"I should talk to him then," Nosrévis smiled, "I had her too, and after that, I hanged her."

"You're kidding me, right?" Esnemia glared at him.

"No, I'm not kidding. I used my powers to control their minds and functions, they were unable to withstand my will, and I relished the humility they suffered. I can still taste her mind, a delicate flower, easily crushed by force."

"It seems you harbor more in your mind than I give you credit for," he backed up a step, "I would hate to suffer something as equally restrictive." He doubted the powers his lord spoke of and forgot that the evil being in front of him knew telepathy very well.

Nosrévis used his will to enter into the mind of Esnemia, gaining control of him in the aforementioned manner. Esnemia turned by force of Nosrévis' will and kneeled before him. It was clear to the returned Cavanonian that this one clearly was in possession of powers unlike he had ever felt, and he would be sure to avoid his wrath in the future.

"Can you now see the humiliation and horror of it?" Nosrévis glared into his kneeling friends eyes, which showed much fear in them. "I simply will it and *you* execute the task. With this form of control, I subjected the entire royal family to a hell unknown to them and they screamed violently because of it." After Esnemia's eyes grew larger and sweat formed on his brow, Nosrévis released him. He coughed a bit, staggered back against the wall, and watched as his new lord willed the same control on all the combating warriors below them. Each one in turn faced him and kneeled on the ground like peasants pleading for mercy. Groveling was not their style and Esnemia knew it, but he watched them prostrating there, helpless to do anything about it.

"It does not matter how many are in the room, all are subject to my will. Quite a useful tool for you to doubt, don't you think?" his lord turned and revealed the darkened creature within. A face distorted, elongated, and dripped blood from his teeth and gums. Red eyes bled down his mired, charred skin, all the way down the line of his jaw, dripping splats of blood on the ground at his feet. In an instant, Nosrévis' face returned to normal, smiling. "Let that be a lesson for you and the others," he warned. "You are safe as long as you hold up your end of the bargain. But, if you should decide to aspire to greatness above myself, then I will show you the true face of humiliation."

While Esnemia collected himself off the floor, his thoughts hid themselves in the back of his mind. Never again must he think clearly without knowing or suspecting that his every cerebral notion was under scrutiny. Esnemia stood back off to the right side of his lord, watching as he stood there with a grimacing look on his face.

"Gather them together, Esnemia," Nosrévis said calmly, "We have much to talk about. I must find out more about this sword of fire. If it is the crown, as you say, then perhaps I should seek out its location as well. Why stop at the pinnacle of my power when I could become feared forever?"

"Yes, Lord," answered Esnemia.

In another part of the galaxy, Othragon sat on his great throne of bones and skulls, hunched over, slicing the flesh off his latest catch that used to be a creature as large as an elephant on Earth. Digging out the fatty tissue and cartilage, his engorged mouth slopped entrails and internal fluids of the creature everywhere about his face, hands, splattering on the floor. Cleanliness did not sit in his mind and there was no need to waste precious time on such characteristics when they meant nothing to him in the first place. To him, there wasn't a creature alive who could challenge him or his ways, much less criticize his disgusting eating habits. However, he did venture over to a nearby watering hole to wash off the mess, wiping off the contents of slop and filth. He realized there *was* at least one reason to wash occasionally, right before praying to his lord. However, this type of ritualistic prayer gave him instant answers.

The big Othragon entered a chamber specifically constructed for just such rituals. Standing in the middle of the room, inside a circle of fire, he prostrated himself in front of the stars that shined above through an opening in the wall. Minutes after his concentration elevated his senses to the point of reception;

lights appeared to gather in the center of the opening, orange, yellow, green, then yellow again. They culminated their brilliance with the color of a dark, arterial red, deeper than almost any red color possible. Seconds afterwards, echoing sounds bounced from wall to wall within the chambers, piercing the stone and soaring around the room in search of purpose, and finding it in the middle of the chamber.

"*Ahhhh, Othraaagoonnn,*" said an eerie voice from the great beyond, "*it is I, your Master and Lord, the Lord of your Father, and the God of your lineage.*"

"*Ellononis,*" he answered, "*the great Father of my line. My lord has heard my call, and I am here to serve him.*"

"*My faithful servant, why have you called on me?*" Ellononis asked him, even though he already knew why.

"*Great Father,*" Othragon said in his deep grimacing voice, "*I have the one who has eluded us for eons. I have found him, though I have made two other mistakes in my search, forgive me, I pray thee.*"

Ellononis spoke up, "*my faithful servant; Cavanon disappeared from my sight ages ago and has not been seen since. I sincerely doubt that he is as trapped as you say. Though your mind and heart are in the right frame, I fear you have been misled yet again.*"

"But, Great Father, I have him here in a prison of ice. Surely, he is the elusive Cavanon who sought to gain another chance at life amongst these mere human mortals."

"*Bring him up at once,*" Commanded the voice of Ellononis. "*Show me this human so that I may see him and confirm that you have been deceived.*"

Othragon did as the spiritual father commanded. He rose the ice block up from the depths of the subzero temperatures that ensured the ice would never melt away, setting the ice prison off to the right of the chambers. Othragon then summoned the energy from his essence and focused his concentration on the ice. The frozen block suddenly began to quake and shudder, as if shedding the frost off its skin. Then, with a powerful blast, the massive ice block shattered completely, and chunks of ice fell off to each side revealing the true contents inside. Othragon was stunned to find that his prize catch was not there. He reached one of his hands into the center and grabbed a handful of the contents, which was nothing more than dirt and grime from the surface above. Throwing it back down to the floor, the enraged Othragon screamed a horrific scream almost shaking the chamber walls to the ground themselves, but instead causing them to weep red and green rivers of blood all around him. These rivers came from the solidified creatures he used to build the chamber walls.

"How...how could this be possible?" Othragon asked. "*I had him firmly within my grasp. I heaved his body inside personally. I threw the switch within seconds of the closing the doors. There is no possible way he could escape, let alone survive!*"

"*He did not survive, my faithful servant,*" Ellononis answered. "*His body was taken before all cells within him truly died. Our enemy, the one being who can ruin all our plans for the future, a physical future for me, that is, has taken him and possessed his body. With this new host, he can defeat us both!*"

"*I will seek him out, even unto the ends of the universe. I will find him, I swear to you, Great Father; no soul shall escape my wrath until I have him dead in my hands.*"

"*I have no doubt of your word and your soul reveals the same message.*" The spirit of Ellononis came to him and stood before him in a haze of smoke and energy. The image of his being came into view for Othragon, and he beheld his creator in his eyes.

Ellononis was quite different from his created brother, Cavanon. His features were dissimilar and horrifying to anyone other than his faithful servant, who shed tears of pain and agony at his sight. The face of Ellononis was demoniac in nature. Fangs of great length protruded downward from his upper jaw. Five each four-inch fangs stuck upward forty-five degrees from the lower jaw outside of the hanging fangs. Catlike eyes slanted upward and downward and ran past the two nostril holes, also slanted the in the same manner. His earlobes hung down below his jawbone, and the upper much thicker lobes ran upwards following the curvature rise of his skull, running past the apex a full twelve inches above him.

Ellononis wore a red robe that shimmered and gleamed with the ancient symbols of his own invented language embroidered in silver and black thread. The symbols, understood by Othragon, read; "Hell is the beginning, and Death is our Father, We are eternal, and so is Ellononis."

A dark hand appeared to Othragon as if the hand of death were about to touch him, personally. "*Do not fear my touch, my faithful servant. Only those of me can withstand my concentrated evil, my blemish of dread and suffering. I shall be quicken you and charge you once again to seek out our destroyer. Beware there are others who seek him out as well. Two seek the Crown of Cavanon for their own deceitful reasons. Though they say they are of us, their intentions and ideas are masqueraded, and they will only bring about their own destruction. Be invisible to them and let them do the work for you. At the culmination of their findings, they will meet together on the planet of the Tnemucodas to begin the ceremony of my reemergence. I shall make you aware of the time and you shall be waiting for them!*"

"*Dark Father, in what manner shall you return? Through what medium do you now exist?*"

"I reside in a host who does not yet know the truth, but he will come to know in time. Although he knows not that he carries me inside him, he is compelled to rise to greatness and deliver me unto this dimension. He knows not his true potential, but he will come to you and you shall help him to find the firesword, and protect me."

"Great Father," Othragon pleaded, "*I beg of you to reveal to me the location of the crown and its holder, so that I may strike now, end his life, and return thee to the physical realm.*"

"*My faithful servant,*" answered Ellononis, his voice and image beginning to fade back into the ethereal of the ancients. "*Although I have the power to see many things, one thing I cannot see is where the crown lies as its essence is hidden from my view, even in the ethereal. Sleep now, rest yourself, and contemplate my words, I shall come again unto you when the time comes. Until then, farewell, my faithful ser-rrrrvaaannnnttt!*"

The dark Lords deep sinister voice faded into nothingness, leaving the echoes of Othragon's screams to filter through the air and dissipate. Othragon wallowed in his pain and screamed a vengeful scream into the air, filling all the spaces within the chambers and out into the other areas. Although his thoughts told him to initiate his own search, his orders were clear and concise, and he would follow them to the letter.

Chapter 8

Time to Wake Up!

On Cavanon, Adoné sat with Laura and the baby prince in the main room of his home staring at the door to the room where the bodies of Xashsa and Sarah transformed their new hosts into their natural Cavanonian form. Xashsa would be able to repair the body of the dead woman, easily. However, Sarah, who had entered her host by force, battled for the right of ownership for the body, against the will of the old host. She would require more time than the Queen would to finish the transformation, but eventually she would awaken as her Cavanonian self again.

Laura saw impatience growing in her father and remembered how it was for *her* when they went under a similar transformation from their once human species to their new Cavanonian state. She also remembered that after she had exited the room of transformation and couldn't get back in, finding out only then that her father had not yet finished the process. The progression took much longer for Adoné than her, not because of size, but rather due to his acceptance of the torturous method of alteration. For the rest of that day either she stood by the door or sat down waiting for him to emerge.

"You know father," she said smiling, "I remember when I waited for you to come out many years ago when we engaged in this process."

His attention caught her voice and he shifted his sight to her, giving her a smile in return. "I remember that. Your mother told me about it later on that evening. I often wondered why you remained there all day long waiting for me to come out."

"At that time, you were the only father I ever knew, and even now the only one I *will* know. If you hadn't saved us from those damn Noleon and Gadnoc idiots, all those humans and myself would probably be dead now. From then on, I didn't want to be away from you any second longer than I had to be. I trusted your instinct, I needed your guiding hand, and you were the sum total of what I envisioned a father to be." Laura walked to him and hugged him, sweetly. "Once we made the change to become Cavanonian, I became even happier seeing what I could do in this new form. If you hadn't suggested I change, too, then I would not be as happy with myself as I am now."

"But," he interjected, "we did go through a pretty bad time a while ago. That was the first of the dark times since our changeover, a sad time, indeed."

"Yes, but after talking with the dormant spirits who reside in the heart of this planet, I have a feeling that in order to overcome our past, we must ready ourselves for the impossible to come."

Startled, Adoné looked up at her. "What do you mean by that?" he asked.

"Some of the spirits I talk with have been around since the beginning of Cavanonian history," she said calmly, "and one or two of them have a secret that they won't tell me. When I ask them what the secret is they become frightened. Mind you, they are ghosts—spirits in the ethereal—and they become scared of my prodding. Can you believe that?"

"No," he answered, his face blurred with question. "Why would spirits get like that if nothing can harm them?"

"Without them telling me, I will never be able to answer that," she shrugged. "One thing is for sure," she paused to look at the door where Xashsa and Sarah lay changing, "We will have to see if mother has found any answers while she was on the other side. I know she listened while I spoke with the spirits and I am willing to bet she has questioned them herself."

"We will have to ask her when she is ready, but first we—" His speech abruptly halted when he heard a sound coming from the room. Just as he stood up, the door opened up slowly. Both he and Laura glared forward in a stare of expectation, wondering if the change back to Cavanonian form was successful. Anticipation rose to an unprecedented height as the staggered back slightly, just as Xashsa's image emerged from the darkened room.

There she stood once again in all her glorious beauty, perfectly fashioned and shapely figured, exactly the way he remembered her in all her previous days of life. He staggered back a few steps, not in disbelief, but in surprise. Xashsa was back, standing in front of him with her white hair flowing from an absent breeze. Her skin had changed from its bluish nature as before to the matched blackness of her husband. Her white sclera eyes illuminated as she beheld the sight of her love, holding her arms up to him, aching to hold him again.

Adoné dropped to his knees in an instant and began to shiver from the excitement and happiness from the burning desires flowing through his veins. His love stood not more than five paces away and yet he could not move. His entire body bowed to his Queen, his life, to show its unbridled happiness at the mere sight of her.

"My King is bowing to me?" she said in that same luscious voice he remembered every moment since she her untimely demise.

"To have you back," he replied, "I would sacrifice myself before Cavanon himself to see that you never have to die ever again," he said profoundly, rising up to his full height.

"Let *others* sacrifice themselves for our sake so that we both may live in each others arms, eternally."

In an instant, they came together in a blaze of passion and fury and held each other close together, so close that even air could not flow between them. Their lips met together and kissed passionately, their very essence telling the other how much they had missed each other; even their spirits proved the strength of their love. Their eyes met together in a blissful manner, illuminated with their feelings and desires. Nevertheless, Xashsa required something, something additional and essential, and she made her desires known.

"My Love," she said, "I need to be complete, more than I am now. Only one thing I require remains in you."

"Take what you need of me," he said, tilting his head back, baring his neck to her, "there is enough in me for the both of us."

She smiled her wicked smile and revealed the deathly cold look she wore years ago. Her complexion changed to match the one in his dreams, and she knew this look excited him. The one facial expression she possessed could bring him again to his knees and keep him longing for more filled his eyes with a welcome fear, causing his body to shiver.

"You're doing that on purpose, aren't you?" he chuckled.

"But of course!" she exclaimed, "your heart asked me to!"

As she smiled lovingly to him, she quickly dropped her smile and her facial features quickly changed into the hideous beast of the warrior Cavanonian she bore within her nature. To a creature ignorant of this trade characteristic, it would seem that a demon had a hold of the King. However, to him, *the* ruling

Cavanonian, the creature that held him demonstrated a trait of hers that would not be as dormant as it had been in the past. As if he could be no more ecstatic, she repeated the same words she gave to him on his day of total transformation.

"*Muye Kasha ke* (witness my undying love)," and instantly, she sank her daggered incisors deep into his jugular vein. Adoné gritted his teeth and felt her teeth penetrate his skin, muffling an intense strain from within his lungs as they sank in deeper. With her left arm holding him against her body, she forcefully tilted his head even farther to the right with her right hand to accommodate the lustful grip her mouth had on his neck. His arms slowly fell to his sides and moans of joyful pain emanated from his throat, signifying his total acceptance of her feeding.

Laura watched in awe, not scared or frightened from the horrifying sight her eyes beheld, but instead happy that a love she did not yet know existed right in front of her. She knew the act that took place; the King was giving his Queen back the true Cavanonian blood her body needed to complete the transformation. This task was not necessary for him to accomplish when *he* came back. Because of his regal stature, and being the ruling Cavanonian, his inherent powers transformed him over completely, blood and all.

Xashsa eased the suction her lips had on his neck, her killer beast dissolved, and her natural beautiful complexion reclaimed its place. Her mouth agape to the air above dripped the blood from her lips down her own neck, her skin absorbing the royal red cells as well. Nothing of him would go to waste, not one ounce of it. Every part of her needed him and now that she was back, she would not let another moment go by without proving it to him.

"The...that" he said, shaking and stuttering, "you...you gotta do that mm...more off...often."

"Is that a command, Love?" she asked, smiling profusely.

He returned a smile almost as big and as his head lulled from the drainage, he managed to answer her, "you, you know it is." His head fell back.

Xashsa carried him over to the waiting couch, cleared off by Laura. She placed him down gently and covered him with a blanket. As he laid there resting from the enjoyable trauma, Xashsa leaned forward to him and kissed him sweetly as she gazed upon him and the immense smile he wore.

"Are you guys at it so soon?" said a voice from behind them all. "Gees, we just got back and you already wore him out?"

"Sarah!" shouted Laura, turning to greet her, "you made it!"

The two sisters hugged each other happily and tightly. "I am so pleased you made it back. But, does this mean you have to feed off him too? I don't think he could take it in his present state."

"Oh!" Sarah said, "so they didn't do the—"

"No," Laura said, shyly, "even *I* know it is too soon for that."

Xashsa stood up and hugged her as well, smiling her happiness of this great reuniting. Sarah knelt down beside her father and caressed his head, giving him a sweet kiss on the cheek. She held his hand and gazed into his face as he opened his eyes to her.

"Sweetie," he said with a proud smile, "I'm so happy you are back, even though what you did was wrong." He spoke of the body she overtook and killed for the sake of her return. Inside, even she knew it was wrong, but she did have her own reasons for such a drastic overtaking of another life.

"Yeah, I'm sorry. But damn it, I wasn't going to sit there and wait any longer. Mom had a way back and I wasn't going to wait for a dead body to present itself. I think the last thing we need around here is any more dead bodies of our own, don't you think?"

"True," he answered, exhausted, "you'll have to give me a day before I can replenish you; your mother did a real good number on me."

"That's okay," she replied as she stood. "Actually, I think we need to get out of these shredded clothing and back into our normal clothes." She hinted to the Queen.

"I suppose your right," Xashsa replied, "even though I wish to remain naked for my King, I suppose I must dress more appropriately."

"You two are something else," Sarah laughed as she excused herself and went to her old room. Xashsa first saw to his comfort and then went off to her own room to wash and dress as suggested. Laura went in first and guided her to the baby prince, who was sound asleep. Xashsa gently picked him up and held him close to her, smelling his sweet innocence and purity. She hummed a soft tune to him as she went over to a solid wall. With a simple wave of her hand, the secreted door revealed itself and inside she roamed through the myriad of clothing that remained in the same state as she last remembered. She went back to the bassinet and placed the prince inside, giving him a tender kiss to keep him in his peaceful slumber.

Xashsa washed and dressed herself in a simple sheer nightgown. She noticed from the apparent darkness outside that time still held the dead of night in its grasp, so there was no need to dress now. Instead, she readied the bed and went to collect her husband. Carefully, she carried him into the room, placed him on the bed, and pulled the covers up to his chest as she climbed in. Adoné was down for the count. There was no way he would wake up at this moment. This she understood, so she put away her desires for lascivious activities and wrapped her arms around him, swiftly drifting off to join him in his dreams.

Sarah and Laura both noticed the time as well and went to bed. Even though Sarah had just returned, Sarah knew the extra sleep would do her much good. As she climbed into her bed, she thought about the act to come of how she would have to drink from her Dad. She thought about the possibility of another way, a simpler way rather than bite him as Xashsa did. The thought lolled around in her head for a while until she had fallen asleep and drifted off into dreamland.

The next morning, Sarah and Laura were up early to greet the day. Sarah welcomed the new day as the first of her rebirth; a Cavanonian reborn has reason to celebrate. Even though her torturous murder was hell on her senses, mind, and body, she instinctively rose above it. In the ethereal, she learned the meaning her father and Xashsa, who she considered now her mother, had tried to teach her years before. Cavanonians rejuvenate life from death, and out of death they rise anew, strengthened, and quickened with a much greater and precise measure of power then in their previous life. Sarah stood on the balcony where the enemy thrust her body over to hang and die in the wind. The pain returned the memory of the torment she endured and her anger rose for the first time in her life. A new instinctive reaction took over, one that she had never known before but was blessed with from the touch of the ancients in the ethereal.

Her hands rose up in front of her and glowed with a marvelous blue light. Streaks of electrical current flew inches in the air aimlessly and then joined the together in front of her. The sensation of electrifying current shot back and forth between her hands and she revealed a smile much like that of her Queen mother. Sensing the greatest exhilaration, she held her hands up to her sides and enveloped herself in a blaze of energy, a current impregnable and dynamic. So full of force was the current that the edge of the balcony she stood on rumbled and shook vigorously, vibrating from the intense energy. Sarah, unaware that her next move happened by instinct as well, could feel a change in her form. Her face changed to the same hideous features she had witnessed on the Queen earlier and as she looked down at the balcony's edge, she drew her hands together and shot a powerful blast of her new energy in that direction, causing the solid stone railing to disintegrate outwards. The rage of energy transformed more than her face. Her whole body had altered into a beast as large as the Srotaderp and stood poised over the remainder of the balcony.

Unaware of other eyes upon her, she loomed over the edge and howled at the sun. The eyes behind her understood the spectacle; Sarah had embraced her gift of form, her new form, the instinctive defense mechanism that would surface any time danger reared its ugly head in her direction again. Her anger subsided and withdrew and the natural force of defense calmed as well, changing her back into her natural loving self.

She heard clapping behind her and as she turned. She noticed Laura clapping, standing with Xashsa as she cradled the baby prince in her arms. The expression in her queen mothers face spoke of pride, evident in her enormous smile.

"It is truly a day of joy and happiness when the last of the Queen's daughters has finally risen to her calling," said Xashsa. "You have attained what you did not inherit when you changed over to our species."

"And what is that, my mother?" Sarah asked, coming closer to her.

"The gift of Cavanonian dominance," Xashsa answered. "You have been touched by the ancients and given the gift of purpose, which is to strike down those who oppose us. You could not do this previously because you were still untrained and unaware of your natural inherent abilities. Oh, you dabbled in the lesser crafts but those are not the sum total of our traits. Now you see what was veiled before. So, now that you've tasted your gift, how do you feel?"

"Like I could take on the world!" exclaimed Sarah.

"Precisely, and that will lead you to the next step: control."

Xashsa hugged and kissed her and felt a little of the residual current on her skin. Laura smiled, too. She knew how Sarah felt now; she felt it years before and had learned the secret from those who resided in the planets core. The spirits were the ones who trained her in the use of her gift and elevated her senses to near that of the Queen's. Now, at the time of Sarah's rebirth, they were both truly sisters.

"So," said Sarah, "does this mean I have to bite my dad the way you did?"

"No," said her father as he came from the back bedroom, staggering a bit from last night's depletion of fluids and rest. Wearing a gray robe, he slowly walked into the room to join her and the others. Nearing her, he handed her a chalice. She took it in her hands and at the same time looked at him with question and surprise.

"I took the liberty of draining a generous amount before I came out. Draining me in the manner witnessed of the Queen is reserved only for her."

"You know," said Sarah, "this would seem sick to us if we were human."

"But we are not," he smiled, "and never will be, ever."

Sarah took a small sip. She raised her head suddenly looking at them all with wide eyes of pleasure. "Oh! Man!" said exclaimed. The taste was very different from what she expected. It wasn't the thickly coagulated taste of plasma and red blood cells, instead it was sugary, sweet like honey wine. Of course, many years ago before she became Cavanonian, she did not consume any sort of intoxicating beverage or wine. She brought the chalice up to her face and viciously slurped and gulped up all of the contents. Again, like the Queen, she held her mouth agape and the streaming blood absorbed into her skin as it trickled down her neck.

"Damn! That tasted better than I thought it would," she said, suddenly feeling dizzy. The chalice fell out of her hands and she braced herself against a nearby wall. She had the look of drunkenness about her and a smile that indicated such.

"I'd better sit down," she said. Laura helped her to a chair. "Am I supposed to feel this way?" she asked.

"Yes," Xashsa answered. "You've never tasted blood before. This is expected the first time, but you will get used to it."

Sarah and Laura both looked at her funny, turning their heads like a wondering animal.

"If you think that is wild," Xashsa continued, "just wait until we find an enemy in our midst. Then, you will feel the rush again as you desecrate them, violently. My mother taught this to me when I was young. I had not the luxury of filling myself from a chalice, though, I had learned in combat much like you will in the future."

"I've got a feeling I am going to like this!" said Sarah, as she felt the rush of royal blood flowing through her veins. The child from long ago had disappeared from her being and surrendered its space to the new creature she harbored within. With this new sensation of power, she would not sit idly by like an addle pupil. It was time to train, and train she would.

"I thought of another slight problem," Adoné said, "that we must take care of very soon." Xashsa glanced at him with question. "Sarah needs to change her name, since the other Sarah is here with Kayla. That would lead to confusion in the others."

"I suppose," replied Xashsa. "What do you suggest?"

He thought about it for a moment and answered as if his mind were already made up. "I suggest she take on your mother's name, to honor her as well."

"That is an excellent idea!" Xashsa smiled. "What a fitting way to pay tribute to her legacy, and it seems fitting for the gift we have already seen."

"So what will my new name be then, if you don't mind me asking?" Sarah, eager to hear the name, edged closer to them.

"Zérnoda!" whispered Xashsa proudly, echoing the name with a hiss in her voice.

"Zérnoda?" asked Sarah, with question in her eyes, "what does it mean?"

"It is pronounced, Zair-no-da, and it means 'Beautiful Predator'," her mother answered.

"Hmm, I can get used to that. It might confuse the others though."

"They will get used to it," her father replied. "Speaking of the others, I wonder how they are faring today. Those new humans must be freaking out by now; we'd better check in on them."

The Helena's were indoctrinating the new arrival of humans who had arrived rather unexpectedly as a result of the time machine power up. The new humans were having a tough time dealing not only with the continuation of the time travel experience, but also the sudden shock of a different sort of freedom. This was freedom in a dissimilar way, but that was not on their minds right now. Instead, they listened in on what the other humans had to say about how they were saved long ago and who their new protectors really were.

The Helena humans tried their best to explain the current situation and promised to guide and care for the new arrivals until they adjusted. However, to these outsiders, it would take some time to get used to the fact that there was no going back. There was no possible way to reclaim their old lives on Earth of the past and the hope of performing such feat did not exist. Some were already questioning the obvious lack of technology absent from sight. They could not perceive living in such a primitive time and did not see the advantages of it. The new arrivals were unaware or forgetful of the certain death that awaited them. Helen tried her best to tell the same tale told to them by Adoné. The description she gave was more gruesome then the new humans could fathom. It was all impossibility to them, unbelievable and much too far-fetched for their shattered minds to comprehend. But, they would understand in time; the Helena's would see to that.

Throughout the day, meeting and greeting the other species of life that existed on Cavanon was another inevitable task. The new humans would have to meet them for obvious reasons. If they were to live on and survive, they would have to know that not all who resided on Cavanon posed a threat to them. The new arrivals must know who is who and what they can do in order to understand the ways of other life forms that existed. Tanazakh and the Anadonians were hideous to them, the Srotaderp scared them shitless, and the Tnemucodas, well, they just frightened them *beyond* description. Still, the forced meeting of all took away the new humans' sense of fear and gave them a little bit of peace knowing these creatures meant them no harm. It was a trying task for a few; the others were simply not as brave. The other humans—Kayla and Sarah—were there to help them.

The outside air gave them a source of hope with the sunlight and fresh air. The sky seemed a bit awkward looking though, as if a tint or shading were placed high above. In the sky, hundreds of Tnemucodas warriors flew through the vast empty skies, effortlessly riding the winds of the upper altitude. Spread out like a huge net, each winged warrior soaked up it share of the twin suns rays, taking solace in a bath provided them by the clouds moisture.

The Srotaderp were busy removing large boulders that littered the once heavily trodden dirt roads and paths created when they first arrived here. They wanted to keep busy with activity and repairing paths and old structures gave them the peace they needed to carry on. To the kings of the underground, sitting around did nothing but make them stagnant and lazy, qualities they instinctively detested. They were workers and they prided themselves for being masters of their trade.

Two miles to the west of Royal Mountain, Tanazakh and his family were fishing on the nearby shores of the Zedgen Sea. Ever since Adoné taught his friend this trick of fishing, Tanazakh had a thing for aquatic flesh; it appealed to his taste. Oh sure, he could easily dive in and spear them or pierce them with his own cylindrical fingernails, but Tanazakh hated the water or rather the idea of getting wet. He bathed regularly, but only when the stench of his body hinted the fact to his family.

The entire area slowly came to life as the morning suns rose up in the sky. A majority of the humans with the new arrivals ventured outside to roam around the area, to familiarize them to the new surroundings. Jade, a woman Adoné saved long ago, told the newcomers of who lived where and why. She also explained that the hideous underground Srotaderp were busy clearing the way for them to reconstruct their old homes. She sighed with relief that soon all would be living above ground again and the return of the King, Queen, his daughter, and the new security forces of the winged warriors meant that they were safe from outside aggression.

As Jade assigned the new arrivals their new living areas, ones they must help clean up and restore, Adoné with his family came down to pay a visit. The King remembered the man, Stan, he single out and questioned soon after he fell through the time machine. He had questions for him, questions that needed answers in order to quell the rising frustration of the unfortunate journey of the new arrivals. The questions had to do with where they were, what they saw, and how did they survive?

Not long after Adoné found Stan, he sat him down on a downed tree and began to converse with him, at first attempting to put his mind at ease since Stan was obviously still frightened of the Kings seemingly abnormal appearance. Was it the teeth or the color of his skin, or the seven foot height? No matter, that wasn't important at the moment.

"Stan," Adoné said calmly, "tell me more about how you came to be in the presence of our enemies, and please be specific."

Stan looked at him with reservation, wondering what good this information would do for him here. He cleared his throat and began to tell his tale.

"It was January, 2006, and I was at the bus stop waiting for my kids to arrive home from school. Several other parents waited there as well, all of us stuck to our own little groups. Obviously, I hung out with the other parents I knew, only a couple."

"So there were three of you standing together?" Adoné asked.

"Yes. Jimbo, Clyde, and I usually hung out together. I think it was because the three of us worked around the steel mills and the others at the bus stop looked down on that occupation. They usually had their noses so far in the air they could have smelled a bird's ass flying by.

"You work with steel?" Adoné asked, curiously.

"Yes," Stan answered, "not the usual metal worker style, mind you, but in the craft of fashioning and forging unusual metals into whatever the customer wanted. All three of us had our start in the steel mills and worked for years, but decided to work in fashioning instead of the industrial sector metals. I guess you could say we had a gift for shaping metals and we all had the same kind of mentality for it. Anyway, we stood there waiting when all of a sudden this weird visual distortion enclosed us. We tried to get out but a filmy substance prevented us from doing so. It was like putting your hand in the air and the air moved, rippled, and waves of air circled round us. A wind blew around us furiously and electrical streaks of light shot around us. I didn't know it at the time, but the area we stood in became smaller and then Boom! Everything went black. When we woke up, we could hear screams, weird screams, as if something were attacking or ripping something or someone apart. It was dark where we were, we couldn't see anything. Then, as I stood up trying to find my friends, other things kept bumping into me, frantically. I kept getting knocked against a wall. Suddenly, a door opened up and at that time, I could see a crowd of things standing in front of me.

I don't know what they were; I saw some humans or those who resembled humans, and a lot of other strange creatures I've never seen before. That's when the wolf headed creatures came in and started beating those in front of me, throwing bodies out the doorway. Once they did that, the screaming grew deafening, almost ear splitting. They were, I...I—"

Caught up in the moment, Stan's speech stuttered and stammered. He appeared to relive what he wished were only a bad dream. Nevertheless, Adoné new what he saw; even the wolf-headed creatures, the Gadnoc. As frightening as it was, Adoné had to hear the rest.

"Its okay," he said calmly, "it is in the past and you will forget in time, go on."

"Well, after the wolf-headed creatures beat us severely, they took some of us away and left the room, closing the door behind them. As we stood there holding ourselves together, a bright light came out of the center of the room and again, everything went black. When we woke up, we were standing in a pit, a huge rectangular pit that had some really ugly looking thugs standing up on the rim of the pit. They looked a little like you, but they were red, like the color of blood."

"They looked like me?" asked Adoné, "are you certain of this?"

"Yeah, I'm positive," answered Stan sharply. "They pulled out the biggest of us, Jimbo and Clyde, too. That was the last time I saw them. Shortly after that, they pulled out some more of us and began pulling them apart, breaking their bones and ripping off their skins, eating them as they went. My God! What were those things and how could they do that to them?"

"I've a very bad feeling I know who and what they were, but first, finish your story and I will give you the answers you need."

Stan wiped his watery eyes and stared blankly at the King.

"They took out the other weird creatures that were with us, leaving only us humans in the pit, about fifteen of us. As the ugly creatures left, again we saw that damn light and ended up in a cave, a dark musty cave, with bones that littered the floor. Some of the bones were human, I could tell from the skulls. But the others, I have no idea what they were. There was a little light in the cave and we all hid ourselves wherever we could find a hole or crevice, any place that we could fit in. Outside the cave, we heard strange sounds of thunderous footsteps banging the ground and they echoed throughout the cave. I thought it was a dinosaur or something huge, but that was impossible. But then again, I thought time travel was impossible. Just then, inside the cave a huge creature emerged and almost filled up the cave inside. While we were trying to figure out what the hell it was, something pulled it outside the same time we saw the light again. Part of the creature was pulled off, I leg I think. Then, outside we heard roars and groans, deep and growling, like a lion or something. Most of us wanted to see what was happening, and when we gathered in the middle of the cave creeping closer to the cave entrance, the light took us again and we woke up where you found us."

Adoné seemed puzzled from his tale and sat there next to Stan wondering.

"Oh wait, I forgot a part," Stan interjected. "I forgot the hallway."

"What hallway?" Adoné asked.

"It was just after the dark room filled with many creatures. We fell into another room. When we got up, a doorway opened up and revealed a hallway that went on for a great distance. The floor was a grating like in a steel factory, and far below it looked like lava or something. We ran down the hallway as fast as we could, turning many corners and going through other doorways. Some of the others with us tried to jump to the walls but slid down to their death; they burned up in flames when they reached the lava. The rest of us kept on running and when we went through the last doorway, we fell again, all of us. We were running so fast that we couldn't stop and we all fell for a long time, until the light took us and that's when we ended up in the pit place."

"Unfortunately for you," the King said, "you had to endure a lot more than I did when I originally came through with my family. I can't explain the purpose for the long hallway; I've thought about *that* one for years, but the rest I can explain."

Adoné knew this was going to be difficult for Stan's limited human mind to understand. Stan understood most of his own story, but did not understand why or who the mysterious creatures were. The King would do his best to break it down for him in terms he could understand.

"Okay, first off you *were* brought forward in time."

"How far in time are we?" Stan asked.

"About four thousand years in the future, near as I can tell."

Stan's mouth dropped open, revealing his true disbelief. "Four thousand years? You have *got* to be kidding."

"I'm afraid not, but let me continue. The dark room you were in was a processing center for an alien enemy force—the Nogzakhs of the Dominion—and they use the time machine to bring in its food. They never go out for food; they just bring it to them. Usually, they can only import three creatures at a time, or so we thought. Now it seems they can move large amounts of creatures around in this time. The wolf-headed creatures are the Gadnoc: a sinister species that are in league with the aliens who control the time machine. They are the underhanded assassins that do their dirty work because it is all they know how to do. The pit seems to be a place of another enemy that used to be human. I used to be John

Rykus, a human just like you. However, when I was brought here I escaped the enemy and found help in some of the creatures you see here. I became another creature, one with powers and authority over a dying race I have yet to restore. The enemy tried to capture me a second time because of what I later discovered was an old prophecy. They thought by capturing me a second time that the meaning of the prophecy would be discovered and the one they sought to capture would be in their custody. We *found* the second me and saved him, he was safe until he left us and went off on his own. The enemy found him and transformed him into something else, something evil. You could say it is the truly evil side of my kind, this Cavanonian race. Apparently, you landed in their own type of feeding pit, where they store their own food until eaten. The cave you were taken to is yet another enemy, but a more powerful and grotesque form of evil. With all these bad guys out there, you'd think they gave evil new meaning, but they are hell bent on the destruction of everything except their own. They seek the crown which I possess, and to stop the fulfillment of a prophecy I do not yet understand."

"I sort of get the part about the bad guys," Stan said, "but the part about four thousand years ago is staggering. I mean, this has been going on for that long?"

"Longer," replied Adoné. "This all started over one hundred thousand years ago in another dimension that ran parallel to the dimension we lived in on Earth. In the beginning of *this* dimension, the Gods created two sons, one Cavanon and the other Ellononis. The latter hated the first with a passion simply because the Gods gave the first created son the crown of authority. His brother became enraged and jealous and swore to steal the crown for himself and give his lineage the blessing of power. That's how good and evil in *this* dimension started, but the form of good and evil that exists here is much different and distorted than what you and I remember of Earth's time."

"I understand the evil because I've seen it, but where is this good you speak of?"

"You're looking at it," Adoné replied.

"But you're hideous; you look like a ghost that fell into a pit of charcoal or tar. How could you be on the good side at all?"

"That is a limitation of your perception," Adoné said sternly. "Goodness doesn't always have a pretty face, it has many forms. The particular form you see in me is the pure form of Cavanon, from the first created son. Our ways will seem very different to you and you will be amazed."

"Oh I doubt that," replied Stan, cynically. "I don't think there is anything you could do to—" he abruptly stopped as Adoné disappeared right in front of him.

Stan looked around on each side and behind himself, but he saw nothing. Suddenly, he felt something touching his shoulder and slowly the King's image remerged above him, upside down.

"There is much you have to learn about us," Adoné said, "you must believe in the unbelievable now."

"I...I don't think that will be a problem."

Adoné flipped right side up and floated in the air in front of the disbelieving Stan. The King flew around in the air in a dazzling display of aerial acrobatics, coming to a soft landing before him.

"How can you do these things?" Stan asked, curiously.

"Easy," Adoné replied, "I am Cavanonian; these are traits inherent in our species. Every one of us can do some of what you saw; others can perform different feats of amazement."

"So anyone who is like you can do this? What about us, we are defenseless in this era of time. Why can't we do these things if we are in the future?"

"Simple," Adoné replied, "you are still human and humans are limited. However, there is a way you could become like us; you would have to die from your current form and be reborn into ours. It's painful, but hey, I did it and look at me now!"

"I'll have to think about that one. I don't like the idea of dying, although I should have after all I've been through."

"You still need some time to adjust to our way of life on Cavanon; there is much you have to learn and you will learn from the others along the way. I'm sure you already have learned much in the past day or so."

"Yeah," Stan answered, "but right now I'd like to get some food."

"My friend Tanazakh is coming and has a load of fish, why don't you help him out and you'll get the sustenance you require."

Chapter 9

Spiritual Enlightenment

    Federoth stood by the window of his guest room watching the hustle and bustle of the thriving community outside on Nomaseri. The sprawling controlled metropolis of Edoratis boasted of complacency and appeasement of all who lived here. Everyone enjoyed the freedom of their unique city and either worked to perform some medial tasks, run about on personal errands, or simply enjoy the luxuries at their disposal.
    Federoth lost himself in the view for the moment and took delight in a scene so very different from that of his own planet. However, a moan from behind him disturbed the vision. His glance over to the bed revealed the inevitable outcome of last night's wild sexual engorgement caused by Eñala. He viewed streaks of red and yellow splashed over the bed that appeared as though a painter had lost control and decorated the bedding, but Federoth knew the cause. He began to contemplate the events of last night and relive the moments one more time. This is what took place:
    After leaving the company of his friend, Rudecor, Federoth followed the servant and headed down to his guest chambers. He lost sight of her through the winding staircase to the floor below and continued to his own chambers. After not seeing her anywhere, he assumed she had retired for the night. He undressed

from the regular garb he wore for the day and slipped into a simple pair of shorts and a robe, tossing wristbands and other decorative items onto a nearby chair.

He spent time by the window, taking in the sights of the spectacular sunset and marveling in its shimmering aura. From the location of his window, the sunset cast a beautiful golden glow over the entire city, streaking its way past the myriad of surrounding pylon towers and other pyramid buildings to his immediate front. After a momentary yawn—and assuming the servant was in no mood for nocturnal mating rituals—Federoth disrobed and lay down on his bed, immediately closing his eyes. Spreading out over the bed proved that there was plenty of room for at least four others should he decide to take up more than one servant at another time. The structure of the bed itself consisted of a stone base with steel grating underneath to support a great amount of weight. The four cornered stone legs rose up, met with the ceiling, melting with the stone above, and gave off the appearance of being carved out of the room itself. However, something tugged at his mind, his conscience. He released the structural contemplation and opened his eyes.

After focusing briefly, he saw that the servant—Eñala—did not return to her own chambers, but instead was already waiting for him in his own room, secretly adhered to the ceiling. She seemed to float effortlessly above him, slowly swaying side to side. In doing this action, he could see she did not float but rather supported by tentacles that protruded from her back, which attached to the ceiling and caused the wondrous spectacle. She had even more tentacles than what were visible to him and slowly each one made their way around her dancing in a snake-like fashion in front of him, hypnotizing his vision, and mesmerizing his already intoxicated mind.

Eñala slowly lowered herself to him until there was almost one foot of distance between their bodies. Federoth attempted to reach for her but a tentacle smacked away his hands before he had the chance to make contact.

"You should come down here," he said, "that way I can satisfy you in my own way."

Eñala had other plans. "You are not familiar with the mating rituals of the Nomaseri, are you?" she said in a soft, fainting voice.

"I'm afraid not," he replied. "I've been meaning to ask, but the chance slipped me by. It has been ages since I've been with anyone, but my firmness will not disappoint you in the least bit."

The servant laughed at him and as she did so, her eye color had changed to a redness to match his. Saliva dripped profusely from her gaping jaws and lips, down onto his chest and face. "Your firmness is not the only thing I am craving," she said, devilishly. "I will acquaint you with our method of satisfaction and then you can deduce for yourself whether or not I am as innocent a creature as you perceive me to be."

Federoth smiled for a moment and saw deep into her red eyes. Suddenly, while captivated by her compelling glare, the extra eight tentacles hidden behind her slammed into him, taking root into his sides, forcibly. Four tentacles on each side anchored into his body from below the armpit, into his ribcage, and lastly into his skin just above the hipbone. Federoth screamed in pain and Eñala joined him with an equally impressive scream to match. The shrieking sounds of suffering ran amuck throughout the chambers and made their way up the stone staircase.

In the floor above, Rudecor engaged in his own pleasuring acts of sexual carnage with a few of his own *male* servants. He paused temporarily as the screams from below made their way up to his chambers and permeated the air as well, only not as severe. From this distance, the echoes gave the screeching voices a hint of the dangerous activity about to take place in the room below. The Nomaseri ruler knew all too well what was about to take place. He knew the ways of their female counterparts and, from experience, did not wish to partake of the hellish appetites of their own women. Rudecor did try to warn his friend but rather than take the time to explain, hinted by Federoth's apparent infatuation of the Nomaseri female anatomy, he figured it would be best for the dark Cavanonian to experience it first hand.

Back in the guest chambers below, Federoth felt the intense agony of the penetration of her slinky members into his body. Before he could attempt to pull them out, Eñala had pulled his body up from the bed in the air almost to the ceiling itself. Bracing her body with her hands and feet against the four bedposts that met the stone ceiling, she lessened her grip on the ceiling and plunged the extra snakelike members into his body as well, deep into his back. Her claw like fingernails scratched away at his chest area to leave her mark—as if the snakelike extensions did not already do that for her.

In addition to her other limbs, her vaginal area itself did not sink down onto him or allow him inside her, but instead it formed into a snakish limb of its own, seeking out its intended prey. Elongating towards him, the vaginal sexual member (green and frothy in appearance) had teeth of its own which encircled the inner orifice. Once finding his standing organ, her membranous appendage engulfed its prey, sliding its inner walls over his sensitive skin, simultaneously scraping the sex organ with its own teeth. Immediately, she began to extrude the vital conduit for which she could begin self-extracted insemination.

Federoth screamed even louder from the traumatic pain induced and could barely keep himself conscious. Upon witnessing Federoth's head swaying and ready to fall back, Eñala had enlarged the fangs in her upper jaw and prepared to strike at him. With a violent force, she sank her teeth into his neck and laid siege to her other intended target.

Her mouth formed over his neck on both sides and began to siphon out the sweet nectar that was his blood. She knew he would never offer it to her freely and so she had to engulf his entire spirit and overwhelm his senses if she were to receive the desired treat. Spurts and streaks of blood and other bodily fluids from both of them shot all over the bed and floor below, painting a grotesque picture of abstract Nomaseri artwork.

Federoth passed in and out of consciousness from the amount of blood the vicious servant siphoned out of him. But, before he could lose total consciousness, he knew that if he did not make a final attempt to save his own life, he would be done for in a matter of minutes. As she drained both the lifeblood and his seed, Federoth drew his remaining strength and with his left hand, he forced her head to the left and viciously sank his own teeth into Eñala, taking in her own blood that would mix with his. This action quickly caused the overpowering servant to loosen the grip her mouth had on his neck and let out an even louder salivated scream. Her sexual member completed its work, retracted its grip, and retreated inside her body. In a surprise twist, Eñala began to loose consciousness, so much that the brace of her hands and feet could no longer support their combined weight and together they fell down, crashing onto the bed below, bending the steel supports in half. Simultaneously, Federoth lessened his bite on her neck as she retracted her tentacles back into her body.

Severely drained of blood and semen, Federoth forced her off him, rolled out of the bed onto the floor, and rested there. Moments later, when he regained consciousness, Federoth crawled over to a nearby chair and put his robe on, dripping blood as he went. Afterwards, he fell into the chair and gathered a drink from a waiting bedside table to replenish lost fluids. While seated, he took in the sight before him. The scene appeared both surreal and nightmarish in his eyes; a damaged bed he would have to either fix or replace, desecrated sheets and bedding stained horribly with their combined red and yellow splashes of blood, and a Nomaseri woman that appeared dead lay in his bed.

As the morning sunlight gently touched the right side of his face, the vision of last night retreated into the back of his mind, left to savor another day.

"*That was one hell of a night*," he thought to himself. "*She definitely knows the type of pleasure I desire, and I will have to experience this again, very soon.*"

Later the next day, Federoth accompanied Rudecor on a tour of his fair city. Through the streets and avenues they traveled by a gliding conveyance that edged forward movement through an already plotted course. The conveyance had plenty of room for the two; bodyguards weren't necessary as the Nomaseri leader explained to his friend that everyone here had an equal amount of respect for the other. Crime was virtually unheard of in this land. All who lived here sought for the same goals as their neighbors; to live in peace and to crush any enemy found. Whenever there was a crime committed, the punishment was swift and severe, and that usually meant death. So strict were the laws that all understood and lived by them for hundreds of years. Rudecor's philosophy was such that such strict punishment provided the necessary means to thwart any idea of committing a crime.

Federoth did not have to deal with crime in the Dominion either; only those who were of high command had any real possessions to speak of. And murder, well that was just part of their way of life at times. Survival of the fittest could best describe the Dominion, and since all worked to achieve Dominion goals, there was no time for crime.

As the conveyance made its way through the city at a medium pace, a bit faster than a range walk, Federoth saw the spectacular sights everywhere in his view. Shops were busy with females and small children gathering whatever necessities they desired, and the males usually hung out around the local weapons shops. Males had all sorts of weapons stashed in their private home arsenal, another reason why there were no transgressions committed against anyone. Why bother when every house was armed?

Outdoor grocery shops provided the freshest of vegetables and meats that anyone could imagine. Federoth did also notice there were hardly any other conveyances around aside from the one he rode on. With the absence of traffic, they moved freely and unobstructed. The city dwellers used their own privately owned vehicles to get around: their feet.

In the northern most part of the city, the area was completely vacant of buildings, houses, or city dwellers. This open area exposed a space at least twenty miles in diameter, still possessing the giant pylons for protection and security. Instead, the entire area possessed a huge grating of sorts, sectioned off into various subdivisions of steel. Giant doors kept the surface clear of traffic, aside from what exited the underground area. The four city pyramids located in the very center of the city allowed the fighters a fast exit and launch should any enemy threaten the city itself, but the Nomaseri stashed the huge cruisers underground to hide their numbers.

As the conveyance came to a halt over a steel door slightly bigger than the conveyance itself, it opened up, allowing the conveyance to lower into the depths of the hangers below. As they passed the one hundred foot surface construction, Federoth's mouth gaped at the sheer size of the underground bays and vast hangars. Brightly luminous lights revealed the size of the underground and as they sank lower into the depths. Federoth could see the cruisers all stacked at an angle ready to launch should Rudecor give the command.

Each cruiser had the capability of housing three hundred Nomaseri warriors and crew. In each cruiser hangar, fighters were stacked and ready for launch the minute the ship was airborne. Federoth marveled at this sight and thought this fleet could rival his own, but not to any great length. Sure, they had much, but showing him they were located underground meant that if the Nomaseri ever decided to try the might of the Dominion, they would lose. Federoth knew now where to strike if such a reason to every came about.

"This is quite impressive, Rudecor," Federoth stated.

"Yes it is," Rudecor agreed. "We did not possess this capability long ago. The last one hundred and fifty years were solely devoted to creating and housing all of our fleet aircraft. Since we lost a battle to the Cavanonians almost two hundred years ago, we learned that in order to escape annihilation we needed to have aircraft. Since then, we have learned not to rely solely on our hand-to-hand combative skills. The Cavanonians of that time were highly skilled and asserted their aggression more forcefully than we previously anticipated. We vowed never to be caught off guard or outnumbered without some sort of advantage, and that is what we have now."

"Well, it is a grand sized advantage you have, but you still have a ways to go to outnumber Dominion forces."

Rudecor laughed, "My friend, we are not running a contest here; we are simply providing the necessary force protection our numbers require. And you are right; we could never surpass the Dominion fleet of dread."

The conveyance slowed to a hover and then moved forward, gliding effortlessly along a predetermined path through the underground expanse. From the distance traveled underground, Federoth surmised that the underground battle area had to be at least four times the size of the city above, maybe bigger. Thousands of Nomaseri workers and aircrew entered and exited the aircraft, performing maintenance checks and services. Non-stop systems checks made sure that every craft was fit for flight in a moments notice. There weren't any deadline aircraft to speak of. The moment a glitch or system malfunction surfaced, either in flight or in the hangar bays, the Nomaseri support crews were there to repair it right away.

"Where are we going?"

"I am taking you to my ship," he answered. "Since you are eager to seek out the location of this firesword, I have decided to aid you in your quest."

"Aside from our friendship, would there be any other reason for aiding in a search?"

Rudecor turned to look at his friend. "Federoth, you yourself have stated that once you have the sword, er, the crown, you would be the ruling authority among all Cavanonians. Is this not true?"

"It is," answered Federoth.

"Then, I trust when you have attained your goal and many a star system is conquered, we shall have an iron clad union of our two forces, and to share in the spoils of war once they are tabulated."

"You wish to join the Dominion?"

"Not necessarily, my friend. It would be best to consider our forces in a joint role, the combined might of our two fleets would be able to secure the galaxy and any system that dare oppose us. Besides, I enjoy my rule and so do my subjects. To surrender the Nomaseri to the Dominion would show weakness in my character, and I am above that."

"I did not mean anything of that nature, Rudecor. A combined joint force it is. It will be made so to my forces and you shall be granted access to our facilities on Samajap and Tiracus whenever you are in the area."

"Splendid! And now we shall board my ship and set off for where?"

"We shall start by having my forces on Samajap search close to the wasted Muidiri system, while *we* venture off to an area I've not visited in centuries: the system of Ellononis."

"You will have to provide the coordinates, of course."

"Of course," Federoth replied.

Once on board Rudecor's private cruiser, the Dominion commander furnished the necessary coordinates and within minutes, the cruiser slowly left dry dock. The huge upper hangar ground doors opened and allowed the ship to exit into the brightly lit green sky above. Once out of the planets atmosphere, the ship gained altitude and shifted into light speed heading out on a set course for the planet of Ellononis.

On Elaveshan, Nosrévis had plans of his own. These came about after a discussion with his hellion warriors had told him much of the details about their sordid, evil past. They revealed much to their new leader and the information given intrigued Nosrévis, greatly. While thoughts of the information raced through his head, the elites at his service wondered.

"Tell me what you know about this sword of fire," Nosrévis said to Esnemia.

"My Lord, during the time I lived on Cavanon, I myself had only viewed the crown twice. In both instances, the sight of it captivated my soul. The glowing, perpetual fire that surrounds the sword is great in intensity, and so luminous that it could easily light up the night sky alone."

"Did not this perpetually burning fire scar the one who held it?" asked Nosrévis.

"It did not, my Lord," the servant replied. "Only the one who rules the Cavanonians can hold it and not be affected by its intense heat and burning flames. You see, according to legends—since that is all it is for us at this point—the sword created by the Gods had been blessed for the first created being, the first Son of the Gods. Since he was their pride and joy at the time, they bestowed on him a sword, engraved with the signs and symbols of the Gods own language. The sword itself contained two parallel blades, one and a half inch in width, with a beveled surface between them down to the cross guard, with air to filter in the middle. The blades themselves formed from the strongest steel and of a composition unlike anything in the universe. The Gods decided that the sword itself did not meet divine specifications and added the element of fire to it. In another twisted blessing, they decreed that the fire would severely burn all who would touch it, save Cavanon and all who ruled after him. Each one in turn had to undergo a serious transformation of character in order to acquire the sword. That usually meant the departing King had to give of his total inner being and power to his successor, causing the departed King to forever rest in the heavens along side the Gods."

"So," Nosrévis said, as he pondered the meaning and surmised the inevitable. "What you're saying is, that even if I or anyone else were to find the sword, we could not touch it because we are not the ruling authority over it, is that correct?"

"Yes," replied Esnemia. "However, there is a glitch in the legend that the earlier kings attempted to contain. Since the ruling Cavanon were only of flesh and bone, if the King were to die, unnaturally, then the sword would become subservient to the next one who touched it. After all, the sword is the crown and must have an owner."

"Exactly where would one look for this sword of fire, if indeed the information you have provided me is true?" asked Nosrévis.

"My Lord," replied Esnemia, "the last ruling Cavanon would still have it."

"But our Lord Federoth told me that he last saw the sword prior to the demise of its owner, the present King. If he is dead, then where is the sword?"

"I know not, my Lord," replied Esnemia. "We were not privy to such information if such an instance did occur. The only one who would have that sort of knowledge would be Cavanon's hated brother, Ellononis. After all, once the Gods created the second Son, they did inform him that to attain their graces over Cavanon he would have information about the sword that would aid him in time to seek it out and claim it for himself."

"That is ludicrous!" Nosrévis commented, hastily. "What are the Gods but crazy to create two sons only to pit them against each other in order to obtain a crown?"

"The Gods rivaled amongst themselves over which created son would be the best to represent them in future times," Esnemia stated. "The best way to do that was to give each son a different power and see which one would ultimately come out a sovereign Lord. Cavanon was given the crown of authority; Ellononis was given the power of perpetual reincarnation."

"Meaning?"

"What I mean is, even though Ellononis passed on after being killed by his brother, he could still return in another generation, in any time or dimension, having never truly died in spirit, only the flesh. And that is why this John Rykus was sought out."

"So, rather than the story I was told, the true purpose for my being brought into this time period was because—"

"Because," Esnemia cut in, "Ellononis is ultimately responsible for the creating the Nogzakhs. The Nogzakhs then discovered the legend written by the second Son himself and believed Ellononis had returned in a different dimension in the form of John Rykus."

"And that is the same reason of why they imported the first John Rykus," Nosrévis said, brushing his chin. He began to pace the floor, back and forth, wondering with each step he took. This was fresh news for him and this information changed his whole outlook of the Nogzakhs and the Dominion. They didn't really bring him here to eat him, but rather to see if he was the one or not. If not, then they would have torn him apart. But now it was a whole new ballgame.

"Since the first John Rykus (now Adoné) had escaped from them on Earth of the future, they sought to capture him and see if he was Ellononis come back.

However, since he did not exhibit the qualities they were looking for, and since he converted and transformed into the Cavanonian race, he couldn't be the one. Otherwise, he would have gone to them." Nosrévis suddenly became wide-eyed and shocked. "So then, this means that *I* could be the reincarnated second son. Ellononis could be in *me*!"

"That would explain why you became hated by the Cavanonians and more forceful in power then they could ever realize."

"And that means," Nosrévis said, with a glaringly evil smile, "that if I were to acquire the sword, *I* would be the ruling authority over all, and Ellononis would live on through me!"

"You would be immortal!" exclaimed Esnemia. "There is the reason of why you found us: to serve you. Our blessings have been given and our lives will be sanctified with the blood we will shed for thee."

After Esnemia said those words, he and all the rest of the elite hellion warriors fell to the floor and prostrated before their lord. Absolutely and without question, they all believed that he, Nosrévis, truly was their ultimate lord and power.

Sinister thoughts grew inside Nosrévis' head. Thoughts of why Federoth had never told him any of this. Maybe Federoth did not know, maybe he just sought the sword out for his own greed and self-esteem. Now that the truth be known, he knew that Federoth must not get the crown…he must not find it. If Federoth did find it first, then Nosrévis must not waste time in killing Federoth for it.

"All of you, here are your new orders," the evil Lord stated. "We shall find this sword, reinstate my rule, and insult Cavanon with it. First, we must find out where it could be, and what better way to find out then to journey to the planet of Ellononis! You will all take a vow of secrecy; whoever whispers a single consonant of this information to anyone outside this gathering shall die, gruesomely, and I shall torment their soul for eternity. So say you!"

"We swear!" all in the gathering shouted this simultaneously.

"It is befitting the punishment I heaved upon the royal family of Cavanon on their own home planet. Now they know who it was that took their lives and sent them to the netherworld. Come, we must leave at once!"

A few days after take off, the Nomaseri ship bound for Ellononis arrived outside the planets atmosphere. Prior to its arrival, the forces of Federoth acknowledge the order to search through the remnants of Muidiri for any signs of a glowing fire or a sword of that nature. The officer on duty reported to Federoth that there was no sighting of such an item at all. With a myriad of tracking and detection devices at their disposal, an item of that nature should be detected easily, but it was not. Even though they did have a few detections of precious metals, those were due to the amount of metal debris in the area and the search would have to continue in order to produce a concrete answer. Federoth ordered the search to expand in that area and provide updates as necessary.

The planet Ellononis itself gleamed of despair and dread. The outer atmospheric cloud covered shimmered dull red and grey colors, with back patches spread out all around. The gruesome redness of the atmosphere alone would be enough to wave off any would be prospector with the courage to investigate. This did not stop Federoth and his friend from breaking through the stagnant cloud cover to explore this new world.

Mountains of grand size stood bent on angles like fangs protruded upward from a lower jaw. Everywhere they looked; these same type stone formations existed poised and ready to lacerate anything that came near them. With a minimal amount of gravity, half as much as that of Earth, rocks and other lose fragments flew about in the wind or rolled about on the ground crashing into other formations and creating even more flying debris.

The red ash and soot that flew about in the wind gave an eerie appearance to the already doomed surface. However, this was only the surface, and Federoth sought to discover the underworld that existed here. From the information he had on this particular system, the long forgotten descendants dwelt in the subterranean realm. This could have been because of the state of above surface conditions; living above ground would have been extremely hazardous for any type of creature.

On the ship, Rudecor activated a scan of the planets surface. An in depth 3D holographic image appeared on a console in the middle of the control room. Detailed images revealed through a series of luminous color motions, matching the outline of the actual surface. Not only did the holographic monitor display the exact contour of the surface, but also any areas of significant difference.

Passing over rocky gorges, vast expanses of black ocean waters, towering jagged mountain peaks, and rivers resembling arteries, the ship finally slowed as the holographic images displayed a great depression surrounded by fierce jagged edged mountains, which completely enclosed the depression. One would not find it without passing overhead and ground movement would have never revealed it. The ship hovered over this area and allowed the ruling Nomaseri and his friend—with a few guards—to descend to the ground and gain entrance into the depression by using a very large dusty stairway. After the ship acknowledged the safe landing of the ground crew, the ship gained altitude above the fierce surface winds and thunderstorms that could threaten the integrity of the ship. There they would remain until called for.

Federoth, Rudecor, and the ground crew proceeded down through the descending staircase into the bowels of the planet. Webs from some creature adorned the toothed archway above them and draped over the way every so often. The archaic walls themselves reeked of some damp musky substance that periodically dripped a type of plasmic residue: red, filmy and gelatinous in places.

Mystery filled the staircase as the ground party descended. Suddenly, torches on both sides of the wall spontaneously lit up and illuminated the way for them, as if something knew why they were there and aided or guided them. Each torch lit further down as they came within a certain distance; behind them, torches that had been lit extinguished themselves to isolate the light in the immediate vicinity of the visitors.

After following the steps down a considerable depth, they were greeted by a doorway bearing the mark of warning that read:

'Only those bearing the standards and virtues of the creator are authorized to enter. Suffer eternal damnation if you are the opposite.'

"We would do well to be on our guard," said the nervous Rudecor. "We do not know what evil we will encounter here."

"Relax, my friend," replied Federoth, "we work for the creator, Ellononis, so we are safe."

"I hope you are correct."

With a wave of Federoth's hand, the doorway rumbled, crackled, and creaked open. The stone hinges emitted a rough grinding sound as the split doors slowly slammed against the walls, allowing the echo of its massive weight to run throughout the newest revelation of tunnel systems. This foyer area formed a circular area fifty feet in diameter and instilled fear in all from the overly grotesque skeletal remains that hung from the ceiling in chains attached to their necks. The difference in these remains puzzled Federoth; they were still viscous and appeared to be decaying. The stench of this room ravaged even their senses.

There were now four avenues to travel and all four passageways had a warning written above them. The center left passageway read:

'Seek and you shall find, but forget your place and stumble you may.'

The passageway to the far left read:

'Stop and you may stare, hesitate to react and fly to destiny.'

The center right passageway read:

'Make haste and crush your fears, lest fear crush you first.'

"I wonder what these warnings mean?" asked Rudecor.

"These passageways are protected with traps," Federoth replied. "It's a game for those who do not understand the very nature of the creator himself. We must discern the safest route and be aware of our surroundings. We must pass the test in order to gain access to *his* lair."

"But which way do we go?"

"I think we should take the fourth passageway to the right," Federoth guessed, "it seems the best way to go and the warning is less vivid than the others."

"What does it say?" asked Rudecor.

"It reads: '*Wonders are this way, reach for them, and find purpose*'."

"That doesn't sound too bad, but we should send in others first, just in case."

"We should send one into each corridor and save ourselves the embarrassment of failure should we be wrong." Federoth tipped his head to his friend.

"A very good idea," replied Rudecor. He then chose eight of his guards and sent two into each corridor to find the safest route. One thing that amazed Federoth about Rudecor's guards, they were fearless and moved out without the slightest hint of hesitation or question. In pairs, they entered into the passageway assigned to them.

In the far left passage, the two guards walked through at a brisk pace with weapons drawn and at the ready position. Instead of paying attention to the floor, they kept their gaze beyond the torches in their hands and stumbled upon something rather large. Slinky, long, and covered with black grungy hairs and scales, the thing that lay before them awoke and bared his teeth happily; in praise for the creators provided sustenance.

The two guards screamed for their lives as they whipped and sliced away at the monstrous creature that now crawled after them. Both the guards turned around and ran for the passageway, not wishing to suffer their lives to this creature. However, before they reached the foyer area, the passageway sealed itself to prevent their escape. Their screams reached ear-splitting levels as they reached the doorway too late. When the door sealed shut, the screams cut offinstantly.

Federoth and Rudecor shuddered in fear and began to rethink the quest.

"I thought you said we were safe from any dangers down here?"

"Yes, I did say that, didn't I," said Federoth. "Maybe it is because they are less than us and *we* are the ones who must go through?"

"Let's see how the others fair first, if then they fail as well then you will lead the way before me."

"As it should be," the Dominion commander agreed, "since I am the one who most likely represents the Creator's creatures more than you. Be on your guard, just in case."

The second center right passageway door began to seal itself after the two guards had gone through. On the other side, the guards walked on, armed and ready for anything that might come at them. Even though they did not hear the screams, something told them to remain alert.

This passageway gave out to a vast expanse in front of the two guards. The area was dark and dimly lit with fires burning in sporadic locations down the one thousand foot drop off. In front of the two guards stood a thin stone bridge with barely enough room for one body let alone two. Singularly and with caution, the two guards proceeded forward. Slowly they edged their way forward and paused every so often to glance around in the air for anything unusual, not really knowing if there were any danger here at all. The distance from the passageway to a stationary platform must have been close to five hundred feet across. Once on the platform, the guards noticed there was no other way out.

On the other side of the expanse stood a huge doorway, brightly lit with red lights, signaling that was the way to go. But how to get there? As the two guards thought about how to accomplish this feat, screeching sounds began to echo faintly throughout the area. The build up of sounds alarmed the two stranded guards and they took up ready positions to defend themselves against whatever came to them. Unfortunately, for the two frightened guards, the noises now surrounded them. Dark and sinister winged creatures flew at amazing speeds round the intruders, creating a whirlwind effect. Quickly, as the air swirled about them furiously, the two guards instantly bolted off toward the bridge, a fatal mistake. Since they had to move at a slow pace to cross the bridge in the first place, both were instantly knocked off the bridge, screaming loudly as they fell to their death. The winged scavengers dove to their prey and tore them to bits, not leaving a single shred of evidence of their ever being there in the first place.

The doorway out of the passage slowly opened up revealing and empty way ahead. Federoth and Rudecor spent a few moments waiting for something to come out, but nothing came and they heard no voices.

"I don't like this," said Rudecor, with a shudder in his voice.

"One of these passageways has to be the correct route to take, but which one?" Federoth whispered to himself.

"There are only two passageways left," said Rudecor, "one of these has to be the way."

"We'll find out soon enough."

In the center left passage, the two guards walked hesitantly forward. Not because of fear of what had happened to the others, they had no knowledge of that. Instead, they followed a squared tunnel system. The walls, ceiling, and floor had lines cut through them as if the entire section had been cut into huge chunks of stone blocks.

"What did the sign above this passageway say?" asked guard number one.

"Something about making haste," replied guard number two.

After the brief answer, the floor in front of them slowly began to rise up and met with the ceiling, barring further movement in that direction. As the two turned around to make their way back, the floor up ahead began to rise up as well. But, before he two could break out, the stone blocks had barred their way; now there was no way out. Up above them, they could hear rumbling sounds, felt dust and pebbles falling on their heads. As they looked up to see the stone above them vibrating, both guards screamed simultaneously as the huge stone block fell on top of them, crushing their bodies to the floor.

As that doorway opened, Federoth and Rudecor now stood shaking in their boots. From the results of the last three passageways, only one way remained; this had to be the way!

Inside the last passageway, the two guards noticed that after walking through the stone passage, the air became dense and misty. Air circulated throughout the enclosure, back and forth it went, pulling and pushing them as they walked forward. Up ahead, the torch light revealed a tunnel different from what they currently stood in. Creeping slowly forward, the texture of the flooring changed to a spongy material that caused the guards to exercise caution. The heated air inside this tunnel system gave rise to thoughts about what possibly lay ahead of them. Before another thought entered their minds, the flooring behind the guards began to rise up, and the two guards grabbed onto bone bars on each side of the tunnel. Within seconds, both guards were now hanging down toward the mouth of the tunnel, desperately trying to hold on. From beneath their feet, down in the long channel below, a great rumbling came up and a howling growl unlike any they had ever heard blasted their eardrums to the point of bleeding. The tunnel now shook violently back and forth until the guard could no longer hold their grip. Both plummeted down into the depths of the unknown.

Outside, a monstrous creature had placed its huge gaping mouth over the cave entrance once the passageway door signaled that prey had entered inside. The creature stood some one hundred feet in height, dragonous, huge, and fierce. The creature, now content with the sustenance in its belly, crept back into the depths of its own cave and waited for another chance to eat.

"So what happened to them?" asked Rudecor.

"I don't know," replied Federoth, frustrated beyond the point of conjecture. "One of these passageways has to be the way through, and I'll be damned if I will suffer what the guards went through. I represent the Dominion, surely that must mean something to the guardians of this underworld. I should—"

"You should what?" said a voice from behind them both.

Both Rudecor and Federoth turned to see his old creation standing their smiling.

"Nosrévis," Federoth exhaled, "Blast it, you could have warned us you were coming, or do you enjoy creeping up on unsuspecting creatures?"

"My Lord, you above all have the power of detection. You mean to tell me you could not detect my presence here? Maybe you had reason not to, or perhaps you were scared?"

"Scared of losing my own life to whatever lay inside these passageways," Federoth scoured. "Each one sent in did not come out, and now we've no idea which passageway is the correct one."

"Ha!" his evil creation laughed, "it's this way!"

"And how do you know that?"

"Federoth, my Lord, would I lie to you?"

All three of them went into the center right passageway, which read: *Stop and you may stare, hesitate to react and fly to destiny.* All proceeded forward to the bridge and slowly they crossed over to the platform in the center of the expanse. Once there, Federoth and his Nomaseri friend reacted in the same manner as the earlier two guards had: they saw the lighted cave and wondered how to reach it. Just then, the screeching sounds came again and swirled around the three of them. The sounds flew closer and closer, and suddenly, Federoth understood the meaning above the doorway.

"This is what killed them," he said. "These winged creatures or whatever they are caused them to stop and stare. And when they hesitated to react, death greeted them below."

"It looks like the same will happen to us unless we do something quickly," Rudecor hastily replied.

As the two quickly shot questions and answers back and forth, they were unaware that Nosrévis had moved over to the far side of the platform closest to the unreachable cave. He stood there with his hands at chest level, palms facing the cave, silently spouting words he had never known before. When he had finished, Federoth and his friend turned to look as the red light from the cave illuminated the entire expanse, revealing the creatures that had caused the guards death.

Huge winged warriors, Ellononis' secret guardians flew at an even slower speed so that the ones below could see their shapes and sizes. Great gigantic lizards, with giant claws and massive bodies, supported by a huge wingspan of up to sixty feet across flew effortlessly around them. All of the creatures, maybe fifty total circled round the platform. Then, as if on cue, each of the creatures stopped sideways in front of Nosrévis. One after the other they stopped until Federoth and Rudecor could now see how to reach the far side cave: over the backs of the dragons. The only way to reach that area was to chant the silent password that Nosrévis somehow unconsciously knew. In addition, as the three of them began to walk on the dragons, the creatures bent up their necks to meet with their tails above them, giving the three crossers something to brace themselves on and avoid a nasty fall. Once a creature had served its purpose, it launched itself back into the air cutting off any escape route. The three of them stood inside the brightly lit cave and wondered.

"Where to now?" asked Rudecor.

"There is another trial for us coming up," replied Nosrévis.

"How do you know this?" Federoth shouted. "Where did you receive this information, hmm?"

"My Lord, on the planet of doomed souls a library exists with knowledge in abundance. I simply read through most of it."

"You've found the lost souls?" Federoth lost his composure and his mouth fell agape. "Impossible!"

"Not quite, for I have freed them and now have a grand force of hellions at my disposal."

"But they are the accursed of Cavanon, you can't control them!" Federoth tried to rationalize.

"They will tell you differently, my Lord. Come, we must keep going."

The new course led them deeper still into the abyss of the unknown, much further than they had hoped. The tunnel system had mysterious black spackled patches of some type of fungus on the walls, moving slightly. With the copious amount of dust and cobwebs in the walkway, it was apparent that no one had come through here in a very long time, possibly eons. As they walked, Federoth began to wonder if his evil creation had indeed found the ancient chamber of lost souls or the vast library he spoke of. As far as Federoth knew, nothing of this elusive planet had ever been written or logged. This should all be new for Nosrévis, yet he knew exactly where to go, which passageway to take, and how to control the winged scavengers.

After an hour or so, the small party reached another foyer type enclosure, one hundred feet in diameter. Huge tapestries hung over the walls, bright yellow, lined on the side with black jagged edges, and in the middle red colors, simulating the splatter of blood but in the shapes of the language of the second son. Rudecor thought it odd to see such works of art this far down in the planet, and he noticed how well kept the area appeared to be. Who or what maintained this enclosure and where did they come from? It was also apparent to him and Federoth that no other door or passageway existed in here. With no other way out, they began to have thoughts of egress routes. Nosrévis heard these thoughts and explained the meaning to them both.

"The language on the tapestries is that of Ellononis," Nosrévis said. "It says the guardian will come and all who are pure shall pass, but those who are of questionable mentality shall dwell in the pit below."

"What pit?" Federoth asked, "I see no pit anywhere, nor even an opening for such place."

"That is because one who is questionable has not yet entered in."

"Strange," commented Rudecor, "I wonder who this guardian is?"

About that time, a miraculous and bizarre occurrence took place. In a scene distorted and warped, the ceiling opened up as one tearing the cover off a tomb, and the walls on the far side peeled apart before their very eyes. In this instance, the guardian the tapestries foretold appeared in the opening and shocked Federoth and Rudecor greatly; Nosrévis was unmoved.

This being emerged through the opening and stood face to face with Federoth's evil creation. Federoth jumped back as the creature resembled Othragon, and he thought it *was* the one time Dominion ruler. The intimidating height of the guardian stood twenty feet high from head to toe. His body was that of a lizard with eight legs like a spider, and a head of a dragon with four horns, two up and two down; a couple of the horns were broken off, possible a sign of some struggle or fight with something else.

The guardian sniffed at Nosrévis for a moment and as if sensing his purity within, off to the right in the middle of the only portion of the wall still standing, a doorway materialized and shown them the way to go.

"Go in," said Nosrévis, "I will join you once you have safely passed."

"Nosrévis, I am not afraid," said Federoth.

"You should be, my Lord."

The eyes in Federoth's head grew large as he glanced between his creation and the guardian, who now looked sinisterly at Federoth, as if knowing his history and deceit. Without wasting any more time, Federoth and Rudecor dashed into the open doorway. The guardian raged in anger, but Nosrévis, held up a hand to him and he slowly retreated into the darkness, allowing the walls, and ceiling to return to their normal state. After this, Nosrévis went in through the doorway.

There, all three stood firm, with all eyes fixed on the shrine that sat in the middle of the five hundred foot diameter area. The walls angled upwards to a point in the ceiling high above them, and a bright spotlight shown down from the apex onto and engulfing the shrine. All three walked towards the middle, gazed upon the perpetual fountain of blood, and read the name engraved at its base: 'Zalestole.'

"I never thought I would actually see this," Federoth said in a state of amazement. "All my life I had heard about it. I had tasted the blood brought back by Cavanon himself eons ago, but never in my life did I think I would actually see it with my own eyes."

"My Lord, if this is indeed your first time, then you may have the honor of the first taste."

Federoth gleamed with pride and excitement as he slowly walked toward the fountain. He picked up one of the golden chalices located round the rear of the base and scooped up a generous portion. As he drank the blood, his senses burned and inflamed the passions in his heart to a point that he staggered from the apparent intoxicating effects. He dropped to his knees facing the shrine and before his eyes, the walls of the enclosure swirled away revealing a picturesque setting all about. Generations of past lives visualized and images of lost friends appeared. Planets of unknown origins and galaxies swirled about beautifully. Federoth showed his appreciation for the images he saw and smiled, greatly.

Rudecor, on the other hand, stood in the background witnessing only Federoth's actions and emotions, and saw nothing of what took place in his friend's mind. The Nomaseri thought this was a remarkable sight. Federoth's attitude had become very different. Instead of the fear he exhibited earlier, he now took solace in this place and became almost as one with his surroundings. What is in the blood that causes him to act in this manner? Was it a natural phenomenon or a condition of the substance he drank? On the other hand, was it totally something his conscience dreamed up? Rudecor would not know unless he drank from the fountain himself.

Nosrévis took his own chalice and repeated the same actions as his creator, drinking a generous amount himself. However, Nosrévis saw differently than Federoth. What he saw was the beginning of the line of Ellononis, the creator himself. Nosrévis held up his hands and the vision of his God did the same in turn. With every action Nosrévis committed, the creator likewise repeated the same action in kind. He also received words of comfort from his ultimate Lord:

'*You are the carrier of my soul, my essence, and my being. You are blessed amongst those who are closest to me. Share your thoughts with no one; trust only those whom you must. Be ready, for when the time is nigh, I will summon you to a secret place where I shall emerge from within you and take up station in this dimension once more. Your reward shall be the seat of my left hand and you shall rule along side me. One task remains for you to complete. Seek out and find the Sword of Fire. Stop at nothing to acquire it and kill all those who oppose you in your quest. Drink from your lineage, generously. Consume your fill until your pores themselves seep the life-giving fluids freely. Once you are fattened, be on your way and complete the task beset you with all haste. Be mindful of those in your company. Give them your trust and bring them with you on the day of calling...I have need of them as well!*'

After the voices ceased, Nosrévis regained control and slowly stood up. As he turned, he saw Federoth and Rudecor looking at him with strangeness in their eyes and an unquestionable expression of wonder. In the back of his mind, his God had given him knowledge of how to locate the Sword of Fire. To locate it would try him to the utmost of his abilities, and test his inner fortitude.

Unbeknownst to Nosrévis, his entire body emitted a brilliant glowing light, as if his aura were strengthened and reborn. The continuous light began to pulsate to accompany the blood flowing through his veins, quickly at first but then slower as his heartbeat calmed.

"You should try this, Rudecor," he said, motioning him to come forward. "Since you are with us in our common goals, you should drink as well and see what will be in your future."

"This blood gives you the ability to see the future?" the Nomaseri asked.

"Only when you drink from the fountain," Nosrévis replied.

"What else will happen to him?" Federoth asked suddenly. "The ability to see the future is not all he will get the chance to see, will he?"

"Relax, my Lord. He will only see what lies in the future, nothing more will happen to him."

Rudecor hesitantly stepped towards the fountain. Nosrévis gathered up a generous portion of the blood from the fountain and handed the intoxicant laden chalice to him. The Nomaseri had no idea what would happen and for a second, he wondered whether it was a good idea to try. The expressions on the faces of his two friends showed no signs of worry at all. Rudecor sipped the blood at first, but after the taste took hold of his senses, he suddenly gulped down the remaining contents of the chalice. Instantly, his body felt the effects of the intoxicants running rampant through his system.

The chalice dropped out of his hands as he staggered forward and fell to his knees behind the shrine. The most spectacular sight spread out over the walls in front of him revealing all sorts of new information and wonders. There would be a battle on a strange and distant planet, new creatures were at war with the might of the Dominion, and beside them fought the warriors of Nomaseri. The size of the forces in battle astounded him greatly and he watched in awe as they smote down the enemy forces and laid siege to the planet, dividing the riches and untold wealth of the planet. Nogzakh machines, Gadnoc, and Nomaseri warriors joined forces once again on the field of battle, clamored in their armor and war machines.

A new force of warriors came into view, ones that Rudecor had never seen before. Ruthlessly this new force attacked and desecrated the remaining enemy in chaotic conflict, effortlessly slashing their enemy to bits and devouring their fresh prey strewn about the ground.

At the end of the battle, Rudecor saw thousands upon thousands of warriors standing together, shaking their fists in the wind, and shouting at the top of their lungs. The next vision he saw was that of a strange place, underground and remote. There were other strange beings there as well, ones he never knew, and some were of the Cavanonians he had helped to destroy long ago. At the end of the scene stood a tall, dark, and sinister being drenched in blood and saliva. Body parts made up the furniture of the floor, and only a few of their warriors were shouting this time. Others in the picture stood in fear, and shackles and chains bound others; perhaps they were the last of the enemy leadership. Rudecor's eyes grew large and misshapen as the face of the grotesque being came into full view in one swift motion.

"*AAAAHHH!*" Rudecor shouted, and his body reacted by jumping back in fear of the face. After that, the vision disappeared and the walls returned to their original normal state. Rudecor shook in fright, forgetting who was with him there by in the hall of the shrine. Never before had he known fear of this magnitude and this disturbed him so much so that his hands and body shook feverously.

"Rudecor, what did you see?" asked Federoth, wondering what had happened to cause him to shake so badly.

"I saw, I saw," he managed to spit out, "I saw a great battle, I saw a strange place with our forces all engaged in a new enemy. I then saw a strange place with strange beings bound and chained. Then, I saw, I saw…I saw the most hideous creature yet to enter into my vision. I know not who or what it was, but I saw fear for the first time in my life. I saw *fear*."

Federoth glanced up at Nosrévis. "What the hell did he see that caused him that much fear?"

"I know not," Nosrévis blatantly lied. He knew all too well what Rudecor saw, because he knew the blood did nothing to the Nomaseri leader but cause him to be more receptive to subliminal suggestion. Instead, Nosrévis substituted his *own* visions into Rudecor's mind. Visions that would guide him to prepare his forces to do battle with a new enemy not previously encountered. He also programmed the vision to instill fear and instant obedience the moment Ellononis returned, thus subjecting Rudecor and his entire planet into the service of his new God.

"It is possible that he saw a new battle that has yet to come. Obviously it is does not concern the Cavanonians since they are no more. However, this new enemy appeared to be well equipped and advanced for it to be so great in size. It would have to be since the vision revealed all of our forces fighting on the same planet."

"Indeed," Federoth wondered. "But who? Who is this new enemy we do not yet know and where did they come from, or better yet, where are they now?"

"More importantly," Nosrévis pondered, "this new species might have the crown of Cavanon with them, since the Cavanonians are no more. But, we'll probably find that out in time, my Lord. After all, the vision was of the future."

"Let us leave this place. We must be ready for war when the time arrives, I do not wish to be caught, how did you say it once—with my pants down?"

"That's the one!"

Nosrévis and Federoth both took out a cylinder jug and filled it in the fountain. Knowing that the blood replenishes itself in whatever storage device held it. They both could have their very own nectar of the Gods to accompany them at all times. If they drank a little each time, it would replenish itself. This gave proof to the rumor of immortality. But, if they drank it all, they would have to return for more.

Once they safely made their way out of the chambers, tunnels, passageways and back up the long stairway, they returned to the waiting ship and departed.

Chapter 10

A Change of Heart

Three months time went by for the humans who arrived accidentally through the time machine brought to Cavanon by the Tnemucodas. Initially, the humans had some trouble adjusting to this new world and new way of life. However, as time progressed, they adapted to their new environment and began to understand their place in this community of mismatched aliens.

A few of the new humans found comfort in the fact that their community had other humans living amongst them. A couple others were bold, daring, and sought friendship with the others such as the Anadonians, Nablah, and the Srotaderp. However, two of the remaining members—Stan and Zach—were intrigued with Adoné and the Royal family. Their appearances grew on the male humans and they were interested in the many powers and wonders the Cavanonians were able to perform, effortlessly. Adoné had listened to their minds and understood their curiosity. He knew in time they would come to him with questions about the Cavanonian race and how they were able to do what others could not.

One day, as Adoné and Laura sat by the Zedgen Sea fishing, the two male humans came and sat with them, both gathering up a pole to join in the quest for aquatic sustenance. The western sun sat high on the horizon, while the other sun hung low in the southern hemisphere, still providing the extra light of the day. The light of the twin suns glistened, shimmered golden streaks over the waters, and gave brilliance to the area. The serene scene gave Adoné something else to smile about.

"I know you both did not come here to fish," Adoné said without looking at them. Laura just smiled and snatched her pole out of the water with a fresh catch.

"Is it that obvious?" Zach asked. "I mean, how did you know we—"

"—Dude," Stan butted in, "they can reads minds, too, remember?"

"Shit! I can't believe I forgot that part."

"Its okay, gentlemen," Adoné laughed, "I understand your concerns and interests. And, in the interest of intelligent conversation, I shall avoid reading your thoughts. It has been a long time since we had anyone around who could speak so—" the King stopped himself. *"Now where did I ever hear that before?"* He thought to himself.

Laura answered his thoughts, *"Mom told me she said that to you when she told me the story of how you two first met."*

Adoné noticed the look of question on Stan and Zach's faces, and apologized for the momentary silence.

"Sorry, gentlemen, but we were talking."

"Between yourselves…dude, that is so cool!" Zach replied.

Laura jerked her head towards the human, became furious because of his comment, and swiftly stood up to correct him.

"He's no *dude*! He is King Adoné to you and to all others. It would be wise for you to be mindful of future address."

"Sorry, I didn't mean it that way," said Zach, with a look of both fear and resentment to her scornful remarks.

Adoné had to calm her anger before she could get any worse. He understood her concerns and it appealed to his senses. Laura took great pains to see that others gave respect to her father, as they should. To her, he was more than just a father, much more, and she would correct anyone who thought differently.

"Its okay, sweetie," her father replied, "I understood what he meant. We used to use that term a lot back on Earth of the past. It's just another friendship term and we are friends here."

"I've got questions that I'd like to ask you."

"About what it is like to be Cavanonian?"

"Yes," replied Zach.

"What's it like?" asked Stan.

"Well, *dude*," replied Adoné, "it's much better than I had ever dreamed. Not that I had ever dreamt about becoming an alien myself, but all those years I used to think about how cool it would be to do things that others could not do, to have powers unlike anyone else. Then one day, after I met the Queen, she told me what it would be like and offered me the chance to accept a temporary change. After that, I accepted the full transformation and since then, I haven't been the same." Adoné smiled. "Now, I have powers beyond what I used to think were possible."

"Do you ever regret not being human anymore?" Zach asked. "I mean, doesn't it bother you that you changed from the way you were born?"

"Are you kidding?" Adoné abruptly put down his pole, stood up, walked out a considerable distance onto the surface of the water, and turned to them. "How *cool* is this?"

The King stood on the water walking as if it were a concrete surface. He held his hands out to his sides and fish came up out of the water and into both of his hands, flopping around in his grasp from the lack of water. Adoné dropped them back into the water and performed another trick that even Laura had not yet seen.

"Your basic Cavanonian has powers similar to mine, but not as much as I, and for good reason."

After saying this, Adoné's clothes changed into a flowing black robe from his neck down to his feet, with large sleeves and a large collar. His long white hair fell over the robe and swayed effortlessly in the wind. The color content of the robe shimmered and flowed within a cloud of grayish-black flames that rose up from below his feet, up over his height. The sunlight of the southern sun hit Adoné just right, causing a spiral effect from the heatless grayish-black flames that consumed his presence.

"But as you can see," Adoné continued, "as a King, my subjects must have someone in power that they can look up to for more than just guidance, understanding, and adoration. As a ruling monarch, I must also provide protection and security as well in whatever form I deem necessary. Because of the extra added advantages, you might say that rank has it privileges."

"Oh man!" said Stan and Zach, simultaneously, "I wish I could have powers like that."

Laura smiled; she knew where this was leading.

"That is possible," replied Adoné. "You can become as I am, a true Cavanonian. Seriously, I suggest you boys think about it for a while before you commit yourselves. Not that I am trying to discourage you in any way, I just think it would be best if you took a hard look at what you will be giving up."

Adoné regained his original stature, walked back to the beach, and knelt down in front of them. He could see in their faces that they were ready to hear whatever he had to say, as if two excited children intently listened to some great story.

"Ask yourself this question: are you willing to do this for your own personal benefit because it looks *cool*, or are you willing to surrender yourselves to this race that is in desperate need of skilled and determined warriors. Look around you, this place once thrived with millions of Cavanonians, but the very same aliens who brought you through time killed all but of few of them, and we are now all that is left. There is much work to be done in order to rebuild our numbers, and if you did change over for the good of the cause, you would be role models for others to follow should they ever think as you do now. This is no sales pitch. I am proud of what I have become, and because of the enemy, I have sworn to fight to the end to see to it that no more creatures suffer at their hands."

"But how long do you want us to think about it?" asked Stan.

"Take as long as you need to; since there is no going back to your old world, you have plenty of time."

"Well," Zach spoke up, "my mind is already made up, and I got no need to think about it."

"Gentlemen, do not accept this blindly. Once you change over, there is no turning back. You will forever cease to be human and will be sworn to preserve and defend the Cavanonian Empire."

"Okay," Zach eagerly replied, "so where do I sign up?"

Adoné could not believe that these two humans were so eager to join their ranks. If these two survived the transformation process, then maybe other humans would see the light and decide to covert as well. It would enable them to be even more capable of defending their lives and their new homeland. Before they departed for Royal Mountain, the King had one final thing to say to them.

"Do you guys remember all those movies on Earth about fierce, horrible aliens destroying worlds and killing many innocent lives, ripping people to shreds?"

"Sure, I remember some like that," replied Stan.

"Well," Adoné replied, "you haven't seen anything yet."

Inside the main audience chamber, Adoné informed Xashsa of the discussion on the beach and gave instructions on the ceremony to take place. The Queen was surprised to see that two humans had taken a liking to the Cavanonian race and decided to changeover. The only other instance of this kind took place when Adoné, Sarah (Now Zérnoda), and Laura changed over. Xashsa smiled at this and beamed with excitement since this would be the very first time in their new legacy of a King performing the ceremony himself. She also knew that if these two (Stan and Zach) made the journey over successfully, they would make fine examples to the others. Eventually, they could even become the new subordinate leadership needed in this community, freeing up the King and Queen to attend to other more important tasks. The current monarchy did not mind the medial day-to-day duties required of them, but having other leaders around would free up some of their time and give the King and Queen the ability to concentrate on other significant matters.

The Royal Family led Stan and Zach into the hallway that showed the pit area that led down into Laura's chambers. The King decided that her chambers would provide an ideal setting for the ceremony; Laura had no objections. She surmised that the aura of the planet itself would play an important role during the ceremony and give it that extra bit of ambience to heighten the Kings powers, giving him the extra edge sort of like the icing on the cake.

Two stone slabs, solid and rectangular, existed in the middle of the room. Laura cleared all the unnecessary furniture away from the area and provided the Crystals to the Queen and Zérnoda. Adoné escorted the two willing humans to the stone slabs and informed them to position themselves on top, in prone positions on their backs. All inside the underground chambers could feel the excitement in the air and as Zach and Stan wondered what would happen next, Adoné went over the preliminaries for them.

"Okay, gents," he said calmly, "there are two ways we can do this: the easy way and the hard way."

Before the two anxious humans could ask a question, Adoné further explained the meaning. "The easy way is to drink the potion in that sacred vessel the Queen is holding in her hands. Once you drink it, you will become numb and then sleep. You will feel no pain; your bodies will take as long as is needed to perform the transformation. When you wake up, you will be a new creature like us."

"So that is all there is to it?" Stan asked, "I thought there would be all kinds of pain and stuff like that, I mean, it has to hurt, doesn't it?"

"Once you become a lesser Cavanonian, there will come a time later in life when you must experience the true form of pain required before you can ascend up the ranks of leadership. If you choose the easy way, the pain will wait until you are ready. Now, if you choose the hard way, well, that is a different story."

"So what is it?" asked Zach, "you might as well tell us both stories up front."

"Fine," the King replied. "If you choose the torturous or hard way, the pain is introduced up front, right away, and you feel everything. Your skin will contract and stretch, bubble and blister until it lessens and eventually cracks. Your bones will break, disintegrate, and reintegrate, providing an excruciating amount of suffering along the way. Your spirits will wrestled and divide, fight, and changeover as well. Every characteristic, attribute, and essence of your being will transform over. If you survive, you will be whole and purely Cavanonian from the very start."

"Good God! That's suicide!"

"Exactly, but it is different than you think. Need I remind you that you wanted to know?"

"We have to go through all that first? But that means we will die, right?"

"Why, of course!" said Adoné, with a smile. "Your present life must die in order to form into a new one, and this ceremony is instituted for exactly that purpose."

"Hey, I don't want to die," replied Stan.

"Neither do I," likewise replied Zach.

"Nevertheless, if you want to be as I am, you must."

After Adoné said that, he caused himself to vanish right in front of them. Both humans looked around the room but could not see him anywhere. They then felt a hand on their chest but could not see the cause, and also heard the Kings voice once again.

"I went through the same thing you guys did, and see what I am now. Sure, it hurt, I won't lie to you; it is dreadfully painful. However, you see what I can do and I went through the same pain once before. The choice is still up to you."

Adoné reappeared in front of them with his hands still on their chests. He backed away from the two and crossed his arms, waiting for their decision. The two humans glanced at each other, wondering what the other was thinking.

"Stan, dude, we gotta do this, and the hard way seems to be the better way to go!"

"I don't know if we should," Stan replied, hesitantly.

Zach sat up, hung his legs over the side of the stone slab, and attempted to explain his reasons for wanting to go through with it. His friend leaned up on his right arm and listened.

"Stan, if we don't do this we will be regular guys like the other humans here. We won't have any powers or any kind of gifts that could make it easier to survive here. We can't go back, so what have we got to lose?"

"I understand what you are saying, but after hearing what the King had to say, I kinda think we should reconsider."

"Aw, come on, Stan. An hour ago it was all you could think about and now you're chickening out?"

"I'm no chicken!" Stan said forcefully, "don't ever call me chicken, I just think we—" Stan abruptly stopped talking and looked about the others in the room; they were mesmerized and had already mentally prepared the way for the ceremony to commence. Stan didn't feel coerced at all, he just didn't like the idea of dying. However, after listening to his friend's words, he eventually gave in.

"Aw hell, let's just get on with it!"

After finally giving their answers, Xashsa understood that the chalices and Zalestole blood were no longer required. Instead, she pulled out two identical swords and prepared to hand them to the King. Laura and Zérnoda both held stakes of the Crystals in their hands and positioned themselves at on opposite sides of the stone slabs, Xashsa stood in front of Adoné a few feet away. Sounds of gentle rumbling echoed throughout the chambers, and Adoné had to prepare the humans to receive the initial shock.

"You boys might want to close your eyes for this," said Adoné, "this is going to be one hell of a ride for you!"

Stan and Zach nervously closed their eyes and began to wonder what the King was going to do to them. Their breathing increased slowly and grew almost to the point of hyperventilating. Their chests rose and fell with a traumatic rhythm between them. Adoné took one blade in his right hand and then took the other in his left. With the blades pointed downward, he placed his arms across his chest and prayed.

"Father above, I come to thee with two willing converts seeking to join our race. They have come to me and have given of themselves freely, desiring acceptance into the Cavanonian realm. Accept their sacrifice, dear Father, and grant them the ability to cross over safely."

At this point, Adoné lifted his head, held his arms high out to his sides so that the two swords were each over the bodies of the humans. The rumbling in the chambers grew louder and more pronounced. Mist and smoke began to billow across the floor, cascading against the walls and gently crashing against the stone slabs. Despite all this, Adoné never lost concentration and continued his prayer.

"Recognize their commitment to our lineage, my Lord, and bestow your graces upon them. Secure their spirits and impart your blessed wisdom into their minds and hearts. Accept this offering from thy faithful servant!"

Within a split second of finishing the prayer, Adoné forcefully slammed the swords through their sternums up to the hand guards, afterwards raising his hands two feet above the grips.

The two traumatized humans screamed in terrifying agony as they tried to grip the swords with their hands. The swords pierced not only their bodies, but also imbedded deep in the stone on which they each lay. The human bodies reacted by curling and twisting on the slabs. Blood erupted from their mouths and nostrils as they coughed and gagged from the blockage in their lungs and throats. Their hands and feet shook from the reactionary spasms within.

The aura around Adoné changed to the same as what they saw only an hour ago on the waters of the sea. His eyes changed into the redness from the surge of energy he summoned up, and as he held his hands above the sword handles, a blast of electrical energy shot into the swords traumatizing the now despondent victims.

One last task remained. The facial features of the King changed and melted away to reveal the killer nature kept deep within. Eyes blood red in color slanted upward to the temples. His nose instantly hid itself inside his face. His lower jaw elongated itself to allow room for the daggered teeth to escape from the upper jaw. The incisors lengthened to about eight inches with the subsequent teeth on the right and left sides arranging upward on the outside of the upper jaws until teeth married with bone ligaments. Viciously, he drove his daggered incisors deep into Stan's chest, protruding through his rib cage and right through his heart, injecting a small amount of royal blood. Likewise, Adoné repeated the action on Zach.

After the screams died off, the air in the room calmed and returned to normal. The Royal family bowed slightly, backed away from the now dead humans, and left them alone to begin stage two of the transformation. How long it would take to complete would be up to the strength of their initial will and their bodies' ability to adapt and accept what the process forced upon them. Before she left, Laura sealed up the room in order to prevent anyone from entering during this stage. The Royal family wanted nothing or no one to interfere.

Since this was the first time Adoné performed the ceremony, he seemed a bit anxious and wondered if they would make the journey. Xashsa felt this in him and comforted him with her touch, knowing he would respond to her, instantly.

"Do not worry for them," she said, "they will make the journey over; I can feel it."

"Yes," he replied, "I am sure they will make it, the only question now is how will they turn out?"

"Much like you did, I'm sure."

"We shall see," he replied. "You know, if more wish to do the same, we might consider performing the lesser method instead. It could be very trying on us to do others in the same manner."

"We will need to fetch more blood from the fountain of Zalestole for that," Xashsa answered. "I'm afraid we've not enough to serve more than a few should there be more. And besides, we could do well with a fresh batch straight from the fountain itself."

"They will need time to finish. Later on, we will ask the Kostejaanians for help in searching out the planet that contains the fountain."

"We must journey to the system of Ellononis as my father did centuries ago."

Adoné thought for a moment and chuckled. "What better way to show these two the wonders of the universe and the dread that is out there."

Chapter 11

Strength in Numbers

Out in the semi-rebuilt community, Tanazakh sat around with his family and other humans, and some of the Nablah discussing the happenings of the day. Most of the humans were busy with their own activities consisting mostly of cleaning, cooking, and maintaining their homes. Some of the Nablah occupied their time soaring through the air with the Tnemucodas in a wonderful display of aerial acrobatics. The view of the sky from below appeared as though the sky filled with tiny insects chased by large bats. One by one, the tiny Nablah creatures followed behind a winged warrior in a game of follow the leader, whisking through clouds and rays of sunshine.

Kayla and Sarah thought this a magnificent sight and laughed at the spectacle. Never before had they viewed such creatures together in flight and the sight seemed almost magical in a way. Laura paid attention to their expressions and smiled. She knew what they needed: a chance to get out and see the planet itself. Maybe a flight of their own would put an even bigger smile on their faces and cause an even greater amount of happiness to fill their mundane lives. Laura did think that the way things went for them really did not give an impression of hope or anticipation, and Kayla and Sarah did not see the advantages of living in this period. Even though they had been here only a few months, they fell into a monotonous routine of their own. Kayla and her daughter performed the regular chores and helped acquire food; they even learned how to skin and clean animals.

Even though it was detestable to them at first, they knew they had to learn, eventually. But, after Laura spoke to Tanazakh of her idea of a small trip, he agreed that a it would do them some good after all.

Tanazakh caught Tejrasels attention and told him what the plan was going to be. Soon after that, Tejrasel went to his brethren and gathered up a few to escort them; the added security really wasn't necessary, but the Anadon wasn't taking any chances. Lokcha even wanted to come and raced off to get Gizmo for Laura. To make things easier for Kayla and Sarah, Tanazakh had secured a couple of the smaller sized Tnemucodas warriors for Kayla and Sarah. They would not only have a much better ride on the backs of the creatures, but they could also swiftly return home if there were any sight of trouble.

Laura went to her father and informed him of her intentions. Adoné had no objections at all; in fact, in his eyes it was a great idea. Rather than be burdened with the trip themselves, Adoné and Xashsa would remain behind and wait for the humans—Stan and Zach—to finish transforming. The others in the community would feel better if the Royal family stayed behind. They should remain here anyway, just in case.

Laura informed her father that a total of eleven would be traveling. The party consisted of herself, Tanazakh, Kayla, Sarah, Two Tnemucodas (Krags and Grussel), Lokcha, Tejrasel, Gizmo, Mengress, and Dachale (Tanazakh's daughters). Laura gave the general direction and approximate distance of travel, as well as a general timeline of their expected return. Adoné suggested that Zérnoda, formerly the first Sarah, go with them. After all, she needed to get out of the house every now and then as well, and with her return back into their lives, she might as well see her new home planet as well. Zérnoda thought it a marvelous idea and went without taking leave of her parents. As soon as Kayla and her daughter boarded the winged warriors, the party set off.

It was about midday when they left. Setting out towards the land on the other side of the now inhabited Tnemucodas mountain range gave all the intended direction of travel. All creatures in flight positioned themselves at various heights and flew forward in a double wedge formation with the winged warriors in the very center. During and after takeoff, Kayla and Sarah appeared a little scared at first, this being their very first flight outside of any type of aircraft, but they did well and soon marveled at the sights all around them. In fact, a majority of the creatures—with the exception of the Tnemucodas—had never ventured very far at all passed the northern mountain range or the Zedgen Sea or Royal Mountain. All in the community stayed primarily in the area of the valley and were in no shape to go anywhere of any great distance. The absence of a great amount of security and the fear of running into danger kept them in their own little world, keeping adventures at bay.

Once over the mountain range, the view to the north showed an even larger amount of mountains off in the far distance and ran all the way east and west. Down below in this segregated valley, even more wildlife of Agemoi ran wild through the great forests and tall grassy plains. A myriad of smaller winged creatures flew about in their own daily tasks, effortlessly taking to the wind and subjecting themselves to the twin suns rays. Off to the very far west, storm clouds were brewing up with seawater preparing to inundate another area of choice with deluge and thunderstorms. The majestic mountains to the north were now underneath the formation and appeared breathtaking in their grand size and colors. The geographical nature of the planet hinted of brilliance and wonder, and removed all notions of danger or dread. Unlike other planets, Cavanon boasted of magnificence and awe. Laura noticed that the inspiring sights totally captivated the two humans and their faces lit up with wonder.

The day was extremely warm, even at this height. Sensing this, the Tnemucodas naturally gained altitude and soared through a nearby cloud formation. The moisture within drenched the winged warriors and their guest riders who were not ready for this action, but Kayla and Sarah took pleasure in the sweetness of the mists and shook their hair vigorously in the winds, laughing as they descended back down to the formation of other flyers.

While the winged warriors enjoyed giving their riders a sudden unexpected bath, Zérnoda noticed an odd depression on the other side of the third mountain range head. The depression had to be immense if it seemed huge from this distance. As they approached, layers appeared inside the giant fissure as if giant steps led them down into the subterranean area. Once over the black depression, everyone's attention glanced downward in wonder.

"What is it?" shouted Lokcha.

"I don't know," replied Tanazakh, "I've no idea."

"I'd hate to think something or someone lives down there and we don't know it!" shouted Zérnoda.

"I suggest we check it out," said Laura, "its better to know for sure rather than return home wondering. Besides, what else have we got to do?"

"My sentiments, exactly," replied Tanazakh.

The formation descended downward and landed at the edge of the vast opening. Standing at the rim, Tanazakh guessed that the circumference easily exceeded fifteen hundred feet, at least. The layers now appeared to be sunken levels of ground that had dropped down from some unseen force, maybe long ago. Each of the party members began to jump down onto the next layer and walk to the edge, and again they saw the same thing. After ten different layers, Tanazakh noticed next layer tapered and leveled off into a huge opening or a cave. Tejrasel and Lokcha hovered overhead and were ready to dive in for a closer look, but some unknown essence felt by Laura and Zérnoda gave the Nablah reason to pause.

"Laura, do you feel that?"

"I do," answered Laura. "I sense spirits here, strange and desperate."

"There is sadness here," Zérnoda said, cautiously walking to the rim. "It's depressing and sorrowful. What could make this feeling come about?"

Laura's expression took a turn and focused her eyesight toward the cave entrance. "I have a feeling that whatever it is its farther down below. Now I know we have to check it out."

"Well, you've got my curiosity peaked," said Tanazakh, "lets go, but everyone stay together. I'll take the point, Krags and Grussel; you two bring up the rear and keep watch."

The Tnemucodas nodded in acknowledgment.

Slowly they climbed down a decayed and crumbling staircase that led down to the mouth of the cave. Kayla noticed scarring in the stone walls by the flight of steps as if something clawed or scratched the walls. The size of the marks appeared to be a little larger than her hand. Whatever was down here must have made these marks, but why?

Inside the cave, the air was damp and dense, cold and clammy. Apparently, the heat of the day could not penetrate this depth and from within the cave itself a cold breeze emitted. The way ahead seemed strange and unyielding in length, and gave no impression of friendliness. The rounded walls and ceiling possessed great stalactites as teeth and caused Tanazakh to keep a close eye out in case any happened to fall. Passing underwater streams and rivers, the cave appeared to run underground for miles. The sound of silence pierced their eardrums in between the impact of their footsteps, and yet they moved on, cautiously, and carefully.

Up ahead, the party saw a purplish emanation glowing afar off. The way had emptied into another great depression, but this one was different. It appeared as though someone had built a vast subterranean auditorium here. There were stone steps or seats situation throughout the area and there were many other caves spaced out every twenty or so feet in this enormous area. In the middle of this stood a rise or stone slab maybe fifty feet square. There were things on it grey and dark, but at this height, no one could really make out its nature.

One by one, they descended another winding staircase that ended at the first run of slab seats. Cautiously, they all made their way to the stone slab that appeared now as a stage. The dark objects on the stage were actually chains, dusty and rusted, falling to pieces with time.

"Chains, here, what for?" asked Kayla.

"Hard to tell," answered Laura. "I've been in contact with many of the spirits of the past and none of them ever said anything about a place like this."

"The sadness is overwhelming down here, can't you feel it?" asked Zérnoda, looking at Kayla and the others. All nodded a negative fashion, except Laura. Suddenly, something caught Laura's senses that the others soon discovered as well.

"What the hell are *those*?" Kayla shouted.

Ghosts emerged out of the walls of the huge auditorium floating effortlessly and eerily from the walls and stone steps and gathered all around the party. This caused the party to take up station on the stage and form a defensive perimeter. Tanazakh did not know what to make of this, and neither did anyone else except the Cavanonians with them. The live Cavanonians stood on the ground next to the stage and experienced the overwhelming sadness Zérnoda spoke of earlier. Each of the other ghosts appeared as Cavanonians but twisted and bent, warped and scarred. The sense of depression felt by Laura and her sister told them that these spirits were once Cavanonians. Laura had spoken to past spirits before, but they never gave off a sense of gloominess or despair, quite the opposite. There had to be a reason why these spirits emanated such feelings. Laura had to find out why and since she had spoken to other spirits in her own chambers, she would do the talking.

"Who are you?" Laura said, looking for one to answer her.

Not one answered.

Laura tried again to stimulate a response. "Can you not speak, or are you forbidden to do so? Why will not one of you answer me?"

"Because they won't," said and even sadder, more forceful voice. The answer came from the other side of the stage. Laura and Zérnoda walked around to see whom it was that spoke and were amazed at the sight of what appeared to be an ancient warrior. He wore the same type of garb Adoné had worn during the marriage ceremony long ago, yet it had a sort of torn and disgraced setting about it. His face showed signs of age and scars covered much of it.

"They will not answer you because they were forsaken long ago."

"Why were they forsaken?" asked Laura.

"Because the King decreed it so," the spirit shouted back.

"The King...which King?" she asked.

"Why, King Cavanon himself!"

This answer stunned Laura and Zérnoda greatly, and even Tanazakh became puzzled hearing this. The first King, the original first creation of the Gods did this, but why would he do such a thing?

"Please," Laura softly pleaded, "tell me why Cavanon would do such a thing."

"The spirits you see before you were punished long ago for disbelief in the King and the Cavanonian way of life. They never accepted the true mission of our race as stated to us by the King and instead decided to live their own lives on their own terms, thus turning their backs on the Kingdom. Because of that, Cavanon tortured each here on the stage brutally in order to force a confession of faith and to have them swear allegiance to the Crown. When they did not do so, he sentenced them to death and a life in this underground realm. Cavanon further tormented their minds by placing this underground region under a plague of despair and loneliness. Since these outcasts wanted their own lives, he gave them what they wanted, and they are subject to it until the end of time."

"So, why is this not written in the ancient holy book then?" Zérnoda stated. "Why would these Cavanonians turn their backs on the King?"

"Firstly, these spirits were to be forgotten in time, never to be seen or read about again. Secondly, the King spoke of a great evil that would eventually come to visit this planet and destroy it. These spirits believed there was no real threat or danger to the Crown. They did not believe in this great evil, Ellononis, or the black arts, and thought it all a lie. Now, eons later, they see the error of their ways and have since regretted their initial decisions and actions. Now, their spirits truly do live in despair, knowing that never again will they ever have the chance at redemption."

"You speak of them and not yourself," said Laura, "who are you?"

"I have not been down here as long as they have. Only a few centuries ago did I come to know this place, unfortunately. I was known as Lazasar when I lived. My crime was of ignorance and self-conceitedness for what I did against a later King's daughter. I won her hand but then treated her wrongfully. I became overbearing in might and unaware that while the King applauded such conduct against other races, his daughter was not to be treated so. Since I did not renounce my faith in the crown as this multitude of spirits had, and since I did not follow the black arts of others, I was sentenced to think about how wrongfully I had treated others and the king subjected me to the same treatment."

"How come we have not heard of you before?" Laura said. "I have spoken with many, many spirits who died long ago and yet not one of them has spoken of you or this place."

"That is because they won't speak to us and they will not tell others about us. They know we are here and why, so they will not associate with us. They know of our punishment and refuse to break the judgment handed down. The spirits you speak of died honorably and have refused to enter into the heavens simply because they were loyal to the Crown and so loved their lives and purpose. The spirits *you* spoke to love this planet so much so that they insisted on remaining here. To them, this planet *is* their heaven and they refuse to go elsewhere."

"I must inform the King," Zérnoda said, "he has to know about this."

"King Solisynas died when the great evil spoken of long ago doomed the planet, and I know he could not have come back as you say," replied Lazasar. "Something else destroyed the planet. We saw this when the fires of energy swept through this place, leaving our destitute underworld in tact and unchanged, but we can only guess at what took place above. You are the first to visit this place since the time of King Solisynas."

"I wasn't referring to King Solisynas; I was referring to my father, the new king, King Adoné."

Lazasar staggered back a few paces. It was clear to Laura that he did not suspect that a new king had surfaced; he did not know. He looked about the multitude of spirits and worried much. "If there is a new king and he finds out about us, he may only heighten our current sentence."

"You don't know my Father," Laura replied. "He is unlike any being you have ever encountered."

"Exactly how many of you are there down here?" asked Tanazakh.

"The current number exceeds the thousands; two hundred and forty thousand to be exact. The number count here goes back to the first created Cavanonians." Lazasar mumbled as he slowly lowered his head. "I shudder to think of what the King will do to us when you tell him, for our sake you must not."

"But for your sake we will tell him," Zérnoda. "I assure you, he will not judge you as you have already been judged. He is kind and generous to those who are willing to help us defend what we have against the enemy."

"We are doomed here and there is no hope for us, so do not fill out heads with thoughts of possibility. We suffer enough as it is. Leave us, all of you, and forget you ever came here."

After Lazasar finished, the multitude of spirits evaporated and disappeared, leaving the visiting party alone in the darkness.

One by one, the party made there way out of the underground area and surfaced, seating themselves on the upper outer rim of the depression.

"What are your intentions, Laura?" asked Tanazakh. "Those spirits below ground seemed to have lost all hope and are doomed as they say. I don't think we can help them."

"I think otherwise," she answered. "We must bring my father here; I know he will help them."

"Then let us dispatch someone to retrieve the King and see if you are right. If he could help them, though I doubt it possible, our numbers would increase significantly. We would not be as small a force as we are now."

"That is precisely why we must try!"

Laura prepared herself and boarded Gizmo.

"I will return, swiftly," she shouted, and immediately took off.

Back at Royal Mountain, Adoné and Xashsa waited for the emergence of the two humans below. He knew approximately how long it would take Stan and Zach to complete the process, but that time had already came, and still they did not appear.

Laura hastily flew into the house and informed her father of her findings. After telling the information, Adoné informed his Queen that he would see to this great sight and return as soon as possible. He would not be gone for longer than was necessary, but still she did not like the idea.

Once back at the depression, the others in the party showed the truth of Laura's tale in their faces and in their minds. Adoné knew then that it was true and without haste, he and the waiting party descended down into the underground auditorium once again.

Adoné stood on the stone stage and waited for the spirits Laura spoke of to emerge, but they did not. The rest of the party became frustrated at this and did not like the idea of appearing as fools. However, the King could sense the dread and despair Laura spoke of and decided to instigate an appearance himself. By using his own spirit, he discovered the multitude of others hidden away in frightful fear of him. They did not want to show themselves; they were ashamed and humiliated already and did not want to further their punishment.

Reluctantly, Lazasar slowly came forth and stood before the King. He puzzled at the sight of this King and saw differences in his being. This King did not stand as the others, and the aura he gave off differed greatly. The King also acted in a way that Lazasar did not expect.

Adoné sat on the edge of the stone stage and motioned for the spirit to do the same. "Come, sit with me."

Tanazakh, Laura, and all the others sat up on the third row of steps to allow the king privacy, and to watch in wonder at what would take place.

"I am King Adoné; you must be Lazasar, correct?"

"I am."

"My daughter has hastily relayed your story to me and I find it very disturbing to know you are here without our knowledge."

"As she no doubt has told you, we are to be forgotten," Lazasar said. "We are to exist only as a memory; it is our sentence."

"Well, I think that is crap!" Adoné replied.

Lazasar did not expect to hear that sort of remark from the King. Instead, he assumed Adoné would agree with their sentence and begin to further their torment as he predicted. But, this was not the case. Adoné continued to explain his reasoning.

"You've been down here for many millenniums already, despairing, and wailing in sadness. Don't you think you and all those others down here have paid your price?"

"You're Highness, they have suffered more than I, and I feel as if my crime did not justify the sentence I received. I do regret my actions and would gladly avoid them if I were offered the chance to repent. These others, they are so far lost in dejection and hopelessness that it would be a miracle if they could come out of it. But, no one can undo the sentence placed upon us. Knowing that, we will always and forever remain in this state of eternal degeneration."

"As far as I am concerned," Adoné spoke up, "a king judged you and sentenced you, so why couldn't another king lift the sentence? *I* am King now, and I have a say in what happens to Cavanonians of the past, present, or future."

"You would attempt the impossible?" Lazasar shuddered.

"Not attempt," replied Adoné, "I would do it, and give you and others the chance of living with distinction rather than suffer eternal shame."

All of the other spirits heard this and one by one began to emerge from the walls, gathering around the stage. The spirits of the past-judged Cavanonians felt the glimmer of hope in the new King's words and could not believe their ears. The more Adoné spoke, the more spirits came forth until the auditorium filled to its capacity. Even the others, Tanazakh and company, became alarmed at the volume of spirits trapped down here. And even *they* were amazed.

"But first," said Adoné, "I must find out exactly who here wishes to be redeemed." Adoné glanced at the myriad of spirits and stood to his full height, rotating his body around for all to see. "And if any of you are willing to follow my reign and defend this planet, our homeland…then I will grant you forgiveness from your past crimes. Yes, we have faced the near annihilation of our species and yes, we have prevailed through the most horrid of times. But, with your loyalty to the Cavanonian race, *our* race, we shall overcome the evil that still exists. You have the chance to bring distinction to your lives if you so chose. If you swear allegiance to the crown and aid us in this our time of need, I promise you that when the evil is defeated, you may once again live your *own* lives in your *own* way. *What shall your answer be?*"

The doomed spirits exhaled when the King finished his speech and all stood up to their full height. Hope had come at a time in their lost existence when they thought it not possible. In a wave like manner, all the spirits dropped to their knees. The motion of the wave slowly made its way around the auditorium and as Adoné turned, he saw all of them kneeing before him. Every single spirit pledged their loyalty and shouted "*Hail*" to the new King.

"Tanazakh," Adoné shouted, "take the others topside and wait for me there, you cannot see this."

"But, Father, why not?" asked Zérnoda.

"Because it would kill you!" he exclaimed.

Once Adoné received a communiqué from Laura, he prepared himself.

Xashsa sat in the main room of her home wondering why he two humans had not come out. What happened to them? Why were they not awake? Had something caused their transformation to go wrong? Was it because the King performed the ceremony? Too many variables left her guessing and she became alarmed herself. She did not want to think that Stan and Zach had died because of failure. They wanted to be like Adoné, Cavanonian, and they gave themselves freely up to the process. Xashsa had killed before, but not innocent beings and she wondered if the others in the community learned of this, would it tarnish the Royal family's reputation for kindness and generosity, and protection?

The King stood on the stone stage praying. He fervently called upon the ancients and concentrated long and hard for an answer. Then, as if instinct took over, he revealed the Sword of Fire from his back and held it up to the air for all to see. All of the spirits revered the blade and beheld its power for the first time in their lives. They all chanted *Adoné, Adoné*, repeatedly until the shouts grew to an immense level. So loud were their voices that the auditorium itself began to shake and rumble.

Laura and the others up top felt the vibrations in the ground and glanced at their feet, witnessing the ground shake as if powerful impact tremors shook the surface of the planet.

"What is he doing down there?" asked Tanazakh.

"He is giving them back their hope and their lives," replied Laura, smiling.

As the chants turned into thunderous roars, the King angled his sword toward the stone stage and at the pinnacle of the roars; he drove the sword up to its hand guard into the center of the stone. The power of the sword took effect immediately and gathered all internal energies together and with one swift blast, the energy shot straight down deep into the planet to the very core itself. At the core, the energies merged and transformed, reformed.

While the energy below combined, the spirits all around began the scream and cry in agony. They felt the most horrendous pain in their bones, as they had not felt physical pain of any nature in eons. Their essence faded in and out of the dimension, billowing up smoke around each one of them. As the energy of the planet traveled through cracks and crevices, it reached each one the spirits and seized their spirituous bodies, pealing away their ethereal skin layer after layer. The heat of the energy caused them to melt down into the stone steps and ground.

Adoné stood above the sword and placed his hands together above his head. Smoke billowed around him and swirled in a brilliant spiral fashion upward, culminating, and joining into a sphere of glowing energy in his hands. When the core returned a forceful blast up into the sword, the energy collected in Adoné's hands he shouted, *"I RELEASE YOU FROM YOUR PRISON!"* and he swiped his hands in front of his body, dissipating the energy in all directions as ripples in a pond.

A great quake traveled throughout the planet and all who lived above and below the surface felt it. Laura and the others with her shook and fell from the violent quake and became fearful for the Kings life.

Xashsa wondered what the cause of the quake was and became alarmed, as did the community of members now gathering outside below Royal Mountain. Simultaneously, as all creatures felt the planetary disturbance, the only two who were dead woke up. The eyes of Stan and Zach opened after the quake had passed and began the last portion of the transference.

The energy collided with the transference of essence and through the ashes of the dead spirits; their bodies began to reshape and reform, growing steadily up out of the ground. As the new skeletons stood, muscular tissue and blood regained their places, and their skins covered the exposed tissue and bone, resealing and reshaping the spirits into flesh one again.

The King stood silent watching the new arrivals gawk in surprise and shock. Adoné gasped and took deep breaths; his adrenaline had hit an all time high and he needed to calm down. The spirits were gone and the flesh of two hundred and forty thousand Cavanonians returned, released once again though they all thought contrary. Lazasar bowed down on one knee to his new King and felt ashamed that he doubted Adoné's words and abilities.

"Forgive me, my Lord," Lazasar apologized, "I should not have doubted you."

"Relax, Lazasar," replied Adoné, as he placed his right hand on his new servants shoulder, "there is nothing to forgive. You had reason to doubt, and I would have done the same had I been in your shoes."

Lazasar stood up and smiled. His eyes watered a bit from the happiness he felt inside. In addition, as he gazed at the others who cheered and hailed their return, Adoné felt it was time for them to leave.

"Come," the King said, "let's get them out of this dreadful place and back into the real world."

Lazasar called to all and motioned for them to follow the King.

Xashsa stood outside the entrance to her home and waited. She no longer felt keen on the idea of being alone in her own home; the horror she suffered long ago cured her of that. She took solace in the fact that her husband remained on this system and not elsewhere in the galaxy. The next time he did leave this planet, she would be with him.

The community members below gathered outside their own homes still wondering what caused the great quake they felt earlier. The quake itself did not damage any of their homes, it was just enough to alarm them all and cause some fear. They hoped that something dreadful did not take place, but still they began to wonder.

The Tnemucodas warriors flew about in the sky on their guard, keeping watchful eyes on the area below. They did promise the King that they would protect and defend this small community, and they worked to keep their promise. A few of the winged warriors caught some spectacle off in the distance to the north. A huge black cloud of something came into view and appeared to be heading in their direction. Nervously, they alerted the inhabitants below and one of them went to the Queen to inform her as well.

"Queen Xashsa," a warrior said, "there is something coming, and we do not know what it is. You should be on your guard!"

Xashsa did not like that fact that she was alone, and after glancing at the empty room behind her, she decided that she would do her best to stand her ground at whatever force came. However, as she began to summon her anger and rage, her heart became at ease and her anger ceased. She stood puzzled at what had done this to her. She then received a communiqué from her husband.

"Xashsa," he said, "*tell the others below not to be afraid. I bring you all a very amazing gift.*"

"What is it, Love?"

"*Just you wait and see! Tell them and then meet me on top of our mountain.*"

Xashsa did as he asked and told the Tnemucodas to spread the word to the others and as soon as she did, she raced up to the mountaintop. Shortly after she arrived, Adoné joined her; the others with the King landed with the other community members and prepared them as well.

From where the King and Queen stood, the darkness coming towards them began to move about the sky as if each part of it had a mind of its own. Xashsa had no idea what it was but soon saw the spectacle in its magnificence. Then she saw the cause of the dark cloud, and gasped as thousands and thousands of Cavanonians raced through the sky overhead. The cheers and shouts of praise filled the skies as each one waved to all below. The last time Xashsa saw this many Cavanonians in one place was back when she lived here with her family long ago. There were so many, everywhere in the skies and now landing on the valley floor below the mountain.

The newcomers did not know what to expect, and hoped that the warning given them was true; they had nothing to worry about. So much excitement caused them to hold up in their doorways; the humans did not think this a natural occurrence, but they would soon learn the nature of this miracle.

"Adoné, what happened?" the astounded Xashsa asked.

"These were the wretched spirits Laura told us about," he answered. "In exchange for their aid and loyalty, I have freed them from their sentence of despair and depression. I felt that they had served their sentence for their crimes and I promised them freedom if they fight for us. There are two hundred forty thousand fresh Cavanonians all willing to serve and ready to fight."

"This is indeed a momentous day for us all," she said, and she hugged him vigorously.

"Come, Sweetie, lets go down and meet them," he said, taking her hand in his. "They need to meet their new Queen as well"

They both flew down to the valley floor and received a relentless flood of cheers and shouts of praise. All new Cavanonians knelt simultaneously before the monarchy and rose up to greet and shake hands with their new King and Queen. Male and female of the species all existed now and gleamed with happiness for the pardon of their sentence. The joyous welcome back into the world definitely brought a welcome freshness to the planet and there was much reason to rejoice.

As Xashsa and Adoné made their way through the multitude of new arrivals, Adoné paused when they arrived at Lazasar.

"My Queen," Adoné said, "This is the one whom I spoke to and who helped to secure their promise. Allow me to introduce—" Adoné stopped as he suddenly heard her voice.

"*Lazasar!*" exclaimed Xashsa.

"Xashsa?" asked Lazasar, truly shocked.

Adoné wondered how she already knew his name. "You two know each other?"

Lazasar stayed on his knee and began to worry all over again.

"He was my *first* husband," Xashsa replied in a condescending tone.

Adoné could not believe his ears. "Him…well, this is definitely a twist of fate, isn't it?"

"I ought to kill you right here and now for what you did to me," Xashsa said to Lazasar, angrily.

"My Queen, have pity on a lost soul. Forgive me my ignorance and the sins I committed against you."

Xashsa felt the passionate urge to sentence this wretch to her own version of torment, but she saw the faces of the others standing around them and decided that perhaps this matter should be dealt with later. Right now was not the time to create dissension among the new ranks. The Queen sensed the uncomfortable silence that lingered in the air and dispensed with it.

"I forgive you, Lazasar," she calmly replied, but very controlled. "But you definitely have a lot to make up for…and stay the hell away from me."

While Adoné and Xashsa, along with the rest of the family and friends mingled with the newest arrivals into their new world, the two humans, Stan and Zach, emerged from Laura's chambers. They had made the journey over and they stood outside the main entrance gazing at the world with their new Cavanonian eyes. Their beings completely changed and appeared to have no apparent side effects either. Both greatly admired each other's appearance and were very happy now that they had become new creatures, just as the King had promised. They saw the multitude below and decided to report to the King and make their new appearance.

Adoné consulted with Lazasar to find out who amongst the Cavanonians had leadership qualities, all the while Xashsa stood alongside her husband, averting her eyes from her *first* husband. She would deal with the problem of her memory of him later, but she understood the reasons for Adoné's search. This multitude needed organization, management, and direction. Necessity also dictated that these new forces be strategically placed around various areas of the city.

In his search, Adoné discovered many more former administrators than he assumed he would. The goal of these administrators would be to stay with those who were familiar with others, there was no sense in placing unknowns in different groups, but then again, Adoné thought they all knew each other for many centuries while in their depression. Maybe it wasn't as bad a problem as Adoné thought. Divided up into divisions, each division had several administrators within the ranks to aid in organization. Decentralization at this level was necessary.

Placed in and around the city, and in outlying regions of geographical importance, the new Cavanonians immediately set out to establish themselves. Housing construction began immediately as well, as did food procurement and fabrication of new clothes. Adoné had no way of knowing that many of them were well versed in various badly needed trade skills. Many were able to create the same type of clothing possessing the magical attributes that Adoné and Zérnoda came to enjoy long ago. Many were skilled in the construction of buildings and had tons of ideas for improving the dilapidated domiciles the original community lived in. those primitive houses simply were not up to standards and would be demolished once new housing areas were developed and constructed.

Many others were very useful blacksmiths, possessing the very early knowledge of weapons development, and a large majority were not only skilled swordsmen, but in production as well. They would create weapons of the finest quality not seen since the first generation of their kind.

Some of the others possessed such trades and skills as physicians, scientists, aerial production specialists (who could bring back spacecraft), power generation specialists, and many, many other badly needed artisans. All were equally important and significant to the world, but those who displayed the natural abilities of leadership interested Adoné greatly. He relied on them to organize, implement plans, and manage this great multitude.

The humans who lived in the original smaller community no longer had anything to worry about. With the sudden increase in population, the humans, Srotaderp, Nablah, and Anadonians no longer secluded themselves indoors. Now, they ventured out normally and without worry, mingling with the Cavanonians of the past and getting to know them. Soon the Helena humans began to learn from the Cavanonians and incorporated themselves into a new routine, and to aid in the great amount of work to come.

Adoné placed Stan and Zach into the division of Cavanonians who began to inhabit the once battle trodden valley on the west side of Royal mountain. There, the newly transformed Cavanonians would learn all aspects of their new lives from those brought back. Everything from concentration, mind control, skills with weapons, the arts of enemy desecration, etc, filled their program. Adoné thought it would be a good idea to take these two on the next journey but he decided against it. They required instruction first and the monarch saw no sense in exposing them to the elements without prior training and experience. Throwing them up against any encountered enemy would be futile without knowledge of their inherent powers.

The original members of Adoné's community remained closest to the throne: Tanazakh, Tejrasel, Lokcha, Ann, the Srotaderp leader, and the humans; he kept Kayla and Sarah very near to them as well, for obvious reasons. These members were part of Adoné's personal council not just for advice, planning, or formulating operations; they were his friends and would always be that.

One day, a few of the Cavanonians came to the King and inquired about something he had almost forgotten himself. Their names were Knoj, Sirenis, Olars, and Khayfaj. Khayfaj appeared to be the representative for this little group and addressed the king formally, then asked his questions.

"My Liege, a great number of the multitude wishes to acquire the blood of the Zalestole."

"Is this a request from all?" the King asked.

"After a few millennium of depression," Khayfaj replied, "it is a requirement they wish to have filled. They have yearned for it since the beginning of the depression and it would bring them great exhilaration to suffer its fire in their veins once again."

"I've been meaning to seek it out, but I have not because our numbers were not enough to both search for it and secure the homeland. Now that we are a sizable race once again, we will make the journey. Gather up fifty of them for the trip; I trust your judgment of character will correctly decide which type will be needed?"

"Absolutely, My Liege," Khayfaj smiled greatly and departed.

After the discussion, Adoné gathered a band of fifty together for the journey. Xashsa insisted that she remain and provide leadership to the planet now that there were many more to worry about. Leadership was required.

Adoné took with him Tanazakh and his sons, Lazasar, and forty-five other Cavanonians starved for adventure and action. Firstly, they would meet up with the Kostejaanians and see if they could provide some transportation across the galaxy. The transportation would also help in carrying back a significant amount of the Zalestole hemotoxin, and a great amount would be required to sustain the multitude. Secondly, they could use the transportation to mask their true numbers and identity should anything else detect a presence. The use of the Kostejaani spacecraft would be temporary of course, until the Cavanonians created their own suitable transportation. That required time to design and to collect the raw materials needed for construction. However, time was all they had presently, and with initiative and motivation in their court, they would use their time wisely.

Chapter 12

The Quest for Blood

On the outskirts of Ellononis, the Kostejaani ship slowly circumnavigated the planet and analyzed the surface features using infrared technology and motion sensors to detect any life forms that may exist. Orbiting the planet allowed for a detailed surface scan and the information collected relayed through a holographic monitor displaying the terrain features and surface composition. The information gathered revealed all they needed to ascertain the location of the fountain, or at least the entrance to its location.

Over the intended site, the ship hovered and allowed the band of fifty to exit the craft and enter into the passageway below. Adoné first sent Lazasar ahead with a team of twelve to secure the passage farther inside. This would allow the remaining members to bring up the rear and keep watch for any possible signs of danger. The Kostejaanian ship departed from the unrelenting atmosphere of the planet and took up station in a geosynchronous orbit above the drop-off point. There it would remain until called for.

Down in the passageway, the first obstacle encountered was that of the initial passage warning. On the other side of the door, they found the four mysterious passages early navigated by Federoth, Rudecor, and Nosrévis, but Adoné and his band did not know the enemy had already been there. All in the room had a similar look of question and concern as to which passage to take. They sensed a danger here and smelled the blood of a recent kill. This was odd.

"Something or someone has been here, my Lord," said Lazasar, "The air is heavy with death."

"No doubt from the dangers that lie within these four passageways," Adoné answered. "But who was here?"

None could answer, and the others checked out the entrances to the passageways, but not one went beyond the archway. Some Cavanonians were wise to the construction of such areas and knew that because of whatever lived on the other side, there would be no chance of escape if anyone crossed the path.

"It's definitely the motif of Ellononis construction," said Naltac, a former builder and warrior. I remember designs of this nature and construction from eons ago."

"And what do you make of it," asked Lazasar, "is there danger imminent?"

"Absolutely, Naltac replied. "Once you cross the line of the doorway, it will seal itself shut and allow the danger on the other side to consume whoever was unfortunate enough to venture in."

"So then, how do we prevent this action then?" the King asked.

"Simple, we take one passageway at a time."

"Or we just take the correct path and leave the others," said Lazasar.

'Er, yes," replied Naltac. "Judging by the nature of the riddles above the passageways, you have simple clues as to the danger that lies within each path. Here, this first path has something that waits for sustenance. This second passageway has winged assassins. The third, we must not attempt or we will be crushed, and the fourth—" he was cut off.

"No need to venture in there," Adoné said. "We will only be eaten if we go that way."

"Then the winged assassins it is," Lazasar said, and ordered twelve team members inside the passageway.

Adoné noticed a willingness in the warriors to place themselves in harms way. They did this instantly and without hesitation, as if they were fearless. Adoné damn sure could have used these guys a long time ago; they probably would have helped to put an end to this evil long ago.

Inside the passageway, the initial point warriors entered into the vast open area and stood upon the huge platform in the center. The screeching of danger grew in volume and fervor, but that did not scare the warriors. From all that they had been through, dying in battle would be worth more than a frightful scare.

Armed to the teeth, the warriors switched their vision and saw the winged menaces circling around overhead well beyond their reach. The winged assassins were waiting to strike, but the warriors did not want to wait.

"My Lord," said Naltac, "grant us permission to feast."

"Feast?" asked the King, curiously.

"Yes, let us show you the techniques of desecration we are well versed in. You will be proud, my Lord,"

Naltac kneeled before him and this amazed Adoné, greatly. His warriors were asking to launch their own attack and instigate trouble before the winged assassins had a chance.

"Such bravery and courage is definitely commendable and just what is needed within our species," Adoné thought and further gave the order. "Then show me what my warriors are capable of."

The smiles of their dormant demons engulfed the faces of the Cavanonians and within seconds, they raced to greet the fluttering enemy in their own way. Adoné and Lazasar watched as the warriors revealed their own arsenal of weapons: larger than normal fanged teeth and unnatural claws on their hands and feet. One by one, the Cavanonian warriors cloaked themselves and attacked each of the winged assassins using coordinated attack efforts, ripping the enemy to shreds of flesh and bone. The winged creatures did not know what to make of it, they could not see the cause of the attack, and they perished in a matter of moments.

Below, Adoné stared in wonder and amazement. These Cavanonians truly gave truth to the myths of their elusive battle techniques. The King stood in the center of the platform, holding his face to the air above and relishing the blood that drenched the platform. Adoné did also notice that other warriors encircled the King, immediately before the attack began. Instinctively, they knew to protect their ruler without orders. This was something that Adoné had never experience before. In the past, he instigated attacks or ambushes himself, and took out the enemy in his own way. However, these warriors now relieved him of that duty; it was their turn to fight, and fight they would.

In a downward spiral, one of the winged carcasses careened and crashed into the far sidewall, revealing the entranceway for the next leg of the journey.

"That must be the way to go," said Lazasar, smiling.

Adoné smiled back.

Through this passageway, the warriors soaked in the blood of their kill moved stealthily forward and came to a large opening possessing the banners bearing the name of Ellononis. Naltac immediately went to his lord and informed him that this would be the most treacherous point in the journey.

"The Guardian sits in there," Naltac informed the King. "Only those who are pure can pass, and he will know our nature if *we* try."

"Then this is a job for me," Adoné replied.

"But, you're Highness," Lazasar stopped him, "you must not go yourself."

"Lazasar, the warriors did their job, now watch me do mine."

Upon entering the enormous chamber, the guardian showed up as Naltac said. The walls and ceiling to Adoné's immediate front pealed away and revealed the lair of the menacing creature.

The Guardian came forward and sniffed at Adoné for a moment and as if sensing his impurities within, the Guardian roared in rage and began to strike at Adoné with his massively large claws. The King pulled out his favorite black blade and furiously swung it at his opponent. The Guardian showed great agility in his quick movements, moving out of the path of the blade, continuing to strike at this intruder. Lazasar and the other warriors grew worried and felt they should intervene against the order given them. However, Adoné read this in their minds and decided that he had toyed with the Guardian for long enough. As the Guardian rose up to strike, Adoné swiped his hands and the creature became stiff as a board. Frozen in place, the Guardian could do nothing more and as the King held the blade to the throat this enemy, Adoné whispered words that only the Guardian could hear.

"Reveal the passageway to the fountain and I will spare you. Conceal the passageway and I will send you into oblivion."

Behind the waiting warriors, Lazasar noticed a doorway materialized and he quickly directed all to enter. Adoné waited until all had passed before he let loose the frozen guardian. However, the guardian had a mind of its own, as Adoné turned to the passageway, the Guardian rose, and drove his body towards his opponent. Adoné was not aware of the enemy's quick decision, but one of his warriors was. With blinding speed, a warrior ran to aid the unsuspecting King and pushed him out of the way, saving the King but losing his own life to the claw that protruded through his back. Adoné jumped up, turned with the firesword, and struck the Guardian, smiting his huge body in half. On the ground, the organs, fluids, and blood soaked the stone, sending up a stench unlike Adoné had ever known. The fatally wounded warrior choked and coughed up his blood as Adoné held him.

"Af, after all these many years of, of humility," the warrior coughed, "I p...pray I have at least honored you, my Liege."

"You have," the King replied. "With your sacrifice, you shall be the most honored amongst our race and it will be made so upon our return."

"Please, my Liege, I beg of you; do not let my spirit rest here. Take me back to Cavanon so that I may join my brothers and sisters."

"I shall carry your spirit and deliver you there, *personally.*"

The warrior smiled, and as his live force extinguished, Adoné placed his hand over the warrior and accepted his soul into his own body. There it would remain until delivered. Even though Lazasar and the other warriors were saddened with the loss of one of their own, they now felt an increased sense of pride in their monarch. Feelings of exhilaration soared through their essence as each turned toward the intended direction of travel.

The Fountain of Ellononis stood solid in the middle of the five hundred foot chamber; behind it stood a stone shrine of some six feet, arched and decayed. Lazasar directed a perimeter search of the area to determine either if there were any other dangers or if there were another entrance or exit.

Adoné walked to the fountain and stared at it. The name '*Zalestole*' inscribed at the base proved that this was the actual fountain Cavanon himself visited eons ago. Adoné secured a handful of the hemotoxic fluid and slurped it up. Instantly, the intoxicating effects he remembered long ago began to fill his head and race through his veins. The last time he tasted this substance took place prior to when he split his spirit, Xashsa and the Royal family had been murdered, and the surface of the planet of Cavanon ravaged by war. This time, the feeling in him felt differently; he knew this was due to drinking from the perpetual fountain directly. As he stood there in a semi-drunken state, the walls and ceiling before him vanished and displayed visions of future events. The visions disturbed the King, greatly.

Images of a war came into view, a war on a strange and distant planet. Strangely, the creatures at war appeared to be a combined force of three different races of beings: the Nomaseri, Nogzakhs of the Dominion, and another force Adoné had never seen before, but he did recognize the face of their leader, his former self.

"*Nosrévis?*" he said to himself. "He changed his name and created his own brand of demonic warriors."

Adoné did not recognize the planet they were at war with either, and the enemy slaughtered those beings horribly. Thousands upon thousands of helpless souls fell to the combined force. Then, in a similar vision of another far away land, also never seen or visited by the current Cavanonian King, illusions of a ceremony lighted the scene. There, the Nogzakhs, the Nomaseri, and the strange creatures loyal to Nosrévis all stood around a great underground temple. Chants grew in thunderous volume and called the name of Ellononis. As Adoné heard the name, the shape of the ultimate enemy came into full view. The horrid features of Ellononis did not frighten Adoné; instead, they only increased his rage. While he saw the enemy face, visions of all the past times suffered by Adoné and all his friends flew past his eyes and filled his memory. All the evil that had befallen them their whole lives directly stemmed from this one being. The face of Ellononis glanced upward and Adoné looked up toward the ceiling, wondering what was up there that caught his eye. Instantly he floated up to the apex of the ceiling and there hung a handle with two ways to go left or right. Adoné figured that since this was the planet of the evil being during his lifetime, the left (or wrong way) would be the way to go. His choice proved correct.

The ceiling opened up to him revealing a hidden chamber above the base and forward over the base and toward the very back of the chambers. There Adoné stood before a great wall with writings on it, strange writings, but Adoné could make them out.

'When the system of Cinodas blocks the sight of Elaveshan and Tnemucoda, the portal will be opened. The Door to Oblivion shall bring about the rise of our God and he shall reign supreme. He shall be brought back through one who is of another time and another dimension. Ellononis shall smite his enemies and lay siege to their lands, gathering all unto himself. Those who oppose his might shall fall and in the end, the first Cavanonian shall bow before him. This is the prophetic vision as seen by his master's servant, Zalestole.'

After reading the inscription on the stone, Adoné returned to the warriors below. Perplexed and dazed, he stood silent for a minute or two. Lazasar accompanied him as the King walked about the chambers contemplating the prophecy written on the wall above.

"Lord, what is it, what troubles you?" Lazasar asked, apparently concerned.

"There is a prophecy that speaks of the return of Ellononis written on a wall in the above chamber. It coincides with the visions I saw of a great battle and then a massive ceremony. The prophecy above speaks of the first Cavanonian bowing to Ellononis and all others are gone. We must get back and speak to the Tnemucodas. I have seen in this place in the vision; it is where the ceremony will take place."

"We make ready to leave at once, My Lord."

"Wait," Adoné stopped him, "send some warriors up to the ship, and have the Kostejaanians determine our location here; I've another idea as well," the King said, eyeing the rear base of the shrine.

A keyhole in the shape of fire existed in the back of the fountain.

Lazasar dispatched five warriors to the surface and roughly thirty minutes later, they returned.

"The Kostejaanians say that have located us underground," Lazasar reported. "They are approximately one thousand feet directly above us."

"Good, have them move off center of our location and wait until the signal ceases, then have them position the ship directly over us. Have them prepare their empty storage tanks as well."

"My Lord," Lazasar said, confused, "what are you going to do?"

"I'm going to drain this fountain and destroy it."

When the warriors returned from delivering the message, Adoné removed the firesword and pierced the keyhole behind the shrine. The sword unlocked a potent energy source that blasted a hole clean through the rock above, sending a larger than life signal through the heavens. The Kostejaanians now knew what signal the warriors mentioned. Afterwards the ship descended onto the rock and had their storage tanks open and ready. Adoné mustered up his powers and siphoned out the Zalestolean blood, shooting it straight up through the rock and into the waiting ship.

Rumblings shook the ground all around and Adoné ordered all of the warriors out immediately. Lazasar insisted on remaining but the King would not have it. All departed swiftly and as the fountain finally ran dry; the inside of the fountain began to implode violently, causing a chain reaction of rumblings and explosions in the underground chambers. Adoné rose up and flew through the hole to the ship, gaining entrance right behind Lazasar. As the ship gained altitude, the planet itself began to implode, as if the entire planet connected somehow with the fountain below. Once out of the planets atmosphere, Adoné and Lazasar watched as the planet shrunk into itself and released a massive blast, sending shockwaves through space. With the blood secured, the ship made off for home.

Xashsa could not believe the amount of progress and advancement completed by the forgiven multitude of Cavanonians. Even though Adoné and his warriors had only been gone a few days, the population at home increased their dwellings and houses drastically. This new society seemed to spring forth overnight. Social order was not a problem at all; all creatures interacted with a profound sense of purpose and belonging, and possessed a natural willingness to promote peace and well-being amongst the population. All creatures treated each other with mutual respect and admiration; even the humans were in a sense revered for their characteristics and attributes, despite the fact that they were absent of inherent powers.

Once the King had returned, he immediately set to constructing a different sort of Fountain for the thousands of gallons of the hemotoxic beverage desired by many of their species. This fountain should not be hidden away such as it was on the Ellononis system. Instead, it would be at the very heart of the city itself, placed inside a temple of its own and guarded over to ensure the population did not drain it all in one night. Cavanonians understood the myth of the bloods automatic replenishing qualities and believed it to be the true source of immortality, though they themselves knew they weren't immortal. Now they would have a chance to see it first hand and witness the spectacular event.

The humans did voice their concern and questions as to the nature of this craved drink, and wondered if it had side effects evident of the very nature of the evil side. Other Cavanonians explained to them that there was no need to worry about that. The King himself knew to add some of himself into the mix in order to counter any other possible effects. The blessing of the king removed any possibility of concern regarding evil residue.

While the multitude served themselves, Adoné wondered about the visions he saw after he first drank of the hemotoxin. They visions disturbed him greatly. Observing a war yet to come and the slaughter of so many innocent victims nudged his senses into considering a plan of warning. He had yet to visit this place, but he did not know its location. He held council with his family and closest friends to discuss the matter.

"The visions I saw gave me reason to grieve," Adoné said, "however, I know this event has not yet come to pass."

"Is there any significance to this race you saw destroyed?" asked Tanazakh, "it would help to know who they are."

"But that's just it," his friend replied, "the vision did not reveal who they are or where they are located, I just saw what will be."

"Then let me see your vision and maybe I can find out," said Xashsa.

Adoné revealed the vision to her mind and afterwards even Xashsa became disturbed, slightly. Even though she detested the killing of innocent beings for no reason, she did find the events of combat arousing to her senses. That had to do with her own visions of Cavanonian warriors, the real warriors currently here, in combat with the enemy.

"That *BASTARD!*" shouted Xashsa.

Everyone in the chambers jerked in surprise, not prepared for her colorful metaphorical outburst.

"Adoné," Tanazakh spoke, "what did you show her?"

"I just showed her what I saw," he replied.

"It was that vile fiend who murdered me," she said, angrily. "He has a big part in this, and the species you saw being destroyed are the Dolumek."

"Dolumek? Wait a minute, didn't you tell me long ago that they were once at war with the Nomaseri?" Adoné asked.

"Yes, well actually, it was the Kostejaanians that told us of the conflict between the two systems. They were presiding over peaceful negotiations and the delegation attending to this became trapped on Earth, shot down by the Nogzakhs."

"So then, why are the Nomaseri, the Nogzakhs, and Nosrévis attacking them? Do the Dolumek play some important role we know nothing about?" Tanazakh queried.

"Not that I am aware of," answered Xashsa. "From what I remember of the Dolumek, they are loyal to no one; they think only of themselves and do not associate with anyone outside their system. It's a wonder to me that they even agreed to peace negotiations with the Nomaseri in the first place. I think the Kostejaanians were just trying to end the Nomaseri aggression in that region."

"Well," Adoné said, "we must warn them of what is to come; they need to know this before they are wiped out, completely."

"You'll have a hard time winning *their* hearts and minds," said Xashsa, "they do not take kindly to anyone being amongst them, friendly or otherwise."

"All I can do is provide them with a warning. If they fail to head, then my vision will become the inescapable result of their own failure."

"Be warned, Love," she said, placing her hand on his right arm, "they are blinded by their own majesty and are dumbstruck by it."

Chapter 13

The Realm of the Dolumek

Halfway between Cavanon and Samajap, not too far away from Kostejaan sat the Planet of Dolumek, tucked away in its own cubbyhole with the Philistoal Nebulas as a backdrop. The brown and bluish-green planet possessed a stronger gravitational field compared to Cavanon. This meant that whatever entered into the planets atmosphere usually struck the surface with greater force. Small meteors or rocks plagued the skies periodically, but never did any damage above what inhabitants considered normal.

The Dolumek land mass covered three-quarters of the planet's surface, with the remaining fourth being an enormous source of water. The standard type of cloud cover came not only from the only source of water on the planet, but from the vast rivers and subterranean waterways, which periodically peaked above ground. Dense forests of viscous trees covered the planet surface and secluded the Dolumek and their cities. The rubbery substance of the viscous became the most widely used material on the planet aside from non-viscous trees used for other odd reasons.

An unknown sentiment of stone made of the composition of Dolumek planet itself. One aspect of the planet that differentiated it from others stemmed from the larger than normal mountains and ranges. One mountain located in the southern most hemisphere, took up the space of one half of the hemisphere. Its height stopped at thirty two thousand feet. The Dolumek themselves or any of the other indigenous life forms never went up there. The reason for this stemmed from the fact that the temperatures at that height were fatal and anyone who ever tried to attempt the climb outside of spacecraft froze to death.

The Dolumek cities did not exist above ground. They enjoyed a peaceful subterranean existence out of sight of anything that may journey over the surface above. Their underground life flourished in vast hollowed out expanses in a secondary ground layer deep within the crust of the planet. The Dolumek did not require surface light. Instead, they enjoyed the ambient light of enormous Slass plants that existed above ground. The expanding petals and pollinated stamen center actually sank up the light from a nearby star and charged inner cells all the way through the lower stems. Underground, these arteries or vessels brilliantly illuminated the subsurface area with a greenish yellow light, sensitive enough to light up the expanses beneath the surface. The Dolumek worked and slept with this light and never had problems. Above ground was a different matter. The intensity of the daylight hours could easily blind their kind and because of the nocturnal nature of the race, they never went out in daylight unless an extreme situation dictated otherwise. When that happened, dark shrouds prevented the extreme rays of the sun from piercing their sensitized eyes and skin.

The city network consisted of structures of stone blocks where stalactites or stalagmites did not exist. Unique in design, the underground buildings rose in height almost to the roof of the expanse itself. Several hundred Dolumek lived in a single structure, and the areas usually had several hundred large cubicle structures organized in rectangular arrangements. The cities did not exist solely out of rock or stone or brick; Steel girders hung everywhere from the roof of the expanse and other layers of community areas leveled in checkerboard fashion. Other areas possessed huge bays and hangars for the multitude of aircraft owned by the Dolumek. Subterranean vehicles followed hollowed out roadways or tunnels that ran through out the subsurface mantle. The greatest amount of the population dwelt at the very center of the planet. A circular structure built upon over the centuries expanded outward to the globular size of approximately two thousand miles in diameter.

The Dolumek enjoyed their planetary seclusion greatly and weren't bothered at all by neighboring star systems, except for one neighbor. The Nomaseri sought to inhabit this planet and from the absence of above surface life, with the exception of the overpopulating wildlife itself, they assumed the planet uninhabited. When the Nomaseri entered into caves or great depressions, they learned the planet did have occupants and thus the initial conflict began. That was when the Kostejaanians decided to intervene on behalf of the Dolumek in an attempt to cease hostilities. The Dolumek did not require interaction with other races or species in the galaxy; they lived peacefully without such socializing and the problems that usually coincided with it.

The Dolumek did know of Cavanon but had never seen any of them. Generally, this species did not seek adventure elsewhere and did not venture out of the planets atmosphere. To the Dolumek, their requirements to sustain life existed here anyway and there was no need for sightseeing or unwarranted escapades. They were content with their own lives and did not typically socialize outside of their own species.

At the very center of the planet, the capital city of Dolumek itself began a new day in the same manner as any other day. The city population went about their own daily business as they saw fit. The governing ruler held councils routine in nature and almost mundane at this point. Courts matters usually consisted of general subjects such as future development projects, refurbishment of housing construction in various areas of the planet, etc.

Today, the Dolumek received a little excitement different from the norm. This they were not ready for and reacted very different from what the visiting party imagined.

A ship arrived outside Dolumek's atmosphere and took up a stationary orbit above the highest mountain in the southern hemisphere. The planetary tracking systems detected the ship and dispatched a force to the underground region beneath the mountain. There, the force awaited further orders.

From the ship, a small delegation of five landed on the surface and began to search for Dolumek life forms. Since Adoné and Xashsa had never met a Dolumek before, Nyfletoné came to advise and assist the two Cavanonian monarchs through the translations of Tanazakh; Lazasar accompanied them as well.

In one of the various entranceways to the subterranean realm, Nyfletoné made his descent down over rocky terrain, knowing that as he descended, eyes of a force watched his every move. Nearing a leveled off ledge to a small river expanse, the force halted his movement. Although the Kostejaanian leader knew their appearances from long ago, he could not see their features through the heavy robes covering their faces and bodies. The Dolumek were secretive even in their dress, not wishing to reveal their nature to anyone who wasn't of them. Recognizing Nyfletoné's species, the guard force calmed their suspicions of the visitor and led him farther in to the planet. After boarding a flat rail transport, they raced off toward the center of the planet to the center figureheads of the species.

While cloaked on the back of the transport, Adoné, his Queen, and Lazasar gazed in wonder and amazement at how seemingly disorganized the underground dwellings arranged themselves. Some buildings rose up, some were sideways, and others hung down from the roof of the expanse. Tunnel systems showed the railway track through stone masses and opened up every so often to reveal another type of city.

Adoné and his delegation now observed the uncovered Dolumek and gazed at their characteristics as they passed by them. Each stood at a height slightly shorter than Adoné himself and had about the same body mass, but not overweight. Hands with only three fingers and a thumb, two arms, two legs; standard features. Their faces differed though. They were similar to the Nomaseri but had different characteristics. Two black eyes, no nose, and smaller rounded ears adorned the box shape head on its broad shoulders. Outward from the head, and on top, a horn came out from top-center of the head curving to the front and downward pointing directly in front of the owner. Males had no hair, but females did have hair but no horn. The two sexes were easily distinguishable from each other not only by body features, but also through their variety of attire.

The small force, Nyfletoné, and the secretive Cavanonian delegation traveled for hours and hours before reaching the very heart of the planet.

"*Too bad the Srotaderp could not see this,*" thought Xashsa, "*they might enjoy a little construction competition, don't you think?*"

"*That they might,*" replied her husband. "*However, I think that our underground lords do a fine job of their own. The primitive nature in them suits their abilities very well and besides, too much advancement is a bad thing.*"

"*You're referring to the ongoing construction projects at home?*"

"*Yes,*" he answered. "*They enjoy the work, but I don't think they will care to learn how to fly. They enjoy the life underground and probably won't ever fly again, not since the relocation from Earth…*"

"*They are content with where they are. Our planet has more room for them to grow and populate.*"

"*Our planet has enough room for all of us to grow and populate,*" Adoné answered happily.

At the planet core, the rail transport slowed a bit and began to navigate the hundreds of intersections, rail crossings, and walkways of the city center. The hustle and bustle of the inhabitants gave the secret passengers something to look at as well, learning life underground and its structural society.

The small force led Nyfletoné to through massive structures and corridors to other hallways interconnected to all of the cities main buildings. The Dolumek force did not say a word through the entire trip and continued to maintain silence. They were under strict orders to say nothing to the visitor; the Dolumek did not freely converse with anyone outside of their own species unless directed; for the most part, they kept to themselves and shunned outsiders.

Nyfletoné halted as the force paused in the great hall that stood before them. The Kostejaanian leader had visited this place many times before, but the secret delegation behind him had not. All of the secretive party stood in amazement at the magnificence of the great hall and its grand size. This construction boasted a size twice as big as the underground depression of lost souls back on Cavanon. The sheer massiveness of the structure itself was a builders dream. Adoné would have to show this to the Srotaderp one day, maybe this would give them new ideas. This grand area had to be at least a good two miles wide in octagonal shape. The ceiling rose to a height equal to the size of the width. From the ceiling hung great spikes of steel, girders welded into unnatural teeth of metal and iron. To Tanazakh, it appeared a frightfully moving setting, but to Adoné, it was a deathly beautiful work of art. Xashsa sensed his thoughts and commented.

"*You are enjoying this sight.*"

"Absolutely, Sweetie," he replied, "*this is spectacular!*"

"*No doubt, you will have a few ideas of your own for our own home,*" she said.

"We'll see," he replied, "*but first we must attend to our mission.*"

"*This construction has your mind occupied more than you think.*"

Adoné forgot his setting and murmured, "Hmm."

The guard to his front turned to look for the cause of the sound but saw no one. After a few seconds, he turned and began to assist Nyfletoné onto a waiting hover transport. Once boarded, they moved at a mild pace so as not to run over any unsuspecting beings on the guided path. Instead of catching the transport, Adoné and company simply hovered over the conveyance and followed, while taking in even more of the magnificence features of the grand hall.

The transport came to rest at a position in front of a very large and spacious metal table, arranged lengthwise above a special set of stone steps. Here sat the ruling or governing council as they presided over matters requiring their attention. To the Dolumek, open councils were a common occurrence; anything worth discussing was worth spreading to all, keeping all members of the race informed in one way or another. Word of mouth usually followed out to the other underground regions and cities if the council discussed something of great importance. Today, they would have much to spread.

The small force led the Kostejaani leader up to a chair that sat ten steps below and in front of the grand council. The escort force took up stations in a row five steps behind the visiting guest.

Nyfletoné spoke to the council and informed them of a situation coming that they must know about. The council did not believe him and instead laughed at him, questioning him about the real reason or intention of his visit. Adoné understood the Dolumek language but still had the Kostejaanian translations provide to him in Tanazakh's mind. Tanazakh could sense the uneasiness in Nyfletoné and informed Adoné that they should do something or else the Dolumek council would throw the Kostejaani out. Revealing themselves would definitely startle and alarm the population within the immediate vicinity of the grand hall and put all inhabitants on full alert of intruders. The Dolumek reactionary forces remain in their population; once danger of any type surfaced, the entire population became their armed force, each one with subliminal orders to defend, attack, or destroy. With so many armed creatures, it would be extremely difficult to destroy them all, or so they thought.

Adoné knew it was time to save the frustrated Kostejaani and he did just that. After informing the others of his intentions, they each took up a space behind the chair in which Nyfletoné sat. Tanazakh, Xashsa, and Lazasar faced to the rear of the area while Adoné himself would take up Nyfletoné's seat. The Dolumek council stared inquisitively as the Kostejaani rose up and stood a pace away. Before they could ask him the reason for this, Adoné answered them.

"I asked him to step aside."

The council rose up as Adoné revealed himself seated.

"INTRUDERS!" shouted a member of the council and immediately all in the vicinity reacted. With drawn swords and spears, they rushed to the steps and barred the escape of the uninvited delegation, attacking at will. Xashsa, Tanazakh, and Lazasar furiously met blades and spears with their own, smacking weapons away, kicking, and punching the gathering opponents. The council stood up and drew their weapons. But, as they attempted to jump over the table, Adoné pulled out his black blade and held it to the throat of the centermost council member.

"*Cease your attack or I will sever your head!*"

The council member shouted back at him, "you are not welcome here; you shall die for this intrusion."

"I think not," said Adoné, and with a wave of his hand, his powers had stiffened the enraged member who dropped his sword instantly.

"You will have a hard fight in your escape," the stiffened Dolumek said.

"Fighting you is not our intention," Adoné replied, "we came to warn you of impending doom. Cease your aggression and I shall tell you of what I saw in your future."

The Dolumek thought for minute and ordered the guards and others to stop. Afterwards, Adoné released him, put away his sword, and sat back down in the chair. The other aggressors behind him held their weapons up to the Cavanonian delegation and awaited further orders. Slowly, the Dolumek council resumed their seats and began to speak.

"Who are you, speak up!" demanded the council.

"I am King Adoné of Cavanon," he answered. "Behind me is my wife, Queen Xashsa, Tanazakh my Anadonian General, and Lazasar, a respected member of my council."

"I have heard of Cavanon," said Ulynas (pronounced you-lee-nas), scornfully, "brutish beasts with unusual techniques for torture and desecration." His tone of voice indicated the degree of resentment and outrage at this sudden visit.

"Your statement is incorrect, Sir," Adoné replied, "we are more civilized than the nature of beasts, and if we *were* such creatures…we would have desecrated your kind the moment we entered into your planet."

"What is this knowledge you have of our future? Tell us quickly before I decide to have your hearts torn out!"

"Well, that's a joke, considering you current inability to act," Adoné said. "I bring you warning of a great war to come, one so great that your entire world will suffer annihilation because of it."

"You would declare war on us?" Ulynas asked.

"Not I, but a great evil that exists elsewhere in the galaxy. I have foreseen this in a vision and read the prophecy written in stone and blood. I bring you this news so that you will ready yourselves when the time comes."

"I see the true nature of your vision," Ulynas said, angrily. "You seek to rule over us as the battle hungry Nomaseri once tried."

"Gimme a break, *Damn!*" retorted Adoné, shaking his head. "Are you that stuck up you can't see that I am here to give you an honest warning? I came here to give you a heads up so you will not be overwhelmed and surprised. Your entire species will face extinction if you do not heed my words."

"Your words are feeble and weak, Cavanonian, as is your pathetic wizardry."

"I suppose if you will not listen to my words, then perhaps I should *show* you instead?"

"Do not move or you shall perish," commanded Ulynas.

"Ooh, those are big words for one so helpless to defend himself!"

Adoné had other plans. It was abundantly clear that this council would not listen to his information let alone believe any of it. He could see now why the Nomaseri once attacked these creatures. With two races of such arrogance fighting each other, they would wipe *themselves* out. Adoné had another way to try to convince them; another method that they would have no control over. Not that the Dolumek had control over him or the delegation, which was not an issue, but the method Adoné chose would show these creatures that they should listen and reduce their animosity towards the visiting delegation.

"Fine," replied Adoné calmly, "I will remain seated and you will suffer fear for your comments."

"The moment he moves, seize him!" shouted Ulynas.

Adoné closed his eyes and sat back in the chair, mentally informing the others of what was to take place, and for Xashsa to guard him, closely. Xashsa stood next to the chair and placed her left hand on his shoulder, glancing at the council, and maintaining her blade towards the crowd below the steps.

While everyone watched the Cavanonian King in his chair, Adoné had already departed his body and spiritually stood behind the council members. With lightening fast speed, he disarmed the council and flung their weapons far off to the side of the room, well out of their reach. All of the council members attempted to stand but could not; instead, their chairs rotated around and faced the wall.

"*Since you will not listen to words,*" Adoné's voice echoed, "*then maybe a little glance into the future will show you the truth I bring you.*"

The King telepathically forced the council to stare into their minds as the images in his vision began to unveil. The vivid descriptions detailed what Adoné had spoken of and after a while, their tension had eased and fear engulfed their spirits. Each one watched as the imagery showed them the horror yet to come. Simultaneously, Adoné portrayed the images onto the back wall in large size and vivid color for all to see. Tanazakh and Lazasar noticed that the defensive stance of the guards dropped and their weapons lowered to the ground. All stood in disbelief and horror at this sight and wondered how a vision of this nature was possible. They saw the Nogzakhs of the Dominion, the Nomaseri, and a newer species of creatures never before encountered. The scenes displayed the near decimation of the entire planet and all its inhabitants; the enemy spared no one, not even the wildlife above ground.

As the images ended, Adoné had already regained control of his body and remained seated. He took hold of Xashsa's hand, informing her he was once again in control. The council members regained their position at the table and stared at each other. Their entire attitude had changed and they began wildly talking amongst themselves and engaged in furious supposition and conjecture. The now crowded hall behind the Cavanonian delegation began conversing as well and their voices grew in volume so much so that they drowned out the voices of the council members.

"SILENCE!" shouted Ulynas, "we shall have order here!" the council leader stood up, walked around the table, and stood before the King of Cavanon, gazing at him with anger. "You are indeed powerful as we no doubt have experienced, but we do not take kindly to visitors who venture into our world unannounced. You are strong willed and impressive in your arts and skills, and we are no match for this unknown ability you have. If we were to release you, what guarantee can you give us that you will not be the leader of this doom that waits?"

Adoné stood up and extended his hand to Ulynas, "something as simple as a hand shake will see to that guarantee."

"A hand shake…that is all?"

"Ulynas," Adoné said firmly, "I did not come here to conquer you or your people; I came here to bring you warning and attempt to help you save your world. I have no appetites of conquering others; we have our own world and our own race of beings to preside over. The Nomaseri are a long time enemy of your people and the Nogzakhs are our enemy. If these forces take over your world, they will gain in strength and prepare themselves to summon up an even greater evil from the great beyond, one that will decimate *all* life. They will not merely kill off your entire species; they will take you over, inhabit your bodies and spirits, and in so doing, add even more strength to their already overwhelming numbers."

"If this is so, then what chance do our worlds have against such a force?"

"We stand a better chance if we were allied, and I've much more knowledge of the enemy then they know. We've gained in strength ourselves after the Nogzakhs and the Nomaseri nearly annihilated our race; I do not wish to see yours erased and suffer the same fate."

"There is sincerity in your voice…unexpected, but assuring." Ulynas accepted Adoné's hand and shook in friendship. "Perhaps we were a bit hasty in our judgment of you. Come, let us dine and discuss matters further."

Afterwards they gathered for more formalized introductions.

In a great dining hall with dimensions exceeding that of one thousand feet, all of the council members and the Cavanonian delegation sat together around a huge dining table. Huge woven tapestries, gold and silver colored, adorned the octagonal walls and concave ceiling. Torches lined the walls, two on each, and an enormous cauldron style torch sat high above the middle of the room suspended by chains; the light reflected from the mirrors attached to the ceiling, giving the entire dining area plenty of light with which to see. A solid metal dining table with an estimated size of thirty feet in diameter, dull and grey in color, sat directly beneath the ceiling torch. Luxurious heavy chairs lined the entire circumference of the table.

Each of the five Dolumek council members and the Cavanonian delegation sat comfortably around the table. The Dolumek treated their guests to the finest drink and cuisine—spared no expense—and afforded the majestic couple consideration befitting of their stature and position.

Dolumek servants served up a hardy dish of meat imported from the surface. Local herbs and vegetables grown underground proved very delicious to the delegation, topped off with variation of fermented red drink. The Dolumek did not think they had pulled out any stops at all; they ate in this manner regularly, as did all Dolumek creatures.

Once the dinner finished, table talk commenced and all generally listened as Adoné and Ulynas conversed in depth about each other's race, how they came to be, and more importantly, about the vision seen earlier.

"So, King Adoné," Ulynas spoke up, "how is it that you came to receive this vision you have shown us?"

"I discovered it by accident, actually," Adoné replied. "There is a substance our growing population required that I had to seek out. When I found it, I saw the vision on the walls of a great underground chamber. What I saw disturbed me, greatly. Since then, I knew that if we did not warn you, the Nomaseri and the Nogzakhs would come and destroy your way of life."

"But what concern are we to you?" Ulynas asked. "We have been able to sustain our lives for many centuries living peacefully underground. We pose no significant threat to anyone. Why do you suppose it is that this vision involves us to begin with?"

"I'm genuinely concerned for all innocent lives," Adoné replied. "As to why the vision involves you, I've no idea to tell you the truth. It may be that the Nomaseri still house some resentment for not conquering you long ago."

"But what of these Nogzakhs and the other species we saw...what about them?"

"I can only assume that the Nomaseri are in league with the other enemy forces and combined they can easily defeat you."

"But," Ulynas hesitated, "we have no special powers, no special qualities, and no vast resources of any kind. For what possible reason would they attack us? We are peaceful if left alone. We keep to ourselves in all matters and go to great lengths to remain out of sight. Because of that, we have survived for a very long time."

"I am as perplexed as you are, Ulynas," replied Adoné. "Still, I believe what I saw and I am convinced they will come...I just don't know when."

"If this vision is true, then you will have saved our entire species, and I assume there is a payment to be made for such service?"

"Oh, hell no," Adoné chuckled. "I seek no payment whatsoever; I don't operate like that.

"Then there has to be some reason other for telling us this, other than saving lives."

"Actually," Queen Xashsa spoke up, "we have a serious vendetta against both the Nomaseri and the Nogzakhs, but more importantly, we have to repay the leaderNosrévisand his third force. All three entities are responsible for the near annihilation of our kind and we wish for more than a little payback."

"Then you will aid us when the time comes?" Ulynas asked, giving Adoné and Xashsa a wide-eyed look.

"Absolutely," Adoné replied, "we will provide what aid we can. But it would be wise to have battle drills ready prior to the commencement of this attack."

"I agree. Tomorrow, I will show you around our core city and then take you up to the crust to view some of our forces and aircraft."

"I look forward to it."

The next morning, Ulynas did as he said and made transportation available for a tour of the city. Situated in circular fashions, the city structures had been arranged to adapt to the gravitational pull of the planet. At the center, the defiance of gravity stood out greatly, evident in the bridges and walkways construction. Within the core, all creatures walked as if the gravity of that sector accommodated the force in that general area. There were no other roads than the main arteries for the transports and conveyances distributing goods and services to the many facilities at the disposal of the Dolumek creatures.

After leaving the city core, the transport drifted through tunnels that periodically revealed other underground cities along the route. Windows in the tunnel system gave the visiting delegation a chance to see life outside the major capital city and showed a much easier setting. As they transport traveled, Ulynas told them about how all of their creatures have invested much time and energy constructing their own unique housing areas. A leader who governs many of these outlying areas visits the core city monthly to present reports and updates as necessary. Due to the location and distances of these areas, traveling to the city core weekly would have been taxing to say the least. Other areas closer to the surface reported to a central location, one member of the grand council collected the reports and took them back personally, thus relieving the burden of the others.

The transport took several turns through the winding tunnel system and entered into a huge hangar area filled with various aircraft and workers. As the transport traveled overhead, far below the activity went on as normal. Daily maintenance checks and services, repairs, and other monotonous tasks seemed to be the routine. Adoné noticed the variety of aircraft and the numbers in this particular hangar.

"You don't have very much aircraft in your inventory," Adoné said.

"That is because we are only looking into one hangar bay," Ulynas replied. "This is but one of four hundred bays at our disposal."

"Whoa, you have four hundred? Tanazakh asked. "Times the amount of aircraft you have in this one bay, that's over thirty thousand aircraft."

"Quite a fleet, it is not?"

"Absolutely," Tanazakh replied.

"But, do you have the necessary pilots for all of these aircraft?" Lazasar asked.

"Yes. Our population numbers around six million. I'd say we have more than enough pilots"

"And a pretty hefty size ground force as well," Xashsa stated.

"Now I can see the reasoning behind the attack yet to occur," said Adoné. "The Nogzakhs and the Nomaseri would vanquish the only other race in this region that could put up resistance. With these numbers under their control they could swarm through other galaxies and subjugate other worlds with their evil leader in power."

"They would be near invincible in that right," Lazasar said.

"But how will they be able to control six million souls at once?"

"If the enemy gets to the leadership first, then they will stand a better chance at forcing over the hearts and minds of all Dolumek creatures. What better way to instill fear than to wipe out the leadership, which is Federoth's tactic as well as the Nogzakhs."

"So what exactly are you suggesting we do?" Ulynas asked.

"Decisive battle plans must be drawn up using whatever techniques you have. Think outside the box in your tactics and make them as ruthless as possible. We've much more to do before we can finalize anything. If there were only some way to infiltrate the enemy bases and find out what they are up to, that would answer lots of questions and also keep us up to date on what their next course of action will be."

"Now that sounds like fun," smiled Lazasar, "it's exactly what I enjoy doing anyway."

"We can discuss that later, but when we do initiate something, be sure you will be informed. If you can establish radio communications with the Kostejaanians, it would be much easier to pass word."

"I shall have my communications personnel meet with them at once," Ulynas said. After which he pressed a button on the console and issued orders to the operator, orders that were to be carried out prior to the departure of the delegation. "My communicators are working on establishing a link as we speak; it should be complete by the time we reach your ship."

"Excellent," Adoné replied.

After boarding, the Kostejaanian crew informed Nyfletoné that communications had been established and the links were clear, no distortion. Adoné thanked Ulynas and his council for the reception, and apologized again for the initial surprise greetings. The warning provided to them gave the Dolumek something to think about and something more to work on as well. Rather than spend there time in complacency, they now had battle plans to draw up and rehearse. In time, the Dolumek would also incorporate the Cavanonian forces as well; more help meant less would die.

While Adoné and the delegation departed for home, other matters were stirring in the Tnemucodan mountain range on Cavanon; matters that would greatly interest the Cavanonian King and worry others.

Chapter 14

Rumor Control

The once spiritually damned Cavanonians brought back much exuberance and life to their home planet. Spread out in and around the city of Solisynas (currently under construction), the Cavanonians had begun to inhabit various areas of strategic importance. With a multitude of two hundred and forty thousand, cramming everyone into just one area would display a wonderful advantage to the enemy if they decided to attack this planet all over again. The Cavanonians, together with the other species of creatures in their midst, appreciated the invisibility shield provided by their King. This meant they had less worries about anything or anyone unfriendly finding them. The atmospheric shield hid the planet very well; it had been lost to history the moment the Nomaseri and Nogzakhs departed after ravaging the planet with war.

The core of the planet reacted to the returned multitude and blessed them with the renewal of their abilities, strengthening their essence once again, after heightened by the Zalestolean Blood brought back by their monarch. Not only did the core crystals of Cavanon give life and bring about change in others, but also increased in strength with more and more Cavanonian lives. The powers of the planet core grew and multiplied greatly, causing all sorts of fruitful life to spring forth in all areas of Cavanon. Finding sustenance did not pose a problem either; there was enough to go round on this huge planet. With the uncharted areas, there was always something new to discover.

Many Cavanonians took up residence in Solisynas and set up domiciles around the perimeter of Royal Mountain. All of the Cavanonians were exceedingly thankful for their return and for what the new King had done for them. In return, current leadership staged domiciles around the home of the Royal family to aid in security and overwatch. The warriors instinctively relocated to various areas of the planet, away from the main city. So, if a new enemy did show up, the warriors would be able to alert others of possible trouble or danger. These returned Cavanonians would surprise the King greatly when he returned. Adoné knew what type of figure he appeared to be in their eyes, but not in the literal sense. These Cavanonians would demonstrate that the King no longer had to do things himself in order to provide for the well-being of his subjects. Now, there were others now to do that for him and do it gladly.

The importation of the Zalestolean Blood gave all Cavanonians another reason to be happy. They remembered its intoxicating effects of long ago and aromatic essence instilled in the body that only heightened the desires of the mind and spirit. This did not compete with the effects of the planet core, nothing could compete with that, but instead the blood gave them more than just a beverage to heighten powers or goals. Cavanonians did not make a daily habit of drinking from the newly built fountain; this was a drink to consume once in a great while. Each Cavanonian knew the effects of the potent hemotoxin, they knew that to drink to often would mean a build up of immunities to its effects. The extra-added advantage the King added to the blood was adding some of his own, so that his own would counteract the tainted version of the original meaning of the blood. This gave each Cavanonian who drank of it their own sample of royal blood to run in their veins, which would elevate the status of all Cavanonians once again. This was the King's attempt at reinstating virtues within these once cursed souls lost long ago. A sense of pride and contentment in the race grew in their minds and gave purpose to the race once again.

With all of the Cavanonians hard at work in their rebuilding efforts, the humans and other species of Solisynas watched in amazement as the city seemed to spring forth overnight. Laura and Zérnoda hung out with the humans and kept them company, not wishing for them to feel left out. They understood what was happening in their fair city and explained to those not engaged in rebuilding efforts that this was only one way of repaying the King for the kindness he showed the once lost souls. Soon all creatures would have a new place in which to live and the accommodations would be very different than the dilapidated housing they currently lived in.

The Srotaderp, on the other hand, engaged themselves heavily in the rebuilding efforts. By splitting their numbers, half worked with the Cavanonians in the rebuilding of the city while the other half worked with the Kostejaanians on the hangar bay projects on the outlying areas of the planet. At their current pace, hangar bays for aircraft would come much faster than previously anticipated. Other Cavanonians worked with the Kostejaanian technicians and production teams in the beginning stages of design and construction of their own aircraft. With Cavanonian designs and motif in their minds, the new aircraft to be built would be menacing in their own right and instill fear the moment they came into view.

Other tradesman and artisans setup shops for the manufacture of weapons: swords, spears, daggers, and other odd tools for killing their enemies. Some of these weapons would be strange and ungodly in appearance, but would have deadly effects once used. Stan and Zach, newly transformed themselves, made use of their previous skills of metal manipulation by working along side of the artisans and metalworkers. Not only did they gain knowledge of the ancient trade and style of weapons manufacture, but they also threw in their own knowledge to aid in more forceful, more formidable weapons design and implementation.

Adoné and Xashsa had no idea if Stan and Zach's transformation would have an effect on the other humans and figured the humans would chose to remain themselves as they have always been. However, since two humans did transform over, the other humans paid attention and saw the advantages of being Cavanonian. Opinions changed and dreams of such possessing such abilities flooded the minds of the humans, giving them dreams of endless possibilities and unattainable qualities.

Every member of this society contributed in one way or another and the production of textiles and clothes increased, as all needed clothing badly. With the construction and manufacture of Cavanonian style wardrobe, all would have reason to be happy. Cavanonian clothing had far more to offer than regular clothing worn by all for far too long. With magical qualities, clothing produced gave all an even greater ability of flight, especially to those who were without such powers. Even though there were so many in their numbers, as new clothing was produced it was issued out to each, starting with the humans, the Anadonians, and the Srotaderp; the Nablah enjoyed their own clothing and did not have need of more.

Adoné and his delegation returned to Cavanon and received a formal update of the overall efforts already underway. To his and Xashsa's amazement, the massive efforts did not stop once word of their return had spread. The King did not wish to be revered in a way that all ceased their work and normal livelihood. Instead, leadership visited the Royal family and expressed the happiness and contentment with the current activities and work. They did however, express concerns of a growing worry; rumors of deceit surfaced from within the ranks not from uprisings or anything of that nature, but rather from sensing a doubt in their midst. Laura echoed this worry and spoke to her father about it while he sat in council with the new leadership.

In the large auditorium located at the base of Royal Mountain, the King sat in court with many of his new generals and his own personal council. After receiving the update status of all general subjects, Adoné informed all of the progress made on Dolumek and the guarantee of alliance between their two systems. The increased alliance now brought their numbers to four systems: Kostejaan, Nylantia, Dolumek, and Cavanon itself. With the number of forces in each system, the enemies' ability to wipe them all out as easily as before diminished. Still, the matter of this looming doubt within this thriving society must be dealt with, and swiftly. If someone or something living amongst them has deceitful intentions, however insignificant, then they must be identified.

"Tell me," Adoné said, calmly addressing all in the auditorium, "who first discovered this rumor?"

Without hesitation, Laura immediately spoke up. "Father, I heard this while walking through the city. It was not the talk of all, only a few spoke of this random conversation."

"And what was this rumor about?" her father asked.

"The gist of the rumor was about a prophecy yet to come; one that could lead to the downfall of our race once again."

"That is a significant rumor, indeed," Adoné replied. "Who amongst our people would start such a rumor and why?"

"I can assure you, my Liege," said Krecian, a general from the western sector, "it is not any of *our* forces."

"Nor from ours," replied another general, and another after him.

Krecian continued. "Our people could not have instigated this rumor and would not speak of such a thing without hearing it from you first. The kindness you have shown them has captivated our people so much so that they would never dishonor the Crown or you're Majesty."

"Then, it must have come from one who is not of our people, our race," commented the King.

"It is not our people," answered Nivlac.

"We humans have heard but have not spread it around," said Ann, "even the new arrivals do not repeat what they have heard; they know better and are afraid of the possible retribution they will face if they do."

"Then it has to come from ones who are fearless," said Lazasar.

"It is not from the Anadonians," Tanazakh boasted, "I will kill my own if I find such deceitful lies being spread."

"But we don't know if it is lies being spread or if this talk it is truly deceitful in nature." Adoné wished to reassure his long time friend that his people were not under scrutiny. "My friend, I'm not pointing the finger at anyone and I am not questioning anyone's loyalty. What mostly distresses me is that something has started within our own society. Something has surfaced in our own realm and we must deal with it immediately. Now is not the time for mannerisms contrary to the collective good, not while we are in the middle of reconstituting our forces and communities."

"What are you suggesting, my friend?" Tanazakh asked.

"I suggest we investigate further into our own, by that I mean each of you segregate your race and question them collectively and individually. See if you can determine who it was that started this rumor. To the Cavanonians, I suggest you convey this telepathically; that will lessen the chance of word of mouth spreading. This must be done discreetly; we do not wish to alarm the instigator and give him or her reason to flee before we can find out more. Once we have the information, then we will decide what to do about the perpetrator."

"We shall begin at once, my Liege," said Krecian.

All stood up, bowed to Adoné, and moved out.

All through the discussion, Xashsa paid attention and used her senses to ascertain if she felt dissention in the characters of those in the auditorium. However, just prior to the end of the meeting, she did notice the winged warriors in the sky overhead; why were they not at this meeting?

"I think there is another source we need to visit as well," she said.

Adoné heard her voice and followed her glance upward to the sky above, and saw the reason for her comment.

"I think you are right, my Dear," he replied. "Now that I see our winged friends, there is one other topic I mean to discuss with them as well; one that I had learned of on the dreaded Ellononis system."

"What did you learn there, Adoné?"

"A prophecy written on a wall mentioned the planet of Tnemucoda, *by name*!"

"What?" she exhaled.

They both went up to their own house out of earshot of anyone else. Adoné needed privacy with his Queen in order to keep what he knew a secret.

"Xashsa, I read a prophecy on a wall that spoke of the return of Ellononis!"

"*Ellononis,*" Xashsa said, shocked to the gills, "you can't be serious?"

"Oh, but I *am* serious," he replied. "This is to take place when the planet of Cinodas comes in line between Elaveshan and…Tnemucoda."

"*DAMN IT!*" she burst out. "Those bastardous beings are within our own borders!" she immediately began to walk towards the doorway, but her husband stopped her.

"Wait…wait, wait, wait," he repeated, pulling her back inside, "let's not jump to conclusions."

"But, why not?" asked Xashsa, puzzled. "We have to deal with this now!"

"Yes, but I kept this information secret for a reason, Love. If I were to tell everyone here that I read about the return of the ultimate evil being responsible for our initial downfall and continued destruction throughout the centuries, what to you think would happen? Each of them might lose hope and fall into despair or hopelessness against this enemy. We've worked so hard to bring our numbers back to a healthy degree and for them to fall again into despair before this takes place would literally take them all out of the fight."

"But, Maillewvan told you about the prophecy of Cavanon's return," she said, "surely that would give them all the hope they would need to be proactive in defense and self protection."

"Just because these beings came to us and told us of *that* does not mean it is true. I've not read it anywhere. I don't doubt what they said, but what I have read gives more weight to it then the word of the Tnemucodas. We must be secret with our information and get to the heart of whoever else might know this. That is the only reason these rumors could have come about in the first place. Everyone has heard of the supposed prophecy of Cavanon's return, but not his evil brother!"

Xashsa became worried and angry at the same time. She did not want to believe their worst fears could possibly come about: the reincarnation of the hatred of Cavanon.

"Adoné," she said, worried, "what are we going to do about this?"

"I've already been working on possible solutions to save us. My ideas will come about the closer we get to this, *rebirth*, so to speak. In the meantime, let us find out ourselves."

Each leader of their respective people or section of inhabitants immediately and discreetly began questioning as ordered. For those without the ability of telepathy, questioning would have to be done indoors and out of the range of unwanted ears. For the Cavanonians it was easy; a simple thought conveyed far more information than mere words could describe. Not only did the leadership convey the meaning or intent, but also the ability to detect difference in character alleviated the concern or worry about the perpetrator being in their midst. Krecian's comments were right on the money; not one Cavanonian had thoughts other than what he spoke of to the King. Their loyalty and integrity were beyond reproach or doubt.

Nivlac found no evidence of an instigator in his people, and neither did Ann in the humans. Adoné and Xashsa would check out the Tnemucodas and see what they could find.

In the Tnemucodas mountain range, Adoné and Xashsa went in and met with Maillewvan to discuss matters of importance. Inside the main audience chambers, the Tnemucodan received the Royal visit enthusiastically.

"Please, come in and sit," Maillewvan said, "It has been a long time since you were last here."

"A problem we shall rectify in the future," replied Adoné.

"May I ask as to the reason for this visit?"

"Certainly," Xashsa answered. "We wish to know more about this prophecy you spoke of when you first arrived. Can you tell us again how it is you came to know this?"

"Ah!" Maillewvan exhaled as his mind drifted back. "I can remember it as though it were only a day ago." The cycloptic ruler seated himself and began to recall how things came to be for them.

"Eons ago, before many of these creatures here were born, Lord Cavanon ruled with authority and an iron fist. His exploits of other star systems were legendary even in his own time. Then, he came upon a system wrecked with war and chaos and sought out the cause of this devilry. This system, Kilisajka, had been devastated by a war and its inhabitants scattered to the four winds. To his amazement, he discovered that his own brother—Ellononis—was the culprit responsible for it all. Lord Cavanon sought to end the conflict of this star system and defeat his brother at his own game. He succeeded in ceasing the conflict but his brother had fled the system before he could be held accountable. Hundreds of years later, Lord Cavanon's health deteriorated rapidly through some unforeseen and unknown disease. The cause was never known but few had guessed that maybe it was because of some infectious bacteria on the Kilisajka system that brought about his untimely death. All creatures touched by Lord Cavanon were sad and grief stricken when they heard that the most feared ruler in the galaxy gave up his spirit and ascended to the heavens."

"He handed down the crown to another before he died, correct?" asked Adoné.

"Of course," Maillewvan replied, "to the next heir, his son, Fesson. After that, it took many, many years for his memory to begin to fade away. Since our service to him ended, we continued to serve the crown dutifully as our way of repaying the kindness shown to us. Then, many centuries later, I—and a few others in my service—received a vision from Cavanon. We did not think it true because we had never known of such abilities before. A visit from a heavenly ancient is unheard of."

"Almost unheard of," said Adoné. "I can relate to you in that area because I had a heavenly visit once before myself."

"Then you must understand how we felt in such divine presence."

"Absolutely!" smiled Adoné.

"As he stood before us, we nearly died from the amount of energy in his aura. Even in death, he was powerful, yet he himself could not do anything to stop the chaos that spread throughout the galaxy, caused by his evil-hearted brother. He informed us of his intentions and told us he would return with a new mission for us if he were successful in his personal task. A few nights later, we received him yet again, and this time, he told us that a way to end the chaos had materialized. He spread himself before he Gods and pleaded for them to hurl his spirit into another form, but one not of Cavanonian nature for Ellononis would know it instantly and come looking to kill him. So, without knowing which form he would be cast into, he took an oath from us to swear on our very lives that when he decreed it so, we should wake up and seek him out. By casting himself into another form, he had hoped to bypass his brother's existence and re-emerge after his brother's death in hopes of putting down his lunatic reign of mayhem, once and for all."

"But what of his brother's power, the possibility of reemerging into this era, isn't that in some sort of prophecy as well?" asked Xashsa.

"I do not have knowledge of that," Maillewvan replied, "and as far as I know, Ellononis does not possess the same blessings as our Lord Cavanon."

"Well, I hate to say it, but there is someone on this planet who *does* believe in such a vile miracle."

"But, who would spread such deceitful lies of this nature?" asked Maillewvan, innocently.

"That is a good question, Maillewvan," replied Xashsa. "We are trying to find that out now, and so are others as we speak. Aside from the rumors, did our first king tell you where his rebirth would take place?"

"Yes," Maillewvan said, happily, "he told me that it would take place on our home planet, on Tnemucodas."

"Why there?" asked Adoné.

"Because of the neutrality of our homeland and because of its location away from Cavanon. Just prior to his demise, he instructed us to build an enormous temple in his honor, one befitting of a king. We did this and today it sits in isolation and solitude, ready for the moment to come."

"Did he leave a time frame or reference as to when this would take place?"

"He did. The planet of Cinodas comes in between Elaveshan and Tnemucodas every five thousand years. We've not long yet to go before this happens, I'd say within two years."

Adoné thought to Xashsa and she began to exhibit signs of question.

"I read about this occurrence on Ellononis," he thought.

"But, what does it mean?" She answered. *"Does it mean that Cavanon shall return, or Ellononis, or both?"*

"I don't know for sure. We have Maillewvan's word and the words written on a wall. But which ones are true?"

During their conversation, Adoné did not sense anything contrary in Maillewvan's character. Since there was nothing out of the ordinary in him, they might as well move on and see if anyone else has found out any new information. After taking leave of their cycloptic host, Adoné and Xashsa departed again for Royal Mountain.

Chapter 15

Surprise Measures

Deep inside a dark and cavernous lair, Othragon stood inside his private cave of food and puzzled over which creature fancied his tastes. Twenty or so hysterically frightened creatures became glued to the wall of a cave unable to retreat or hide from the hideous dragon that loomed over them. A woman, scared beyond her abilities, passed out cold. The ominous dragon reached out for the woman and mercilessly wrenched her body up off the ground. He paused for a few moments, either from noticing something or from entertaining a rather twisted and bizarre thought.

"*Hmm,*" he thought, "*this female human may be of some use to me.*"

While holding her body in one of his right hands, a left hand and the other free right hand ripped a male human off the wall. Othragon wasted no time in twisting the head from the body, holding the body up to catch the flowing blood that poured out from the neck area, coating Othragon's throat, and jaws.

"*Ahh,*" he salivated, dripping blood between his teeth, "*so exquisite the taste of human fluids.*"

After licking his deranged, whiskered lips, he chomped down on the head in his jaws as his free hands savagely ripped the human body to pieces, stuffing in limbs and body parts to fill his oversized chops. The remaining humans that saw this were terrified and horror struck and what would soon be there own death, but that wouldn't happen now. The snack seemed to fill Othragon's stomach for the time being and the rest of the human menu would wait for their time to unwillingly provide his belly with sustenance.

Back in his main audience chamber, he placed the human female body onto a table and stood back, contemplating sinister thoughts. He knew that Federoth and the Dominion still existed, but by now, they surely have given allegiance to another. The one-time Dominion ruler could easily return and claim his forces once again, but the secrecy of his existence remained uppermost in his mind. While he remained hidden, no one could thwart the prophetic plans of the return of his lord, his creator, and the god of war who would seek punishment of those who fought against Ellononis' objectives. Besides, once Ellononis returned to the physical, all forces would inevitably belong to him and with Othragon by his side, Othragon would once again be in charge of the Dominion its fragmented empire.

As he walked around the table containing the female human, devilish thoughts stirred in his cerebrum and developed purpose. Unnatural feelings of a hellish creation permeated his pours and caused him to smile greatly; knowing full well that forces in his previous command where formidable, but a creation of his own? The possibilities seemed endless and staggering to the son of Zalestole. Intent formed and after continued moments of decision-making, the perverted mind began to formulate an ingenious plan.

"You shall be the mother of my creation," he said through a crackled, low drenched whisper. *"I shall humiliate the human species by creating the ultimate demon for my service and domination. Once they have served my purpose and the purposes of our great God after his return, I shall unleash them unto the world of Earth and conquer it. The humans shall never be blessed by the Gods or chosen as mediums for other beings to emerge. The human species is intriguing, and yet you can so easily be manipulated and changed, reformed and restructured with no resistance whatsoever, save one that was of you a long time ago. Nevertheless, even he shall bow down to our God and serve him painfully, for all eternity. The King of Cavanon shall never ascend to the Gods favoring."*

After spouting words to an incoherent human body, Othragon gently picked up the female and headed into his own room of horrors. In this chamber, plain, vacant, and overly dreary in nature, the hellish creature of twenty feet bound the female human with chains around her wrists and ankles to a stone slab. Completely stripped of clothing, Othragon did not care for the beauty of the naked female anatomy at all and did not consider the thought in any way. Instead, with precision and detail, he used a fingernail from his hand to carve the symbol of his soon to be creation into the belly of the human; a jagged cut "X," trickling with red blood and hideously cut.

Maliciously, Othragon pried apart the human jaws and removed the tongue with his teeth. Then, Othragon coughed up his own blood from within and allowed the syrupy substance to drip profusely into the human's mouth, filling up the orifice completely. As if the grimy substance possessed a mind of its own, Othragons blood instantly flowed through the human body destroying anything in its way along a predestined route for another part of the body, the ovaries. There they found purpose and infiltrated the egg laden organs, transforming and recreating their nature on a cellular level.

The female ovaries began to swell up internally, gaining in size from the amount of converting eggs contained within. All at once, the ovaries burst and the oversized eggs flowed on course to the outlet, the vaginal area. Othragon sensed their emergence, picked up the female by the neck, and held the body over a large vat, allowing the concentration of eggs to gather in a single place. Flowing freely out of the body, the drainage coated in what was left of the humans blood and sat in a frothy disgusting mixture, ever expanding in the vat. Once Othragon tossed the body aside, he carried his minions outside the surface of the planet and there, he scooped up handfuls of eggs spreading them out over the ground. The amount of eggs covered at least one thousand feet, and Othragon was meticulous in his work. The monster stood before this spread and blessed his creation, his private force of demons whose purpose would be to become the guardian force of the creator when he returned.

The ground under each egg began to sink into the planet surface, lowering the egg as if lost to quicksand. Underneath the ashen soil, the eggs would incubate, grow, and form into the intended form of Othragon's vision. Once these creatures emerged, Othragon would train them in his secret arts, secrets that only he knew about. Still, that would wait until later, right now Othragon's belly rumbled; time to eat, again.

Zérnoda had taken leave of her parents and gathered up Sarah and Kayla taking them on another trip around the areas of the hangar bay construction. The Cavanonian princess changed her views of slight animosity towards the humans and decided to include them in on as much of the goings on as possible. They should be aware of what takes place in their world and be a part of every facet of Cavanonian life, just in case they might decide to change over as well.

The Cavanonians and Srotaderp construction crews performed extremely well in their efforts and most of the work completed ahead of schedule. The last of the tasks to be completed were the large outer doors. Once finished, they could top it off with a localized camouflage covering for total concealment, in the event the outer planetary shield failed to thwart anyone accidentally finding in the invisible planet. Zérnoda did mention this to her father once before; he should implement another type of shield defense since the Nomaseri and Nogzakhs know where to look for the war-ravaged planet. Forming a new type of planetary shield would give the enemy the impression that the planet had doomed itself and died after the war. However, that was a problem for her father to deal with; it was much too big for her to tackle and she would not put forth the effort for no reason.

Sarah and Kayla followed the princess around through the myriad of construction materials and workers who diligently attended their tasks. They were astounded at the level of work underway; this was much for them to comprehend and understand. Never before had they witnessed construction of this magnitude or grandeur, never this huge or massive, or well attended. Of course, back on their own world, they would not know facilities such as this or even dream about its manifestation. To them, it was unreal and unbelievable; facets their human minds would have to shed if they were to begin to accept their new surroundings totally.

Despite all that took place around them, Sarah had questions for the princess, questions that had nothing to do with the workers or the construction underway. Instead, the questions she had dealt with her species and what Zérnoda had went through for the change.

"Zérnoda," Sarah called to her.

"Yes," she replied, "what is it?"

"What's it like?"

"What's what like?" Zérnoda asked, knowing already what the nature of her question entailed.

"What's it like to be you, you know, this Cavanonian that you are?"

Zérnoda had to think about how to answer that one. She never thought about it before, not in this sense, although she did entertain the thought long ago while after meeting her beloved Aila. Zérnoda lost herself for a moment and her mind drifted back to the days when Aila were still alive.

Days before the evil Nosrévis secretly infiltrated Cavanon, a calm peacefulness caressed the surface of the planet and enveloped all who dwelt in this land. The King and the search party members set out to find Rykus who had fled the planet rather hastily. It appeared to be the calm before the storm, just when everyone felt more at ease with the return of the King in their midst. Zérnoda had a conversation with her sister that resurfaced shortly after her re-emergence into this world along side the Queen. As Zérnoda gazed up to the heavens, she could visualize Aila in front of her; she could hear her voice and feel her touch once again, as if she were actually there. Aila's voice filled her head from the last conversation she remembered having with her dear sister, and it was in this manner said:

"What is wrong?" asked Zérnoda, "you've barely said anything today. It is as if you are distant."

"I'm sorry," Aila apologized, "but I've been doing a lot of thinking. Questions have surfaced, bugging me, begging for an answer and I have none."

"Sweetie, you must share this with me, if you don't, I can't help you now can I?"

"You are my happiness, but I fear as if something will change for us, something dreadful, something bad. I worry about us and what it means."

"How can you tell something bad is coming? I don't sense anything and I haven't heard anything either. You have to think positive and don't worry, it will all be fine."

"Dear sister," Aila sad, sadly, "I wish I could think as you, your thoughts are comforting and soothing, and only you know how to touch me and make me forget. But this time, it's different, like a dream that won't go away or a vision that plagues the mind until the only recourse for it is to come to life. What I feel is dreadful and I am scared for us both."

Zérnoda hugged her sister delicately and caressed her soft skin, gently fingering the hair away from Aila's face.

"My sweet sister, what reason is there that you feel this?"

"I don't know," replied Aila. "Call it woman's intuition, perception, a hunch, whatever. All I know is that deep within me something tells me we are in danger."

"Relax," Zérnoda said softly, "I know how to take your mind away. You are with me and I will let nothing happen to you."

Zérnoda clenched herself as she remembered the last intimate moments they shared together, lost in each other so heavily that time itself could not pull them apart. Blissfulness engulfed their spirits and minds, revealing itself, illustrating a version of heaven, that of being together as they had been for so long.

While Zérnoda saw the images of her love in her minds eye, Sarah and Kayla looked on in wonder, confused about the expressions on the face of the princess.

"Zérnoda!" exclaimed Sarah.

The voice took the princess totally off guard and shocked her senses, so much so that she almost drew upon her inner self to the person who disturbed her vision. When she turned and saw the reactions of the two humans, the princess calmed herself and eased her emotions, still dwelling on the sadness of the loss of her dearest departed sister.

"I'm sorry," she apologized, "I was lost in thought."

"I see that," Sarah replied. "You were about to tell me what it is like and you drifted off somewhere."

"Listen," Zérnoda faced her, "when I was still human, I thought I knew happiness. I thought I knew much more than I did and I never thought I would ever be happier than being human. But, since my changeover into this species, my happiness has surpassed what it once was. I never felt freer to do what I can now, and I never looked back. I have been blessed with more than anyone on Earth could ever wish for or hope to attain. Powers? You can't believe what it is like to have the ability to do what I can, to feel what the Cavanonian spirit feels—the emotions, the heightened sense of awareness, the total ability to read your surroundings and others. To you, these are all attributes to dream about and stare at in wonder. But, to *feel* them, to feel the power running through your veins and to know that what you have become is real, *that* is a feeling almost indescribable in nature. I tell you, if I had to do it all over again, I would do it in a heartbeat."

Sarah just stared at the princess as they walked along a catwalk over the construction below. The look on her face told Sarah she was not joking; the sincerity of her feelings were genuinely real. Sarah continued to stare, but in awe of her elucidation. In the past, Sarah rarely heard such feeling or emotions poured into a simple explanation, and she thought it intriguing.

"So," said Zérnoda, "you are seriously contemplating a change, yes?"

"Is it that evident?"

"Yes, it is."

"But," Sarah said, "all I have is your account, aren't there rules to follow? I mean, isn't it a sin to do what you did?"

"You're still thinking like an earthling, like you are back on Earth. Humans are limited to the rules back on Earth. Here, in this dimension, we have a completely new set of rules and are not bound to the laws of nature or others of the old world. You have to start thinking in terms of *this* world, *this* time, *this* dimension."

"That would explain a lot," Sarah replied. "But, isn't it painful to change?"

"Not if you take the easy way as I did," the princess answered. "There is a potion you drink that makes you sleep. When you wake up, you will be a new being, completely transformed over, and changed into our species; all your human imperfections will be erased for good."

"Are you trying to sell this idea to us?" asked Kayla, "it sounds like a sales pitch to me."

"I don't have to sell you anything," Zérnoda replied. "You are free to make up your own minds."

"We humans can do great things ourselves," Kayla said proudly.

"Yeah, sure, like walk on air?"

"You know we can't do that."

Zérnoda stepped off the catwalk and the two humans screamed in fright. They stopped when they saw the Cavanonian holding her position in the air away from the catwalk, walking around as if she walked on a solid surface. Zérnoda just looked at them and calmly replied to Kayla's statement.

"Of course you can't. Human imperfections prohibit you from doing so."

Sarah and Kayla just watched in amazement.

"I'm sick of being amazed all the time," Kayla said scornfully. "Can't anything happen around here without amazement being attached to it?"

Kayla and Sarah then heard Zérnoda's voice in their heads and she looked at them without saying a word.

"Human imperfections..."

The activities of the Cavanonians below ceased and another scene developed that instantly put all into frenzy. Zérnoda saw this and wondered what all the commotion was.

"Stay here, I'll find out what is going on."

Down below, the Cavanonians were boarding onto one of the smaller ships donated by the Kostejaanians—a short-range transport with the ability to carry one hundred individuals.

"What's going on?" Zérnoda asked.

"There is a ship outside of our atmosphere not far away."

"Do we know who it is?" she quickly asked.

"No, and it isn't one of ours!"

Once she learned of the cause of the alarm, she quickly returned to the humans on the catwalk. "Come, we're going to find out what this mysterious ship is and who it belongs to."

"You want us to come, too?" Sarah asked.

"Sure, what else have you got to do?"

Fifty Cavanonians boarded the spacecraft; Zérnoda, Sarah, and Kayla were the last to board. All hands on board (except for the two humans) were eager to find out whom the mysterious ship belonged to. If it were friendly, the ship should know the location of the planet, or maybe the camouflage did a better job than the inhabitants of the planet were aware. If not friendly, then there were plenty on board who wished for combat. All on board were well aware that if the size of the mysterious ship were too big, they would disengage and return home to report their findings. However, all of these Cavanonians wished the strange ship were unfriendly; that would give them the ability to exhibit their wrath and demonstrate their destructive potential.

The ship left the hangar bay on the western most sector two hundred miles away from Royal Mountain. As it ascended into the heavens, the pilot, Solen, cloaked the ship and set a course for intercepting the vessel in question. After locating the ship on radar, the small fighter followed behind and caught up with the ship, which turned out to be an enemy after all.

"Crap!" exclaimed Zérnoda, "that's a Dominion ship!"

"Are you sure, how do know?" asked Solen.

"Because, that is one of the ships I saw descend onto Cavanon and aid the Nomaseri in the war that tore us apart."

"Is this bad?" asked Kayla.

"Only if they catch us, but they don't seem to be alerted to our presence or they would have slowed down."

"What's the plan, princess?" asked Solen.

"I say we take them out," said Crees, another Cavanonian thirsty for blood.

"And how shall we do that?" asked Zérnoda.

"Simple, we follow above the enemy ship, hover on top and dock with it. Afterwards, we secretly infiltrate through a hatch and attack everything in sight!"

"It would be prudent to knock out the ships communications and radar capabilities," said Solen, "that way they can't radio for help and send their last known coordinates or trajectory."

"Well," Zérnoda said to Sarah and Kayla, "it seems we fell in with the right crowd!"

"So what do *we* do?" asked Kayla.

"You two will stay on the ship with Solen and remain where it is safe," the princess replied.

"You don't want us to come with you?" asked Sarah.

"We can cloak ourselves and remain invisible to the enemy, you can't; human imperfections…remember?"

"Yeah, I got it," Sarah said, frustrated.

This was exciting to them and they wanted to see more. Sarah and Kayla could never do anything like this before. They were never in a position to just take off on a whim and do anything this reckless, and it felt good to them.

Solen gained in speed and caught up with the Dominion ship, following closely above, and there was no indication of their detection either. Zérnoda noticed that this wasn't a ship like the big cruiser that landed on Cavanon, this ship was much smaller, maybe twice the size of the ship currently occupied. Solen positioned the ship over a hatch and carefully docked with it. Once docked, they opened up the lower doors on the second level and began to work on the outer hatch to the enemy ship. Once opened, fifty cloaked Cavanonians entered in and resealed the hatch; Solen disengaged from the ship and followed close behind waiting.

"Solen, can you hear me?" Zérnoda telepathically communicated.

"Yes," he replied, "I hear you fine. Watch yourself, remain cloaked, and get back with me when you have something."

"Right, I'll do that."

"Remember," he added, "take out their communications first, take out the radar second, secure the ship, and then see if you can find a homing beacon."

"I got it."

On board the enemy ship, the slight fear of detection exhilarated the senses of the Cavanonian borders. Adrenaline peaked at an all time high as they made their way through the ship. It seemed a lot smaller inside then what the outside revealed. Discovering only two floors, they split their efforts and covered both floors simultaneously. As they communicated to each other telepathically, Solen could hear their chatter and relayed the scene to the humans on board the ship.

Slowly and with careful footing, the upper party found the ships control room with only a few crewmembers at the helm. The boarding party paused as the crew officer spoke to his two pilots.

"Send the crew chief to check out the hatch, something tripped the outer seal."

"Right, Sir," answered the co-pilot.

"I'll be glad when this trip is over," said the Dominion officer. "How the hell we got stuck with this deep space search I'll never know."

"We shouldn't run out of supplies, Sir," pilot one replied, "we've got enough to last for six months, at least."

"Yeah, good thing there is only ten of us; otherwise we might be in bad shape."

"*Only ten?*" Zérnoda thought, "*this isn't as bad as I thought it was going to be.*"

"*Princess,*" Crees called to her from the lower level, "*we're in position. We've got seven here just itching to die!*"

"*Right, she replied.*"

"*Crees,*" Solen called, "*have everyone position themselves behind their prey, and then pull them away from their consoles before they have the chance to initiate a signal.*"

"*I'm ready!*"

"*I want in on this,*" Kroneg said, "*I've been waiting for a chance to kill an enemy ever since I can remember.*"

"*As do we,*" commented four others with the Princess.

"*Fine,*" she motioned, "*knock yourself out!*"

All elements positioned themselves behind each intended enemy. Since the Cavanonians were ready to do battle, they had changed their outward appearance from the normal nature into the warrior beast within. Zérnoda did not know how fierce her brothers could be and would find out as soon as she initiated the signal to attack. Without hesitation, all ripped the enemy from where they stood or sat and viciously assaulted their prey, ripping them to shreds and gore, splattering everywhere. Once the Cavanonians smelled the blood of their enemies, the feast was on. They didn't eat the bodies; they just drank up all of their blood and screamed in delight at the top of their lungs. From the obvious cheering and screaming, Solen knew his brothers had performed the mission successfully and relayed the information to the humans.

"They have taken the ship!" said Solen.

"Woo hoo!" shouted the two humans, who jumped up and danced excitedly around the floor.

"What are they doing now?" Kayla asked Solen.

"You don't want to know," he replied, smiling.

"*Solen, we have the ship, as you can probably tell, shutting off comms now; radar is already dead.*"

"Good, now find the homing beacon."

"*Already found it,*" answered Crees, "*its too bad there weren't more of these bastards, I'm still hungry.*"

"Patience, Crees, there will be more another day."

"*Zérnoda here, we are turning around and heading back home.*"

"Who is flying that thing?" Solen asked.

"Kroneg."

"Good, I shall follow you home, but allow me to enter in the atmosphere and dock first; otherwise, they might think you are the enemy coming to attack."

"*Affirmative,*" Kroneg acknowledged.

Adoné and Xashsa arrived back at their mountainous palace and sat outside with Laura and the baby prince. The baby was his usual self, happy, giggling, and always smiling to his parents. Xashsa cooed and held the baby up returning his laughs with hers, gleaming in pride and happiness at their beautiful bundle of joy.

Adoné thought it unusual that they had never heard the baby crying. Why was it that he was always in a pleasant and delightful mood? The baby never gave of a colicky impression or carried himself in any other manner and it amazed his father.

While sitting there basking in the warmness of the suns rays, a commotion rose up from below the mountain. Just then, Laura saw Lazasar approaching rather fast. Something must be wrong for him to move as fast as this.

"You're Highness," he said, bowing, "there are two ships approaching from the western sector, rather rapidly."

"Are they ours?" asked Adoné.

"One is, Sire, but the other we don't know."

"We'd better check it out," Adoné glanced at Xashsa. "Let's go."

By the time they arrived at the hangar bay, the Kostejaanian ship arrived and docked. Solen exited the ship with Sarah and Kayla in tow and immediately ran topside, informing the others of what was coming.

Adoné and the others with him arrived not long after that and went to the gathering outside as the ship in question descended into the atmosphere. Before he could exclaim a few colorful metaphors, Solen came to him and began to explain.

"You're Highness, we received word that a ship had passed by our system, and we went to check it out."

"And what did you find?"

"The princess identified the ship as belonging to the Dominion."

"WHAT?" the Queen shouted.

"The princess went and put your lives in danger just to see this?" asked the King.

"No, my Lord, we all volunteered to go before she could order it. She wanted to come as well and brought the two humans, Sarah and Kayla with us."

"I don't believe I'm hearing this," he said, clenching his fists.

"But, my Lord, we captured the ship and killed the enemy on board."

"Well, that's good news at least," said Adoné, with a smirk.

"We shut off comms and radar and disabled the ships homing beacon immediately after we seized control of the ship," Solen said, standing rather proudly.

"Anyone injured?" Adoné asked, glancing upward, he saw the ship descending.

"No, my Lord, just the enemy," Solen smiled.

"And where is the princess now?"

"She is on board the ship, my Lord."

Zérnoda sat in a command chair and saw the gathering outside of the hangar bay, and instantly she knew that her father was waiting for her.

"Oh Shit!" she said, with a little apprehension.

The ship carefully lowered inside the open hangar bay and the door closed behind them. In the docking area, the princess emerged from the ship with the others and stood outside waiting for the heated ass chewing to commence.

"That won't happen here, dear daughter," he said coming round the ships hull.

Xashsa had to voice her concern, "but I would like to know what possessed you all to do this?"

"It was the heat of the moment," Zérnoda replied. "We heard about the ship and decided to do something about it before they could."

"But didn't you think it was a bit risky on your part? Not to mention the fact that you took Sarah and Kayla with you, did you not think about their lives as well?"

"Well, actually, we wanted to go," said Kayla.

"Did you?" the Queen replied, "and just what did you think about this little unwarranted excursion? Please, tell me, I would love to hear it."

Kayla did not like the Queen's tone of voice, but she also understood tact, and used it. "Queen Xashsa, these warriors of yours—both male and female—did an outstanding job of using tactics to counter anything the enemy might have been capable of. They planned their strategy and used caution every step of the way. They even kept us informed of what was going on and *we* were stuck in the other ship. I think you should give credit where credit is due, but that's just me."

"So, basically, what you're saying is…you enjoyed the whole thing, is that it?"

"Yeah, actually," Kayla replied, with a stern look in her face. "Sure, we knew it was dangerous, but I'd rather have a little hint of danger every now and then as opposed to this boring life us *humans* live. In fact, I would like to go on the next mission as well!"

"Great!" exclaimed Adoné, "we already have volunteers."

Adoné moved closer to Kayla and told her a few more words that he felt needed to be said.

"Kayla, I admire your courage, but not every mission will turn out as easy as this one. There will be times when our warriors will not come out unscathed or uninjured. You got lucky on this one. Just keep that in mind before you decide to volunteer yourself for future missions. Besides, we honestly do not want anything happening to you or Sarah; we would never forgive ourselves if you should perish because someone jumped the gun on something such as this."

"I understand, you're Highness," said she calmly, "but I still think they did a good job."

"So do I," he replied, "they did an excellent job. For this little unnecessary mission has proved to us that these warriors are fearless, jumping into a situation like this and using their abilities and minds to outwit the enemy. I'm not angry, not in the least bit…just concerned. We can't afford to screw up even once, and definitely not because of acting without considering of the consequences of failure."

"So that means we're off the hook?" the princess daringly asked.

"For now," her father replied, "in the meantime, has anyone done a thorough search of the ship?"

"Yup," she answered sharply, "did it already and found a few weapons, some yucky food stuff, and a few maps and charts."

"What about the ships mainframe computer?"

"Password protected," she answered, "but I was able to crack it and found a plethora of information."

"I'll be damned," Adoné said, smiling. "Let's see it then."

They boarded the ship and moved towards the bridge, glancing about the ship as they went. When they arrived, Kroneg had already downloaded all of the information into the Kostejaanian ship as well, for backup purposes.

"We analyzed the data, my Lord, and came up with an abundance of information about the Dominion—troop numbers, base and ship locations, trajectories, everything."

"What about future operations?" the King asked, "anything of that nature?"

"This particular ship was sent out to find the whereabouts of the Sword of Fire, the crown, Sire."

"What?" Xashsa said.

Adoné couldn't believe it either. "Why are they looking for that?"

"It doesn't give the specifics, only that it is to be found and with the utmost sense of urgency."

"Just this ship?" asked the King, "why would they send out only one ship?"

"Not just this one, Sire, there are at least fifty other ships out there looking for it as well."

"Aw shit," the colorful metaphor came out.

"This is not good," said the Queen, "are there anymore headed this way?"

"No, my Queen," Kroneg replied, "this is the only ship out this way, all the others are searching through the remnants of Muidiri, the Dominion planet that exploded. They only sent one out this way because the information here indicates that this planet no longer exists."

"Well, that's a relief," Xashsa sighed.

"But also says in another file that this planet has been camouflaged and all life has been destroyed. There are some who know Cavanon is here, but there is no indication of visiting us again."

"Well, that proves that the cores Crystals are doing a much better job than we realize. Still, I will have to come up with another method to convince others that this planet was, in fact, destroyed and make it appear as such. Now, show me where these bases are located."

While others outside the ship were giving the ship a once over, Kroneg revealed the information the King had asked for. Each planet with a Dominion base or ally revealed on the monitors in the bridge. The King and Queen were startled to see the systems spread out over such a wide area. In this galaxy, the planets occupied by Dominion authority were in three of the four corners, with the Cavanon system in the fourth. Conjecture and supposition riddled the Dominion and its commander, Federoth, as to where the crown might be located at this very moment. The data also pointed out the commander of the Elaveshan system situated in the Red Nebula region, and Rudecor, the commander or ruler of Nomaseri.

This was a great amount of intelligence to collect in one whack and once again gave the Cavanonians the upper hand. The previous thoughts of reprimanding his daughter had all been erased and he now realized that these were the same type of qualities that must be inherent in not only all Cavanonians, but of every creature who lived on Cavanon. If these two humans, Sarah and Kayla, were eager to go and do something like this, then if all were to act this way, there would be no stopping them. But, that was something Adoné would have to work on, after all, leadership has to provide purpose, motivation and direction.

Another piece of vital information that Kroneg discovered would give the King his greatest chance to plan yet, and he would begin to devise plans the moment Kroneg relayed this information.

"My Lord," Kroneg spoke up, "there is another file I found in this database that tells the crew just how long they have to search."

"You're kidding?"

"No, my Lord, here take a look. It counts downward to a point slightly less than two years and the cursor points to a strange planet, but it does not give a name."

"Something is going to happen when the clock runs out, and they need the crown to do it. Something big is supposed to happen there, and we have to find out what it is."

"What should I tell the others, my Lord?" asked Kroneg.

"Spread the word about what you've discovered; inform all Cavanonians and the other creatures as well. Keeping everyone in the loop would be most beneficial, indeed. If everyone knows what is going on, then everyone will not be misinformed or left out when the time comes to act. They will have intent and purpose already instilled. You have done well, Kroneg." The King patted him on the back as he walked out.

"Thank you, my Lord."

Xashsa and the others met Adoné outside the ship, escorting him around and showing the ships other features. Adoné did not like the idea of a VIP type escort, but he let them carry on anyway. The faces of those who participated in this incident gleamed with pride as the King congratulated them all on a job well done. They provided not only valuable intelligence information vital to their own survival, but also gave them the ability to prepare countermeasures or counter offenses against the enemy the next time they struck, if ever. The Cavanonians could also plan and rehearse for covert or clandestine missions to infiltrate the enemy when they least expected it. Having the element of surprise again amplified the feeling of their increased survivability and strengthened their tenacity to overcome great odds.

On the way out, Xashsa stopped her husband for a little private conversation, away from the others.

"I have a feeling that Kayla and Sarah are having second thoughts," she said.

"Second thoughts, about the mission?" he asked.

"No, Love, about remaining human."

"Do you really think so? I didn't sense anything."

"No," she said, "but our daughter told me about it. She said they didn't like the idea of their *human imperfections* getting in the way."

"Oh really?" asked Adoné. "If they do decide to change, then perhaps that is a ceremony *you* should perform. They might feel a little…uneasy with my being there."

"Perhaps, but we will discuss that when they come to us."

"Absolutely…"

CHAPTER 16

▼

MYSTERIOUS OCCURRENCES

For many months after visiting the Ellononis system, Federoth's forces scoured the galaxy for signs of the Cavanonian crown, the elusive Sword of Fire, but it was nowhere to be found. By dispatching ships in all directions, Federoth ordered them to visit any system within a reasonable distance of their projected course, seize and search any and all vessels encountered along the way, and bring back anyone who had information of the Crown's whereabouts. The scale of the search was massive; the largest armada in the galaxy ventured out to all areas and left nothing to chance. The concentration of forces would easily sway thoughts of possible enemy contact; the armada of ships would easily decimate any enemy opposition encountered. All ships were to maintain weekly communications if they had nothing significant to report, if otherwise, they should report it immediately so that command could analyze the information and determine its priority.

Samajap and Tiracus emptied nearly all of its hangars and flight docks of available spacecraft. Each of the Dominion commanders were eager to aid in the search as it finally gave them something worthwhile to do. Sitting around within the confines of their own offices or ships bridges did nothing but make them stagnant and bored. Their troops and equipment gathered dust and laziness in between repetitive exercises and routine immediate reactionary drills; this did nothing for morale, although morale did not concern their superiors.

Each ship had been assigned a sector to search and a follow-on trajectory once an area had been cleared. All spacecraft were assigned areas of responsibility. The ships in the sector of Samajap searched through the remnants of the destroyed Muidiri system. Elaveshan dispatched the ships in their area out around the systems within the immediate vicinity and to the outlying areas past the Planet of Lost Souls. Federoth's ship, with a few of the Nomaseri subspace vessels, returned to Earth and searched through the planets in that solar system, wondering if they would ever find the elusive item. The search would apparently take quite a while due to the number of systems to investigate, not to mention the uncharted systems viewable on navigational charts and deep space radar.

With all of the ships out searching, only a slight amount of Nogzakh forces remained stationed on their home bases; this did not worry Irol (the Nogzakh hierarch leader) at all. Despite the lack of adequate forces available at his disposal, there would be no chance of an enemy attack here. The base defenses in and around the perimeter of the above surface installations would prevent any attempted landing or infiltration.

Of the ten thousand Nogzakhs left attending the bases, one thing Irol did not have to think about was their supply of food. The dreaded time machine securely situated deep within Samajap ran at maximum operation and continued to import all manner of creatures for their continued sustenance. Unknown to any enemy was the fact that the main portal time machine on Samajap happened to be the primary mechanism for importation. From there, the Nogzakhs dispatched or sent victimized creatures through a localized time machine network to the other time machines located on Tiracus, Elaveshan with its six surrounding systems, and secretly to Cinodas to curtail Othragon's insatiable appetites.

Of course, each fortress cruiser capable of morphing into the oversized Labyrinths did possess a smaller version of a time machine onboard and graciously imported from the hub system on Samajap. If a situation required a fortress cruiser to infiltrate and claim a certain system, the organic time machine housed within the fortress could accept primary responsibility of Samajap's importation protocol; a fail-safe system developed in the unlikely event an unknown force or cataclysmic occurrence destroyed Samajap. Naturally, the original creator of this system did not foresee the need for such redundancy, but his progeny did. Having redundant capabilities gave the Dominion and its forces a warm and fuzzy feeling with their safety net.

On Earth, Federoth's ship had landed on the outskirts of his once great fortress. Walking amidst the melted steel, volcanic rock, and deformed remnants of the destroyed machines, he became disgusted all over again because of the devastation heaped on his forces by a seemingly insignificant enemy. Had Federoth known about the abilities the enemy once possessed, he would have thought twice about the activities engaged by the Nogzakhs and a planetary defensive system would have been established. At that time, he surmised that the Nogzakh patrols were enough to secure their formidability and deter any hostile force from ever plotting such an attack. As it stood, the enemy had greater capabilities than Federoth gave them credit for and he regretted underestimating his opponents and overestimated is own forces abilities. Even though the enemy had been destroyed, wiped out, or murdered, Federoth still wished he had the chance to seek vengeance against the enemy for what they did and the headaches they incessantly gave him in their quest to destroy him. Stepping over obstacles and debris brought it all back to his mind.

"Perhaps, digging out the underground wasn't such a good idea," Federoth said, kicking around rocks with his feet.

"What makes you say that, Sir?" asked Slagis, his first officer.

"If we hadn't carved out the underground areas, then the enemy would not have infiltrated the fortress from below."

Federoth stared into the massive reformed lava that solidly sealed up the massive depression that led straight down into the Earth's crust. Signs of the immense eruption littered as far as the eye could see, painfully evident of the choices he had made.

"If we hadn't dug through the ground and rock in the first place, then they would not have had the avenue with which to destroy the entire fortress in one stroke." Federoth glanced up Slagis, "the enemy, Sachom, was responsible for this as he was *in tune* with the planet so to speak. The Cavanonian King gave the order and Sachom obeyed it without hesitation. Fortunately, for us, we have Sachom's spirit stuck in the spherical prison on board."

"And how is that fortunate, Sir?"

"Because, history will not repeat itself, Slagis," Federoth replied. "If there is one thing I have learned through all of this, its not to underestimate the enemy, no matter how insignificant they may seem to be. Take them out of the fight, and the rest will fall. Nosrévis proved this when he murdered the Royal family."

"So, if they are all gone, Sir, why not go back and search Cavanon?"

"Because it was destroyed," the commander sharply answered him. "You were there, you saw it, and don't you think that if it were there we would have known about it?"

"But, Sir," Slagis tried to reason with him, "we did not know about it when the enemy carried it throughout Muidiri and into Othragon's chambers. If we didn't know then, maybe we cannot detect its presence for some other unforeseen reason."

Federoth thought about it for a moment. "You have a point there. I guess we should check it out, once more, just to be absolutely sure."

His eyes wandered about the countryside reminiscing about the old days; visualizing the Nogzakhs out on patrol, the demon beasts, and their chaotic ways, and the sky filled with aerial flyers.

"Ah, those were the days," he thought, *"how I would love to see them that way again."*

After catching Slagis' impatient pacing around the rocks and stones, Federoth motioned for them to board the ship. There was nothing more to do here and it was high time the searched elsewhere.

Once out of Earths orbit, Federoth set the ship out towards Triston—the system where the second emergence of the old John Rykus took place. He knew there wouldn't be any possibility of the crown being there, but as Slagis told him, if they couldn't detect on Muidiri, maybe they couldn't detect it at all. After all, Federoth did not sense its presence when his enemy first revealed it in the Labyrinth on Earth. Therefore, any place they came upon should be searched.

While Federoth scoured the Triston surface, Nosrévis and his own search party checked out the systems in their side of the galaxy, wildly searching through any and all of the systems they found. One system displayed on the center monitor on the bridge and its darkened outer skin and atmosphere caused the evil commander to tilt his head slightly. Morbid, sinister in appearance, and dreadfully sickening…the exterior surface intrigued him, greatly.

"What system is that?" Nosrévis asked.

"The navigational charts say it is 'Cinodas', Sir," replied Esnemia.

"I wonder what lives there," Nosrévis wondered, gently touching the monitor with his right hand. *"There is something tantalizing about this system.* Set a course for this system, I want to see it up close."

"Right away, Sir."

As the ship arrived in the outer atmosphere, Nosrévis gazed in amazement at the sight of the black clouds that covered the planet. Gloomy, ash filled, and thickly layered, the clouds offered up no avenue of approach. Black filmy chunks of high altitude blackness splattered over the outer hull and caked onto the ship as it descended. Once through, the planet boasted of its youth apparent in the ominous volcanic eruptions shooting into the heavens, coughing up its contents into the sky as a cancerous matter sticks to skin.

"It's beautiful!" Nosrévis said, joyfully.

Esnemia glanced to the left of him but never moved his head, realizing that the look on his face could be perceived as contrary to his commander's opinion of the planet.

Passing over jagged, towering mountain peaks, Nosrévis viewed a huge expanse gouged out of the planet, surrounded by even larger serrated peaks of volcanic sentinels. The scene appeared as if monstrous jaws of a demon had formed with the soil and inhaled. Directing the ship toward what Nosrévis perceived could be a nose, the ship landed at the entrance to the nostrils, setting down just in front of the openings.

Once outside, the blistering hot winds swept through the lowered hangar blowing ash and soot inside the ship. The commander, Esnemia, and a large contingent of the hellions swiftly exited and went into the left entrance. The ships hangar doors closed immediately after and inside the clean up began.

While making their way through the cavernous entrance, covered in loose rocks and falling debris, all of the ground party heard howling winds swirling throughout the cavern. The entire sight was breathtaking to the evil commander, despite what his hellions thought. Their thoughts did not dwell on the gruesome features but instead thought that a planet is a planet. But, this was not in the mind of their leader.

As they moved deeper into the planet, Nosrévis began to hear whispers in the dark, faint, distant, yet somehow recognizable. His curiosity got the better of him and he began moving at an even faster pace. The faster he moved the louder the whispers became until all at once, they stopped. Nosrévis halted and searched with his ears to find the source, the cause of the emanations. Suddenly, unknown screams echoed from deep within the cave approaching, slicing through the air. Screams of torture, of pain, and of fright filled his head with a murky bliss! This greatly captivated Nosrévis and without waiting another second, he took off straight forward, determined to see the cause of this great sight. Rounding a corner to a two hundred foot area surrounded by walls of blackened stone and volcanic ash, Nosrévis stood in the center of the area and waited. Esnemia and the others with him spread themselves out behind their leader and waited for him to make a move. Nevertheless, he did not move, instead his feet were firmly planted as he was convinced that the cause of the screams came from another entrance to his immediate front. His guess was right, and a few seconds later, the cause emerged.

The great dragon form of Othragon crept out of the opening and became large in their sight. Teeth unlike anything they had ever seen resembled daggered swords in a row and lined its jaws, upper and lower. Horns fearsome in sight adorned his devilish head, complimented with sharpness that could pierce solid rock. His eight spider like legs moved the lizard shaped body effortlessly and spread out in a wide area to brace the massive weight of the twenty-foot tall creature. Four opened arms held out this the gathering to his front waited for the moment to strike this new smorgasbord of delight.

Nearly all stood in frightful terror as Othragon let out a monstrous roar that consumed the entire enclosure. Nosrévis did not budge and never flinched an inch to the blood drenched jaws that now stood inches away from his face. The heated breath and stench exhaled from the dragon would cause the others to collapse instantly, but the evil commander stood firm. The others behind him were ready to strike the moment the creature took any action, but their strike would not come, not after seeing the shocking display that took place next.

Without a word or a hint of recognition, Othragon eased his expression and sensed something he knew, something natural, something welcome. He saw what the others behind Nosrévis did not see, and in a split second, Othragon fell on his face and prostrated before Nosrévis. Esnemia did not know what to make of this, and the other hellions did nothing but lower their guard. Hearing their thoughts of doubt, Othragon whisked into action and used his entire body to surround that of Nosrévis.

"*Fooooools!*" He hissed at them, "*...have you know idea who now stands before you?*"

They all looked at each other and back to him.

"*In front of you—inside this body—is our lord and creator, our God, and the father of our great lineage. It is He, Ellononis, my Father!*"

"Him?" asked Esnemia, shuddering in fear, "but...but this is *Nosrévis*, our leader and savior. I do not see our Lord in his character."

"*Idiot!*" shouted Othragon in his deep toned howl, "*our Father's spirit lies deep within, waiting to emerge when the time is nigh. It has been foretold throughout the centuries of his return. You should consider yourselves fortunate indeed to be pawns in his service, unless you have other intentions, ay?*"

Othragon hugged Nosrévis to him and caressed his hair gently, something unlike what the great beast should exhibit. "*I am surrounding my Father, once *again. It has been ages since I sensed his true spirit amongst my own. COME,"* he shouted, *"we must make feast to your arrival."*

Esnemia tilted his head to this and stood paused; Nosrévis turned with a look of suspicion, but relaxed his gaze and winked at his followers.

"He said, come, and now we must follow," Nosrévis whispered.

They trailed the great beast through unhallowed halls filled with the stench of death and decay, brought about through rotting corpses and skeletal remains of freshly skinned victims. Blood from earlier bodies flooded the floor of the entrance into his underground lair, his hiding place, his chamber of horrors. Nosrévis glanced around and thought about the wonders of this setting, how amazing it all appeared to be. So elegantly decorated with the bones of past kills, from all shapes and sizes of creatures brought in from all over the universe; it literally consumed his senses.

"I love what you've done with the place, Othragon," Nosrévis commented, "you simply must decorate my chambers like this."

"I'm delighted you approve, my Lord," Othragon replied.

"Oh, but I am not your Lord," Nosrévis commented, while continuing his study of the interior, "and you shouldn't address me as such. It is I who should be addressing you in that manner."

"Nonsense," the great dragon replied. "You are the *keeper* of my Father's spirit. Therefore, it is you who are blessed and should be addressed so."

"As you wish," Nosrévis smiled.

"It seems that the Nogzakhs of my previous Dominion guessed correctly when they brought you forward in time."

"And how is it that they knew which being in the entire universe possessed the great spirit?"

"That took some time to isolate and will now take some time to tell," Othragon said, and continued to explain. "My Father visited me and told me of Cavanon's flight through time in an attempt to return. My Father simply gave us warning that he would do the same in order to beat his brother and return as well, but to destroy his brother and all they stood for. In the spirit realm, he sensed the point in time and the system in question. When the Nogzakhs focused the time machines inhibitors, they discovered the Earth system. Since we did not know exactly which creature housed my Father's spirit, we simply began randomly importing them. The advantage of searching gave us a never-ending supply of food. After several years of trying, we thought we found him, but instead imported your nemesis. After learning of his skills and successful escape from Federoth's fortress, we assumed that we were on the right track as this human elevated to more than the mere human we assumed him to be. Federoth had orders to capture this elusive being but failed miserably. Therefore, assuming that we had the right human, but the wrong time, we needed to isolate the exact moment when Ellononis assumed his spirit into this John Rykus, and after importing you again, the enemy captured you and took you back to Cavanon. Federoth found you and changed you over to the hellish side of the Cavanon, a form that Ellononis instigated himself as another means of tormenting his brother. Once we learned that, and after you condemned the Royal Cavanonian family to death, we knew we had the right one. Since then, you have become even more powerful that Federoth was aware of, although he still regarded you as his pawn to control. The foolish idiot betrayed me while on Muidiri and brought your nemesis to my chambers. I thought I had him securely within my grasp, until he performed a trick that only Cavanon would know. By splitting his spirit from his physical form, he secretly saved himself while I ate his body. Later on, I discovered that after another attempt to capture Cavanon himself in the same form, but your spirituous enemy had stolen the body I had frozen in my cryoprison. However, a revelation from my Father told me the truth of the matter and revealed to me that the enemy replaced the frozen body in my prison with the grimy soil from above ground. Your nemesis had assumed the dead human body and now lives again and that means he has the sword in his possession."

"Really," Nosrévis found this to be very interesting. "And who else knows about this?"

"Only you, I, and my Father," Othragon replied. "It should stay that way as well, my Lord, and for good reason."

"But, we should search out this bastardous creation and take the sword for ourselves!"

"Patience," The dragon eased towards him. "The sword is required in order to bring the father out of you and back into the physical realm. If we are impatient, we might disturb the forces already at work with the enemy."

"You have secretly infiltrated his location?" asked Nosrévis.

"No, my Lord," he replied. "I mean to say that he will come to the place where the ritual is to be performed. He will receive a calling, yet he will not know the meaning. He will follow the call and it will lead him right to us."

"But, if he discovers the nature of the calling, he might hesitate and not show up."

"He will be compelled to come, because he will believe it to be the return of *Cavanon*."

A sinister smile came across the evil Cavanonians face, delighted with the facts presented to him. "Then we should have nothing to worry about."

"The only thing we have to fear is if someone kills your nemesis and takes the sword for himself, in this case...Federoth!"

"Federoth told me he wanted the sword for himself, damn it!" Nosrévis cursed. "If he finds the sword then it will be a hell of a lot more difficult to ensure the father's return."

"Perhaps, we should inadvertently aid our nemesis and keep Federoth off track."

Nosrévis glanced at the dragon and smiled, "delay him and keep him from following the true course to the enemy, hmm, the only problem with that is...the enemy is where?"

"It would be wise for you to search along side of Federoth and his forces. I shall remain secret and when the time comes, I shall prepare the sight for the ritual of doom."

"Sounds like a plan to me," Nosrévis nodded his head. "So, what's there to eat around here?"

The great dragon laughed hysterically and dashed off to the cavern of horrified screaming creatures.

Adoné and Xashsa sat outside on a large outdoor balcony high above the main steps of the front entrance to their home. There, the royal couple sat with Laura; Xashsa fed the baby, as it was his time for nourishment. The excitement of capturing and enemy ship made all of the subjects on Cavanon happy. This news really hit home in a good way and gave everyone that extra sense of a worry-free atmosphere that was so very different from the way things had been.

All of the inhabitants of the newly constructed city below went about their daily activities of continued construction, acquiring food, or tending to their own homes and loved ones. Tanazakh busied himself with some of the returned Cavanonians, helping them with weapons design and construction. Together, they fabricated some unique weapons and slowly mass-produced them in order to equip everyone with their own blade or battle-axe. After they issued a weapon to nearly everyone, they began to produce a surplus of weapons just in case. Not only did Tanazakh, the other Anadonians, and the Cavanonians help, but the two new converts—Stan and Zach—threw in their two cents worth and gave the other metal workers some serious competition. Blades of forged steel, equipped with stylish cross-guards adorned the blades and with the added power of the Crystals, extra powerful capabilities dominated the blades as well. So well manufactured were these blades that one of the designs caught Tanazakh off guard when he saw it. Of the many powers placed into their works of art, none caught the eyes of Adoné's best friend more than the one Stan currently held up to everyone.

"This is some chemical composition to do this to a sword," said Stan, "I've outdone myself this time."

The sword in his right hand burned of flames that engulfed the blade of the weapon, glowing with an immense fire yet one that did not burn anything, and was not harmful to the touch."

"This is like a magic show or something," replied Zach, smiling ear to ear.

"By the Gods!" exclaimed the big Anadonian, "you might want to let me have that one; I must show the King what you've constructed."

"Do you think the King will approve?" asked Stan.

"Oh, I've no doubt about that, and he will be forever in your debt should you decide to present it to him yourself."

"Then let's go see what he has to say about it!" Zach enthusiastically said.

On their way to the front steps of the King's mountain castle, Kayla and Sarah stopped Stan before he reached the steps and asked for a few words with him.

"I need to ask you something," Kayla stated, "that is if you don't mind."

"Nah, go ahead, what's on your mind?" asked Stan.

"Well, I need to know if it's worth it or not, to change over, I mean."

"Ah, hell, if I had to stay human, I would have gone nuts!" he said with a smile. "But, being this new creature, it's like getting an extension on your life, plus you get a lot of benefits from being this Cavanonian creature."

"Don't you regret it?" Sarah asked him.

"Are you kidding? I should have done this a lot sooner. Are you two thinking about it?"

"Kind of," Kayla replied, "but I'm not sure if it's the right thing to do."

"Its up to you," Stan shrugged, "but, take it from me, you will like what you can do with the new you, should you decide to take the plunge."

Kayla and Sarah stood alone after their conversation, thinking seriously about '*taking the plunge*' as Stan had put it. They saw the benefits already, but that sense of hesitation or hint of danger greatly influenced their decision-making abilities. Both of them talked often about the differences in those who did change—Adoné, Zérnoda, Laura, and now these two Stan and Zach. None of them seemed to mind what they were and now, frankly, they were very happy indeed.

The only thing stopping these two females was the courage to walk up the steps and inform the royal family of their decision.

On the way up the steps of Royal Mountain, Tanazakh approached his friend and greeted them in the usual way, with strong-arm grips instead of mere handshakes. Tanazakh had a smile on his face, the others did not see it, but Adoné could. He knew his friend for a very long time and could easily tell what expression stood on the Anadon's face at any given moment.

"So, Tanazakh," Adoné said, "what are you smiling about?"

"I bring you something that we rarely see around here," his friend answered.

"Oh, and what is that?"

"Stan has something to show you; it is something he built himself by hand while we fabricated weapons for the multitude."

"Ah, and how are we sitting as far as weapons status?"

"We've produced many more than required, and with that, I will let Stan show you his latest creation."

"You're Majesty," said proudly stood up front, "I bring you this as a gift."

Stan held up a replica fire sword to the King and Xashsa gasped at its sight. Adoné squinted at this new blade, yet with his left hand, he sensed that the crown was securely within his secret arsenal. Without saying a word, the King took up the sword and glared at its magnificence, its splendid design and engraved artwork, not to mention the impeccable craftsmanship poured into this blade. A few seconds later, Adoné walked off the balcony and hovered in the air some ten feet away to allow for some swinging room. The fire flew around with the blade and did not extinguish with the swirling air. Through every stroke, swing, jab, the fire maintained its brilliance and luster. Off to the right of the balcony, the beautiful waterfall gave Adoné one last idea as to a way to test the blade completely. He held the sword up to the water and watched as the mist caused the flames to flicker a bit, and by holding it under the falls itself, the fire went out. Adoné frowned a little and hoped it would have been a worthy substitute when the time for deception. When he returned to the balcony, everyone else saw the flames had died out and all wore a frown as well, not from the King's sighs, but from the hope that he would be well pleased with the construction of the sword.

"Its okay guys," he reassured them, "it is still a very well crafted blade and I—"

A miraculous instance cut off Adoné midway through his comments; the blade ignited on its own and once again burned magnificently in his hand. The faces of all present lit up again with pride but not as much as Stan. He swelled with contentment because *he* created this sword and many pats on the back for such excellence in his work.

"Dude," said Adoné happily, "this is much better than I thought it would be and with the delayed reaction, it is certain to fool anyone who thinks it isn't the real crown."

"Exactly what are you thinking, Love?" Xashsa asked, trying to suppress her excitement.

"The enemy is out looking for the Sword of Fire, so, we will simply place it in an austere environment for them to find and with some difficulty, of course."

A few moments after the serious congratulations to the proven skills of these new artisans, Kroneg arrived rather suddenly and very excited about something. Zérnoda showed up with him and called to her father.

"Dad!" she exclaimed, "Kroneg has something you should see."

"What, what is it?" he asked, surprised by her conduct.

"You're Majesty," Kroneg said, "I've picked up some radio traffic from what I think is the enemy. I'm not sure who it is, but they are speaking about an ongoing search for a certain item."

Kroneg set the radio transmitter down on the outdoor table and the chatter continued.

"How did you get this to work without the ships power?" the King asked.

"Oh that was simple, my Lord, I just gave it an alternate power source which seems to supply all the power needed for this device. Here, the chatter is still ongoing."

All in the house listened and paid attention to the verbal communication coming through the airwaves. It was obvious that the enemy had no idea their channel was being monitored by other than their own forces and apparently, there was no need for radio silence. The cross talk continued:

"*Affirmative Senas 6, understand and acknowledged,*" this first communicator said. "*What is your present course?*"

"*Dissention 7…our current projected course has just taken us from Anadon onto the next system in our trajectory. The planet on our scopes no signs of life, but will check it out for signs of the enemy as ordered.*"

"*Understood…our trajectory has led us past the Triston system and are enroute to a secondary planet. What is projected rendezvous?*"

"*Dissention 7…will rendezvous with you on Nomaseri as planned.*"

"*Negative, Senas 6, alternate plan established. Once you've searched the next system, rendezvous with us on outskirts of Cavanon, we must check it out once more.*"

"CAVANON?" exclaimed Xashsa, "they're coming back here?"

"Shit!" shouted Adoné, "Tanazakh, better get everyone to battle stations, we don't want to be caught with our pants down again!"

"I'll alert them all at once!" his friend replied.

"And so shall I," said Zérnoda and Kroneg in unison. "We can fly out faster to the others and warn them as well. But what shall we do if they arrive?"

"All those without the power of invisibility will hide underground. All Cavanonians will ready themselves for covert action. Have them secret themselves; if and when the enemy arrives, wait until they land before assaulting the objective. If they land, they are *NOT* to take off again, understood?"

They all nodded in acknowledgement.

"Also," he added, "have a strike team ready for each ship that lands. They are to take out the enemy communications transmitters, disable the ship so they can't retreat."

"You mean to destroy the lot of them?" asked Tanazakh.

"I mean to wipe them all out, every last ship that lands."

"Love," Xashsa said, becoming angry all over again from the remembrance of the last invasion. "I'm not going to stand for another enemy defeat, and I'm not staying in the house either."

"I don't expect you to, Love. However, we will need Laura to secret the baby underground as she wisely did before."

"Way ahead of you, father," Laura replied. She quickly took up the baby and headed off to her secret chambers down below, deep inside the mountain itself.

"I've got one other trick up my sleeve that I need to try and install before they get within sight of the planet."

"What is that?" she asked.

"I've got to come up with an alternative solution to the planetary camouflage," he replied. "They know where the planet is now, but it is obvious they do not know we are alive."

"Then take me with you so that I may see this great sight as well."

"This will be a first alright," he smiled, "remember the first time you took me to see the Crystals while in your house on Earth?"

"Oh, this *is* a switch!"

In Laura's underground chambers, Adoné walked Xashsa through the same method of concentration taught to him by his daughter. He remembered her lesson well the first time she instructed him on how to tune his essence into the planet core itself. By guiding his Queen through the exact same instruction, in no time at all they felt their bodies suspended in mid air, the temperature in the room had dropped drastically, and within seconds, their spirits were on their way to the core.

Amidst the swirling current and electrical charges, a dazzling lightshow of purple emanations filled the entire area of the enormous space around the core. Velvet streaks and bolts of electrical charges filled up the vastness and the volume of the core was immense, staggering to behold. With Xashsa there now, the two of them together began to receive their quickening at once. Xashsa had begun to receive her initial quickening from the core when a lasting bolt of energy grabbed hold of her. Together, they both became poised in their immovable stance. The energy they received filled their spirits with delight, permeated deep into their essence and elevating the status of their combined spirits. Adoné and Xashsa hovered in the vastness. In unison, they reached out for the other and as they came together, Adoné telepathically whispered into her mind.

"Xashsa," he thought, "*see the vision in my mind; see the visualization I wish to place over the planet and join me in its manifestation.*"

She saw the vision he spoke of and as they hugged tightly together, a massive bolt of energy engulfed them both and seized their spirits, testing the strength of their combined will; an authentication procedure which could only be answered by the true rulers of Cavanon.

Outside the atmosphere, a swirling current of energy transformed the outer camouflage covering that secreted the planet and changed it into the vision in their minds. Once the change completely consumed the outer planetary atmosphere, the current at the core subsided and returned the Royal Monarchs to their relative state of control. As they journeyed back to their bodies, Laura sat in her chambers rocking the baby ever so gently. For some odd reason, the baby prince slept through almost any kind of event that took place. He did not act like a normal baby and exhibited signs above that of what a normal infant should display. Still, she sat there with him, rocking gently back and forth. The sudden rise in temperature an increase in lighting told her that her parents were on their way back; even the fire, which had died out at the beginning of their concentration, flared up again.

Once back in their bodies, steam emitted from their pores as if their bodies had made the trip as well; signs that the energy enlightened them more than they had realized. Adoné opened his eyes and gazed at his love as she floated in mid air, wearing a soothing smile on her complexion.

"Love, what is it?" he asked, curiously.

"Remember when you took the temporary transformation back on Earth?"

"Sure, I remember it as if it were only yesterday, why?"

"I remembered the words you said when you came out of the room, you said, *'that was one hell of a trip'!*"

"Yeah, and it was all over again."

"Do you think it worked?" she asked.

"Well, there is only one way to find out!"

Back up on the surface, the entire population prepared as if an enemy attack were immanent. Not one creature left anything to chance. All of the humans, the Srotaderp, and the Nablah secured themselves in the old underground caverns once used after the war brought on by the Nomaseri. The Tnemucodas hid themselves in their mountain range while the other Cavanonians saw to the camouflage covering over the hangar bays and docking ports spread out over the regional area. With everyone busy with tasks, Adoné summoned a warrior flying by and ordered him to instruct Solen to take a lone fighter out of the atmosphere for a look around, and then immediately report back to the King at Royal Mountain. The warrior did as instructed and sped off with all haste.

"We'll know soon enough if we were successful in our endeavor," Adoné commented.

Solen wasted no time in carrying out the King's orders. The door controllers opened the hangar bay long enough for Solen to zoom out of the half opened entrance and out into the atmosphere. Out in space, Solen turned the ship around and became shocked at the sight, and without knowing the King and Queen's actions earlier, he immediately assumed something happened. Knowing that he had just departed the planet, he dismissed the idea and knew it as a deceptive tactic, a ruse. As the ship descended back down into the planets atmosphere, Solen was astounded to know that what he saw from space…was only a lie.

After landing the ship, he swiftly reported to the King as ordered.

"Well, Solen, what did you see?" Xashsa asked.

"You're Highness," he said, almost out of breath, "it was amazing. I questioned even my mind at what I saw, but I realized that I had taken off from a safe planet. Out in space, I saw the planet in fragments as if a gigantic explosion had ripped the planet apart, burning, and on fire. Chunks of the planet were missing and the core had disintegrated. It was incredible!"

"I guess it worked!" she answered with a huge grin.

"That should cause the enemy to think twice before attempting to land!" Adoné said with pride.

"My father would be very proud of your use of the powers he gave you."

"Yes, I'm sure he would," he said, hugging his love close and giving her a sensuous kiss.

A few days later, Federoth's ship, Dissention 7, had the approximate location of Cavanon on the monitor. Up ahead he saw a glow of red and yellow, grey and black colors spackled the glow from afar. As the ship came into view of Cavanon, Adoné and all in their mountain home listened in to the transmitter, just to see if they could catch some feedback or damage assessment.

Federoth stood at the window on the bridge and wondered about this sight. Slagis came to his side and broke the silence.

"Sir, what happened to the planet?"

"Slagis, isn't it evident?" Federoth answered. "One would think something amiss here, but I know otherwise."

"Is it trickery, Sir?"

"Please, Slagis, have you ever known a system to survive an asteroid collision?" Federoth frowned at him. "It's obvious that sometime after the war an asteroid or something equally great in size struck the planet. Look inside; even the core crystals have been destroyed. There is no way anything could have survived, nothing. With an explosion that big, everything was laid waste, so there is no need to search it. Besides, with the instability of the fragments, we would endanger ourselves and the ship if we ventured too close. Radio Senas 6 and tell them what we found. Inform them that we will change course to the watery planet."

"Yes, Sir," Slagis acknowledge.

On Cavanon, all were eager to hear whether their ruse had fooled the enemy or not. It would be a miraculous feat to beat the enemy at so simple a disguise.

"Senas 6...this is Dissention 7, do you read?"

"Dissention, this is Senas, we read you loud and clear. What is status?"

"Have arrived at Cavanon, disregard previous order, and assume your regular rendezvous point at Nomaseri. Cavanon has suffered a cataclysmic event, some asteroid or other destroyed the planet. We are proceeding to watery planet next."

"Affirmative...Senas out."

Cheers and loud shouts of praise and happiness echoed throughout the royal house and down to the steps below. Swiftly, Solen, Tanazakh, and Zérnoda went down below to inform all the others that the attack had been thwarted and the enemy fooled, again. With the new planetary defense in place, no one would land on Cavanon ever again, unless allied and knowledgeable.

Chapter 17

▼

The System of Nylantia

The waters on Nylantia raged through the air, crashing waves sprayed their mists high into the sky and added to the mystique of the atmosphere. The nearby sun elevated the above surface temperature considerably as the youth of the morning gave way into noon. By all accounts, it was a perfect day for all undersea creatures as the water temperature rose to a degree mildly warm enough to those below living in the capital city of Sirrahsew.

Life for the Nylantians went on without incident, primarily because they had disappeared from existence except to those who knew of them. Left alone to live out their lives in peace, the Nylantians greatly cherished their solitude and isolation, even though nearly one million of their species thrived in the seawaters.

This species did not have aspirations of celestial exploration, galactic dominance, or otherwise. They relished the fact they had survived for thousands of years without such appetites and wished for their existence to remain as such. They were not opposed to new ideas or alternate methods of increasing the quality of life for their species, but the thoughts and ideas they came up with primarily focused on their current environment and did not go beyond that. Each one of these amazing creatures had a wealth of knowledge and wisdom at their disposal inherent in the ruling class that oversaw their daily activities. All of the Nylantians understood and obeyed their inherent social order, otherwise inconsiderate antics (such as Adoné and Tanazakh suffered once back on Earth) would spring up all over again. Gahnepoc swiftly dwelt with the little instigator and put an end to his unruly behavior; that was also the moment an alliance with the Cavanonians came about.

Gahnepoc did not like the idea of relocating from Cavanon to this planet, although he greatly appreciated having his own planetary aquarium. The decision to relocate came after the Nomaseri raged war on Cavanon. Gahnepoc saw the devastation and tragedy heaped upon the surviving members on Cavanon. In their state of sadness and depression, they did not have the means to provide security to the other creatures who resided on the planet. Gahnepoc and his Nylantians were limited to the water and could not survive for very long above ground. Sensing the depression, guilt, and failure to provide what was necessary, the remaining ground dwellers became lost and destitute. Gahnepoc simply sought to take away their worries and concerns by relinquishing those duties that fell to the once powerful royal family prior to the attack. By taking his entire population to Nylantia, the Cavanonians and remaining inhabitants on Cavanon only had to worry about themselves and not anyone else. Gahnepoc knew where to find them should they ever have the means to return, but space travel was not well liked among his kind, for obvious reasons. If ever the Cavanonians did return to a healthy number, a few of the original members knew where Gahnepoc lived.

Early one morning, a few of the Nylantian submariners swam out on a routine patrol taking in the sights and gazing at the myriad of undersea life. With the sun nearby, the intensity of the suns light penetrated a considerable depth into the seas, illuminating all sorts of aquatic specimens and creatures, revealing their brilliant colors and characteristics. The warmness of the suns rays was also prevalent in the waters at each depth. The higher a creature swam the warmer the waters became; the very surface of the waters proved to be too much for the undersea creatures to withstand. At the planet core, canyons and tunnels running throughout the center had the coldest of temperatures. Even at a thousand feet below sea level, the Nylantians could submerge without worries or fears. Each indigenous creature of the planet had a natural resistance to the pressure at those depths. The only thing the Nylantians did have to worry about were the large unruly creatures that lived at the very center of the core. Very rarely did they ever come out from below, but if they did, the Nylantians would place themselves on alert and be ready just in case trouble came to them.

On this day, swimming only a few hundred feet below the surface, the Nylantians went about their daily swim without worries or fear. That was until a strange object crashed through the surface and descended to the depths in front of them. This was strange, as they knew the only creatures that lived in the extreme heat above were supersonic birds of prey that dove into the waters only up to fifty feet for food. To see a new object in their waters immediately warranted investigation.

The object descended a considerable depth before coming to a halt. The submariners came within twenty feet of the five-foot circular object and wondered what it could be. Fears heightened a quickly as the face of he object turned to them and flashed a series of lights, blinding the unsuspecting Nylantians for a few moments. The object had been programmed to perform such an action and the powerful transmitter inside shot the images taken back to the ship that launched it.

"What are those creatures?" asked First Officer Slagis, "I've never seen those before."

"Ha!" laughed Federoth, "so, we have discovered the whereabouts of the Nylantians."

"The who, Sir?"

"Nylantians, Slagis," Federoth sneered. "These creatures had a hand is assaulting my forces on Earth a long time ago while they secretly remained in the waters. I think it is about time for a little payback. How many of the armed probes do we have on board?"

"Two thousand, Sir."

"Not enough," the commander frowned, "but, no matter…have Senas 6 relocate to the far side of the planet and launch all of theirs as well. Let's give these underwater bastards something to really fear."

"Yes, Sir," Slagis replied.

No sooner had Slagis put the call through, Federoth depressed a pulsing red button on the arming console.

"Swim away from this you damned sea mutants!" he sneered.

Instantly, the probe in the water revealed two arms from its sides and fired shots of lasers at the underwater mariners, killing them all in one swift stroke. The probe received new orders: kill everything sighted and update status after each kill. Turning slightly right and down a few degrees, the probe moved out on its search and destroy mission.

Another Nylantian—briskly swimming through the waters—had not a care in the world as it went. After swimming around with a large school of fish, the Nylantian became unaware of the thick mucus secretions in the water. After noticing the substance on its feet, the Nylantian looked beyond the substance he rubbed between his fingers and saw the head of one of his brothers floating in the waters a few feet away. Panic struck the young creature and he swiftly darted off toward home.

In another part of the seas a few hundred miles away, other Nylantian creatures witnessed the same objects shooting deep into the waters. In a similar instance, the probes blasted the unwary onlookers and burst their innards and blood in the waters, dissipating with the current. Other onlookers saw this and immediately swam for home, unfortunately falling victim to the probes that pursued fast behind them.

In Sirrahsew, All manner of creatures swam about and tended to their own agenda for the day, unaware that the enemy force they had beaten before had discovered their whereabouts and were enroute to the city. Suddenly and with swift speed, a few of the Nylantians who had seen this horrid sight quickly raced to King Gahnepoc to relay the information.

"My Lord," coughed one of the mariners, "there is trouble headed this way from something we do not know."

"What trouble are you talking about?" asked Gahnepoc, "describe it to me, quickly!"

"Round objects, steel in construction, with arms that shoot energy have already killed a few of our brothers."

"Where are they now?"

"Far beyond the great divide, but headed this way."

"Alert the city, sound the alarms and be swift; we must warn our people!" he king quickly dismissed the Nylantian and swam off to warn his councils and court members. Whatever was coming, it obviously was not friendly after killing a few of their creatures already.

The messenger signaled for the alarm to sound and within minutes, great white creatures, five times the size of the large whales on Earth positioned themselves over the city and released a sound so horrific in nature, all Nylantians knew that when its frightful scream released, there was immanent danger. All available submariners reported to their respective battle areas to defend the city against outside aggression, but this would definitely task their forces.

Disruptions in the underwater current flowed in substances not seen in the city before, and they soon discovered that it was blood from their own species. Within minutes, the trouble spoken of had arrived. Blasts of energy from the probes laser guns struck key areas around the city, destroying gates and overwatch towers. Indiscriminately, several of the probes attacked hardened structures while others shot after the Nylantians themselves. Many of the submariners attacked the probes and swarmed over them, but to no avail, the circular object easily traversed and spun on their internal axis to shot out any of the creatures that came within distance of its guns. Up above, other submariners launched large boulders that crashed down on the probes and, unable to sustain the massive weight of the rock, they exploded with great force, sending out shockwaves that rippled through the city. The shockwaves toppled several of the buildings before dissipating in the current.

Gahnepoc called for his aid and asked for a status update.

"My Lord, one eighth of Sirrahsew is fallen and our forces are desperately trying to secure the western half of the city."

"Where is the strongest concentration of the enemy?" Gahnepoc demanded.

"My Lord, they are on the western side shattering the city."

"Get the trained pilots to the ships at once, and have them launch immediately!"

"Yes, Sir!"

The ships Gahnepoc spoke of were gifts courtesy of the Kostejaanians, in the unlikely event that they needed aid and assistance. The only way for the Nylantians to let someone know they were in need was to send someone and Gahnepoc had no natural means with which to do this. Two of their species trained in the aspects of flying and in the capabilities of the craft quickly prepared to depart. With aquatic aids installed, Nylantians could breathe for a lot longer in space then they thought. They would not like it and could not survive for an extended period of time—but they could survive long enough to get to Cavanon. These ships had been programmed to head for Cavanon the moment they were launched.

These particular models had been constructed a little differently from many of the other Kostejaanian ships. Constructed of a highly strengthened off-breed of titan steel, the crafts components were completely waterproof. Doors were not needed on the slender fuselage, and the water flowed through the craft freely from one door through the next. This allowed for faster boarding and a much quicker take off.

The two pilots boarded and quickly departed, pressing controls that started the global positioning system. Once the controls locked onto Cavanon, the ship automatically turned toward the quickest route. All the pilots had to do was control the ship through the underwater canyons and tunnel systems. Nevertheless, there would be more to do than provide manual guidance as they soon found out.

Behind them, four probes had locked onto the signals and sped up to pursue the speeding crafts. Unfortunately for the two ships, the guns on these were on the front end of the craft; no need to fire back, all they thought about now was outrunning the enemy. Through tunnels and crevices, gorges and through forests of stone the raced, swaying back and forth to avoid the laser blasts as they shot by them erratically. Up ahead of the craft, a narrow gorge revealed a passage only big enough for the two Kostejaanian made ships. Once through in the gorge, two of the probes crashed in between the rocks and became lodged in between the massive stone walls. The impact of the crash caused the two helpless probes to explode after impact, creating a huge ripple in the underwater current that quickly caught up with the fleeing Nylantians. The two other probes ascended above the gorge and calculated their exit from the on board sonar. Soon after, they caught up with the fleeing craft and commenced the pursuit.

By now, the Nylantians were on the dark side of the planet. With no light available, the probes relied on their tracking systems and analyzed topography to navigate through the tunnels and canyons; the Nylantians had no trouble with the absence of light, their vision was best suited for periods of low visibility and continued without hesitation.

Up ahead, the water density lessened as the ships surfaced. However, fate it seems was only with one of them. From out of nowhere, the probes shot bolts of energy towards them, striking one of the craft dead on, causing it to explode furiously; the other ship made it safely through the waters and blasted through out of the surface into the sky. Just before emerging from the waters, the Kostejaanians installed a device that automatically sealed the inside of the aircraft for spaceflight. Energy shields formed over the areas where doors should be and sealed in the water within the interior of the craft to allow the Nylantian some water to breathe in. A few minutes later, the craft sped through space on its intended destination.

Tanazakh stood outside the entrance to the underground caverns where the Srotaderp held up informing all below that the enemy had passed a while ago it was once again safe to venture outdoors. All creatures returned to their normal lives but every so often, they glanced at the heavens; a habit they thought they had broken. The Cavanonians returned to their normal schedule, as did the other creatures, humans, and Nablah as well. Tanazakh returned to producing weapons, the Srotaderp continued to construct domiciles while the Tnemucodas emerged to guard the skies once more.

Kayla and Sarah finally built up the courage to speak with Xashsa about the process for changing, something that Xashsa thought they would decide eventually, but she did not realize that it would take this long. Xashsa did not want to rush them, after all, it was their choice, and for them to go through with it they would have to have the intent, unsolicited and without use of pressure, threats, or intimidation.

As they stood outside the main entrance, Xashsa sensed their presence and called for them.

"Come in ladies," she calmly said to them. "There is no need to stand in fear at the door."

"Yes, that we know," answered Kayla, "but how did you know we were—" Kayla stopped as Zérnoda entered in from a back room. Kayla remembered the words the princess said a few other times and it finally clicked. "Ah, our human imperfections gave us away."

"Actually," chuckled Xashsa, "the sunlight cast your shadow into the doorway, dear. But I do know why you are here and I will answer any question you have."

"We, my daughter and I, have discussed this more than once and we've come to the conclusion that perhaps it would help us a great deal if we made this change. My only fear is—"

"—is of the unknown?" the Queen asked.

"Yes, that was my answer." Kayla sighed. "I'm frightened of the thought of something going wrong, something happening to us and we won't be able to come out of it."

"We've never experienced problems of that nature before, not even in the old days when a creature would come to us and request such a process. The only thing you have to fear is the enemy; fear itself can never kill you, but it can allow the circumstances for which you can be killed."

"I understand that, I guess I just want some sort of reassurance that nothing will go wrong."

Xashsa went over to the couch and sat with Kayla, attempting to put her mind at ease, although she could not give the definite assurance the human sought.

"Kayla, as I have told my husband many times, everything happens for a reason. Regardless of what we want our lives to be, or how to turn out, or how long we want to live, in whatever manner we are to live and die we shall. The forces of the universe act in mysterious ways and we can never know our true purpose or our eventual outcome. What really matters is how we use the time given to us and in what way we chose to live—honorably or otherwise. If you have it dead set in your mind and your hearts that changing over is the best way to give your lives new meaning and true purpose above what you normally experience, then you have attained enlightenment."

"Enlightenment?" asked Kayla, "but, aren't we supposed to become priests or monks to get that, I mean, I'm not one to study religious beliefs."

"Sweetie," Xashsa smiled, "enlightenment to a Cavanonian does not mean studying religious beliefs. What it means is you have found your vision of purpose, of truth, of enlightenment. Your dormant spirit within has heard the call and is seeking to attain that which you thought was not possible, and those possibilities are within the Cavanonian spirit. So, in essence, you have received enlightenment."

"Ah, now I understand. But, this changeover process…is it painful?"

"You've heard about it from Stan and Zach haven't you?"

"Yes, we did hear it from them."

"Well, they chose that way, but there is an alternative method in which you feel no pain, none at all. You might be a little sore for a while afterwards, but that is to be expected from such a transformation of mind, body, and spirit."

"I suppose we must wait for the King to get here before we can begin?"

"Not necessarily," Xashsa smiled and rose up, offering her hand to Kayla, "I performed the same ceremony on the King himself a long time ago, as well as Laura and Zérnoda."

"Oh, really," Kayla perked up. "In that case, I feel much better already."

Solen and Kroneg sat with the King reviewing the surface scans of their home planet after a squadron of aircraft returned from their overflight mission. The details provided to them allowed them to begin formulating plans for planetary defense should an enemy breach the newly installed image of the outer atmosphere. From the analysis of the surface scans received, precise points throughout the planet were isolated for occupation and support. By placing a few divisions of Cavanonians in and around these areas, they would be able to hold off an attack until reinforcements arrived. This would also aid in passing information of an incoming force and to what location. Others would monitor the skies and upper atmosphere for any other flanking attack from another area. Perhaps it was a bit of a long shot, but they learned from their past mistakes of under estimating the enemy.

While Adoné and his general plotted positions for their divisions, one of the Tnemucodas warriors spotted an inbound aircraft breaking through the atmosphere and followed it. The small one man craft glowed from the heat of penetrating the atmosphere and inside, the warrior could see a creature that appeared to be asleep. Suddenly, the spacecraft appeared to lose altitude and fall sharply towards the mountains. The winged warrior grabbed hold of the small spacecraft and guided it towards a safe spot on the valley floor on the far side of the Zedgen Sea, close to the King's location. Once the spacecraft landed safely, the warrior touched the impenetrable shield around the doors of the craft, not knowing how to open it. One of the Cavanonians who saw this rushed to the King and alerted him to this sight.

"My Lord," the Cavanonian said, "we have captured another craft, outside close to the sea."

"What? Is it another one of the Dominion ships?" the King asked.

"No, my Lord, this one is much smaller; it is only a one man spacecraft."

"One man? This is odd. Show me where it is," he ordered.

Once they arrived on the scene, Adoné recognized the occupant and knew he was in trouble. Knocking on the door did nothing to wake up the Nylantian inside, and Adoné became worried for him.

"Smash it open!" he shouted, "but do not harm him."

The big Tnemucodan took up his weighty hammer and smashed the front panel of the craft. The shielded doors vanished, emptying the water and spilling out the Nylantian.

"Take him to the water, swiftly!" Adoné shouted.

At the sea, the warrior lowered the Nylantian into the waters and waited to see if he would recover. Within minutes he began to stir, coughing and wheezing under the water until all at once, his eyes opened.

"King Adoné," the Nylantian spoke suddenly, "My Lord, there is no time to waste, our kingdom is under attack, and our gracious King Gahnepoc needs your help."

"What?" he shouted, "an attack, who is it, who's attacking your people?"

"I know not," the Nylantian replied, "but they are swift and cunning with their circular machines; they are destroying everything. Please, you must send aid to our King."

"We shall leave at once!" Adoné stated. "Solen, summon up as many as you can quickly, we need to leave immediately."

"Yes, my Liege," he replied.

"Kroneg, go get Tanazakh and tell him to meet me at Royal Mountain, have our ships pick me up when they are ready to leave."

Kroneg wasted no time in dashing off with his orders. All others in the area with the King were already preparing themselves to do battle. They didn't care what enemy it was, as long as they could let loose their dormant demons in the heat of battle, it was well worth whatever risk lay before them.

At Royal Mountain, Adoné rushed in to inform his Queen of what took place on their friend's planet and his plan for aiding them. He walked in right when Xashsa led Kayla and Sarah down the hallway to the chambers to perform the transformation ceremony. Without asking her schedule, he informed her where he was going and how many of his warriors he would be taking with him.

"I know you will guard yourself well," she told him.

"Yes, that I will do, no doubt about that," he replied. "There will be plenty of warriors, the Srotaderp, and the Tnemucodas here to watch over you should anything happen while I am away."

"That I am not worried about, but do be careful. When you return, we will have a surprise ready for you."

"Great, I apologize, Love, but I gotta run; the Nylantians need help!"

"Go, we'll hold down the fort."

Adoné and a force of approximately fifty thousand secured aboard many of the transport ships provided to them by the Kostejaanians, many of the fighters they had escorted them towards Nylantia. While in flight, Adoné received a sitrep from the Nylantian who came to them for help. He provided them with the basic schematics of where the attack was taking place, which side of the planet the enemy came from, and where the most likely spot to land their ships. Although it was unclear exactly who this enemy was they all knew that their must prepare themselves and put on their war faces. Many of the Cavanonians had not seen battle in eons and jumped at the chance to kill an opponent. From the short story the King told, they knew that these creatures were friends of the Crown and must be saved from annihilation. Back on Earth, these creatures played a part to help rescue the Queen once, and since then the King was in his debt. Now, it was a chance to repay that debt.

As the ships neared the planet, on the horizon Adoné saw the ships that had launched this silver circular death probes and was shocked to know them.

"Those bastards!" he exclaimed, "it's those damn Nogzakhs!"

"I knew we would run into them again, sooner or later," commented Tanazakh, "I just did not think it would be this soon."

"Well, if I hadn't come up with the new outer planetary shield, we would have found out much sooner than now."

"So what's the plan?" his friend asked. "If they see us, then they will know we still exist."

"True," replied Adoné, "I suggest we find a suitable landing area and then we'll launch the counter attack under water."

"That won't be easy," said the Nylantian. "The probes move quite fast underwater and we've no idea how to destroy them."

"Well, they are machines," said the King, "if we can crack open their outer skin, the water will do the rest."

"So how do we get close enough?" Tanazakh curiously asked.

"Fifty thousand warriors on board have the power of invisibility," Adoné smiled. "We swim for the city, approached with stealth and cloak just before we strike. If everyone splits up and takes a probe, and attacks swiftly, that will confuse the enemy. They will spend time trying to find out what it is that is causing their machines to go down, while we launch the remainder of the attack inside the city, destroying any enemy that remain."

"But then the enemy will know there is a significant force here and perhaps they will send more ships."

"Yes, but I have an idea that might surprise them," Adoné puffed up with pride.

"Do you think it will work?"

"Possibly," replied Adoné. "But first, let us deal with the immediate goal first and save the Nylantians."

"Sounds good, now all we have to do is get the word out to everyone."

"Already ahead of you there." Adoné pressed a button on the console and said, "all craft report, does everyone understand the plan?"

One by one, the other ships returned the call. "Affirmative, all Cavanonians cloak before striking, secrecy is paramount in this operation."

"Excellent," the King replied, "begin landing. Come, my friend," Adoné said to the big Anadon, "you ready to kick some ass?"

"I think I finally understand what you mean by '*kicking some ass*,' HA!"

Each ship landed on a semi level surface and emptied its contents onto the rocky terrain. With all of the warriors exiting at once, the rock surface became immediately crowded. So, with plans set and approach paths assigned, each division dove into the seas moved out along its intended course. Through the open areas and large canyons, each of the five companies in a division subdivided their efforts and split off from their large group, doing as the King instructed. After furiously traveling a considerable distance, rumblings and underwater impacts could be felt all around. Each of the Cavanonians initiated their own camouflage of invisibility and entered into the area of action.

Up ahead, brilliant flashes of lights lit up the city below unmistakably from the enemy attack that continued to plague the city. Time for the Cavanonians to exact retribution from long ago, and with their telepathic communications, all received the signal to commence their own attack.

Clouds of murky greenish colors occupied patches of the water (possibly from something losing its life) and as the warriors swam through the substance, body parts of the victim floated along the slow moving underwater current. Warriors caught site of the first batch of probes and initiated maneuvers around the enemy. By using coordinated efforts, the warrior quickly pushed three of the probes together as they were engaged in firing their lasers. By pushing them directly into each other's line of fire, the probes took themselves out, exploding from the concentration of energetic beams.

Other warriors pushed probes closer to the canyon walls while their brethren toppled large boulders that fell down from the higher elevations crushing the probes into pieces. With the myriad of chaos in the city, the Cavanonian warriors were busy extracting Nylantians out of the enemy line of fire, allowing the laser blasts to miss their target and confuse the enemy. More warriors took rocks and other large blunt objects and used them to bash the probes causing small leaks, which was enough to allow the seawater into the cracked casing to do its job. Once the water hit the electrical circuits, the probes disintegrated forcing pieces of the wreckage in all directions.

"Slagis," Federoth called, "what is the status of our probes? Why are they disappearing from the monitors?"

"I know not, Sir," his first officer replied, "they seem to be getting caught up in the falling debris."

"I know we built them better than that. Have the quartering party launch and bring back the leader of this resistance."

"At once, Sir."

It was obvious to Adoné and Tanazakh that there were more Cavanonian warriors than there were enemy probes. Suddenly, Tanazakh could see another ship of some kind descending into the middle of the city. On a platform close to what appeared to be a main hall corridor out of a very large underwater building, Adoné saw King Gahnepoc being escorted towards the descending vessel. With Tanazakh and Adoné secured in their own air bubble, a little trick taught to them by Gahnepoc, they were in no position to engage the object. But, other warriors read their minds instantly and bolted off with a plan of their own. By taking up spears from the fallen Nylantians, the Cavanonians simultaneously rammed the outer hull of the ship, causing the leaking vessel to shake and shudder as it attempted to retreat toward the surface. While this happened, Adoné and

Tanazakh secretly dashed through the waters, grabbing Gahnepoc and securing him in a hiding spot out of danger. Tanazakh instantly created another air bubble for breathing comfort while Gahnepoc sat struggled to see whom it was that had saved him.

"Adoné!" he exclaimed, "…is it really you?"

"Absolutely, my friend," The Cavanonian King answered.

"But I thought you were *dead* lost in the spirit world never to come back."

"It's a little trick a few of us can do, and you know me, I couldn't stay away for very long."

"Unfortunately, you came at a bad time, as you can see," said the underwater ruler. "We are no match for the enemy firepower, and I've no idea how many of my people have perished already. We don't even know who it is that brought their wrath to our peaceful planet."

"Not to worry, my friend, we've brought help with us! And the enemy is the Nogzakhs, again."

"The Nogzakhs?" asked Gahnepoc in disbelief, "but how could they have found us?"

"They are looking for the crown, the Sword of Fire that I possess, and they are searching each and every system looking for it. They want it badly and will do whatever it takes to get it."

"And for what possible reason could they desire the crown other than greed," Gahnepoc threw his hands down in disgust.

"Its not greed, my friend," Adoné placed his hand on the shoulder of the underwater ruler, "it's much worse than that. First, let's take care of your little problem here, and then I will explain all to you."

"There are too many of them for us to destroy, and my Nylantians are too weak and overwhelmed to get them out of the water."

"And I know just the way to do it!" Tanazakh replied, and then he relayed his plan.

Adoné communicated with the generals submerged in the area and instructed them to pass the word for exacting the remaining probes from the area. Groups of four Cavanonians each took up a position below the probe and with coordinated efforts pushed the probe upwards towards the surface. Below, all remaining Nylantian creatures saw this and halted in amazement.

"They are leaving!" shouted one underwater creature.

Gahnepoc glanced at Adoné with a raised eyebrow, "did they just give up?"

"Not hardly," Adoné smiled at him and Tanazakh. "Soon the enemy will be scratching there asses trying to figure out what the hell is going on. By then, it will be too late and they will receive their own shock!"

Up above the surface of the waters, the Dissention 7 ship hovered a few miles over the general location of the underwater city. The landing party that attempted to snatch up the underwater King surfaced with smoke billowing out from between the cracks and crevices created by unknown creatures. Once the air got to the ship, flames flared up along the fuel lines and the ship exploded halfway between the waters and the waiting mother ship.

"What the hell happened to the quartering party?" asked Federoth.

"She must have sustained damage from something below," replied Slagis. "They did report objects under the water falling against the ships hull. That may have caused the damage sufficient enough to cause the explosion."

"Then tell me why our probes are surfacing as well!"

Outside, the probes of havoc shot through the surface and bolted through the air, their intended direction was the mother ship itself. There were many more than Gahnepoc and the others were aware of, but not near enough to cause the Cavanonians any degree of worry.

"Slagis!" disengage the probes and return them to the main hangar for inspection."

"Yes, Sir."

Despite his efforts, the first officer had no control over the probes, pressing buttons, levers, and various controls did nothing to stop the probes from automatically ascending toward the ship.

"Slagis, have you got control of them yet?"

"No, Sir, and I can't get control, I don't know what is going on, they aren't responding to the commands."

"Then shut them down, *Slagis*!"

"According to the controls and indicators, *they are* shut down!"

"What the hell?" Federoth's eyes widened. "Launch the ship, get us out of here!"

No sooner had he said that, the remaining probes, around six hundred or so, zoomed towards the ship at full speed towards the ships main generator area.

"*Brace yourself for impact*!" shouted Federoth.

One by one, the probes smashed into the ship exploding on contact. As the ship ascended into the upper atmosphere, more and more probes smashed into the hull as well, creating havoc inside the ship with the roaring flames and secondary explosions in other parts of the ship.

"*DAMAGE REPORT!*" Federoth shouted.

Over the intercom came the reply. "Sir, we've sustained heavy damages to the main power generator. Secondary explosions are causing fires to breakout on levels three and four.

"Have fire control put out the flames in level four immediately, before they reach the armory."

"Affirmative, Sir."

"Engineering, how much power do we have?"

"Sir, not enough for distortion travel, but enough to limp to Nomaseri for repairs."

"Do it," Federoth said, disgustingly, "*Navigation!*" he shouted, "Plot a course for Nomaseri and get us the hell out of here."

"Yes, Sir."

Below the surface of the seas, the devastated Nylantians gratefully praised their secret saviors and welcomed them warmly. As the Cavanonians revealed themselves, all of Gahnepoc creatures were amazed to see how many of them had come to their aid. Each one of the warriors were taken into other open areas of the city and gigantic air bubbles generating out of the ocean floors enveloped the Cavanonians, releasing them from their continued use of their energy. Gahnepoc staggered to see the amount of forces his friends had brought with them. Unknown to the underwater ruler, Adoné relayed the story of how they found them and the process of bringing them back to life, thus restoring honor to their once depressing lives. With the clearness of sight at this depth, the Cavanonians swam in a circular pattern above the city before descending into the air bubbles below. The numerous creatures mingled with the other undersea warriors and engaged in handshakes and thanks as well for their efforts and assistance.

"This is definitely a momentous occasion for us all," Gahnepoc said while gazing at the myriad of warriors. "This was the very first time in my existence when I honestly thought we were doomed."

"I can understand your thoughts," Adoné replied, "you had no way of knowing we had increased our numbers. When you departed Cavanon, there were only a hundred or so creatures left alive. But, fate has shined its face on us once again and blessed us with an increase in our population. The Cavanonians you see swimming before you have sworn to defend the crown and our allies. From now on, you will have nothing to fear."

"You are too gracious, my friend," Gahnepoc smiled.

"Nonsense, you aided us in our time of need, I am simply returning the favor."

Later on after a calm sense returned to the Sirrahsew, Gahnepoc treated his saviors to healthy portions of fish meat and other undersea delicacies. This enormous force needed to be thanked and that is what the Nylantians were doing. Despite the gigantic air bubbles, the Nylantians had no trouble passing in and out of the air, but the Cavanonians were not as gifted in that area as their new friends were. Cavanonians could breathe for extended periods of time, but not indefinitely. While all below dined on healthy portions of food and drink, Adoné began to elucidate his earlier response about how big the problem of the enemy had become.

"So the enemy has grown much stronger than our previous assumptions?" asked Gahnepoc.

"Yes, much stronger, indeed," Adoné replied. "The only reason they are out in force like this is to find the crown. They need it for an ultimate plan they've developed that will destroy many lives and many star systems if they are successful."

"But what plan could be so great as to destroy all life?"

"They plan on bringing back the original creator of their hellish lineage," Tanazakh added.

"Say this isn't so," Gahnepoc could not believe his ears. "Do you realize the magnitude of what will come should they succeed?"

"Yes, I do," replied Adoné. "That is why we have gone to great lengths to hide our population and remain secret. If they know we exist in greater numbers, then they will go to Cavanon to destroy us."

"But if they know you have the crown they are looking for, then surely they will find you."

"Not if I can help it," Tanazakh answered.

"We also know of a battle that is coming as well," Adoné added. "They will attack Dolumek and its inhabitants in preparation for an even greater battle that will emerge when their evil God returns."

"Then the Dolumek must also be—"

Adoné cut him off, politely, "we already warned them. They are aware of the enemy's intentions and are preparing themselves even as we speak."

"Who else is on our side besides the Kostejaanians and the Dolumek?" the underwater king asked.

"We have the Tnemucodas; one thousand winged warriors that came to us a while ago. We also have one hundred and ninety thousand additional Cavanonian warriors at home as well."

"You've grown to a healthy number once again, that is good to hear."

"Yes, but I will need more before my comfort zone is fully satisfied. For now, we are doing well, and if we maintain our secrecy we will to continually strike at the enemy without their knowledge of what is eating away at their forces."

"So, what will happen next?" Gahnepoc asked. "They have retreated from this little conflict and surely they have other intentions as well. They won't just give up because of a small defeat."

"No, I shouldn't think so," Adoné wondered. "But, they are up to something, even if it is to continue searching other systems. The only ones left now to warn are the Kostejaanians. Though they themselves are secreted below ground, they must be prepared in case the enemy forces land in their system as well."

"We've no more ships left to send to warn them," Gahnepoc said in a worried tone.

"I'll take care of it," Tanazakh spoke up. "I'll take a couple of our smaller craft and a few warriors with me and go to them. Once I have successfully alerted them, I will return to Cavanon."

"Right, my friend," Adoné and his friend shook in their bonded fashion, "Be careful, and I will see you when you return."

"Be mindful, if I should encounter danger between here and there, I will return here first, depending on the level of danger encountered."

"We will set you up if you should see refuge," the undersea king waved.

"I must be returning home," said Adoné, politely, "I'm sure you've much to do without having me around to tend to."

"I must thank you again for your help," Gahnepoc shook his hand firmly; "we are indebted to you."

"Our continued friendship pleases me greatly, that and seeing you are once again safe and secure. So don't worry about a debt, for to me there is none. I'll be seeing you again soon, my friend."

After that, Adoné summoned his warriors and the headed back to their ships. Once boarded, they headed for home.

Chapter 18

Sins of the Heart

Back on Cavanon, Xashsa had just finished the transformation ceremony for Kayla and Sarah. Both of the humans were now tucked safely away within the confines of the sacred roomleft to gestate and incubate thereafter. For Xashsa, the ceremony gave her the renewed feeling of pride and contentment in her race. These were the fifth and sixth humans to changeover so far and she wondered if there would be more in the future. If there were, eventually they would come forward after seeing how the others reacted to the transformation. It made perfect sense to the Queen, after all, each creature should have a fighting chance and if they all had the same inherent powers they would be more dominant and motivated to take chances.

There was another who sought to test the waters and see if something remained of a long ago relationship, one that flourished in its initial stages, but turned out dreadfully opposite. As Xashsa strolled through her home wearing her normal dark blue body suit and her husbands majestic heavy black robe, she went over and stood before the large mirror in the extra family room adjacent the main living area.

In front of the mirror, Xashsa gazed at herself and thought about how wonderful she felt in her Kings robe, the one he normally wore everywhere. The robe itself dragged the ground behind here a little, but it suited her aura. The large collar rode slightly up her neck and met the bottom of her earlobes. Black was the major color of the robe as black was his color. Adorned with intricate silver and gold inlaid stitching on the collar and front seams, Xashsa posed a bit wishing her love were there to remove it from her body and hold her in his arms. Her thoughts gave away the mood within and she wished for her King to come and sweep her away. Yet another sensed this and made his thoughts known to her.

"Remember when we felt that way together?" said a voice from behind her.

The Queen whisked around to see the owner of the voice, but she already knew who it was. "Lazasar," she hissed, "You have no right to intrude into my thoughts!"

"I was not intruding, you're Highness, and I was merely reading the air as I came in. Surely, there is no punishment for what is naturally felt."

"There is punishment for any who has unnatural thoughts or ideas when it comes to me," she sternly said. "You would do well to turn around now and leave."

She turned to the mirror again and rearranged the robe, posing in the mirror and trying to decide which in pose she looked her best. She knew her husband loved any which way she posed, but she continually wished to surprise him when he least expected it, and that meant looking her best in any pose.

Lazasar stood some odd feet behind her reminiscing in his mind of the first move he made on Xashsa long ago. At the beginning of their courtship, she was young, naïve, eager to step off the straight path and live a little on the edge. During the times when she would play hard to get, he tried to win her over but found it difficult. Repeated attempts to control her thoughts and cause her to think only of him failed each time; his methods were less than successful. However, another Cavanonian who did not follow the correct ways all the time showed him a trick similar to that of mind control. This trick worked primarily on the heart, the areas of feelings, emotions, etc. The trick focused on the one place in the body's consciousness that no creatures could not survive without. During this era, creatures could be walking zombies, neither dead nor truly alive, displaced, and could still survive without the brain. The heart was a very different matter.

Lazasar trained with this not so well liked Cavanonian and learned well from him. He learned so well in fact that other subjects he experimented on drove themselves crazy from jealousy of one another. When the time came to attempt the ultimate deception, he went for Xashsa. She fell for him completely, and believed in his implanted feelings so much that she honestly felt the love was real. When the time came, the King found out about it and dealt with Lazasar's trickery by sentencing him for this and other crimes to the depressive underground prison. However, during Lazasar's sentence, he learned a thing or two from one other, and now was the time to see if it would work.

"Xashsa," her former ex-husband crept closer to her, "don't you remember how it used to be for us, back when we first fell in love? Wasn't that magical?"

"It was magical because it was the very first time I ever fell in love," Xashsa smiled slightly, "and it seemed so real at the time. But, you broke my heart, you crushed it with your lies and spiteful deceit." She continued to primp her hair and pay attention only to herself in the mirror.

"You know," he said as he crept up behind her and stood much closer than he knew he should, "times like that can be visited again, and brought back, relived and elevated beyond your wildest aspirations. I did what I did to strengthen you." Lazasar secretly harbored feelings for Xashsa. He knew how to entice her and guide her thoughts to a specific point of interest, his interest, as he knew she was prone to mystical speeches and glorious visions. But, he also prepared the power within, one in which he could guide another's thoughts and conscious moves.

"Don't you realize that of all the creatures in existence today, *you* are the most worshipped of all the females in the kingdom?"

"That isn't true," she said faintly, "The *King* is adored by all, and I am equal to him as I should be."

"But, it doesn't have to be that way," he whispered in her ear. "You can be the sole heir of all adoration, become worshipped by all instead of he, and worshipped like a Goddess." Subliminally, his concentrated thoughts had already begun to weaken the Queen's inner protected measures, taking control and prohibiting nature defenses.

"What you say is treasonous and treacherous in nature," her voice quivered as his hot breath glistened its moisture on her neck, "you cannot do this."

"Ah, but I am, my Queen, and there is nothing you can do to withstand my touch. You knew this when we first married long ago."

As Lazasar spoke, something seized Xashsa's inner being and awoke a spot long ago held by him and it clutched her spirit tightly, spiraling inward in a fashion of mysticism, and all at once, it enveloped her heart and seized it.

"Ugh!" Xashsa sharply inhaled, as her body tightened up by an unexplainable seizure. Lazasar knew his psychic incantations hit the exact spot within her…and he continued to speak.

"Back then, you not could withstand the will to submit your body to my hands, and even today you exhibit the same lack of will to resist."

While her body quivered, Lazasar secretly whispered a very potent spell into her heart, one that would captivate and seize control of her regular faculties, changing all that she knew so that she would know no other than her first husband.

"You...you m...must leave...while you still ca...can," she forcibly stuttered, as her inner self began to fight with itself.

"You know I cannot do that," he chuckled and whispered in her ear, "not until I've felt myself inside you once more."

"That will not happen," said a voice in his head; a voice that was not under the influence of his heart control processes. Moreover, before Lazasar could turn around, a great hideous beast behind him wrenched his body from the ground and slammed his body into the stone floor. A crashing foot of the huge beast centered itself on his chest and applied great pressure causing him to scream in agony.

"Get your filthy hands off me, decrepit wench!" Lazasar shouted.

The creature was the unnatural dormant being within Laura, the one who constantly watched over her parents, although they were unaware of it at times. Laura took it as a treasonous insult that this fiend should even think of possessing the heart of her mother, let alone dream up thoughts of a sexual nature. Yet, Laura was unaware of the damage already done to the Queen.

"You piece of shit!" Laura scorned with her drooling saliva dripping profusely over his face and chest. Her howling deep depressive tone thundered as it basted Lazasar's face. "Do you really think you could get away with your vileness in *our* own home? Who are you to try the will of the Queen and break the bonds of my parent's hearts? You have no idea what they have been through, what they mean to each other, and what they mean to the Kingdom. I will personally see to it that I escort you to *hell* for mocking the king's forgiveness of your damned soul."

"The King will kill me if you say a word," he cried, attempting to institute a subliminal message into her brain. "You mustn't tell him a thing."

"Fuck you, bitch! I'll tell him any damn thing I want."

She applied more pressure to his chest as her full weight rotated over the leg that pinned him. He screamed in pain from the heaviness of her creature and the screaming penetrated Xashsa's ears enough that she shook her head fiercely.

"Mother, snap out of it!" Laura's creature yelled.

"She cannot," he laughed, "and if you kill me, she will be lost in the spell I have cast on her heart."

"*AAAAHHHH!*" The creature furiously roared as she picked up his body and slammed it into a wall, causing a crack in the stone to appear. Another wrench of his body slammed him back onto the floor, followed immediately by another crushing pound of her massive foot on his chest. "You had better release her or else."

He coughed and choked up blood and other putrid stomach contents before he could finally answer her in a cynical tone, "or else...what?" he laughed. "You can do nothing to me, *fool*. I can easily win your heart over as well, as you may yet sense yourself."

Her hand wrathfully bashed the side of his head causing even more blood to spurt out from his jaws.

"You'll be dead before you can try that on me, fuck shit!"

"Ooh, fuck shit, that's rather bold language for one so young and tender inside," he said, focusing his eyes, staring deep into hers.

Laura had the slightest tingling sensation inside her, tilting her head as if she were reading something of his mystical high-pitched whispering. Before Lazasar could do his dirty work, she whipped out a pair of swords, whirled them in the air, and drove them deep into the stone floor on both sides of his head, cutting off his ears. Lazasar screamed in fright as the blades came down and felt the sting of her steel against his bare skull. Her demonic jaws coughed up mucus and spat in his face, all the while dripping salvias enzymes on his choking face.

"I would proclaim myself Queen of Hell to own your soul and torment you forever for your vileness."

"You will see hell, my dear child, but not rule it," he retorted, "and you cannot save the Queen now!"

Laura's creature heard the sound of drawn steel, and as she turned around, she saw the Queen holding her own blade to her daughter.

"What?" Laura said in shock. "Mother, it is I, your Laura, can't you see me?"

When Laura lowered her guard, she became herself again and that gave Lazasar the chance to throw her off him and escape out the window. The Queen still held her blade to Laura, walking slowly toward her with the gleaming white steel shining in Laura's face.

"You sought to control my heart didn't you, Laura," Xashsa said softly, yet in a forceful manner.

"Mother, what are you saying? I was just trying to defend you."

"I do not need your defense little one. I have survived for thousands of years without the help of another, so your life means nothing to me now."

Laura was convinced that the spell cast by the traitorous Lazasar was so powerful in nature that it seized her mother's soul. Laura knew this was not her mother speaking for if it were, then the Queen would know that she did not speak the truth.

"Because you have harmed my love, then you will be harmed in kind."

"Mother," she screamed, "wake up, it's me! Listen to me, you have been poisoned with a spell, come to your senses, *please*!"

"Time for you to pay for your harm done to my dear Lazasar!" replied Xashsa.

The Queen raised her sword to her daughter and wrathfully swung it down to her. Laura froze in place by her mothers actions, too paralyzed to act and watched as time slowed to a crawl with every inch of the blade coming toward her. But, the blade did not find its target and was blocked by another. Adoné held his black blade out and stopped her swing dead in flight.

"Someone wanna tell me what is going on around here?" he said forcefully, with a raised left eyebrow.

"You!" gasped Xashsa, shocked as if she had never seen him before, "what are you doing here?"

"Xashsa," he answered, confused, "what's wrong with you?"

"Foul bastard!" she screamed, and swung her sword at her husband. Adoné blocked it and blocked several more after that.

"Xashsa, what's gotten into you?" he quickly ducked to avoid another swing of her sword. "What the hell is wrong? Stop swinging your sword at me!"

"You want to kill him, you want to kill my love," she shouted scornfully.

"What? I am your love, what the f—" she cut him off with a few more swings and jabs, and he blocked them all, smacking her sword away with each return swing.

"Xashsa, stop," he yelled, but she did not listen, "I said….*STOP!*"

Adoné simultaneously held up a fist in front of his face, quickly extending his fingers and the power in his action caused Xashsa to fly up against the wall in a spread eagle stance a two feet from the ground. Her sword dropped from her hand and clanked on the floor below.

Adoné did not realize that her actions had summoned up his inner anger and his eyes had reddened as they normally did when he became irate. Laura half sat, half lay on the floor crying and wailing in fear, tears of pain dripping profusely from her bloodshot eyes. The others in the room, Zérnoda and Tanazakh (who had just returned from Dolumek), did not know what to do or what to say, they were both petrified at what they saw. This was the first time ever that Adoné had summoned up his anger against the Queen, his wife, his love, and this staggered the minds of all in the room. Adoné's hand began to tremble slightly as he understood what he had done. The Queen never acted this way before and he knew it. Feeling the urge to scream choice metaphors, he knew that the only one in the room who would have any sane answers was Laura, and as he looked over at her, he saw the look of fear on her face and calmed his anger. His right hand held up the Queen in her current stance and held the other hand out to Laura.

"Sweetie, come here," he said calmly.

Laura ran into his arm and hugged him tighter than ever before. Adoné sensed that something terrible had happened for his daughter to react in this manner.

"Calm yourself, sweetie, and tell me what happened; why is your mother acting like this?"

"It…it was Lazasar!" she cried.

"What?"

She cried more and after a few moments of her crying and Adoné's shocked expression, she continued. "Lazasar said something to her, he *did* something to her, and now she's turned into someone else."

"What the hell was Lazasar doing in here in the first place?"

"I do not know why he was here." Laura buried her face in his clothes and continued to cry. All Adoné could do was look at her in her torment and pain, and then glance up at Xashsa, weak and near to passing out. His power forcefully affected her more than he knew. Adoné motioned for Zérnoda to take her sister and he raced over to catch the Queen as he released her from the wall; she fell limp into his arms, draping over towards the floor. After carrying her over to the spacious couch, he placed her limp body on it and sat with her, straightening her position to allow her to rest, comfortably.

Laura came over and sat on the floor beside him, resting her hands and head on his thighs.

"I'm sorry, Father," she said tearfully, "but I tried to stop him, I tried to stop it, but I could not. When mother drew her sword to me, I lessened my force over him and he escaped."

"Why would Lazasar do such a thing after I freed him, after he swore on his life to serve the crown?"

"I don't know," the little one answered. "After we performed the transformation ceremony on Kayla and Sarah, we returned here. I went to see to the baby and when I came out, Lazasar was standing behind her, with his arms around her, whispering something in her ears and speaking sexual things."

"That bastardous liar," her father sneered and gritted his teeth. "I'm willing to bet he still harbors feelings for her from his failure after their wedding. I think there is another reason of why Xashsa's father sentenced him to the underground prison."

"Adoné," Tanazakh slowly walked forward form the door, "what if he attempted to obtain the crown from his vile actions long ago, what if he sought to obtain the crown by trickery?"

"At this stage, I would not rule out that idea. It is feasible, but why lie to me, to us…and why now?"

"What is wrong with mother?" Zérnoda asked delicately.

"Give me a minute," he replied, "I must look into your mother and see if I can discover the cause of her abnormality."

Adoné placed is hand inches above her chest area, closed his eyes, and tilted his head slightly up. In his mind, he guided himself through her aura and inside her spirit. Channels of brilliance, light, and inner celestial bodies of wonder swirled inside of her body. The magnificence of her inner being astounded him greatly. Through the myriad of lighted tunnels, caverns of feelings, and the austere essence of her inner demon, he traveled until he came to the area in question. The dome of her love, the singular conscience of life did not glow of its normal brilliance. Instead, a shield had been drawn up around the core of her essence, her heart, shielded and enslaved by this metal mind covering. Adoné attempted to pry and peal away at the force field but it was not use, it reshaped and reformed over the areas pried open. While continually attempting to penetrate this wall, forces from the shielded area lashed out at him and caused him to open his eyes, jerking his hand back a few inches.

"Some sort of shield, a mystical force has formed over the essence of her heart, preventing her true feelings from escaping."

"How can we make her well again?" Laura tearfully asked.

Anger grew in his eyes, as he knew whom he must deal with. "We must find Lazasar."

While all in the royal manor thought about the possibilities for such deceitful nature, Solen came to the doorway and announced his presence.

"My Lord," he said, bowing, "Lazasar has been injured."

"He has?" Adoné answered, as if surprised. Glancing down at Laura, she nodded her head and whispered in his mind.

"*I did that earlier trying to stop him*," she thought.

"And where is he now?" the King asked.

"He has fled to the prison are we once were condemned to," Solen answered. "He believes that you mean to harm him, is there truth in this?"

"And what if there is, Solen, what would you do about it?" Adoné stood up and walked towards the door with contempt in his eyes. "What do you know about the activities that took place in my house prior to my arrival? If you know, I suggest you tell me now."

"My Lord, I know nothing of what took place earlier. I could not know for I was with you on Nylantia."

"And why is it that I sense displeasure in your mind regarding what Lazasar has stated to you?"

"My Lord, forgive me my ignorance," Solen said, carefully, "but he...he is my friend, he has been with us for many centuries in the prison. He has taught us many things in our defective state. Surely he is regarded of high quality with you?"

"Did he teach you of treachery, of seduction, the will to dominate? Did he show you these things during your friendship in the prison?"

"He would never teach us things of that nature, my Lord," Solen said. A look of question came over his eyes as he stared at the King. "Lazasar could not possess such thoughts; that is impossible."

"Is it now," Adoné stared into Solen's eyes. "You know this for a fact, or are you merely guessing?"

Solen coward as the King rose up over him. "My Lord, I mean no disrespect. I only know what I sensed."

"Then for your sake, Solen, I will prove it, if you truly believe in your King?"

"With my life, I do, my Lord."

"Then do this task for me," the King said, in a forceful voice, "and tell no one, reveal nothing to anyone, including Lazasar. I shall show you what I know and enlighten you with truth." Adoné used his powers and gradually raised Solen to his normal height. "Go find Lazasar and tell him that will make any deal he wishes in order to save the Queen."

Solen jerked back, "huh?"

"Do as I have asked of you, Solen," Adoné said forcefully. "State the words exactly as I have given them to you. Go now, and tell him we will meet with him in the old prison area within the hour."

"Yes, my Lord." Solen bowed in obeisance and dashed off.

Tanazakh approached his friend and watched as Solen flew off rather quickly.

"Do you think he will tell anyone else?"

"Of course he will," Adoné replied. "If I were told something like that, I'd tell you in a heartbeat."

"I'm glad you trust me so much, of course you know I would never—"

Adoné abruptly cut off his explanation. "My friend," he said, putting a hand on his friends shoulder, "you have been with me since the beginning, and you have always been there when I needed you, even in times of despair when I was not myself. You and I know we would never betray each other, so there is no need to doubt or explain how you feel. I know you and you know me. We are like brothers, you and I."

"And that we will always be," the big Anadon smiled. "So, what's the plan?"

"I need Stan and Zach to come with us. Please go and tell them I need their assistance, and for Stan to bring his fire sword with him."

"Oh, this *is* going to be good!"

As Tanazakh left to fetch the ones his friend asked for, Adoné went to his daughters and gave them instructions as well.

"Dearest daughters," he said, hugging them both, "don't worry, everything will be alright."

"What are you going to do, father?" they both asked.

"I'm going to save your mother," he replied. "But, while I'm gone, I want you both to stay here and guard each other well. Watch over the baby and make absolutely sure that no one comes in here without my authority. I hate to distrust, but it seems that even *we* have traitors in our midst and we must be on our guard."

"Okay, but please hurry, we are fearful for mom," answered Laura.

"Remember, guard each other well, and I'll be back before you know it!"

At the old prison area, Lazasar tended to his wounds and told twenty other former prisoners a tainted version of what took place in the royal manor. The story he told did not have all the facts, and for obvious reasons. If he told them the truth, he would be alone at this very moment, and Lazasar knew it. Still, if what Solen told him were true, then this would be the one chance Lazasar would have to get what even *he* sought to obtain during the marriage to Xashsa long ago. But, he also knew he should have a backup plan. Knowing how the King felt about his Queen, Lazasar knew that if he did not come up with an alternate plan, he would be doomed, but then again so would the Queen.

"Are you sure he said he would be here within the hour?" the panicky Lazasar asked.

"Those were his exact words," Solen replied. "Why would the King threaten your life?"

"Its like I told you, he wishes to harm me because I merely spoke with the Queen, alone. He is convinced that because she has fallen grievously ill that it was all my doing. I would watch myself around him if I were you."

"That won't be necessary, Lazasar," the King said as he entered into the underground expanse and approached the stone stage. Tanazakh carried Xashsa, laid her down on the stage, and stood over her, ready to react if she tried anything harmful. Adoné telepathically communicated his intentions to Stan before boarding the stone alter. Stan had the sword contained within his body and walked on the Kings left side, Zach walked on the right.

"Stan, stand behind me on the stage. When I give the signal, hand the fire sword to me when I offer my hand to you behind my back. Let no one else see you do this."

"You got it, er, Sir," Stan replied.

"So, Lazasar," Adoné said, standing on the stage, "you do possess deceit and treacherous ways after all."

"Ha, see?" Lazasar pointed at the King, "do you see how he judges me for merely speaking alone with the Queen." His look of contempt did not leave the King's sight. "He wishes nothing but ill to my character and jealously rages his spirit. Is this the way of a King?"

"Lazasar," Solen said, very confused, "the Queen is his wife, and he has a right to act in whichever manner he chooses for her well being."

Adoné slightly raised his eyebrows after hearing Solen's remarks.

"He has tricked you all and will doom anyone who speaks to her, alone."

"Perhaps you should tell them what you did to her, Lazasar, or I will," said the King.

"I did nothing but merely bring up old times, where is the harm in that?"

Adoné reached out his right hand to Lazasar and his powers seized control of his body, paralyzing him in place so that he could not move.

"Now, let me tell you what *really* happened," the King said, approaching Lazasar with a vile look of hatred in his eyes.

"Lazasar is not as innocent as he has portrayed himself to be," Adoné stated. "True, he did bring up old times as he said, but during his chat with the Queen, he whispered something else into her ears: a chant, a mystical incantation of which has seized the heart of the Queen and turned her into something else. She is not herself and in a staggering change of character, she has pledged her love for him." He pointed to Lazasar.

"Lies, all lies, I tell you." The accused did not move but could speak. "If she is this way, then prove it to them."

"As you wish." The King snapped his fingers and Xashsa woke up. Upon sight of Tanazakh, she stood up, saw Lazasar, and dashed toward him. Adoné swiftly applied the same technique to her, causing his wife to freeze in the air a few feet away from him, while maintaining eye contact with the accused.

"Release me!" she shouted, "I command you to release me at once!"

"My Queen," Lazasar said, "do not fight them, they are deranged."

"Lazasar, my love," she replied.

Adoné stepped down off the stage and walked around to the others who had gathered to see this. They were those who Solen spoke to prior to his arrival, knowing this was against what the King had ordered.

"Since I released you from your prison," Adoné began to say, "you have seen the Queen on many occasions. You have witnessed her conduct and you have heard her speak, does this sound like the Queen you know?"

All the others behind and around Lazasar looked at each other with question, not knowing if they should answer or not.

"This one here," pointing to Lazasar, "has a hidden agenda that you are not aware of. He seeks the Crown, the Sword of Fire for his own treasonous reasons. He once sought to obtain it long ago when he seduced the Queen with the same type of mystical speech. Knowing that he could not attain the Crown on his own, he married the Queen and then sought to obtain the sword from her father. However, the King was not ready to relinquish his kingdom to this new prince so soon after their marriage. So afterwards, he treated her wrongfully, abused her, neglected her, and disavowed the wedding. That is why he was imprisoned here, although I think he did not tell you this when he arrived."

Lazasar remembered the scene long ago and the King told it as it here were actually there to see it. In his heart, Lazasar knew he spoke the truth, and the truth got the better of him.

"What right had the king to deny me the Crown," Lazasar's true self came out. "I did all that was asked of me, I practically kissed the behind of the King in his own court. I should have been given the crown right then and there."

The rest of the Cavanonians around him began to back away. Even they knew he just sentenced himself all over again, and they wanted no part of it.

"Ah," Adoné paused his pacing, "and that was supposed to oblige the King into surrendering the most sought after item in Cavanonian history? What would you have done with it, Lazasar, even if he did give it to you…hmm?"

"I would have done what any normal Cavanonian would have, I would have unlimited authority to do whatever I wished and not be subjected to the whims of others."

"And that attitude is why the king would not grant you the right to be his heir to the throne of Cavanon. However," Adoné glanced at the Queen, remembering the real reason for being there in the first place, "I will make a deal with you for the life of the Queen."

All who heard this stood in shock. Would the King yield to the lies of a traitor?

"I will give you want you wish to obtain, provided that you give me back my wife."

"My Lord, I must object!" Tanazakh played along, adding a more convincing performance to the deception. "You cannot give up the crown to this traitor."

"I will do it for her!" he simultaneously shouted and pointed to Xashsa. "She is my life, and without her there is no reason for me to continue living."

"You would to this?" Lazasar asked, as if the King were seriously considering it.

"Without question," Adoné forcefully said. The seriousness of his answer shown in his eyes and in his face—hoping it would fool the traitor. "*She* is all that matters to me."

"And what guarantee will you give to allow me to leave this place without harming me?"

"By giving you the Crown, you will be in power of all who live on Cavanon. *That* is your guarantee."

Lazasar smiled a devilish smile, feeling as if he had won by default. "Very well, I shall release the Queen, but first, show me the crown, reveal to me the Sword of Fire at once!"

"Yes, my Lord," replied Adoné. He bowed and returned to the stage.

All who witnessed this became greatly confused. No King would ever do this for a woman, so why would he do this now?

"This is blasphemy against the Crown," replied Solen. "You simply cannot do this for the life a wife?"

"You do not see, you do not hear, and you no doubt do not understand the true nature of things as they really are, Solen," Adoné said angrily as he gave him a furious look. He reached behind him as if to retrieve the crown from within, but Stan quickly provided him with the replica fire sword, hoping it would fool all except those who wise to the plan.

"By giving up this sword, it shall burn me for only the one true leader of the Cavanonians can wield its power!" Adoné said this as if he had rehearsed his little speech, and in his mind, he heard Tanazakh's comments.

"*Ooh, that was good!*" The big Anadon thought. His friend quickly erased the smile that wanted to surface on his face. Lazasar gazed at the sword and became mesmerized by its flickering flames, its mystique, and magnificence. The magnificent crown he wished to have all his life was now only inches away from his face.

"And now," said Lazasar, "bring the Queen to me so that I may whisper into her ear."

Tanazakh did as he requested, bowed before him, and then forcibly turned the Queens head to Lazasar's face. Xashsa struggled a bit, but the Anadonian held his grip. Shortly after Lazasar whispered into the Queen's ear, she regained her normal self. Dazed and confused, she looked around at her location and wondered why she was here.

"Adoné, where am I?"

"Xashsa, you are at the former prison of the depressed. Come to me, please."

Xashsa went and hugged him tightly. Adoné could sense that it was she and the restraining effects of the mystical incantation had vanished from her essence.

"Now, release me and give me the crown, I command you!" Lazasar shouted.

"As you wish, my Lord," Adoné replied.

Xashsa did not know what was going on and tried to stop him. "Adoné, what are you thinking, you can't do that?"

"I must," he answered, "I made a deal to get you back, I did it for you, my one true love."

"But you can't give up my father's Crown, you can't!"

Her husband whispered his own words into her mind, "*just watch this, Sweetie; you are going to love this!*" He paused slightly, "A deal is a deal, Love, and I will honor my end of the bargain."

Adoné released the mental grip on Lazasar and walked towards him while he regained his stance on the steps below. Adoné really played it up well, so well that he wished the others behind him would stop laughing in their minds. It was causing him to cry tears of laughter, but Lazasar was unaware of this and thought the King truly did cry for being beaten so easily.

"Here is your Crown, my Lord," he said, handing him the sword. And, as Lazasar grabbed the sword, Adoné yelled, "Ahhh!" and jumped back, holding his hand as if the flames burned him.

"That will teach you that you can never again attain what was originally supposed to me mine." Lazasar swung the sword around in the air and smiled greatly.

"Now, slave, I command you to kneel before me."

"Why?" Adoné asked, smiling himself.

"Because I am your King, fool, and since you have decided to question my authority so soon, you shall be sentenced to the imprisonment I was once subject to."

"Do your worst, dipshit, I bow to no one."

"Traitor!" shouted Lazasar, "seize him now so that I may slay this wretch."

The others who had already backed away from Lazasar backed up even more and did not hearken to his orders.

"What insolence is this to the new King?" Lazasar said in disbelief, "I gave you an order, do it now!"

"Hey, dumb ass," Adoné said, and revealed the true Crown secretly kept within his own body. "They know the face of deceit when they see it!"

"You liar, you tricked me!"

"Yes, and I did it for the Kingdom, *and* for my Queen."

Xashsa wore an immense smile and the others behind the King began to laugh hysterically.

"And now, I shall judge you for your treachery against the Crown and the Kingdom." After Adoné said this, he seized control of Lazasar's body again, forcefully pulling him to his knees on the ground. The King jumped off the stage and stood before Lazasar, holding the sword dangerously close to Lazasar's face.

"Do you really wish to hold the real Crown in your hands? Do you want to see what happens to anyone who holds the crown in their hands and has not received the blessing of the Ancient ones?"

"No, no, my Lord, please I beg you, have pity on a lost soul," Lazasar pleaded.

"Oh," the King laughed, "we are *way* past forgiveness, my one time friend. Give my regards to those who are in oblivion, will you?" Adoné grabbed Lazasar's hands and placed them around the handle of the Sword of Fire. Lazasar shouted in terror as the flames from the sword engulfed him. Once the sword had detected that a non-sanctioned creature held it, the flames burned of a glorious white color, signifying the most intense heat possible. Lazasar's body burned out of control and soon after, his cries of pain subsided and died off. His charred and burnt body fell to the floor once the King removed the sword from his hardened grip.

"And that is what happens to any who would attempt to take the crown by any other means," said the King, glaring at the others who all suddenly dropped to their faces, prostrating before him.

"I withheld information from you in order to see where your loyalty actually lies," the King said. "If you had acted to the contrary, you would have joined him. But since you did not, you are blessed and trustworthy."

"*Adoné,*" Xashsa thought to him, "*I am so ashamed of myself, how can you forgive me for what I did to you?*"

"*You did not have control, Love, and it was not your fault. Do not worry yourself, this type of danger will not harm you again.*"

"Solen," Adoné called.

"Yes, my Lord," he quickly replied, stumbling over himself to rise up.

"Take Lazasar's body and the replica sword and place them into one of our smaller ships. Launch it towards Nomaseri."

"Right away, my Lord," Solen stood up and looked at his friends standing behind him, "What are you waiting for, the King has spoken, let's go, and move!"

Tanazakh looked at his friend curiously, and his friend answered.

"The enemy is looking for the Sword of Fire, and they will find one. Come," Adoné said to his friends and wife, "Let's get home so we can tell the others, they will laugh their asses off!"

Chapter 19

In the Hands of the Enemy

Dissention 7 limped through space wounded and smoldering after Federoth's unsuccessful attack on the Nylantians. It was unclear to the Dominion Commander as to why the probes strangely and unintentionally had returned to the ship. The damage to Dissention 7 was critical enough for Federoth to head for Nomaseri an allied system that would assist in repairing and refitting the ship. Federoth pushed his crew into forcing the ship to cough up all the power it had in order to arrive safely on Nomaseri. If they were to stall in space before successfully arriving at their destination, the ship would begin to fall into the deep space freeze and float aimlessly until discovered. With the limited number of life pods on board, a large majority of the crew would not survive the extreme cold temperatures; space itself was unforgiving to anyone caught in her web.

However, Federoth's ship did arrive at its intended destination…barely. Additionally, after a bad emergency landing, Federoth and his crew disembarked from the vessel and began assessing the damage. From the ground, they ascertained the total damage done by the probes and knew that it would take a hell of a long time to repair. With that in mind, Federoth went to his friend, Rudecor, and asked for assistance. With his help and access to a plethora of spare parts and equipment, Federoth organized and ordered maintenance crews and technicians to begin repairs. Rudecor could not wait to hear what trap Federoth had fallen into this time, not that he doubted his sinister friend's abilities, but he knew that Federoth's wasn't always sharpest spear on the rack.

Back at the pyramid palace complex of Rudecor, Federoth showered up and washed off the outer casing of soot and debris his charred ship attached to his skin. A nice hot wash and clean clothes would help him to feel a bit better, despite the nagging frustration mounting inside him from this sudden defeat or failure, whatever it was. As he showered, he could not put his finger on why the probes acted the way they did. Why did they return to the ship without programmed orders? Why didn't they follow their original orders and destroy the rest of the Nylantians? Did the Nylantians themselves have certain powers of reprogramming the probes? Did they have extraordinary powers to use in case of just such a sudden attack? What was the reason for his failure? These and other questions plagued his mind as he walked through the stone-decorated halls of the palace. His attention was definitely not on his immediate surroundings as Eñala playfully pointed out.

"Did you miss me?" she asked with a sly look on her aroused face and ran her hands along his chest.

"Not now, Eñala," he bitterly replied, "can't you see I'm in no mood for your lascivious cravings?"

"Maybe not now, but you will be," she hissed at him, licked her puffy moistened lips, and seductively walked away to tend to other errands.

Federoth reluctantly watched her enticing strut, knowing he did desire her company, but not at this moment. There were times for spanktacious sexual carnage and right now was not one of them.

"Crazy nymph bitch," he said just below a whisper, "she's going to kill me with her body, or better yet, I'll kill her; either way her sexual drive will be the death of us both."

"Oh, don't let her hear you say that," Rudecor spoke up, hearing the painful remarks, "that will only entice her to show you what she *really* finds devastatingly gratifying."

"Rudecor, far be it from me to turn down a worthy sexual opponent such as her, but isn't there a limit as to how violent the Nomaseri sexual nature can get?"

"You haven't thrown each other around the room, slashed each others clothes off, and ripped away shards of skin yet, have you?"

"No!" Federoth cringed.

"Then you haven't seen anything yet!" Rudecor laughed and invited his friend to sit and dine on fresh Boradus meats.

The sinister Cavanonian stood in place contemplating over Rudecor's sexual description and became aroused as he pictured the scene in his mind.

"Perhaps I should not have said anything," Rudecor smiled, "I might have taken away the element of surprise for you."

"Nonsense,' Federoth replied, "just experiencing such an act would be surprise enough. If it is worse than the last encounter I had with her, then I know I will enjoy it."

"Well, I would have warned you about the ceiling initiation, but that would have prepared you and heightened your guard to the intended attack. Without knowledge of the ambush that waited, your body was relaxed, rested, and ready for the sexual waylay she unleashed." Rudecor picked up his chalice and swished the contents of green hemoglobin drained from the Boradus. "I remember the first time that happened to me, I was in pain for four days. After that, I tried it several more times, but if you know it is coming, your mind doesn't react the same way and the act loses its flavor."

"So, why not try something else more adventurous?" Federoth asked.

"I did, but afterwards every sexual act performed on my person by a female did nothing to arouse my...awareness, so to speak."

"So, what did you do, give up on sex totally?"

"Oh no," Rudecor laughed, "our male servants can be just as deviant in those arts."

"Uh, sorry, my friend, but I would rather not talk about that aspect of erotic affairs," Federoth said, wishing he had never heard the idea.

"Suit yourself, but I have a feeling you will be drawn into yet more pleasurable acts; Eñala has a rather large repertoire to choose from. You will be dead before you can experience them all."

"We shall see!" Federoth grinned.

Rudecor stripped off a few shards of the seared meat situated in the middle of the rather large dining table and treated himself and his friend to another round of the green florescent Ghegnas blood. He studied Federoth's character and noticed his friend sat very quiet and staring into nothingness, preoccupied with some other thoughts, perhaps the failed assault.

"So," Rudecor spoke up, gulped more of his drink, and continued, "what happened back there?"

"That is a good question," Federoth replied.

"Did you notice anything out of the ordinary, something unusual or strange?"

"Well, yeah, the activity of the probes has my mind stumped. Why would they act that way? Do you think it was the water?"

"I don't think so," Rudecor answered, tearing off more meat. "If the water did damage the probes, then why did it take so long? Didn't you state earlier that this happened well after the attack had taken place?"

"Yeah, and we were winning, too. We nearly had the underwater city secure. Of course, there were plenty of enemy creatures left to destroy and we were working on that, but then the probes just stopped, all of them, and then they came towards the ship. I don't understand it."

"Did you see anything strange, other than the actions of the probes, anything else at all?" asked Rudecor.

"Nothing, nothing strange at all," replied Federoth.

"I'm willing to bet that something or some *things* pushed them out of the water."

"Rudecor, if something had pushed them out of the water then we would have seen it."

"Not if they were invisible, my friend."

"Just what are you saying?" Federoth glared at his friend.

"If something threw them out of the water, then the probes would have been able to stop on their own. But, if something pushed them out, and were invisible, then you would never know. Perhaps there is another force at work there aiding the Nylantians that you are unaware of."

"And what force would that be? What other force is there with the power of invisibility that could—" Federoth stopped himself. "That's impossible," he murmured.

"What is?" asked Rudecor.

"There is only one creature I know of who could perform that feat, one who is well versed in the art of deception, and the expert use of the ruse."

"And who would that be, besides the Nogzakhs themselves?" Rudecor's curiosity peaked. Before Federoth answered, he himself disappeared right in front of his friend.

"Cavanonians," the invisible Federoth shockingly said. After reappearing, he continued to explain his assumptions. "I can't believe I forgot about them."

"Wait a minute," Rudecor shook his head, "they were all killed during the war, we left none alive, and so there is no possible way for it to be them. It has to be someone else."

"But, who?" asked Federoth. He rose up and began to pace the floor, analyzing the facts. "He is alive," he whispered to himself.

"What was that?"

"He's alive!" Federoth repeated his answer louder this time.

"Who is alive, who are you talking about?" Rudecor was thoroughly confused at this point.

"My enemy, Adoné, the *King of Cavanon*, that's who."

"He can't be alive, Federoth, because you said you saw him last in Othragon's chambers. You saw him pinned to the ceiling with webbing. If he is alive, then how did he escape before the planet exploded?"

"I don't know how he did it, but he must have," Federoth said, chuckling internally and forgetting his friend's presence. A moment later, he began talking to himself.

"I remember a story long ago about a king of the Cavanonians who had the ability to escape out of nearly any situation. He could do miraculous feats in defiance to the laws of nature. Of course we do that now, but anyway..." Federoth turned to his friend and stared at him. "Do you realize what this means?"

"No," Rudecor answered, "and I've no idea what you were talking to yourself about either."

"It makes perfect sense." Federoth went and sat down next to his friend. "Back on Earth, Adoné had friends in the oceans that helped to destroy some of my forces, and they attacked from the waters. Somehow, when they relocated back to Cavanon, the must have placed these creatures on Nylantia again, and that means that the King must be living there with them. It's a place for him to hide, knowing that his planet is in pieces, he could never survive on the rocks of Cavanon, such as it is."

"So how did he *survive*, Federoth?"

"He must have either escaped from Othragon at the last minute, or learned to use his unlimited power given to him by the Crown. If he did that, then his body would have died in the explosion, and that means he would have infiltrated another form, another body in order to come back. But, if he did that, then in what body is he now?"

"Federoth, my friend, you are spouting gibberish. There's no way a creature could do that."

"Not just any creature, but the King with unlimited power could easily distort and twist the natural elements to best suit his purpose. He has the ability to assume control of any creature, though it is not his natural habit to take a life just to reanimate himself, which would be against Cavanonian law."

"Well, if this is indeed true, then you know where he is, and that means you can go and destroy him when your ship is repaired."

"Yes," Federoth smiled, "but until the ship is ready, I must plan my attack. If he *is* there, then he will be expecting us, and I must pull out all my best tricks to deceive *him*."

Federoth now had an appetite and began to dig into the main course that sat in the middle of the dining table. As he stuffed his face with meat and tore of a huge chunk of flesh and bone to gnaw on, one of Rudecor's guards came in and made a startling announcement.

"You're Excellency," the guard kneeled and said.

"Yes, what is it?" Rudecor replied.

"Our sentry ships have encountered a strange craft entering into the atmosphere."

"Where is it now?"

"Our sentry ships have seized it and are enroute to the main city hangars now."

"Excellent," Rudecor said, rising up out of his chair. "Come, my friend, let us see what we have captured."

As Federoth and Rudecor approached the outer hangar doors, the sentry ships descended and slowly lowered the captured craft to the ground, off to the side. Once on the ground, the sentry ships resumed their normal flight pattern high above the city.

The two leaders walked over to the craft and stood puzzled, attempting to discern the outer markings and scars scratched deep into the hull. The glass appeared black and smoky, as if burned by a fire. One of the guards that accompanied the two leaders pressed a depressed switch and the hatch immediately opened upwards. Thick clouds of black smoke billowed out from inside of the ship, and the two leaders waved their hands in the air as if to aid its dissipation. The inside of the cockpit had been badly damaged by the fire and in the pilot seat sat a charred body of some form. In his lap lay a sword, plain, ordinary, and burned as well. Federoth reached in a grabbed the sword with his right hand, and held it up to his face.

"Hmm, this is unusual," he said. "...yet it looks very peculiar."

"You've seen this sword before?" asked Rudecor.

"No, but it does look strangely—" His words abruptly stopped as the sword miraculously caught fire in his hand. "What the—" Federoth pulled the sword away from his face, "I don't believe it, it can't be, it is, *it is!*"

"It is what, Federoth?" Rudecor jerked away from his friend, "what is it?"

"It's the Crown!"

"Oh you've got to be joking; surely a thing of that nature cannot simply turn up so easily."

"Well take a look at this poor sap," Federoth pointed to the charred body inside the craft. "He obviously succeeded in stealing it away from the King and he has paid the price for his theft."

"So, why aren't you on fire? If this is the sword, and you have stated that only a ruling Cavanonian can hold it, how it is that you are able to wield it in your hand without the same punishment?"

Federoth studied the sword intently, gazing at its splendor and magnificence. "That is simple," he replied. "The Sword of Fire must have an owner, as stated by the Cavanonian forefathers long ago. I can wield it, Rudecor, because I *am* Cavanonian. And now it seems that I am the last of my kind, for if I were not, then the sword would have destroyed me already."

All the others who stood around him gazed at the crown in amazement. This was reason to celebrate, and they would have such a celebration to attend to.

Nosrévis' ship landed a few kilometers outside of Nomaseri capital of Edoratis. Once grounded, a reception party escorted the senior occupants of the ship to the capital city. Nosrévis had been here before, but not to the city itself. The closest he came to this area was when he exited Dissention 7 just after his body had finished the transformation process. Of course, at that time, he was on another mission and did not concern himself with other matters; the matter of locating the enemy was uppermost in his mind and that was all he could think about.

From the upper balcony of the main palace pyramid, Federoth and Rudecor viewed guests arriving from the back way of the city. The main avenues through the city were jammed packed with forces of Nomaseri warriors in sort of a modular demonstration to the hierarchy of their latest capabilities. During these demonstrations, the population, who were also part of the planets armed forces, was privileged to a live display of current technological advances in spacecraft designs, armor, and weaponry. While Rudecor and Federoth watched from above, Nosrévis made his way up to the platform where the official party observed the demonstrations. Nosrévis wore a fashionably colored blood red robe heavily adorned with golden threaded emblems of his inner God; the material was unlike anything he had worn before. While on route for the Nomaseri system, the spirit inside Nosrévis instructed him on the fabrication of an outer garment that would suit his aura and signify his status and importance. As his evil creation came closer, Federoth became a little nervous and perspired a bit.

"Ah, Nosrévis," Federoth greeted him, "and what is it exactly that brings you here?"

"It's good to see you, too, my Lord," Federoth's evil agent replied, raising an eyebrow to his lord's question. "I came to aid you in your search for the crown."

"Oh," Federoth hastily replied, "well, we obviously haven't found it yet and we've searched a majority of the surrounding systems from Earth to Cavanon. We haven't found a sign of it anywhere."

The sweat poured out of Federoth more and more as his mind continued to fight the urge to reveal what he did find in the captured ship. Knowing that Nosrévis possessed the same telepathy characteristic, Federoth kept his thoughts at bay and did not let on his little secret seep into his conscious thoughts.

"You are intimidated by my attire," Nosrévis said as he walked over to the edge of the balcony and glanced to the multitude below.

"Yes, that is *precisely* what I was thinking," Federoth lied. "Where did you get such unusual clothing? It is as if you were born to wear it."

"In fact, I *was* born to wear clothes such as these, and I received…inspiration as to its design and fabrication." Nosrévis paused and changed the subject. "I noticed that your ship has sustained some minor damages, should I be concerned with whatever did that to your ship?"

"I had discovered the aquatic creatures that used to live on Earth," Federoth answered. "They were once allied to the enemy and their resistance against our attack was unexpected."

"Then they must be dealt with."

"Yes, but in due time," Federoth slightly waved his hand in a downward motion. "You see, they are trapped on their watery planet and cannot live outside of their aquatic atmosphere. They are isolated and will remain there, permanently."

"I should think that a fortress cruiser would be able to wipe them all out with one swift blast of energy, why didn't you do that?"

"We didn't have time. We sent probes into the planet and they malfunctioned, returned to the ship armed, and exploded when they arrived."

"Sounds pretty unusual to me," Nosrévis answered, leaning over the balcony railing. "Umm, prior to this, did you seek out the sword on Cavanon?"

"No need," Federoth replied, "Cavanon itself has been destroyed."

"It was camouflaged before, quite brilliantly, therefore, it could have easily fooled even the best of us."

"Yes, but this time it was no camouflage. The system had sustained massive damage from an asteroid; the remnants of the system exist now only as fragments of the planet."

"And you saw this, first hand?" Nosrévis glanced at his lord from his peripheral vision.

"Of course," Federoth sounded sure. "We saw the planet after it had been torn apart, as if it had happened only moments prior to our arrival. The planet fragments still glowed from the fires and devastated energy of the core crystals."

"It just seems rather odd to me that the entire system would suffer total destruction that way."

"What is odd about it, Nosrévis?" Federoth asked and turned to him. "It is only befitting that the entire system be destroyed since the Cavanonians are no more. What better way for the Gods to erase the useless bastards from history, *completely*. It is as if the remaining embarrassment of the Gods did not exist at all."

"Except for us," Nosrévis pointed out.

"Yes, but we are of different circumstances, my friend. The Gods have favored us as we have come out supreme in the fight of the two great races. It was wise for us to unite with the lineage of Ellononis."

Nosrévis kept his immediate thoughts hidden. The blasphemous tone in Federoth's voice gave instant rise to Nosrévis' hatred. To brand Ellononis' name on Federoth's pithy goals was an insult that his evil agent would not tolerate for long. The keeper of Ellononis' spirit knew that he must put up with Federoth's attitude until the Sword of Cavanon emerged from its elusive state. After that, Federoth would just be in the way. Despite his self-conceited attitude, Federoth did provide some amusement for him, although Nosrévis knew the real story. Calculated intimidation regularly entered Nosrévis' thought process.

During a long uncomfortable silence, Federoth stared up in the heavens at a nearby system that revealed its distinctive features. Close, conveniently located, and bright, this system appeared large in the daytime sky. Glowing of gold and patches of blue waters and green landmasses, this planet looked inviting as it occupied half of the visible sky.

"Rudecor," Federoth said to his friend, "what is that system up there?"

Rudecor looked to the area where his friend pointed and smiled, "oh, that is the Celceloris system. Beautiful, isn't it?"

"Yes, very. Is it occupied by anyone?"

"No, that is our very large moon; it orbits our planet on a weekly basis."

"I would like to see it," Federoth said, staring.

"If you are thinking of inhabiting the system, you are welcome to it. We've too much space on our own planet to even think of inhabiting another."

"I have an idea to relocate my forces there," said Federoth as he scratched his chin and thought.

"Which ones?" Nosrévis asked.

"My forces on Samajap and Tiracus," replied his lord.

"That might take a while to complete. What will you do if we encounter any enemy during the relocation?"

"We have enough forces here on Nomaseri to take care of that," Rudecor spoke up. "Besides, anyone who even thinks of trying to take out both systems will be in for a big surprise."

"With the two systems so close, no one would dare oppose us. The combined might alone would be more than any force could handle."

"I hope you aren't seriously considering that I move my forces there as well," Nosrévis turned and commented.

"Not at all," Federoth smiled. "Your forces have a secure grip in your region and there you will continue to operate in that capacity. There is no need to relocate everyone, just those back at home. Who knows, they might even enjoy the chance of living outdoors for a change."

"You'll also be happy to know that there are already a few bases established on Celceloris. They are much the same construction as these on Nomaseri, but they are ready for habitation."

"That will do nicely."

Federoth and Nosrévis entered back into the main palace and made their way out towards Dissention Seven. Once there, Federoth entered inside and proceeded to his quarters. There he pressed a few buttons and within seconds a transmission with Delushan on Samajap.

"Yes, Commander," Delushan said in his usual disinterested tone of voice, "what is it?"

"Delushan," Federoth replied, "I have good news for our fleet and the Nogzakhs."

"What is this good news, Commander?"

"You are to evacuate Samajap and Tiracus and relocate out forces to the Celceloris System at once."

"What?" Delushan asked. "Did I hear you right, Commander; you want us to relocate all of our forces there?"

"You heard right," Federoth said, smartly. "Take a look at the surface scans I am sending you. They are totally opposite of that lifeless void we currently inhabit. From this new system, we will be within striking range of a large majority of the systems in this vicinity. Send the fortress cruisers ahead first full of troops and equipment. They will anchor deep into the planet on all sides so they can establish bases as soon as the ships arrive. I imagine all of our forces will relish the idea of breathable air without the need for gravity equipment."

"I will brief the commanders here on your orders," Delushan said, looking over the images of the surface of the new planet. "But, know this, Commander, not every creature will leave this planet, especially not the ones who have been here the longest. They have grown too attached to it."

"Be that as it may, I want as many of our forces on their way here within the next few weeks. Leave those who wish to remain behind, they may yet decide to move once we've sent back proof of new life."

"As you wish," Delushan signed off.

"Well, there you have it," Federoth prided himself. "They are preparing themselves for relocation. In the meantime, we should check it out ourselves and claim which of the pyramid complexes there is the largest. I for one could use my own palace; you can have a guest room, if you like."

"I feel so honored," Nosrévis sarcastically replied.

Not long after issuing orders to the Dominion Command, Federoth and Nosrévis, together with their Nomaseri escort, boarded a small transport and headed off to see their new home base. The flight would not take them very long, maybe an hours worth of travel, but nothing to over bearing or taxing on their system. While in flight, Federoth knew it would not take his forces very long to vacate Samajap and Tiracus since most of the fleet were out scouring other systems in other parts of the galaxy. With the new orders already in their ships computer mainframes, plotting a course would require no difficulty at all. The remaining forces on the outdated and lifeless planets would see to securing the most valuable equipment and resources, and then transport them to Celceloris within a few weeks.

Irol did not have any plans of evacuating the premises, as this had been his home planet for centuries, even before Federoth came about. During the course of his habitation, Irol learned to see the inner beauty of the planet and relish the peace and quiet that abounded in the zero gravity atmospheres. Samajap would not be totally abandoned, Federoth did give orders that anyone who wished to remain could do so. Eventually, they might see that life on another more resourceful planet would be to their benefit. If not, then it would be there loss and not of any great concern to Federoth.

The surface of Celceloris resembled much of Nomaseri and Earth, and in some respects, it even resembled Cavanon in such beauty and magnificence. Not that Federoth showed any appreciation for the Cavanonian countryside, he more or less paid attention to the natural resources the planet had to offer. Anything past that was a bonus.

Spacious yellow and gold plateaus, vast dark green forest regions, high altitude purple mountains, and ranges adorned the surface of the planet, all equally surrounded with sparkling silver streams, incredible cascading waterfalls, and enormous blue oceans. The plentiful water sources meant that they did not need to drill for it, and basing the fortress cruisers in strategic locations would preclude having to install extensive pipelines.

As Rudecor mentioned earlier, palace pyramids were built here long ago in the event a catastrophic occurrence were to fall on the Nomaseri system. Since they did not feel this would ever come about, and since they had never experienced anything of that nature yet, the great steel structures would provide suitable refuge for these Dominion occupants. The marvelous Nomaseri construction techniques certainly dominated the housing market of the future. With such use of steel and stone materials, the Nomaseri prided themselves with the inexplicable knowledge in the fabrication of these immense pyramids.

There were only twelve pyramid structures on Celceloris: one palace complex, four fighter hangars, and eight general population compounds. With these structures and the fortress cruisers (capable of morphing into huge Labyrinth bases), there would be no shortage of housing areas for the Nogzakhs or their other secretive force of assassins, the Gadnoc. Even though they made their presence known on only two occasions, they would return in full force once they acclimatized themselves to this new environment.

Once before, on Earth, the Gadnoc secretly ventured out onto the planets surface to eliminate any enemy opposition. Unfortunately, for the Gadnoc, they were not as successful as their reputation led others to believe. They discovered this through the failure to recapture the escaped humans, Adoné and Zérnoda, formerly John Rykus and his daughter Sarah. Months after their escape, the Gadnoc searched and found them again, but lost them to another race of beings also secreted away from Gadnoc and Nogzakh sight. This unanticipated aid helped them to become more than the mere humans they started out as and gave the new *Cavanonians* the ability to elude and evade the enemy, further preventing the Gadnoc from capturing what the Nogzakhs considered a prophetic return of their ultimate enemy, Cavanon. This prophecy had been kept confidential from

Federoth as others in the Dominion had other plans should they in fact find the enemy. Instead, Adoné had become their number one target; if they found him, they would find the Crown. But, through their actions and perseverance, the new Cavanonians did more than just become a pain in the Dominions ass. With the obliteration of Muidiri, the Dominion realized they were dealing with more than just a capable enemy. This being put up quite a resistance and dealt more blows than the Dominion hierarchy, and Federoth, envisioned.

Now, Federoth knew inside that his enemy must have perished since the Dominion Commander had the fire sword in his possession, obviously hidden away from anyone's sight. He would not tell a soul of this or reveal its location to any until the inevitable day came, which would arrive in just less than a year's time.

Federoth and his party entered into the main palace and immediately organized the chambers inside. The Commander himself would occupy the upper level himself, no doubt to show his supremacy over the others in the Dominion. Slagis took the level below that and Nosrévis, not really wishing to have a permanent residence here, took a spacious guest room as Federoth mentioned earlier on in the day. The sinister keeper of Ellononis did not appreciate the motif of the palace complex, but instead preferred his hellish mountain paradise in his own version of hell on Elaveshan. In his mind, the Creator would prefer the violent volcanic atmosphere of Elaveshan compared to this already domesticated planet. Such scenes of beauty and magnificence would be erased when the time came for Ellononis to return, and then he would brandish these systems with his own version of disarray and chaos.

Out on the balcony, high above the other steel pyramid complexes, Federoth greatly admired the sights that surrounded this region. To his far left, an ocean existed with cloud formations high above ready to drop their rains over the lands. To his right, a great mountain range traveled from behind the local area to the distant horizon. In addition, ten miles or so to his immediate front, he viewed the largest canyon he had ever seen. The other side was not visible, even from this height, the enormousness of the expanse must have occupied hundreds of miles of territory. The only way to ascertain the actual dimensions of this great canyon would be to map out the entire planet and provide holographic images of the analyzed topography. Those operations would be taken care of once the first few squadrons of ships arrived, the Nogzakhs would have a great time with all there was to be done.

With nothing more to do now but rest and relax, Federoth curiously looked about his upper chambers and discovered many fascinating areas of secrecy. One in particular would suffice as a new home for his Fire Sword, which could be secured within the central pillar of his main room. There, the sword would be kept away from prying eyes and Federoth would not have to worry about its detection on his person. He felt that if he did not have it on his person, namely hidden inside his body, as Cavanonians were prone to do, then the possibility of someone finding its presence in his mind would be erased. All Cavanonians had the ability to secret their weapons inside their bodies by absorbing them completely. This is the main reason of why the Sword of Fire has remained so elusive throughout the millenniums.

Several days later, a few of ships that had finished the search in their respective target areas arrived outside of the palace complex, now formerly named Dnajdun (pronounced Na-june). After landing very near the outer pyramid structures, some of their ships contents—the Nogzakh white machines, aerial flyers, various communications equipment, and such—were off loaded. However, the most important item extrapolated from the ship was its time machine. Inside one of the four fighter housings, the lowest level of the structure had been converted into a processing plant for importing, processing, and storage of food specimens. By isolating this structure from the others, they now had a central facility where processed food, namely imported humans and other alien life forms, could be transported throughout the city. Refrigeration systems were also installed but would not be widely used as the Nogzakhs and others of the Dominion preferred their food freshly killed and dripping of its natural fluids. Federoth relished the idea of hearing the screams of their unwilling victims in the air and the eerie echoes as they rose up to his chambers. In his mind, that was all this city needed, the peace and quiet would soon be gone and they could once again feel right at home, *above* ground level.

Alone in his chambers, Federoth removed his hooded black robe and placed it on a nearby table. While removing his shirt, he thought about the possibility of sleeping for a few hours; a nice rest would do him some good and replenish his energy. The day seemed long and dragged on longer than a day should have. He did not know yet that this new system had a full forty-two hours of daylight. This system rotated on its axis much slower than other systems and that meant he would have to adjust his sleep habits, slightly.

Federoth showered in a room filled with the natural underground water piped in through interconnected steel tubes that ran throughout the palace pyramid. The entire room was the shower and the floor drained the grimy leftover residue and processed it through the water treatment facility incorporated in the foundation. This meant he did not have to worry about cleaning up after himself. However, one creature would see to this task, not as a burden, but as payment for services rendered.

After drying off, Federoth stood naked by his bed preparing to flop down for some badly needed shuteye. Unbeknownst to him, that wouldn't happen right away, and not in the way he thought it would either.

"Ah, I see you are ready for me," said the sultry voice of Eñala.

"What?" he turned and asked in surprise, "how did you get here?"

She winked her left eye and sashayed across the floor towards him, seductively.

"You did not expect me so follow you?" she asked, "Obviously, you do not remember our leader's instructions that I am to be yours for the duration of your stay."

"That was the last time I visited, and that duration is over."

"But, I am eager for a continuation of my services...unless you are too tired to play?"

Federoth could not resist the mesmerizing look in her eyes and soon found his senses giving up on resistance. "So, what do you have in mind?"

"I thought I would give you a hug and envelope you in my love," she said innocently.

"That's it?" he asked, "that's all you want?"

"Yes, and afterwards your passions and abilities will escape you."

"Oh, really," he chuckled, "very well, envelope me then."

Federoth had totally forgotten Rudecor's words of warning when it came to Nomaseri women. They are innocent on the outside, but their passions and violent nature retained within unleash whenever their sexual deviance is aroused.

Eñala wrapped her arms around her prey and gave him a huge passionate kiss, tenderly at first, yet growing in intensity. Federoth actually let his guard down as he felt the heat from her velvet skinned body through his hands as they caressed her engorged breasts. The rough palpitations of his hands only heightened Eñala's desires and elevated them beyond the level of control. From out of her back, her concealed tentacle appendages surrounded his body and forcefully entered into his back, pounding into his spine to weaken the intended victim. Ten to twelve of these tentacles pulled his body into hers and completely surrounded the two of them. With her mouth widening and elongating over his entire face, Federoth was now paralyzed to do anything about it. It seems that Eñala knew that to weaken his defenses, she must penetrate his spinal cord and apply her own method of anesthesia.

Down below in his guest room, Nosrévis heard a blood-curdling scream, loud and sadistic in nature, and it did not emanate from a *female* either. After hearing this, he raced up to see what the commotion was about, after all, if something sinister went on above him, he would not want to miss this!

Federoth's chamber doors were unlocked and they opened up rather easily with a slight push. As Nosrévis entered in, he could hear moans and muffled sounds of exasperation, drowned and gurgled. He searched about the grand chambers and concluded that the sounds must have come from the back room. As he entered in, he jerked back a bit from the sudden shock of the view on the floor.

"What the fuck is that?" he exclaimed.

On the floor, surrounded in gooey green and red liquid, a rather large yellowish-green membrane wriggled and twitched. Nosrévis could see Federoth's legs sticking out from underneath and the membranous cocoon totally engulfed his head up to the base of his neck. Nervous twitching caused Federoth's feet to jump about underneath the creature, perhaps trying to escape. Nosrévis walked over and crouched down next to the thing, poking it with his right hand.

"Federoth," he said, "what the hell have you gotten yourself into this time, literally?"

After a few more repeated annoying pokes of his fingers, the creature let him know that the action was unnecessary.

"Be gone at once, I am not finished with him yet!" Eñala's voice shouted back.

"Far be it from me to stop my lord from having a good time, but if you intend to kill him, will we have a problem."

Eñala's head formed from out of the membranous creature and hissed at him, spitting saliva, and blood in his direction. "Fool!" she shouted, "he will be around in a few days, but you cannot have him until I am finished with him."

"Hey," he laughed, "knock yourself out then!"

Nosrévis did not have time for this anyway. Prior to hearing the screams, he had contacted a Nogzakh below and ordered some carryout. Just after returning to his own guest quarters, a couple of Nogzakhs came in with the food requested: two human females, feisty and very frightened. The sinister being stood up and went to the two hysterical humans and snapped his fingers, instantly freezing their bodies and emotions.

"Oh don't worry ladies," he said calmly and politely, "after tonight, you will not feel a thing...*ever*!"

Chapter 20

Into the Unknown

After Adoné had rescued his Queen from the clutches of her first ex-husband, they returned to Royal Mountain to resume their lives, peacefully. This little scenario had taken its toll on Xashsa's pride and her husband sensed it, despite the assurance given to her. He knew she did not harbor feelings for any other, which was evident. Her feelings of guilt came once again from betrayal, but not from another love, this time it came from lowering her guard. Adoné knew the Queen possessed one of the most potent creatures in the Cavanonian race and she could let loose a torment that could decimate an enemy once unleashed. The Queen rarely ever used it and her husband thought that perhaps this reason was the basis of her guilt. She possessed a trusting soul and since they did not perceive a traitor in their midst she had no reason to distrust anyone. Unfortunately that would bring about a change in her character, one that Adoné would have to deal with. Aside from this predicament, they arrived at home to another startling drama.

Zérnoda and Laura stood by the main entrance with Sarah, who had recently emerged from the transformation chamber, but Kayla was not there. The three Cavanon women awaited the arrival of the majestic couple so that they could inform them of the events that took place prior to their return. There was a new dilemma to report; one that resulted from a slight mishap with Kayla, but no one knew that a problem had surfaced. Everyone expected the transformation to go smoothly as it had for the others who engaged in the process.

After talking with Zérnoda, Laura, and Sarah, the majestic couple went down into the transformation chambers. There, lying on a seven by four foot stone slab, Kayla lay motionless, stagnant, and decaying. Her skin had contracted and shrunk onto the bones, legs and arms were deformed and twisted, and everything appeared to have sunken inward into and through the very middle of the slab. The stench of rank death lingered in the air erasing the sweet aromatic ambience created earlier by Laura. No one could say what happened here. Adoné had to find out, not only for Kayla's sake, but also for any others who may consider this way of life. This was the first time anything of the transformation process had gone wrong; six out of seven wasn't bad, but Adoné wanted a perfect record. These brave souls placed their trust and confidence in the majestic couple's assurance that all would turn out well, and Adoné did not want to ruin the name he and Xashsa had worked so hard to maintain. As they both knew, trust was a hard thing to come by these days, evident in the latest bout of trouble with Lazasar. Still, they did not want to risk a blemish on their name.

"Xashsa, what do you think happened?" her husband asked, as he approached the slab, glancing at the degenerated carcass that used to be Kayla.

"I'm not sure," she replied. "I've never seen this happen before."

"Was there something wrong with the potion?" asked Laura.

"If there was something wrong with it, then it would have done the same thing to you, Zérnoda, and Sarah when you went through this." Adoné commented while running his hands inches above the remains. He attempted to ascertain whether her spirit still existed within the shriveled up mess, but he felt no such entity. "Something else had to have happened. From the looks of things, something appears to have pulled her down into some unknown void; everything has been sucked inward towards the middle of the stone."

"*That is correct, Father,*" said an unusual yet familiar voice.

"How do you know that?" Adoné asked, looking over at Laura and Zérnoda.

"We didn't say anything," his daughters commented.

"Nor did I," Xashsa added, staring back at her husband, the glancing about the room.

"Well, if no one said anything, then who answered?"

The air about the chambers became cold and calm and an eerie mystical smoke began to form in the air on the opposite side of the slab. As all in the chambers looked to one another for answers, Adoné glanced at the far wall on the other side of Kayla's remains and witnessed a sight they never imagined they would see.

There, in front of the living, the spirits of their once devoted servants singularly emerged out of the wall. Jasmine, Leila, Sharizar, Ariel, and finally....Aurora had appeared. Faint, mystical, and very surreal.

"*It was we who answered you, Father,*" said the spirit of Aurora.

"Aurora!" Adoné said in amazement, "It is good to see you again." He collected his excitement and calmed his adrenaline. "I thought that you were now living amongst the Ancestors of the past. Surely, you are secure with them?"

"*Yes, Father,*" she replied smiling, "*and the Ancestors are generous with their blessings not only for us but also for you and our growing family.*"

"I trust the Ancestral spirits are pleased with our conduct?" he asked.

"*Yes, and they are even more profound in their blessings to us after you graciously forgave the condemned who dwelt in their underground prison. The Ancestors have seen more in you than they originally perceived and that has given them the proof they require to bestow even more help in this new crisis you now face.*"

"Aurora, I mean no disrespect to the Ancestral spirits," Adoné moved closer to them, gently clutching his right hand to his chest, "but since I have become the sanctioned King of our ancient species, what more proof do they require of me? Haven't I already aspired to greatness beyond their vision?"

"*Father, even a King has much to learn,*" Aurora smiled. "*True, the tests and trials you faced in the physical realm have elevated you to greatness, and you've mastered the abilities to transfer from the physical to the ethereal as well, but you, are about to trod where your inner fears will greatly affect you.*"

"I don't understand, Aurora," he replied.

"*I will explain, Father,*" said another spirit that emerged from the ethereal realm.

"Aila!" gasped Zérnoda, Xashsa, and Laura. "Is it really you?"

"*Yes, it is, and I am alive and well for you.*" Aila went to her mother and sisters and smiled at them with beauty in her face. "*I see you have done well with your reemergence into the physical, but I have missed you, greatly.*"

"You should come back as we have," Zérnoda said to her.

"*Patience, my sweet sister,*" she replied, touching her ethereal hand to Zérnoda's face. "*Everything happens for a reason, as we will all find out in times to come. But, right now, I must get back to my instruction.*"

Turning to the King, Aila began her explanation to the King, and what she had to say would trouble him far worse than anything he had been through before.

"*Kayla has suffered through the transformation process with great pain and agony. Before her good spirit could elevate its status, the older demon inside was not willing to give up its place within her. You yourself felt this resistance after you transformed over, when your older demon tried to kill you off. However, with Kayla it is different. She cannot finish the transformation process until her spirit is released from her captors, and unfortunately, she is being held in the worst place imaginable."*

"Let me guess, she's gone through time travel and the transformation just to be kidnapped and held in…*Hell?*"

"*Not Hell itself, Father, somewhere else.*" Aila became sad and fearful for him. "*There was no easy way to tell you all of this, but you had to be told in order to mentally prepare yourself for your worst nightmares. If you should go to save a single soul who willingly entered into our race, then you not only must journey there to find her, but you must also face your relentless fears along the way.*"

"No bullshit, Aurora, will I again be powerless like the time I had to face my own personal demon?"

"*You were not powerless when you split from your old form, when the enemy devoured your physical body, or when you returned. You will have what your spirit has possessed since you became King!*"

"Great," he huffed. "Can I have help or do I need to do this alone?"

"*That, Father, is the other reason of why we are here.*"

"Well, that is a relief!"

Adoné prepared himself for a journey into the unknown. By placing himself on Laura's empty bed, Xashsa came to him and sat beside him, wondering if saying goodbye would be the right thing to do.

"No, Love, it is not the right thing to do," he answered her thoughts.

"I don't want to lose you, not again."

"I'll do my best to see that doesn't happen," he reassured her, "but I will need you to watch over me while I'm gone."

"I will see to it that nothing happens to you, and I will not be alone in that task, either."

"Then wish me luck!"

After a sensual kiss, Adoné fell back on the bed and mentally rested his body for the journey over into the unknown. What new horrors would he have to face in a strange and unknown world? What would he encounter here that required warning and what would elevate his spirit higher than it already was? The only way to answer those questions would be to find out first hand and get on with the task. With the faithful of his former house along side of him, it couldn't be that bad.

As if splitting from the physical were a common occurrence to him, Adoné lifted himself out of his body and gazed at his family through surreal eyes. Their aura shined through their bodies like a light from a brightly lit flame, beautiful and enlightening. Adoné tool solace in knowing that his wife and daughters were of pure intentions; their spirits glowed with proof of their virtue. Somehow, he knew they would overcome any obstacle the future would put in their way…no matter how difficult or trying. Even Xashsa, his love—despite her regrets of past failures—possessed more than she thought. In time, he would enlighten her spirit and erase her regret to the point that it never existed.

Standing there watching them, he felt the touch of Aila. Her hand on his arm proved to him that spirits have the power to feel as if they were in another realm of physical matter, but on a more translucent scale. One by one, Aurora and the others came and hugged their dearest Father, tightly. Even though he was not their true father, in their hearts he treated them as such and never looked down on them in any way, shape, or form. To Adoné, they were his daughters, all of them, and he cared for them all equally. By doing this, they considered *him* their father and would always refer to him as such.

Out of the same wall that Aurora and the other spirits emerged, a dark portal opened up to them, only visible to those in the spiritual realm. The immense portal must have been at least twenty feet in diameter, surrounded by the shadows of flames and vaporous hissing. The blackness within instilled doubt and fear of the unknown and gripped the King with intrigue. Even though this appeared to be nothing more than a portal to another world, it was a world that Adoné had seen only once before, but the version he experienced was only the polite version and even then he did not understand it, not fully.

One by one, they proceeded into the murky abyss. Once through the door, the darkness loomed over them and became heavy as if the weight of guilt or sorrow had taken on form. This was quite a different mood to experience, as the gateway did not reveal its sinister aura prior to entrance. On this side, Adoné began to realize the nature of the warnings given to him, and even Aurora and the others now understood the meaning of trying the king's spirit. In front of them, the portal changed into an eerie path through dimly lit tunnels of ghostly white flame, which burned from ethereal torches spaced out fifty feet or so. In the obscure distance, the tunnel appeared to have no end.

Along the tunnels, the walls came in and out of focus, blurred, and distorted, giving the illusion they were not traveling through mere solid matter. Glimpses of other areas below told Adoné they must be descending through time itself, rapidly giving him the impression that this place was not subject to the passing of time as in the physical reality of Cavanon. Here, laws changed and abated, transformed and mutated, twisted and warped. Even though this was enough to cause slight hesitation in forward movement, still, Adoné had to proceed.

At the end of the tunnel, a great area opened up in front of them. Vast unimaginable entities swirled about this enormous area and heightened their sense of fear. Energies circled above and below as they progressed over a bridge of light, clouded and mystical in appearance. Soon, Adoné began to see images of other creatures; humans, Cavanonians, those of line of Ellononis, Nogzakhs, Gadnoc, all creatures who inhabited the underworld dwelt here. Adoné and the other faithful followers behind him proceeded in awe of the spectacle that took place around them. As in the physical, these creatures were here fighting each other, as if the never-ending battle for the domination of a species continues even in the hereafter.

Adoné became lost in the sight of the battles raging in front, above, below, and on both sides of him. Suddenly, ahead of him, a spirit he recognized as Gadnoc raced towards him. White flames surrounding the spirit appeared to be raging wildly out of control, but before he could reach the King, a Cavanonian spirit, whom Adoné did not know, came to his aid and stood firm between the King and the spirituous enemy. The unearthly speed at which the two spirits struck at each other surprised even Adoné, and he watched with great admiration. Still, the looming feeling of despair filled the air and did nothing to offer hope of safe passage.

After the Cavanonian spirit defeated the Gadnoc, he turned to Adoné and quickly bowed to him, returning to his defensive stance with his back to the King.

"Forgive me, my Lord," the spirit said, *"I am Sestanon, I do not wish to disrespect, but I must protect you."*

"Sestanon, what is this place?" The King asked.

"This is the punishment of purgatory," the spirit answered, *"and there is no rest here for the wicked or those who wish to attain a greater glory."*

"Purgatory? But, this can't be purgatory, that's a place of expiation for past sins."

"This is not the same type of punishment you know of, my Lord," said the spirit, *"what you know of purgatory has to deal with exactly that, but this is a place of suffering, for those who have not fulfilled their commitment to their species. Here, we fight for honor and the graces of our God. Each race must fight for the right to ascend, and if they don't fight, then they fall."*

Adoné looked over the edge of the light bridge but did not see the fires of Hell below them. He didn't see anything down below except more and more spirits in the heat of battle.

"Hell isn't down there, my Lord, it is in another realm, the realm of chaos!"

"And when you fall, you fall into the next dimension?"

"Exactly," the spirit replied. *"Make haste, my Lord, we have to get you out of here and on your way."*

"But, where do we go from here?" Adoné asked.

"You will journey through the land of regret," said the spirit, *"and I must warn you, there are few who ever make it through to the other side."*

"Well, we have to try."

"So be it, come!"

As the faithful spirit cleared the way in front of him, the distance between them had opened, which allowed another spirit to challenge the King.

"I never thought I would see your damn face down here, what was it you called me? Ah, yes, I remember, it was…dipshit!"

"Lazasar!" Adoné shouted, *"what the hell are you—, oh never mind, I guess this is the right place for you."*

"I shall ascend to greater glory above the sentence of death you placed on my soul."

"I think you would be better off descending to your doom, dipshit!"

Lazasar swung his sword down towards the King, but Adoné moved out of the way and secured his black blade within his right hand, bracing himself as the force of the next swing met his steel. Sparks flew even in the spiritual realm, and with each crashing blow exchanged, the heat of battle had consumed even them. Behind the King, Aurora and the others with her commenced to fighting other spirits as well, each of them battling with Gadnoc, Nogzakhs, and hellions of Ellononis.

"Adoné" Aurora shouted, *"we must get clear from here or we will be delayed in our task."*

"Well, I'm kind of busy at the moment," he replied, striking Lazasar's sword again and again.

"I will see you fall from grace and into the darkness deep for your cruelty to my person," Lazasar boasted, *"witness my inner self and all its glory!"*

Instantly, Lazasar's inner demon viciously transforming his body into a two-headed snake, with wings and monstrous centipede like legs. *"Time for you to die, great King!"* Lazasar shouted and snapped at the king with enlarged jaws.

"I don't have time for this," Adoné said to himself.

Off in the distance, another portal opened up in the same fashion as before. This sight distracted the King long enough for Lazasar to snap at the king, grip the black blade in his teeth, and fling it to the other side of the abyss.

"*Defenseless, now you are finished!*" Lazasar shouted as he reared his head back for one last strike.

"*Not so fast, traitor!*" Another Cavanonian spirit came to the aid his Lord and stepped in between them both. This spirit raged with fury and swung a huge spiked hammer in Lazasar's face, causing Lazasar to soar upwards.

"*Run, my Lord, run, get to the portal!*" The spirit screamed.

"*Aurora, come on!*" Adoné shouted and bolted off towards the portal entrance, dodging other battling spirits in the way. Aurora and the others kept up their defense and swung viciously at others as they ran.

At the portal, Adoné turned to see Lazasar striking at the spirit who saved the King. His lord had to do something to repay his help, and at that moment, Adoné got a clever idea. By summoning up his energy, he threw a powerful bolt of lightening at the winged menace and shouted to the expanse in a raging voice.

LAZASAR HAS THE CROWN!

The energy he threw at his enemy turned into a fake sword of fire stuck into Lazasar's side. The entire population of wicked spirits saw this and immediately assaulted the winged menace attempting to claim the crown for their own. Lazasar screamed in a horrifying sound as the multitude struck him down repeatedly. The other Cavanonians who were on the side of the King came and stood around him, witnessing the act of thousands of wicked souls fighting each other over a mirage.

"*It seems their lust for the crown is their own undoing,*" Adoné commented. "*I thank you for your help, but we must be going.*"

"*Take us with you, my Lord,*" replied the other spirits. "*We wish to further aid you in your quest.*"

"*Can they do that?*" Adoné asked Aurora.

"*Only if you wish them to,*" she replied.

"*Hell, why not, we can use all the help we can get!*"

"*That might detract from the test of your spirit, my Lord,*" said Ariel.

"*I'm sure the Gods won't look down on me for allowing a few good souls to perform virtuous deeds along the way,*" he replied, "*besides, what else do they have to do down here?*"

All together, they proceeded through the portal into the next dimension, the one the spirit told the King about, the realm of regret. In this dark and gloomy place stood a great ancient cathedral style building, so great was it in size that the walls themselves seemed to touch the highest clouds above. A light from a bright star pierced through the overcast skies and illuminated the very center of the structure. Secured in a great emptiness, this building once stood as a grand temple to the under lords of this realm. Age and eons tore its greatness from her stature so now only the shroud of despair remained. Regrets of all past, present, and future beings were kept in here either waiting for assignment, returned for fulfilling their task to the living, or were engaged in haunting the living.

In this place, Adoné, Aurora, and the others felt the sensation of internal uselessness, feelings instilled for the failures of their lives. All of the feelings they once harbored and sought to rid themselves of were here to remind them that they never go away, they are just swept out of the path of progress. Here, there was only one way to pass and that was to come face to face with their failures.

As they walked through the threshold of the great stone hall laced with decadence and morbidity, one by one the party members began to fall victim to the voices in their minds. Whispers of fear swooshed by their heads, glimpses of fleeting spirits shot through their eyes until each one met with their regret, head on.

Adoné watched as all in his party began to fall to their knees and wail in sorrow, the agony of their failures hit them much harder than they could ever guess possible. Each spirit of the damned lay claim to their victim and induced the trauma of despondency and disappointment, as if the biggest guilt trip ever suddenly filled their heads with the vision of collapse. Adoné thought this odd, as he did not experience anything like what he saw in his followers. He stood there emotionless, puzzled, and confused.

"Aila," he said to himself, "*what does she know about regret, she is only a child!*"

He went to Aila as she knelt on the stone ground. As he turned her to him, he could see her face riddled with guilt and felt the pain of her own insignificance.

"Aila, what have you to regret? You've done nothing wrong!"

A darkened entity lashed out at him from inside her spirit, "*she is mine to torment, be off for your time is coming.*"

"*Why should she suffer torment of regrets when she has none?*" The King asked. "*What rights have you to needlessly suffer her to dread?*"

The dark entity came to him and again said, "*she is mine to torment, she has lost all hope and will fall into the deepest despair imaginable. She will never again leave this place.*"

"Well that's bullshit," Adoné replied. "You can't hold a soul simply because you want to, she has to have done something wrong before she can have true regret."

"*Ah, and you know much about regret, don't you, fool of a king,*" the entity scorned.

He revealed his true self and to Adoné's disgust, the entity took on the shape of the hated Gadnoc form to further instill hatred in the heart of the monarch.

"I suppose I can ease her pains temporarily until I have satisfied my hunger with you."

"You can do your worst on me but leave the others alone," Adoné demanded. "They have fought valiantly and have attained honorable status amongst those in the heavens. If they did harbor true regret, they would not have attained their place with the ancients."

"However, you are another matter," the entity pointed out. "You have not yet ascended unto the heavens and therefore you are prone to failure simply because of your pithy regal status."

The entity walked very slow circles around the King, pointing out the mistakes of his life along the way.

"You think you are so high and mighty, untouchable by anyone, and infallible to sin…but you have the most to lose and much to regret. Was it not you who failed to save your wife from the black fortress? Was it not your fault for turning yourself into another creature simply because you were a failure as a human? Was it not you who doomed your daughter and another to an unnatural creation as well? Did you not provide the means with which to allow your enemies to capture your beloved Queen? Did you not fail to save them in time before they were murdered? These are only a few of your faults. Your failures to provide that which a king must, security, peace, tranquility, purpose are numerous! You were charged to provide guidance and leadership, assist those in need, and afford all creatures under your rule the peace and security of protection. Yet, you did none of the things I spoke of. Instead, you have focused yourself on worldly matters such as creating armies for war, changing more creatures over from their natural creation to another, and desiring this putrid thing called "Love." What is love but a useless feeling that is the soul of all regret? Wasn't it lusts of the heart that doomed you to change into this wretched failure of a king?"

"You can't stop regret from happening, it's a natural part of living," Adoné replied. "Without regret, what would we have? There would be no backstop for failure, nothing to help us to learn from our mistakes, which is what regret is: a tool to learn by. Regret helps to remind us of our experiences and teaches us to take on the next situation with a little more grace and dignity. If all creatures sat around feeling sorry for themselves because of failure, then no one would have a life."

The entity continued to walk around the King, periodically tugging at the King's clothes as he went. As he did this, Adoné learned something and continued to speak and guide the discussion towards his benefit.

"Another thing, I do not regret anything that I have done. What has been was meant to be; otherwise, it would not have happened. Speaking of Love, have you even seen my wife? If you did then you would understand my lustful desires of what she has *rightfully given to me, freely, and with all of her heart. There is no sin in that, and if there is, well then I'm guilty as all hell."*

"Nevertheless, I shall teach you the true meaning of regret." The entity threatened.

"Fine. You teach me, but let the others go free."

"As you wish, fool of a king!"

No sooner had the entity answered; the others in his party began to feel the force of humility lift away from their spirits. Each one slowly stood up and glanced at the others, checking to see that everyone was okay. Adoné felt better knowing they were free from the despair placed on them needlessly; now to have a bit of his own fun.

"Speaking of regret," Adoné started; "*don't you regret that you've not done something better with your life? Don't you feel bad for ruining so many lives because of your failure as a spirit to help anyone? Hell, I'd feel like the lowest piece of shit in the universe if I were guilty of that, and I'm not immortal, you are!*"

"Your reverse psychology will not work on me, fool of a king," the entity laughed. "*Now I shall teach you the full measure of humility!*" The entity poked Adoné's chest to get his point across, but that did nothing to instill understanding, just piss off the King.

"Adoné, we must hurry, the portal is open!" Aurora shouted.

"*GO!*" he shouted staring at the entity, "*I've no time for you now.*"

"My Lord, hurry!" Aurora shouted again,

"Fool of a spirit," Adoné said forcefully, gritting his teeth and throwing a crashing blow to the face of regret, "*the only thing I regret now is not being able to kick the living shit out of you! If you really* were *the spirit of regret, you'd know that I'd never be able to touch you.*"

"*Adoné!*" Aurora shouted as the portal slowly began to close.

"You had better not be here when I come back through!"

Swiftly, the King dashed to the portal, jumping through at the last second before the portal sealed up.

"*Whew, that was close,*" Aila said breathing a sigh of relief.

"Everyone alright," Adoné said.

"I think so," Aurora answered, "*we'd better get moving, my Lord, we must still find Kayla's spirit.*"

"Where are we now, anybody know?" Adoné asked looking around a dimly lit red tunnel.

"We are at the entrance to the Cavern of Fire," Sestanon replied.

"Oh, great," sighed the King, "*this just keeps getting better.*"

"It would be wise to be on our guard, my Lord," Sestanon warned. *"There are spirits here that do not sleep and have no will but the will of the great lord himself."*

"You mean, Satan?" Adoné asked.

"Oh, no, Satan is way above this one, but he is just as despicable."

"Great, I can't wait to meet him," Adoné's sarcastic voice came out, trying to hide the concern and worry for himself and the others.

On the path ahead, red glowing embers dimly lit the way through a narrow tunnel arched over with cobwebs and ash. Through the murky rocks and debris, those in front could see an opening, an area that emptied out onto a large cobble stoned floor with pillars to support an impressive upper stone roof. Out on the stone floor, the area to their front opened up into an enormous cave, with walls that shot up to the dark clouds high above the expanse. Below, rivers of molten lava flowed gradually from the left off a reservoir that collected the lava from the falls high above the expanse. That way seemed to be the way to go.

Through an estimated distance of maybe ten miles sat a great huge chair in between the lava falls. The picturesque view looked as if the lava flowed from two great glowing eyes way off in the distance. From this distance, the chair had to accommodate a being that stood an estimated two hundred feet tall. The entire area glowed reddish orange from the brimstone and fire down below and added a sinister look to the surroundings, billowing smoke all around.

Out on the leveled off floor, Adoné stood puzzled at this sight, wondering what could be the significance of this place. What was its purpose? The area seemed deserted, but he knew better. The empty chair told him that something huge ruled this area, something greater than anything he had come up against so far.

"Let's find a way down; toward the end has to be the way to go," Adoné commented softly.

Over the far right edge of the level was an buildup of large boulders, from there they proceeded down onto somewhat level ground and view a path which turned to the left and right, eventually leading to the huge throne chair off in the distance. A ledge on both sides ran the distance of the expanse; with around forty in their party, Adoné split them up into two squads, one to the right, and the other to the left, he himself took the lone path in the center. The area was absent of activity aside from the constant flow of lava, which continued to flow menacingly fast underfoot.

After moving forward the entire length of the expanse, Adoné came within a few hundred feet of the colossal throne and gazed at its grand height of at least fifteen or sixteen stories. The dominating scene above the chair gave Adoné chills in his spine; lava flowed from slanted eyes and plummeted to the reservoir on both sides of the throne. Together with the stench and smoke and great roaring flames, the picturesque sight warped and distorted with the heat and illuminations, and gave the Cavanonian King the immediate impression that his skills and powers would be no match for the creature that held this region in power.

Faintly at first, Adoné and the others could hear thumping sounds echoing throughout the expanse and with each moment, the sounds grew larger. The thunderous volume of these pounding sounds caused all of the visiting party to glance upward. In the sky above, they could now see the impending doom that waited as thousands of winged creatures filled the air below the dark red glowing clouds above. Their features were unascertainable at first, but after diving a considerable distance the shapes appeared in the form of winged demons with four arms, two legs, a long whipping tail, and a head with the biggest jaws seen on any creature; all of this complimented the impressive set of bat like wings that protruded from the creatures back.

The winged demons took up stations all around the area in front of and behind Adoné. On the ledges off to the sides of the expanse, other winged demons stationed themselves on both sides of the divided forces of Adoné, roaring and sneering at those who had infiltrated their hellish paradise.

Just as Adoné summed up the numbers of the opposition, the cause of the thunderous thumps descended downward and took up his seat on the ominous throne. When Adoné turned around, the menacing creature sat in his seat and directed his piercing glare at the insignificant speck that stood not more than a hundred yards from his feet.

"And what have we here, my winged warriors of doom?" The creature said in a sinisterly delightful tone. The momentous volume of its deep, deafening voice was enough to cause Adoné's spirit to shudder and quake. This clearly gave the King something to worry about since he did not know fear of this magnitude.

"Who are you to come into my house uninvited?" The ominous creature said.

"I am Adoné, the King of Cavanon, and I come to—"

The massive stomp of the creatures' huge right foot shook the ground with tremendous force and caused Adoné to fall back a bit, cutting off his answer.

"Fool!" Shouted the creature, "*I know who you are and what you represent. You are a part of an insignificant species destined for extinction. Although I know why you are here, I am curious as to what it is you hope to accomplish by coming into* my house."

"*I—*" the creature quickly cut off the king's explanation.

"*Silence!*" The echoing thunder spread throughout the area and ran the length of the expanse to the far side. "*Do not speak, impetus fool; you only insult me with the foul stench of your pitiless squeaks and squawks. I can read your mind as easily as you can think with it. You are searching for a puny soul, the soul of a human attempting to crossover as you have, and you have the tiniest hope of saving her; that will not happen.*"

"I came for her soul, it is true," Adoné quickly blurted out, "but what I can't understand is why Satan himself would want her, she is unimportant to the likes of your kind."

"Satan? Ha! You could never venture close enough to witness my father's hellish form, the mere sight of his evil alone would cause you to suffer great pains of death. I am no match for my father's wrath, but you are no match for mine, either!"

"Just give me the soul I have come for and I will be off!"

The creature laughed at his request and stood up to his full height, towering over Adoné as if he were a mere speck in size. With thunderous quakes, the ground shook violently with each step the creature took towards the king. The gigantic beast spread his wings before Adoné so that all he saw were a membranous wall of red searing flesh, with pours breathing fire themselves.

"*Such an intriguing fool you are,*" the creature said. "*You display fear like that of a youngling before a beast of prey, you shake and quiver from your own insignificance, and doubt threatens to consume you. Yet you are brash enough to request the soul of another, despite your fear.*" The creature slammed his right foot down in front of the king, and he fell back on the ground; lava rose on both sides of him as the ground cracked around him.

"*I shall never release her soul to you foolish king, but you are welcome to take it, if you can overcome your own death!*"

With an enormous ear-splitting roar, the hellions of the deep began attacking the other Cavanonian spirits on both sides of the expanse. Whipping swords met with lacerating claws and jaws filled with credulous amounts of daggered teeth, and as this went on, Adoné was in for a different sort of pain, one that he did not see coming and could never envision.

The creature summoned up Adoné's spirit into the air with his mere thoughts. Once at eye level, the creature reared his head back, roared again, and thrust his jaws forward gulping up the Kings spirit out of the air, swallowing him whole. Aurora and the others did not see this, as they were too busy fighting for their own spirits, hacking away at the threatening demons as they continued the attack.

Inside the creature, Adoné slipped and fell through the throat cavity and into the creatures' stomach. There, mixed with a different type of acid, inner demons formed out of the inner flesh and began to grab and pull Adoné as if attempting to rip him apart piece by piece. Other inner flesh demons slashed and tore the kings' spirit, violently trying to dismember not only his body, but destroy his inner will to survive. There, amidst the blood, acid, and demons, Adoné began to fall into despair. Inside, his soul began to loose hope and slowly it prepared itself for the inevitable doom that waited in the next dimension. In his eye's he saw a fleeting glimpse of his life, his accomplishments, and his family & friends. He had done so much with his life by saving others but in his last fleeting moments, he was unable to save himself. As his life force began to fade away, he saw lasting images of his family, the one regret he did harbor at this moment was not being able to say goodbye to them.

The ominous creature laughed and howled into the winds as if he had triumphed over a great adversary, and his winged demons roared with him, giving the desperate Cavanonians a moment of rest and wonder.

"*Where is the King?*" Aurora asked, "*I don't see him anywhere.*"

"*I don't know,*" Sestanon answered, "*we must find him and get out of here...this is hopeless!*"

Inside the belly of the creature, a small spark lit up in Adoné's mind, it was faint yet noticeable through the dreaded thoughts that helped to send him into oblivion. The spark formed into an image in his mind, a figure that had guided him before, a figure warmly familiar and comforting.

"*Adoné,*" a voice said.

"*Father?*" Adoné said, staring at the figure of Solisynas, Xashsa's father.

"*You are destined for greatness,*" Solisynas replied, "*as it has been foretold. Therefore, you cannot perish here. You must rise above your fears and conquer that which threatens you, your inner demon. He is trying to take you over yet you have the power to control him. Seize his strength, draw off it, and unleash your potential. Save yourself before the demon consumes you!*"

The King heard his father's words and understood them. There, in the belly of the beast, Adoné summoned up his courage and regained his strength by taking over the force of his own inner demon. While praying to the Ancestor's, he called for the Sword of Fire and began to hack away at the fleshy demons that gripped and tore his being. Blood and chunks of putrid flesh flew wildly inside the oversized organ, and after freeing himself, Adoné began to climb back up the throat of the ominous beast.

Outside, the huge demon began to cough, gag, and he gripped his throat to attempt to suppress the bile from rising up. The fierce creature shook his head savagely as Adoné climbed in his mouth. The king summoned up his internal energy and forced the mouth cavity open enough to fly out and into the air, simultaneously slashing the creatures' eyes with the fire sword. The creature's hands flew to his face, screaming in pain from the wound inflicted and the unbelievable idea of being struck by an insignificant soul.

"*I shall see you in hell for this wretched fool of a king!*" The beast shouted fiercely.

"*Not if I can help it,*" Adoné replied.

Hovering over the lava flowing rivers and hordes of demons, Adoné called upon the powers inside his spirit. By placing his hands high above his head, he would use a power that had only been used on two other occasions of the past.

"Aurora," he shouted, "*get the others to the entrance, be swift!*"

She heard his call as did the others, and immediately they flew up and away to the stone level to the tunnel entrance. The hordes of winged demons paid them no attention as they saw the king floating in the air in front of their wounded master. With anger and wrath as their guide, they lunged for the king, at precisely the same time the king released the built up energy. With one fluent motion, Adoné raced his arms downward and spread out the energy, obliterating the winged creatures and turning them into streaks of spewing gore and body parts. The force created a rippled effect that knocked the huge creature on his back, the crashing blow of his fall sent shockwaves of thunder throughout the expanse.

On the stone level, Aurora and the others with her heard the monumental blast and saw the glowing energy of Adoné's release spread out through the interior of the expanse, echoing of thunder and the shaking quake of victory. Fires erupted out of control and the lava eyes above the huge throne cracked and began crying tears of glowing fire. The ground ripped apart with enormous upheaval as the molten lava underneath shot forth and into the air, racing half the distance to the gloom clouds above.

While they watched, Aurora could see the ball of energy as it floated effortlessly and untouched toward them. Adoné set himself down on the stone flooring in front of them and glowed of anger and contempt. Sensing it was over, the mounted energy subsided and he once again became himself as he looked over his shoulder to he devastation in the distance.

"*My Lord,*" Aurora bowed, "*I thought we were done for.*"

"*As did I,*" he replied. "*However, I think I understand why this was to be, but that explanation I will save for when we return to safety. In the meantime, we must get out of here.*"

"But, we've not found Kayla's soul yet," she cried.
"Yes, we have."
Next to the King, Kayla's soul appeared and stood glowing from the residual energy of the monarch. She had been safely secured and brought back from a place they would never have guessed. At once, Adoné and all in his party raced to escape from the area and begin the trek home.

Xashsa stood her silent vigil over her husbands' body, waiting intently, yet impatiently for his return. She rose up, went over poured herself a drink, and sat beside Laura. As they gazed at the bed, the energy in the air had risen, and the room began to glow brighter and brighter. Without warning, Kayla's body began to convulse and quake; the rejuvenation of dead tissue evident through the transformation process picked up where it had been disturbed. Those in the room watched in awe at the spectacle and gasped in sheer astonishment as other lost souls of the deep emerged from out of the walls along side of Aurora and her sisters.

With their eyes on the spirits and the rush to greet them back, Xashsa did not see the King's body as it began to glow and shimmer, coupled with a smoky mist that emanated from the pours of his skin.

The glow in the room became bright, almost blinding, forcing others to cover their eyes. Adoné woke up and climbed out of Laura's bed, then went and stood over Kayla's body as the transformation process continued unabated. Xashsa ran to him and hugged him tightly, and as they gazed at each other, Aurora had to ask where the King found Kayla's soul.

"Her soul was in the belly of the beast," he said, "and as I despaired, I found her there. I thought I had spoken with my father, but he really spoke his words of hope through her spirit."

"Was this supposed to happen?" Xashsa asked.

"I'm not sure, but it did," he replied, "and I'm glad that is over with."

"Who are they?" Xashsa asked, glancing over at the other new arrivals.

"They assisted us in the deep dimensions of the underworld. I brought them back from their hopeless state and now I must reinstate them with flesh."

"My Lord," Sestanon spoke up, "you seemed to have forgotten this."

Sestanon handed the cherished black blade back to his lord, and Adoné thanked him for his gift as he secreted into his private arsenal once again.

"I knew you'd renew our race," Xashsa grinned, "but I never thought it would be like this!"

Her husband smiled and gazed back down on Kayla.

Chapter 21

Dredging the Gutter

Federoth emerged from his chambers some four days later, after Eñala's unsightly and unimaginable sexual assault, and limped slowly into his main audience chambers on the main floor of his palace. Already present were Nosrévis and Rudecor, who both sat patiently waiting to find out exactly how bad off their friend suffered. Rudecor knew that Eñala was vicious and forceful in satisfying her lustful cravings, but it seems that this new event would raise considerable questions in the mind of the Nomaseri ruler. Federoth did not appear to be the worse for wares, but his limping right leg, pale complexion and the new scars on his face told them otherwise. He would surely fall over if not for Eñala's support and aid over to a large chair adjacent to his friends.

"Damn, Federoth," Nosrévis commented, "you look like you've been through hell."

"Oh," the limping Federoth replied, "you've no idea."

"Eñala, what did you do to him?" Nosrévis asked.

"Nothing that he did not wish to be done to him," she answered.

Rudecor chuckled, folding his hands in front of his chest, "she is a veritable cornucopia of lasciviousness whose persistence surprises even me."

The Nomaseri vixen slowly assisted the drained Federoth into his chair, kindly fetching a drink for her victim while he adjusted his bearing. As he rested his back on the back of the chair, Eñala pulled up a small footstool and positioned herself on his right side. Her normal everyday apparel barely covered any of her private areas and attracted Nosrévis' eye, but only for a moment. Eñala felt the dance of his eyes on her lightly scented green skin and sneered in his direction.

"My wares will only be to his benefit and for his satisfaction," she said, gently removing the hair away from Federoth's eyes.

"Benefit?" asked Nosrévis. "I have no such appetites for the likes of you. Besides, I have already had my fill of sex and food, and I assure you my methods are not as...*affectionate* as yours."

"Nevertheless, I am his possession."

Sensing that the others did not require her presence at this time, the Nomaseri lass stood up and graciously walked away to tend to the mess she left in the upper chambers. Nosrévis knew where she was going and thoughtfully added a few additional comments.

"While your up there, you should stop by my guest room and see how nicely decorated it is."

"You clean your own quarters, evil one," she scoffed.

Nosrévis chuckled to himself as he read her mind; his words gave her something to think about and she would look anyway just to satisfy her curiosity.

"I must admit, my friend," Rudecor said, "I did not think you would be incapacitated for this long."

"To tell you the truth," the sore Federoth replied, "I had no idea what to expect, and I did not know I had been out for four days."

"What the hell did she do to you that caused such a condition?" the curious Nosrévis asked. "I mean, hell, even *I've* never experienced a sexual encounter that knocked me off my ass for that long."

"Honestly, I had no idea at the time," Federoth said, wearing a blank stare. "I remember her kiss and after that it was lights out." He visualized the scene just before the event, when Eñala gave him a deep and sensuous kiss. This is what she did:

After her tentacle appendages slammed into his spine, he lost all control over his functions and his body then was hers to do with as she pleased. He remembered blacking out, yet he consciously felt everything; her stimuli, the arousal, the throbbing sensation in his lower region, and her method of semen extraction. What Federoth did not see, and was not aware of, was that Eñala had reformed her body, changed her shape, and became a wriggling glob of membranous flesh that cocooned around his entire body. Within her transformed fleshy shell, hundreds of needle-sized teeth had penetrated through his skin to all of the pressure points in his system, causing immediate and total relaxation. Once she did this, her inner cells injected venom into his bloodstream, causing instant paralysis. To other creatures, moreso with humans, this would be deadly, but to a deranged Cavanonian it was the ultimate in sexual release. The visualizations of her mind focused in his eyes as the effects of the venom initiated in his veins. When that happened, he saw whatever she wanted him to see, and she viewed the entire contents of his deepest thoughts as well. She saw the fleeting moments of his ancient marriage to Queen Xashsa and how bleak her sexual prowess had been. Detesting the sight, Eñala removed that worthless memory and placed her *own* essence into his mind, subliminally programming him to love only her and remember only her pleasuring acts of gratification and satisfaction. With the residue of the injected venom absorbed into his body, his mind then became responsive to subliminal suggestion; a reaction would trigger instantly the moment she uttered a certain word, a word that only Federoth would hear. Had he known this would be the outcome of such an encounter, he would have declined the engagement. This was not the case and Eñala was well aware that he couldn't say no, and now he never would.

"Aside from the pain and fervent soreness," Federoth continued, "I've never felt more satisfied. She has unleashed something in me, something in my mind that I could not get rid of, and it's almost as if she not only cleaned out my loins, but also certain areas of my mind."

"Did I not tell you that Nomaseri women are very efficient in the sexual arts?" Rudecor said, standing over to the right at the table of drinks. "I distinctly remember telling you this."

"Yes," his friend replied, "but you did not state the extent or the methods involved."

"Well, it would have taken all the fun out of it if I did."

Soon after Nosrévis began to roll his eyes at this conversation, one of the Gadnoc mercenaries that arrived early that morning entered into the audience room and kneeled briefly. Once Federoth acknowledged the effort, he motioned for him to come forward. This Gadnoc appeared much different from his predecessors back on Earth. Trolton, as he was known, retained much of the deformed wolfen features with spiked teeth protruding erratically down past the lower lips, feral lidless eyes, grayish Mohawk hair, and doglike ears. The skin on his arms held a charred like skin texture, as did the rest of his body underneath the leather and tarnished metal plated armor. The metal laden boots made stomping sounds when taking simple steps, sounds that would give off the impression of the wearers' brute strength.

"I was wondering when you would get here, Trolton," Federoth said.

"Commander, we arrived only a short while ago," the Gadnoc replied. "Had it not been for the mere chance capture of a wayward ship, we would have been here earlier."

"Stray ship you say, from where?" Rudecor asked. "I trust it isn't one of mine."

"No, this one is has been identified as Dolumek."

"Dolumek," Rudecor replied in surprise, "then surely, it is an unmanned ship. The Dolumek do not stray very far from the surface of their planet without sufficient numbers of protection."

"This one had occupants," Trolton smiled, if he could smile through the sinister set of teeth in his face. "There are three in captivity, Commander."

"Three, how fortunate this is," Federoth said, sitting on the edge of his chair. "And where are they now, Trolton? I would very much like to see them."

"Finally," Nosrévis burst out, "someone to torture, it's about bloody time!"

"Not so fast, my evil friend, we'll let them sit in the cells and hear what their minds have to tell us. If their minds are uncooperative, then you may inject your nihilist suggestions into their cerebrums."

"I was thinking more along the lines of a blood sacrifice," the evil agent smirked.

"As was I," Rudecor stated. "Have you ever tasted Dolumek blood? It's exquisite!"

"Makes my eyes red just thinking about it," Nosrévis smiled.

There was no limit to the horror these three compiled in their collective minds. It became clear to all of them that this would eventually turn out quite messy, but then again, what were they if not without their instinctive savage tendencies. In nearly all forms of torture or information extraction, all of the victims ended up on someone's dinner palate. Federoth chose to exercise restraint before the feast. New creatures meant new forms of information and new thoughts to collect and analyze. What better way to learn of this new species than to infiltrate the minds of the prisoners without them ever knowing it.

Rudecor knew of the Dolumek, far too well. They were once at war with them long ago and would have succeeded in conquering the Dolumek system had it not been for the persistent nagging of the Kostejaanian peace negotiators. Back then, the efforts of the negotiators caused the temporary cessation of hostilities in the region, and eventually led to a full withdraw of forces. To this day, Rudecor wondered why they never went back to annihilate the Dolumek. Maybe, it had something to do with no resources to collect or consume, but Rudecor did not know what riches existed below ground level.

Outside Federoth's main pyramid palace, the streets filled with Nogzakh white death machines all in formation marching in and out of the city as if stretching their enormous metal legs. The thirty-foot tall machines appeared formidable in formation and the menacing sight caused immediate appreciation for the forces in their war arsenal. Federoth thought for a moment about the sheer awesome power contained within these machines and they would be no match for any army. Then, his mind went back to the Earth fortress he previously commanded and he remembered the devastation done to his once proud army. As the thought processed through his mind, he said to himself, "that will never happen, again!"

After the column of machines passed, Federoth and the others with him dashed across the street and followed Trolton into the sublevel basement area of the adjacent building. The dimly lit halls gave off an eerie feeling of suspense and intrigue as they passed through a myriad of walkways, doors, and security checkpoints. Security was another necessity that the Nogzakhs maintained. Even though they were the only inhabitants of this new system, there was no need to lower the standards for anyone…just in case.

After passing a checkpoint equipped with an x-ray machine, the four of them made their way into the detention level, peaking into each of the cells along the way to the cells in question. Obviously, there was no need to inspect the other cells, as they were all empty, except for three. Outside the laser barred force field, the prisoners sat against the rear walls of the respective holding area, bloodied from previous beatings that forced them into a semi-submissive state. Standing in front of each cell, Federoth, Rudecor, and Nosrévis glared at them with puffed up pride, as if they had singled handedly captured the prisoners.

Federoth and Nosrévis studied their prisoners and began to read their thoughts of hopelessness and despair. The Dolumek's immediate inner thoughts were of knowing they would never again see the light of day. The information extracted was slight at first, but Federoth attempted to dig deeper into the enemies' subconscious thoughts, knowing there had to be more than just what dwelt in the cerebrums surface. However, as he concentrated more, a sudden outburst abruptly halted his focus.

"That bastard!" shouted Nosrévis. "I can't fucking believe this!"

"Can't believe what?" Rudecor answered, Federoth turned to him as well.

"Adoné, that bastard, he lives!"

"What?" Federoth exclaimed.

He could not believe his ears and instantly, his mind was full of shock and awe for only one reason: he had a sword of fire in his possession. If the statement Nosrévis read in the Dolumek's mind were true, and a ruling Cavanonian did still exist, then how is it that Federoth can hold the sword? Did the charred body in the ship captured a while ago actually take the sword from the ruler? That would explain why the body caught fire, but then if Federoth were able to hold the sword and suffer no damage, then maybe he was in fact the *new* ruling Cavanonian. Brilliantly, he put up his on mental block before Nosrévis' wandering mind power could come across this information. Federoth smiled slightly, but still held up his act of surprise.

"How do you know our old nemesis is still alive?" Federoth asked.

"This one's mind revealed the image of my enemy, there on Dolumek," the evil agent answered. "He is there on that system and I'll bet he has been living there this whole time, secretly living out his life deep underground."

"Then that would mean your theory of his aiding the Nylantians is incorrect," remarked Rudecor.

"Perhaps, and if he is living on Dolumek, then that means we now have provocation to destroy that system and its underground occupants."

"That is quite an undertaking," Rudecor commented, "exactly how do you intend on accomplishing this feat?"

"Patience, my friend, an attack of that magnitude doesn't come up in a moment's time. For that, we must plan, organize, strategize, and prepare. Once we've done that, then destroying the system will be easy. Since the enemy is there, then that means the system also contains resources which we can collect for our own benefit."

"And all these long years I thought the Dolumek lived only on the planets surface, no wonder we couldn't take them out."

"With the might of our combined forces," Federoth spoke aloud, "we will systematically wipe them all out and claim the system for our own use."

"So why not just wipe out the entire planet with a fortress cruiser?" asked Nosrévis. "It would only require one blast of energy; wipe out the planet in one moment."

"That is quite possible, my evil creation," Federoth smiled, "but this time, I want to make sure that our enemy is dead once and for all. There will be no room for conjecture or error. Trolton," Federoth called, "have the prisoners secured in the interrogation room and instruct the Nogzakhs to prepare the serum needed to begin the process."

"Right away, Commander!"

"Don't administer anything to them yet," Nosrévis interjected, "I want them drug free, it will be more meaningful if their body functions are not interrupted."

"As you wish," Trolton bowed.

Leading the frightened prisoners into a vile chamber of horrors, two of the unwilling captives were forced onto upright steel beds, their hands and ankles bound by manacles. The last prisoner was forced into a chair and anchored onto it by shackles and chains, but one arm was left free for a purpose that would be painfully revealed in a little while. Each of the interrogators positioned themselves around the room outside of the bright light that shown down from the ceiling into the faces of the soon to be victims. Nosrévis would start the process of method extraction and produce results much sooner than expected. Although Federoth was well known for his forceful methods of torture and information withdrawal, he would see just how effective his evil creation could be. These new skills would rival Federoth's to a great degree, and become more fearful with each step.

"Since we will start with you," Nosrévis began to say, "you will now have the opportunity to tell us what we were not able to obtain from your cerebrum ourselves."

"I can tell you nothing," answered prisoner number one, "and I shall do no such thing."

Nosrévis chuckled at his answer as he went over to a nearby table filled with surgical and other objects of torture. Picking up a shiny form of cleaver, he walked over to the prisoner and stood in front of him.

"I would kill myself before I freely tell you anything of value," the resisting prisoner added.

"Very well, here, I will give you the pleasure of killing yourself by chopping off your own body parts, and do not worry about the mess, there are others who are hungry just waiting for tidbits of your carcass."

The prisoner slightly smiled as he grabbed the cleaver and held it up as if to throw it at his captor. But as he began the forward thrust of the blade, Nosrévis froze the prisoner in place with a wave of his own hand.

"Oh no," he laughed, "you said you would kill *yourself*, not me, so begin."

Sweat began to drip off the prisoners' fearful looking face and his eyes bulged from his eye sockets as his own hand, against its will, suddenly came down chopping off his own left hand. The prisoner screamed in agony as his detached hand fell onto the floor, blood flowed freely out of his severed arm squirting over the floor and slightly onto Nosrévis' boots.

"Aw," Nosrévis shirked, "look what you've done, you've stained my boots." Levitating the severed hand into his grasp, he held it up to the gasping prisoner's face.

"Now, where is the Cavanonian King now?" Nosrévis said forcefully.

"I...I don't...know," screamed the prisoner.

"Nope, wrong answer," his tormentor quickly replied. With another wave of his hand the prisoner brought the cleaver up and more forcefully cut off his right leg from the knee down. Screaming at the top of his lungs, the prisoner choked and cried in severe pain from the trauma forced on him. The other prisoners began shouting words of hatred and vile contempt at the hellish being standing over their brother.

"Ah, so you two want to play as well," Nosrévis added, "very well." He nodded his head to Rudecor and Trolton who both began beating the other prisoners almost senseless.

"You see, it would be much easier for your brothers as well to tell us what we want to know, otherwise we will be here for much longer than you care to be. Besides, you still have more appendages to lose yet."

One of the beaten prisoners spoke up, attempting to cease the horrid acts of his seated brother.

"He...he was there, at our planet," the prisoner coughed. "He was in the midst of our hangar bays inspecting the armies of our planet, he and his Queen along with our grand council."

"Ah, see Federoth," his evil creation smiled, "he is there after all."

Walking over to the upright restrained victim, he sneered into his face and proceeded with more questions.

"And why would he inspect your armies? Is it possible he is there to recruit your species in order to attack the Dominion?"

"I don't know; we only saw him for a short while. They escorted them back into the planet core, the city. We haven't seen them since."

"So, he is living in the very center of the planet," Federoth said, just above a whisper. "What an excellent place for a coward to hide where no one could find him."

"How many are there in your hidden army?" Rudecor asked.

"We have millions," coughed the other restrained prisoner. "There are too many of us for you to conquer."

"Oh I think that is an overstatement, if I do say so myself," Federoth grinned. "Where is your base entrance located?"

"It is hidden, you will never find them."

"Oops! Wrong again," Nosrévis replied. After waving his hand again, the seated prisoner swung the cleaver around and chopped off his left arm from the shoulder. The screaming prisoner cried and screamed again from the torturous pain inflicted. Trolton picked up the severed hand and arm, sniffed the limbs, and threw them across the room to other Gadnoc creatures that waited patiently for the remains of either of the prisoners.

"You're running out of limbs and I'm running out of patience," Nosrévis sighed. "What are the intentions of the King and your grand council?"

"I…I do not know that," prisoner two shouted, "we only know what we are told."

"We do not know anything," shouted prisoner number three, "we live peacefully underground, away from the sight of others. We've no intentions of any kind other than to remain secret."

"So why were you out flying in your ships?" Federoth asked. "why were you found so far away from your planet?"

"We strayed off course and were captured. We were just flying!"

"Maybe he is telling the truth?" Rudecor asked, plunging his right fist into the prisoners' stomach.

"Perhaps," Nosrévis replied, "if he is, then maybe we should let them live?" with a quick glance to Rudecor and Federoth, he made his own decision. "Nah, I think not."

Another wave of his hand caused the seated prisoner to sever his own head clean off his body. The cleaver fell to the floor as Nosrévis released the tension from the gripping hand. Afterwards, he motioned for the other shackled prisoners to face the seated Dolumek and forced their heads to watch as the other starving Gadnoc came and stood round the chair.

"You will now witness your fate and see the end of your brother first."

A quick snap of his fingers and the Gadnoc warriors began savagely ripping the retrained body into pieces, feasting on extruded organs and dismembered appendages. Others fought over the head and other dislodged bones, burying their faces into the carcass, sucking up the inner fluids while stuffing loose intestines and other bile covered organs in their mouths.

Rudecor went over to one of the upright prisoners and drove a dagger into the prisoners lower abdomen area. As the blood of the prisoner profusely poured out, Rudecor held a metal cup up to catch the life draining fluids.

"Federoth," he said, "didn't I tell you that Dolumek blood is exquisite? You simply must taste this!"

"My friend," Federoth replied, "you're doing it wrong. We Cavanonians have a rather different way of extracting the life out of any creature."

Federoth smiled as his face reformed and changed into his inner self, his inner demon. Forcefully, he drove his angular teeth deep into the chest cavity and began to suck the life out of the prison, who reeled in agony, convulsing. The frothy discharge formed around Federoth's enlarged mouth and not only did he suck out the blood and internal fluids, but opened up the cavity to extrude the inner chest organs with his internal interoperating teeth.

"That's not how you do it, boys," Nosrévis sparked up, "I'll show you how to eat fresh food!"

Standing in front of the last remaining live prisoner, Nosrévis smiled and hung his head back, staring up at the ceiling. The prisoner screamed in horror as the jaws of his killer enlarged and grew up and outward. Teeth elongated, deranged, and shined, dripping his own blood from the tips. As Nosrévis lowered his head, his eyes had changed and slanted up and down, his ears and risen above his head to a point a full foot high. With a snarling howl, Nosrévis rose up and slammed his jaws down over the head of the prisoner, snapping it clean off, remaining in place to excrete the blood shooting out from the throat and exposed arteries. The body of the prisoner convulsed and went into shock from the sudden loss of its most important part. Nosrévis slowly closed his mouth and chewed, chomped, and crushed the head in his mouth into tiny fragments of bone and brain tissue. Saliva, blood, and liquidous brain matter dripped and spewed out from between his reddened lips. Federoth and Rudecor watched as if in shock themselves, never really witnessing a spectacle such as this. After the vile creation swallowed the contents in his mouth, his facial features returned and calmed.

"Nosrévis, where did you learn to do that?" Federoth asked.

"Oh, that," he replied, "it's a little trick I learned from a dear friend inside."

"let's leave the rest of this mess to the Gadnoc," Rudecor said, "they are more hungry than we are."

"Yes, that is true, come, we must begin preparations," Federoth replied.

"Preparations for what?"

"For war, what else? We aren't just going to let the Dolumek live in peace, not while they are harboring my greatest enemy."

"So then, what is the plan?"

"We must begin preparing our forces, get them ready for launch, but first send out reconnaissance patrols and ships to surround the planet to prevent anyone else from escaping."

"Why not just destroy the planet itself, killing everyone in one blow as Nosrévis stated earlier?"

"Because," Federoth replied, "it has been eons since our forces were engaged in real combat, and they have become stagnant with no one to destroy. So, we simply let them fight and annihilate the enemy on their own. We take over the planet, destroy everything, and work our way toward the core from all sides, to further isolate the King of Cavanon so that I may destroy him, personally."

"Great, you do that," Nosrévis smiled, "I've got something else I need to see to first."

While the Gadnoc warriors finished scarfing up the remains of the prisoners, Federoth left the interrogation chambers with Rudecor and Nosrévis in tow, headed for the command center. There, the Dominion Commander issued orders to his forces to prepare for war on Dolumek. Recon ships were to be dispatched and provide overwatch on the unsuspecting system while the main body of the Dominion forces prepared themselves on Celceloris.

Chapter 22

Controlled Chaos

Outside the atmosphere of Dolumek, one squadron of Dominion ships placed themselves in orbit around the planet to provide eyes on the target sight in order to get a heads up of any obvious enemy activity below. The Dominion commanders on board would exercise patience and follow Federoth's orders to the letter; do not engage the enemy, observe and report only. From this vantage point, 3D holographic images in their ships imagery section revealed the contoured intervals of surface landmasses and possible subterranean access routes.

While the enemy above analyzed the terrain, Ulynas and his grand council deep in the city core center watched on similar consoles of the formations of enemy ships in the heavens. It was clear that the time for an impending enemy attack drew closer than they originally thought possible. The Dolumek ruler knew that he had a formidable amount of forces to do surface battle and give the enemy a good run for their money, but the fleet of dread was another matter. For this, Ulynas decided it was a good time to enlist the aid of King Adoné and his secret Cavanonian forces. Ulynas' plan was for the Cavanonians to keep the fleet busy while the Dolumek concentrated their efforts on the ground force attack.

With word of warning sent throughout the planet, all Dolumek prepared for war.

From the southern most point in the lower hemisphere, Ulynas dispatched two small fighters capable of eluding the enemy ships to Cavanon. While secretly exiting the surface, they proceeded with all haste to the allied system in hopes of reaching the required support before hostilities broke out.

On Cavanon, Adoné and Xashsa were busy tending to Sarah and Kayla, assessing their conditions from the changeover to their new creation. It was trying on the King and his party who entered into the unknown to rescue Kayla's spirit from the evil spirits unwilling to let her go. After thanking them, Aurora, Ariel and the others who came to his aid, patiently waited in the ethereal for another chance to aid their King.

While feasting on a hearty dinner, Adoné began to tell Xashsa and the others in the home of what took place on the other side. The tale he told gripped all and kept them on the edge of their seats, tales of the other side were rare, so anything brought up was instantly exciting and perilous.

From outside the royal mountain palace, Sestanon came in with two Dolumek pilots. The immediate and unprecedented arrival of these two caused all a slight degree of worry.

"My Lord," Sestanon said, bowing in respect, "these two Dolumek have come with word from their grand ruler."

"What is it?" asked Adoné.

"Our Ruler seeks your aid and assistance," replied pilot one.

"Dominion ships are orbiting our system and our ruler believes they are staging themselves for an attack," pilot two added.

"This is an unexpected move on the part of the enemy," Tanazakh stated. "Why would they go after Dolumek?"

"Because they are bent on domination and destruction," Xashsa replied.

"There is no other reason for it," Adoné added.

"They captured three of our personnel not long ago and we've not seen them since."

"Then that means they are dead already," Tanazakh said with anger rising.

"But, if they read their minds before they were killed—" Xashsa began but was cut off but her husband.

"Then that means the enemy has learned of the interior of the planet, but this doesn't add up," Adoné leaned back in his chair and thought. "There is nothing of importance on Dolumek that the enemy would want, so why attack it?"

"Unless it is like you said, they are going to destroy it just for fun."

"Possibly, but we can discern that later." Adoné rose up and motioned for Sestanon to come forward. "Go and alert the division commanders, have them meet here as soon as they can."

Sestanon did as ordered and wasted no time in exiting the premises on his mission.

I smell a plan brewing, eh?" Tanazakh smiled, "I know that whenever you get that look, something is forming in your sneaky mind."

"You got that right, my friend," Adoné replied, "and I've just the thing to do it, too. Zérnoda, go and fetch Stan and Zach for me, please."

"Yes, Father," she replied, taking of swiftly as well.

"The main thing is to see that our forces are all on the same sheet of music as far as the plan goes, we also must see to it that our forces here are on alert and ready to defend the homeland, while the rest of us are on our way to wreak havoc on an unsuspecting enemy."

"So, what's the plan then?" Tanazakh asked, "you know I'm on pins and needles here."

"Yes," Adoné replied, "but first, I want all the commanders here so that we can go over this in stages. Afterwards, we can refine it and hone it into shape. This is going to require coordinated efforts and cunning. What we will do is attempt to draw the enemy away from the main effort of the planet by pitting the enemy against…themselves."

"Ha!" Tanazakh laughed, "this *will* take some doing."

When all of the commanders arrived, they entered in and witnessed the King in the main audience room of his palace. Xashsa seated herself in her throne chair directly behind her husband and watched. The excitement in his voice and eyes of the plan brewing in his mind gave her a feeling of anticipation and heightened ecstasy, knowing he could not think of sexual matters at a time like this, but he could later.

All had gathered around a floating image of Dolumek, the illusion provided to them and the King by the Queen herself. As they watched the image rotate around in mid air, the king began to describe the plan and surrounding obstacles.

"Okay," he started, "here is a visual representation of Dolumek, and from the information provided to us by the Dolumek pilots, the enemy ships are located approximately in these locations." He pointed to the various spots around the planets outer atmosphere. "The most likely course of action for the enemy will be to land a large portion of their ships and begin a ground assault. Knowing how the enemy thinks, from personal experience, they will overwhelm the surface with ground troops, machines, and other unimaginable death contraptions."

"Do we have an accurate number of ships in their possession?" asked one commander.

"Not yet," the King replied. "Right now, I would guess that the ships presently in orbit around the planet are recon ships, to report any surface activity that the rest of their forces should be aware of prior to their arrival."

"Has the enemy begun landing troops yet?" asked Sestanon.

"Not that we are aware of," Tanazakh spoke up, "and that is probably due to the fact that the main body of their forces has not yet arrived. It would be wise to assume that once they do arrive, they will land in full strength and occupy by force."

"So what are we to do about this then," asked Kroneg, another commander.

"Simple," Adoné replied, "my plans involves two stages. One, we load up as many of our medium transport ships with as many of our warriors as possible, cloak them before arrival, then one by one they secretly dock with the orbiting enemy ships, slowly and secretly taking out the ships occupants. Stage two begins after their ships are in disarray and chaos; at that time, the bulk of our forces will travel through the portal systems in space and land on the surface of Dolumek, providing the much needed turmoil on the enemy ground forces. A weakness in the Nogzakh machines are their exposed hydraulic tubing located in the back of the head. Strike there and the machines will fall. The any other troops will be yours to dispose of as you see fit. The main priority throughout the entire operation is to remain cloaked. I don't think the enemy believes any aid will come to the Dolumek, otherwise they would not have sent recon ships to orbit so close to the system."

"How many of our forces will we deploy?" asked Sestanon.

"I plan on leaving at least fifty thousand here to defend the homeland, all the others will deploy into combat."

"It's about time!" exclaimed Kroneg, "I can't remember the last time I did battle with an enemy and this will be just the motivation our warriors need!"

"Then prepare your warriors, the ships launch as soon as they are loaded. Disseminate the plan to all, I want everyone to know what is to take place and tell your warriors to make me proud."

A simultaneous bow from all filled the Kings heart with pride. Long ago, their numbers were not so large and could barely defend themselves, but now, these warriors of old would seek vengeance against the enemy, knowing that the blood of the fallen will not be shed in vain.

"How do you think they will hold up through all of this?" Tanazakh asked, curiously.

"My friend," Adoné said, placing his hand on Tanazakh's shoulder, "you will see battle unlike anything you've ever seen before. They will make themselves heroes in the Cavanonian race and death will not be able to deter them from their quest."

"Then I'm coming, too; I damn sure don't want to miss this!"

While the rest of Cavanon was preparing to go to war, more and more Dominion ships arrived on the outskirts of Dolumek. Close to fifty ships encircled the planet allowing no escape possible. Federoth arrived in his aptly named Dissension Seven flagship, dispersing the fleet and giving the command for ground forces to be taken to the surface to begin the operation. To most of the ground forces, the true motive for launching an attack was unclear and not necessary information to have. However, what *was* clear was that once they hit the ground, they were weapons free and any opposition encountered was to be considered hostile.

Giant sized Dominion ships landed on the surface of Dolumek and after touchdown, the white machines began marching out of the lowered bay doors, each one taking up a sector of fire to their immediate front. In one simultaneous instance, close to five hundred thousand Nogzakh machines emerged and began forward movement in their dispersed patrols, a walking perimeter that scoured the countryside over the surface of the planet. On the surface, nothing but the enemy could be seen, and in the distance, Dominion ships anchored into the ground to provide bases for repairing and refitting damaged machines, if that time ever came. Since the Nogzakhs and their commanders assumed it would be a fight to the finish to battle test all of their forces, bases were needed to maintain the effort.

Above the surface, the enemy seemed to have control, but below the surface, at every hangar bay and docking portal, the Dolumek waited. The entire planet was on alert and prepared even before the enemy had begun their descent onto the surface. Each Dolumek creature armed themselves with either energy bombs, futurific flame throwers constructed from their own form of chemical energy. But, unknown to all, even the Cavanonians, the Dolumek harbored massive super weapons with which to decimate and enemy force. These weapons were not powerful enough to take out planets or fortress cruisers in a single stroke, but they were powerful enough to put a hurting on the invading force.

After hours of troop landings and off loading, the Nogzakhs crushed the natural plant life underfoot in search for hostiles. Dispersed throughout the planet, radio traffic ran amuck through the speaker systems on board Federoth's flagship. Federoth knew the enemy was down there, he read it in the minds of the prisoners captured and tortured days ago. The only question now was where to gain entrance into the underground. The Dolumek must have sensed the enemies' apprehension, and began to prepare to emerge themselves. While the Nogzakhs stood around scouring the area, all seemed quite and calm. That's when all hell broke loose!

In a massive coordinated effort, all outer doors on the planets surface opened up, and wave after wave of Dolumek creatures raced out to meet the enemy head on. Dolumek fighters ripped through the skies at great speeds firing at will on the surprised Nogzakh machines. Each Dolumek creature began going after the enemy in the manner the Cavanonian King had warned would work best. By taking out the exposed tubing on the rear of the machines head, the Nogzakh toppled over and crashed to the ground with tremendous force. Millions of Dolumek creatures swarmed over the planet in all directions and from the skies, it appeared as if a flood of energy swept over the surface.

Nogzakhs fired blasters and energy from their guns, exploding on the ground, creating impacts and upheaval of dirt and rocks, and Dolumek creatures. Unfortunate victims caught in the blast were trampled and crush under the huge Nogzakh feet. Glowing energy flew erratically in all directions, striking everything and anything, even their own forces. Monstrous six legged gargantuan Nogzakh transports emerged out of the greater ships and began to reinforce the battling machines. Greater amounts of firepower took out large sections of Dolumek creatures, slowly reducing their numbers and adding to the death toll currently rising.

Dolumek fighters soared through the skies firing down on the machines with minimal effort, until the Nogzakh aerial fighters showed up from the higher ships still in orbit. Dogfights broke out in the skies above with violent energy shot towards the enemy prey. Aircraft hit with laser blasts spiraled out of control and crashed onto the surface over whatever force lay in its unguided path.

From above, the scene look as if millions of insects engaged in combat, explosions shot forth, crashes lit up in brilliant flames, and bodies flew through the air.

"Release the probes," Federoth commanded, "have them penetrate into the hangar doors and infiltrate as far into the planet as possible."

"Sir, we may loose the signal of they are too far underground," said a console controller.

"I don't care," he sneered, "just get them moving. I want them to strike at the heart of the Dolumek."

As ordered, the probes were released from underneath of the fortress cruisers in orbit. Thousands of steel-balled probes descended downward towards the surface, entering into the planet through the now exposed outer doors. On their way through the myriad of tunnels, canyons, trenches, and passageways, they drove deep into the subsurface area.

"At this rate," Rudecor said, "we'll be done with the attack in no time."

"We still have to overwhelm their numbers," Federoth replied. "Once we've lowered their numbers to an acceptable level, then, we infiltrate the planet itself and that will give our forces more to do and more to kill."

Unbeknownst to the visiting enemy, cloaked ships approached to the lesser cruisers and secretly docked with the outside doors of the various ships. Each of the invisible Cavanonian ships emptied their contents of warriors into the bowels of the enemy ships, immediately detaching and veering out of sight to a predetermined rendezvous point not far away. Inside the Dominion vessels, the Cavanonians, fifty in each load, divided their efforts and split up to each of the different levels within. From their, they began their own form of wailing on the enemy, striking mercilessly at each and every Nogzakh and dominion creature lurking in the way. Swiftly and effortlessly they hacked away at their opponents, trashing equipment, destroying consoles and energy generators, and emptying cargo and hangar bay contents into space. From a distance, the ship appeared to be flickering with energy, and trash seemed to drop out from the bottom of the ships.

Once the Cavanonians did their dirty work, the cloaked ships returned to pick them up, taking them to another ship to repeat the same work.

Federoth noticed one of the ships appear to be leaning and pitching off level of its normal status and wondered what the problem was.

"Senas Six, what is your status?" asked Federoth, but he received no answer. Frustrated he repeated the call, "Senas Six, acknowledge, what is your status, come in."

Still, there was no word. Federoth walked to the window and peered out in the direction of Senas Six. Suddenly, Senas Six exploded right in front of his eyes! The shockwave of the explosion rocked and shook the Dissention Seven vessel slightly, but enough to cause the crew to stagger about and regain their footing.

"What the—" shouted Federoth.

Pieces of the wreckage exploded outward hurling the remnants in all directions. Federoth's flagship suffered minor damage as fragments of the once great destroyer struck the hull, piercing one or two major oxygen valves. Quick thinking on the part of the Nogzakh repair crews alleviated and fixed the problem before it could get any worse.

The shocked Dominion Commander gazed outside in awe and wondered how this could be. Concentrating his efforts, he then commanded the ship to descend into the cloud cover to avoid contact with whatever it was that caused the dominion ship to explode. There were no signs of enemy, no craft, and no space debris that could have smashed into the ship, so what caused it? Federoth studied the surrounding areas from his position at the window.

"Sir," called the navigator, "we're directly over an opening on the planets surface."

"Good," Federoth replied, "remain in this position, the cloud cover will secret us from whatever it was that took out Senas Six."

"*No, it won't.*" Federoth heard a familiar voice in head. This immediately caused him to look behind him and all around the inside of the ship.

"What the hell?" he said to himself. When he returned his glance out the window, he got the shock of his life when, there, suddenly, the image of his nemesis flickered in front of his face.

"*SHIT!*" he exclaimed, "*Battle stations*, the bastard is outside on the outer deck!"

"I'll get him," Rudecor shouted back.

"Too late, he's gone!" Federoth raged in anger. His innermost thoughts began to worry. Even though he knew the idea was to find him, Federoth did not think he would see him so soon. He thought it would be more difficult that this, or was it the king's way of tormenting the Dominion Commander? Maybe it was a trick or test to see if Federoth would lose control and his mental incapacity warped enough to disrupt the flow of operations? Federoth wasn't taking any chances and realized that to be a sitting duck like this would only make things worse.

"Take us out of here and past the orbital rings."

With thousands of Nogzakh and now Nomaseri warriors engaged in the attack on the planet, the Dolumek increased their fight and brought out their own secreted weapons. Machines of great size and strength climbed out of the hangar bay doors and began firing in all directions. The massive forty-foot monstrosities moved on four metal legs, a rounded body covered in spikes that shielded gun turrets in the front, back, on both sides, and one on top. Moving and great speeds the machines crashed through the Nogzakh white menaces, blasting away at their pathetic metal covering. Unlucky enemy creatures were either caught in the stomping metal claws as the Dolumek would give the enemy the same courtesy they received, none.

Once the Dolumek spotted the Nomaseri warriors, the old vendetta raged with intensity and the heat of battle focused more on their old enemy. While up above, the cloaked Cavanonians had opened a hole in the enemies armada of ships, clearing the way for the multitude of Cavanonians now making their way onto the planets surface through the many secreted space portals. In their covert action, they invisibly descended onto the planet and wreaked havoc on the enemy forces. The surprise of seeing Nogzakh machines exploding for no reason caught the enemy off guard, as they stood puzzled. Nomaseri creatures ripped apart and splattered in the air from the unseen force, body parts and blood flew in all directions. A wave of some unforeseen energy ran over the planet surface, consuming all in its path, killing Nomaseri and Nogzakh creatures and machines. While witnessing this event from the safety of his ship, Federoth could not believe his eyes and had no explanation for what he saw.

"What the hell is happening down there?" he asked.

"It appears as if the Dolumek have a formidable weapon to use against us," Rudecor replied. "I've never seen anything like it before."

"But I don't *see* any weapon; it's as if some kind of power or shield spreads over the surface!"

"We'd better pull our forces out now before it reaches the bulk of our forces."

"Give the order, retrieve our machines, get the Nogzakhs back into the ships, and up into orbit, while we attempt to figure out a way to counter this new weapon."

"Slagis is on the Senas twelve," Rudecor said, "we'll get started with him."

No sooner had Slagis received the order, all of the nearest Nogzakh and Gadnoc began fleeing back to the ships. The multitude of the enemy raced back to the closet ship in their sector, but many of them did not make it. The invisible force continued to flood over the planet, destroying many of the creatures in its path. Fratricide was common and understood by the Dolumek, but with the amount of creatures in their numbers, they would not harbor ill-will toward the Cavanonians helping to eliminate the enemy and remove them from the planet.

In orbit, Federoth began to receive casualty reports from those who had managed to escape the planet. The amount of damage sustained staggered Federoth but did not cause him a great degree of worry, only surprise.

"Two hundred thousand lost?" Federoth asked, "but how could that be?"

"When Senas Six exploded she held at least seventy five thousand alone, sir," replied an operations lieutenant.

"Damn it!" the commander exclaimed. "Has anyone found out what caused the last of the casualties?"

"Not yet, sir, we're working on it."

Back on Celceloris, a unique occurrence suddenly attracted the attention of Nosrévis while relaxing on an outdoor balcony. A disturbance or presence filtered through the air and attracted his interest, faint at first but growing in intensity. He felt as if a sensation of enlightenment heightened his already alert state of awareness and gave rise to expectation. Inside his mind, he discovered the reason for this ethereal arousal and its reason for permeating his senses.

"*The time is drawing nigh, my faithful carrier,*" said the voice in his head. "*You must begin the preparations for my return to the physical realm; journey now to the system of Tnemucodas.*"

Nosrévis understood the voice to be that of Ellononis himself. Receiving the wake up call sent his senses into overdrive with excitement and anticipation. This would be a glorious time for the Dominion and bring the wrath of their God down on all who opposed their rule. He called down to his faithful servant, Esnemia and ordered him to ready his ship and have his personnel hellions board at once. While Federoth and Rudecor were busy at the moment, he decided to send a message to them requesting their immediate presence on Tnemucodas as well. Othragon *did* instruct him to bring them along as well as he had need of them, too.

On the bridge of his ship, Esnemia established the commlink with Federoth's flagship.

"Federoth, Nosrévis here," he said.

"What is it," the impatient commander replied, "we're kind of busy at the moment, can't it wait?"

"No, Sir, this is very important. I have just received a call from a higher authority; we are to journey to Tnemucodas at once and prepare for the emergence of Ellononis."

"Ellononis?" whispered Federoth, "now, here, in this realm?"

"That is correct, my Lord," Nosrévis smiled. "His instructions were very specific, too. The ceremony is to begin in one weeks time. I am beginning takeoff now and I should be there within three days. I suggest you pullout the remaining forces and rendezvous with me on the surface of Tnemucodas."

"We're already doing that now. We'll call back when we approach the system. Federoth, out."

Rudecor saw the shocked look in Federoth's face and it appeared as if his own skin turned pale, if that was even possible through his darkened charred skin.

"Rudecor, have Slagis mop up and collect the remaining forces, have him rendezvous with us on the outskirts of Tnemucodas. Send the coordinates to the other ships and have them depart immediately."

"Right away," he replied.

"Tnemucodas, huh?" Sestanon said, while two other Cavanonians held the Dominion first officer prisoner on board his own ship. "Thanks for your ship, Slagis, we'll take it from here."

The escorts beat Slagis senseless on the way to the detention cells to await his doom. While the other Cavanonians secretly killed off the remaining bluish Nogzakhs, Adoné entered into the ship and proceeded to the bridge. When he arrived, Sestanon informed him of what transpired and the new information he received over the commlink. While they conversed, Sestanon ordered the ship to land for a brief period. While on the surface, they would inform the Dolumek of the new events and collect up the rest of the Cavanonians who came by way of the space portals. Once the leadership exchanged information and orders, the captured dominion ship departed on route to Cavanon.

"I thought you said this would be the hour of Cavanon's emergence, my Lord?" Sestanon asked.

"So did I," Adoné replied. "It seems that there is more going on than meets the eye. If this is indeed the time for Ellononis to re-enter the realm of the physical, then we must get there and stop it from happening."

"I know that once he does come back, there will be no stopping him, he will be invincible, and we will all perish under his malevolence."

"I must find out why the Tnemucodas told me otherwise, regarding the emergence of Cavanon instead of Ellononis. Something this important should not have been over looked. They told me they were hidden away from anyone so that Cavanon could emerge when the time was right. Why the mix up?"

"We can ask them that when we get there, My Lord."

Chapter 23

Courses of Action

Back on Cavanon, there was a semi-joyous welcome for the returning warriors who assisted in thwarting the attack on Dolumek. Many of the fallen were remembered in a brief graveside ceremony to commemorate their spirits to the ancestors above. The ceremony had to be short as they all knew the King had much more important matters to attend to. Not that he thought less of those who fell in battle, far from it, all of the Cavanonians knew that the King cherished his subjects greatly and he would attend regardless of other matters, but they also knew that there was something else in the works, which required his immediate attention.

After returning to Royal Mountain, Adoné informed Xashsa of what took place on Dolumek and all events that transpired while they were away. To further sense the drama, her husband willfully allowed his queen into his mind so that she could *see* exactly what took place, but in a shorter fashion. She saw all the highlights and heard about the future event through the intercepted radio traffic on the captured enemy vessel, which was grounded several hundred miles away outside one of the underground hangar entrances.

There were many things to attend to, namely the interrogation of the prisoner, Slagis, and the questioning of the Tnemucodas who were also waiting to speak with the King personally. Rather than let one important matter wait for another, Adoné left the fate of the prisoner into Sestanon's capable hands, since it was he who originally captured the Dominion officer in the first place. The only order that was not to be ignored consisted of not killing the prisoner. Instead, the King had another purpose ready for him. The King also charged Sestanon to see that the enemy ship was retrograded with Cavanonian equipment and refitting with more space for more of their warriors. The division commander only surmised the idea floating in the King's mind but did as requested.

Knowing that Laura and Zérnoda remained safely within Royal Mountain watching over the young prince, both Adoné and Xashsa headed off to the Tnemucodas mountain range to speak with Maillewvan and find out why certain key facts within the prophecy had been omitted. The royal couple had all of the information they needed, now it was time to piece it all together.

As they arrived on the landing platform of the cave entrance, Maillewvan personally greeted them, eagerly and overexcited. His jittery actions caused them a slight degree of hesitation, as they knew this was not Maillewvan's normal display.

"Maillewvan," Adoné said, "what's all the excitement about?"

"My Lord," he replied, "don't you feel it? Don't you sense it? Isn't the energy flowing through your veins with such profound sensations?"

"I'm sorry, my friend, but I don't feel anything except for the loss of some of our warriors. Why am I supposed to be feeling excited?"

"Because it is time, it is time for the awakening to begin. It has been signified through the stars and the energy of Cavanon's return has touched us again as it once did when we awoke."

"My friend," Adoné said, "we feel nothing of what you speak and it is apparent to me that your awakening coincides with some other beings who sensed this as well, but not of whom you speak."

"But who else would sense this?" he asked, rather innocently.

"The enemy feels it, too," Adoné replied, "but they do not feel the awakening of Cavanon, instead, they feel the coming of his hated brother, Ellononis."

"That is not possible," Maillewvan stood up to his full height. "We know of the awakening because Cavanon himself foretold us of his return. He said nothing of the other."

"Well, the enemy knows it; all too well I'm afraid. We intercepted a transmission on the ship we captured. The enemy is now traveling to Tnemucodas for the reemergence of Ellononis; they said nothing of Cavanon coming back."

"This is not good," Maillewvan said sadly, "I would hate to think that our admirable Cavanonian lord would have given us false information."

"I don't believe he would do that to you or anyone else for that matter. I'll bet there is more going on here than meets the eye."

"Suppose that Cavanon is remaining dormant for a reason," Xashsa stated. "Perhaps the reason why we feel nothing is because Cavanon does not want us to rush in getting there and be needlessly slaughtered by the enemy."

"That would make sense," Maillewvan replied.

Adoné added his own thoughts into the mix. "Maybe, if Cavanon plans on reemerging as well, he told the Tnemucodas of the awakening in order to prepare *us* for it, to give us a heads up of when it would take place. The chance of capturing an enemy ship and overhearing of their plans and destination gave us the information of what they are really up to. Without anyone knowing about Cavanon's planned 2nd coming, no one could ruin it, or prevent it. If he is anything like what I've heard about in stories and from the ancients themselves, he will show up at the last minute and from a source no one will expect."

"Then, we must pave the way for his return," Maillewvan proudly. "We must engage the enemy while they are on my homeland and destroy them while we have the chance."

"Patience, my friend," Adoné patted his giant arm. "This has to be thought out, planned, and resourced before we can jump into something this hazardous. We're talking about the two greatest beings in our history, Cavanon and his hated brother; you can't get any higher up the ladder than those two…unless you went straight to the Gods themselves."

"It sounds like you've got something else up your sleeve, Love," Xashsa smiled, reading deep into his mind.

"I've got the weirdest idea and the will to carry it out; I just have to figure out if it feasible."

"What idea?" the Tnemucodan leader asked.

"Its time to turn on the time machine again, Maillewvan," Adoné smiled.

"But, my Lord, why?" shrieked the Tnemucodan.

"Because," he replied, "the enemy is currently occupied and very busy with the impending ceremony that is coming. They will not be able to get away to check out a disturbance in the time dimension. By turning it on, we can weaken their forces by draining their food supply and save the lives of untold numbers of humans in their storage houses. We will need to move the time machine outside so that there will be plenty of space when the new arrivals begin to fall into our world."

"I'll have it moved at once, my Lord."

"Excellent," Adoné replied. "In the meantime, I will send word to the Kostejaanians to come and assist; we will need their expertise with the machine."

"We will also require Nivlac's aid in building more domiciles for the new arrivals," Xashsa confidently added. "How many more do you think we will need?"

"For the sake of planning, I suggest he work along the entire foothills of this range," Adoné said, pointing all the way down the range to the west.

"They will need help; I will get one thousand of the female warriors to assist. They will be able to use the cave digging techniques you love so much, plus they will add a more homey touch."

At the same time as Maillewvan started in on the tasks given him, the King and Queen stopped off at home to inform the others of the new tasks to be performed. Adoné instructed Kroneg to send a couple of fighters to Kostejaan and seek their aid with the time machine operations, along with another few key pieces of equipment that the King wanted. Nivlac received his task with great enthusiasm; Adoné told him of the events to come and the Srotaderp leader felt it would be wise for some of his forces to remain behind while the excitement took place elsewhere. Not all Srotaderps wanted in on attacking the enemy during the ceremony.

While this went on, Sestanon engaged in interrogating Slagis, rather forcefully. The King gave Sestanon specific instructions not to kill the Dominion officer, only to break him down, weaken his spirits, and extrapolate all information contained within his cerebrum. The King had another ingenious plan in mind that would allow the Dominion officer to serve a more useful purpose for the Cavanonians rather than waste the enemy officer, even though that was the immediate thought of the interrogators. Through the constant beatings, mind probes, sleep deprivation, and shock treatments, Slagis gave them pretty much whatever they asked for. Since they could read his mind willfully, the interrogators knew instantly if Slagis' thoughts were contrary to giving a truthful answer.

From the information extracted, the Cavanonians now knew the entire matrix of the time machines locations, operation cycles, and Dominion priorities. This also told them that the main time machine protocol had been transferred from its once great seat on Samajap to Celceloris, the new Dominion base. The priority of effort shifted the moment Dominion commanders relocated and Celceloris became the new major hub to all of the outlying region time machines. Sestanon became shocked to know that Celceloris supported seven other sites—eight if they counted Samajap—but that system did not import as often since only a skeleton crew remained there. In all actuality, the machine on Samajap had been shut off, considering that the zero gravity environment outside provided an adequate area for an already overabundant food supply.

After issuing out the guidance to his trusted friends, Adoné called for all of the division commanders and his own personal council to discuss plans for the inevitable event to come. This would require meticulous planning and precise timing if everything were to go over somewhat smoothly. Adoné knew that no mission was without consequences though, and that thought remained uppermost in his mind the whole time. Still, the others had to know this and the King had to instill this in the minds of his commanders as well. Since there was not nearly enough room in the main palace chambers for everyone, Adoné held the meeting in the outside auditorium at the foot of the mountain. A slight feeling of anxiety swirled around through all of the creatures present, giving them all the same sense of uncertainty and doubt. Adoné sensed this before the meeting began and decided to give his own little pep talk before the planning commenced.

"Everyone," he said while gazing at all of their faces, "as it has been stated to me many times in the past, everything happens for a reason. Whether we know or understand that reason is another matter, what does matter is that we use the time we have wisely and to the best of our ability. Amongst us, we have the finest creatures in the galaxy, brave, courageous, fearless, and extremely talented with their gifts and powers. Some of you have known me since my beginning in this dimension, and others have privileged me with their introduction on many other occasions. I say that because you know me, but some of you have known me for a lot longer period. Therefore, you will understand why I say the task before us is not impossible to accomplish, *improbable*, yes, but not impossible. We are about to undertake the most significant and dangerous mission we have ever come up against and some of us may not return. But, we must do this to ensure that the great evil—which threatens to destroy us all—does not come into this realm. If he does, then all will be lost and everything we know, everything we've ever worked for will be gone. The creatures who live here, in nearby systems, our allies, even those who are innocent of any sinister knowledge do not deserve to suffer the dread that will come forth should Ellononis be allowed to reemerge unchallenged."

"But we've never faced anything equal to the likes of him," said Crees, one of the division commanders. "Aside from the fact of his emergence, we still do not know what other evil we will have to face."

"And what about other enemy forces," Kroneg asked, "how many will there be?"

"We do not yet know who else may be involved," said Tanazakh, "knowing would help to isolate which forces would best be used against the enemies arsenal of troops."

"Sestanon has information of the enemy composition," Adoné said, pointing him out.

"Yes," Sestanon stood up and walked to the middle of the auditorium. "We were able to extract a lot of useful information from the prisoner. It's a good thing we captured such a rarity, his head was a virtual gold mine of information. From that, we ascertained that the Nomaseri, the Gadnoc, the Nogzakhs, Nosrévis and his evil hellions will all be involved in this. There is also one other that I've no knowledge of that will play a part as well."

"And who might that be," the Queen asked.

"A being by the name of, Othragon," Sestanon said looking around at all the faces, hoping to find a glimpse in one who might know this being. A couple others knew him by name, but only one actually saw this being, face to face.

"I know him," said Adoné, calmly, "all too well, I'm afraid."

"Isn't that the one who tried to kill you back on Muidiri?" Tanazakh asked.

"That's the one, and if I hadn't split myself then I surely would have ended up dead."

"So, how will we defeat him this time?" Tanazakh pondered. "From a standpoint of strength, we will face Federoth, Nosrévis, Othragon, and Ellononis if he makes it out."

"Uh, there are also the hellions Nosrévis created from the souls of the long since banished Cavanonians; they are to be reckoned with as well."

"Not to mention the Nogzakhs, Gadnoc, and the Nomaseri," Xashsa added.

To a few, the situation looked bleak, almost a no win situation. With so many foes concentrated in one location for the same purpose, it would be extremely hazardous indeed to tackle that lot.

"That is why we have to plan out the operation, entirely," said the King. "Everything has to be taken into account, nothing overlooked. What do we have in our arsenal? We have numerous Cavanonians, the Tnemucodas, Tanazakh and his Anadonians, and of course the Dolumek and Kostejaanians."

"I suspect the Kostejaanians will not be participating in the battle of the century," Tanazakh chuckled. "They seemed rather squeamish after the battle back on Earth."

"We won't require them to do battle, that is for the other forces," Adoné replied. "What they will do is much more important and it requires their technical skills and brains rather than strength or numbers."

"What about the Srotaderp?" Nivlac spoke up, "we are ready to do our part as well."

"Yes, I agree," answered Adoné, "your great strength is needed for the battle as well, but we should still leave behind a sufficient number to see to the multitude of new comers that will be arriving very soon."

"Have you any idea at all about where this great emergence will take place?" Sestanon eagerly asked.

"Yes, Maillewvan here has intimate knowledge of the location and its surroundings. The ritual ceremony will take place in an ancient stone temple. Inside is a rather large and unique enclave full of stone pillars. We can use his knowledge to plan out our attack, strategic locations from which to strike, and assume the most likely course of enemy action."

Tanazakh started to laugh aloud. Everyone looked at him strangely, wondering what it was he found so hilarious.

"This sounds just like the time back in the new Helena village where we planned out the destruction of the black fortress," Tanazakh said to all. "It sounded just as interesting back then as well. Tell me we can't win this?" he said staring at Adoné.

"Either we win," Adoné replied, "or we die trying."

"That's just what I wanted to hear!" the big Anadon replied, waiting for the tactics to come out.

This complex attack required many stages to complete. Stage 1 required the Kostejaanians to commence start up of the time machine and begin draining the food supplies of the enemy while they were busy with the impending ceremony of their evil God. While the time machine imported the untold number of petrified humans and other alien creatures from the enemy holding facilities, Cavanonian warriors would begin reprogramming the five thousand Nogzakh white machines secured in the bowels of the captured enemy ship. Cavanonian warriors would secretly operate these machines after the captured enemy vessel landed south of an ancient stone temple on Tnemucodas. They would begin to assault the enemy while the attack continued, blending into the myriad of other enemy fighting machines, taking them out one by one to significantly reduce their numbers without giving themselves away.

Stage 2 involved the majority of Cavanonian ships, graciously donated by the Kostejaanians. These ships would land a great distance away from the main battlefield and the ground forces would travel overland to a mountain range on the north side of the temple where the ceremony would take place. From there, field commanders would ascertain where best to place or reroute friendly forces to engage and distract the enemy away from the main effort.

Stage 3 would commence the moment the enemy displayed a significant decrease of forces around the temple. At that time, Adoné, Xashsa, Tanazakh, along with two hundred Cavanonian warriors, the Srotaderp, and the Tnemucodas themselves would enter into the temple enclave inside to kill the evil enemies within, thus attempting to stop or prevent the evil God from returning.

Stage 4 would commence after a squadron of Cavanonian fighters relayed word to back to the Kostejaanians for a surprise attack on the time machines themselves, taking them all out in one swift stroke. This would entail sending an enormous build up of Crystal energy from Cavanon through the time machine to the others in the various Dominion bases.

Stage 5, if they survived, would commence once the captured enemy vessel loaded up with friendly forces and ascended into orbit. From there, they would completely finish off the planet by destroying it, further reducing the possibility of escape for any enemy who may have survived.

"So what about aerial fighters?" Sestanon asked.

"We have some of our own stationed in flight patterns out of enemy sight," Adoné replied. "They can intervene the moment they see any flying activity."

"What if the numbers are too great for them to fight off? What if the bigger ships begin to ascend?" Sestanon asked, a bit worried this time.

"The bigger ships can't take off if some of our forces get in and sabotage them before they have that chance," the King replied again. "There are many things that have to take place while the attack is ongoing, so it's crucial that we all use out intuitive intellect and think outside the box."

"My friend," Tanazakh spoke up, "we could really use those warriors of old again, is there any chance of that happening, too?"

"I can't say for sure," Adoné said, wondering. "The last time, Aurora knew about them and told me they would come, but I'm not sure if it will work this time or not. All I can do is ask."

"Then ask, please. I would feel a lot better knowing we had another ace in the hole rather than wish for one." Tanazakh stood up, stood next to his friend, and continued to speak. "Hell, I'm going along either way, with or without them if need be. But we would do well to have a go to hell plan."

"I'll see what I can do."

"Uh, Sir," the voice of Stan came from behind the King. "I couldn't help overhearing about this battle coming up, and I thought you could use our help."

"And how did you hear about this?" Tanazakh asked.

"The Srotaderp excavating the new homes told us," Stan replied.

"Yeah, we figured we could help out," Zach spoke up, "you know, kick some alien ass along side you guys, no offense meant."

"I'm not trying to discourage you two, but this is a little above your level of experience," Adoné said calmly.

"Well, I thought you could use a bunch of these new swords we made up while you guys were gone," Zach said. "I think you could use them."

"What can these swords of yours do exactly?" Sestanon asked.

"Well, this one shoots fire," Stan said, holding the sword upright, shooting flames up from the tip at least a hundred feet in the air.

"Whoa!" Tanazakh fell back on the ground.

"This one here shoots firebombs," Zach said, aiming the sword into the sky, shooting a huge blast of energy that soared into the air, exploding several hundred feet in the air.

"This will blow the ass off anything that comes near it, and this one—" Adoné cut Stan off from further demonstrations.

"Guys, you got the job."

"And how many of these swords have you made?" Tanazakh enthusiastically asked.

"Oh, I dunno, a couple thousand, maybe?" Zach replied. "They were easy to make with the materials of this planet. These things practically made themselves and—"

"Guys," Adoné laughed, "I said you can come."

"Excellent!" Stan shouted.

"Dude," Zach said to his buddy, "this is going to be fucking sweet!" the both gave each other a high five.

Adoné looked at all the other Cavanonians and creatures in the meeting and stated what he thought needed to be said.

"See that, that is exactly the kind of mentality we need; everyone coming up with ingenious ways of killing the enemy. Just look at the enthusiasm in their eyes, the will to destroy and wreak havoc. But, that by itself will not be enough. Each of you must unleash your slayer instinct, your inner being. This is your chance to release your inner demon and let him have his chance at desecrating and destroying the enemy through any means necessary. You must unlock your true potential; your most diabolical hellion must come out and seek vengeance against those who seek to wipe us out. This is a one-time shot and you must keep that in mind, as we will not get another chance."

All eyes lowered and all heads filled with thoughts of the king's speech. This would be their test, their trial, their ultimate tribulation to overcome. Simultaneously, visions of the battle filled their minds and shown in their eyes, the determination, the intestinal fortitude to go into battle facing overwhelming odds. This would heighten the Cavanonian spirit to an unprecedented level and elevate it to an unparalleled status. If they were successful in their quest, they would forever be known as the most feared in the galaxy, unmatched and unequaled. The King sensed the overwhelming rush of adrenaline in their bodies and the blood racing in their veins.

"That," Adoné said, "is exactly what I want you to feel when we go. Remember, we are to kill the enemy, period, not one enemy lives, no mercy, as they have shown us none in abundance. According to the information from the enemy officer, Slagis, the ceremony culminates in seven days—and on that day…they all die!"

"Well, hell, what are we doing sitting around here talking for?" Tanazakh stood up and said, "we've got things to do!"

"Fuck yeah, let's get started!" Stan shouted.

Everyone else stood up and shouted, yelling praises and words of cheer.

"Alright," Adoné said smiling, "let's get to work."

"We're all crazy, you know that?" Xashsa said, smiling at her husband.

"Yeah, you may be right there," he replied. "They will fight as warriors, but you will see the blood of heroes shed on the battlefield."

Chapter 24

A Call to Higher

While the enemy forces of Nosrévis began landing on Tnemucodas, Federoth and his ships resumed a course for the same system, after a brief stop in Celceloris. Federoth wasted no time in racing to his palace chambers to secure his fire sword—the one he *thought* was authentic. Once back on the ship, Federoth ordered the flagship to join up with the remainder of the fleet already enroute.

What Federoth did not realize was that he had a stowaway on board.

The Dominion commander did not feel as excited about the upcoming ceremony as the other sinister beings felt, that really wasn't on his mind right now. Instead, he worried about what would happen the moment he saw Othragon again. The last time he saw the Dominion ruler was in his own chambers on Muidiri and even then, it was only brief. Once Othragon sensed the presence of the enemy in his midst, he forgot all about Federoth and knew nothing of the plan to assassinate him. Federoth still hoped this was the case, otherwise it would make things more difficult than he envisioned.

The mentally occupied commander walked through the halls of his ship pondering all sorts of "what ifs" on his way to his private chambers. He left word with the bridge of his intentions to get some shuteye, but after dreaming up possible events and different scenarios of what was to come, he knew he would not sleep unless he fell out from sheer exhaustion. Federoth was resilient in his overwhelming thought process. There were times when he would collapse in place from over-thinking, extinguishing his strength to the point his body could no longer take the long days without sleep or rest. When something bothered him, it showed, and no amount of consoling or reassurance would ease his conscious mind until he had attained a certain degree of comfort.

This worry also encompassed the reemergence of Ellononis. If he emerged, then Federoth had reason to worry. He knew Ellononis would read into his character, his being, his secreted mind. Once Ellononis discovered Federoth's long ago hidden agenda for assassinating Othragon, Federoth would perish, violently, and in a manner even *he* could not imagine. The horrors Ellononis was capable of would rival even those who dwelt in hell and give them serious opposition if the second creation ever decided to fight the entire underworld. The Dominion commander had to come up with his own strategy and quick. The fire sword gave him hope that he would survive if the great evil overlord discovered his hidden sins. If Federoth only knew the sword was fake he might have abandoned his current thoughts and retreated to the far edge of the galaxy.

Feeling the warmth of his chambers, Federoth poured himself a drink of the blood wine gathered from the planet of Ellononis. There, standing in front of his spacious window, he watched stars fly by at incredible speeds, illuminated nebulous clouds that lit up in glorious fashions, and dimly colored planets all snuggled in their own private sanctuary of peace, oblivious of what was to come.

"I know what you need," said a feminine voice from behind him.

Federoth spit out the contents of his mouth on the window before him.

"What, you?" he shrieked, "Eñala, what the hell are you doing here?" he asked angrily.

"I knew you would be weary since you've battled with the Dolumek," she replied, softly, "and I knew you could not go on without my loving touch."

Eñala came to him and attempted to place her arms around her sexual prey, but her arms did not find purpose. Instead, he quickly threw them away and pushed her back out of arms reach.

"Foul temptress," he sneered, "I've no time for you now and you have no right to be aboard my ship."

"So, this is how you treat the love of your life?"

"Who said you were the love of my life?" he asked, "I *never* told you that."

"That is what I read in your minds eye during many of our passionate encounters. You cannot hide what your heart secrets."

"Stupid bitch," he retorted, "there is nothing in my heart that would even think to suggest those words. Your minds eye is clouded and has deceived you."

"Your playful banter amuses me and only heightens the eroticism flowing in these veins." She gasped air as her head fell back and then forward again, wearing a fuming look on her face. "You have been such a bad commander, and I am just the one to punish you."

As she snapped into action, lunging herself towards him, Federoth held up his hand and froze her dead in the air. Her eyes grew large and glanced to the left and the right, then centered back to Federoth.

"Not this time, fool of a wench," he said, sinisterly. "I've no time for your sexual prowess; you will cool your blood in the cells on board until I come up with a use for your carcass."

Federoth called for two Gadnoc thugs to enter in and take control of the sexually deviant lass, and further ordered them to take her to the detention level. There, they were to show her their own form of sexual molestation and violent nature, but not kill her…yet. In the cells she would remain until Federoth needed an object on which to thrust his anger should the need arise. The unfortunate vixen would grow angry in her cells, much more than Federoth would ever dream.

Nosrévis landed on Tnemucodas and took in the sights of the drab and dreary scenery of the planets atmosphere. In the distance, Nosrévis viewed a ship emerging through the darkened thunderclouds, approaching steadily towards them. He knew all too well who it was and he eagerly went to greet the occupants as they emerged from the lowered ramp.

"Ah, my Lord, it is good that we meet again," Othragon said. "The time had summoned me and I hastened to its call. I am here to protect and serve you, and to see that the emergence of our great God comes to pass without stint or error."

"My servant," Nosrévis replied, "I am sure you will risk all for our great God. We must begin preparing the site at once."

The evil carrier glanced at the numerous creatures exiting from the ship, wondering not only who they were, but also *what* they were. Nosrévis had never seen such creatures before. Standing a full seven feet in height, broad shoulders, and enlarged arms clad with armored coats of steel. Oversized boots laced with shards of iron and spikes crushed the ground with every step of their feet. Large shrouded heads adorned their shoulders down to the spot where a neck should be, but there wasn't one. The oversized arms held menacing weapons—swords, spears, clawed battle-axes, and solid iron mallets covered in jagged spikes.

As Nosrévis walked through the ranks inspecting the new arrivals, Othragon walked beside him and paused in front of the largest one. Encased in armor plating, the formidable size of the creature staggered even Nosrévis, who then approached the creature to within a foot of distance. The creature instantly dropped down on one knee and bowed his head in respect.

"They are wise to your being and know very well who you are," Othragons looming voice said. He pulled back the shroud from the creatures head, revealing a red demon, menacing, intimidating, and wicked. Their likeness resembled that of Ellononis with their red slanted eyes, high rising pointed ears, erratic rows of razor-sharp teeth, and depressions of where a nose should be. The most noticeable feature of the creature was the smoke that billowed in and out of its mouth with every breath it took.

"They are Xhenutian warriors," Othragon proudly said. "I created them from the eggs of a human female and the soil of Cinodas. I used her essence, fears, and demonic spirit to create an elite force of guardians in the likeness of our God's image."

"They are very impressive, my servant," Nosrévis smiled, "and I'm sure they will serve their purpose most admirably."

"They are to secure the perimeter of the temple while the ritual takes place and they will deal with any opposition, swiftly."

"You assume their will be opposition?" Nosrévis asked. "We've wiped out our enemies to the point near extinction. Nothing will bother us in the least."

"It would do us well to prepare for anything."

"You are correct. These warriors must meet my hellions; together they will double the force of the perimeter and see to it that no unauthorized intrusion takes place underground."

"Come, my Lord," Othragon motioned forward with his outstretched arm, "we must awaken the portal."

"Yes, of course," Nosrévis replied, gazing at the impressive Xhenutians.

The sinister procession made its way west through rough cut crags and deformed knolls to a hilltop overlooking an extremely spacious plateau. Down in the center, the great stone temple towered up to the heavens with various stone branches drooping toward the ground as if the temple were once made out of wood. Eons ago, this mysterious temple came into existence and through wind and time it suffered, aged and decayed, until its day of use eventually arrived. However, stone walls a prison do make as the interior led them to believe. Down through winding rock staircase, three on each side of the temple, Nosrévis and Othragon descended. The Xhenutian warriors took up stations outside of the temple itself, half inside on the first floor, and half outside; Nosrévis' hellions took up stations on the other side to block the entrance of anyone unauthorized.

Down below in the only other floor of the temple sat a grand hall with a dimensional size of thirteen thousand square feet. Stone pylons inside of the hall rose from the dust layered ground and married with the u-shaped ceiling. Nosrévis and Othragon lit torches secured on the giant pylons on opposite sides of the hall, giving the level of ambience desired for just such a setting. The dimly lit hall had no other distinct features about it other than one gigantic wall at the far end of the hall and, in the middle of the great hall, a rock, huge and immovable, stood firm and tall. Over the ages, fragments had fallen off the rock through natural erosion of wind, littering the floor around it. At the end of the hall, the plain wall, ordinary, and outlined with a fifty foot chiseled border, would serve a unique purpose for the ritual, and Nosrévis was about to find out that purpose.

"There," Othragon said, pointing to the empty wall, "when the planet Cinodas comes directly in line between Elaveshan and Tnemucoda, the great Doorway of Oblivion will open up to us."

"Oblivion," Nosrévis stated, "isn't that the place of the forgotten?"

"Yes, it is," replied Othragon. "That is where the masses of our fallen go when they perish. They are to remain there forever, never again to see the light of any star. However, it also is the place where Ellononis will send his enemies when he returns. Once he emerges, he will vanquish all those who stand in his way. Here they will be brought and cast down into darkness, forever."

"How long will the doorway be open?"

"Not for very long, only a few minutes," Othragon replied. "It hasn't been used since my father, Zalestole, roamed free in the galaxy. If the doorway opens and a Son of the Gods are not present, then oblivion seals up for another five thousand years. But once Ellononis stands before it at the precise moment of alignment, it will open and remain so until Ellononis passes on once more."

"Too bad my old nemesis isn't here yet," Nosrévis cringed, "I would so love to cast him in myself."

"That time will come, my Lord, have faith, we still have a few days yet before the alignment takes place."

"It's a shame the builders of this great temple are not around to see this," Nosrévis commented.

"They have long since disappeared ages ago," Othragon replied. "It was only after their eventual demise that the doorway had been created. Had they know what this temple would be used for, they would not have built it."

"Too bad for them," his lord stated.

Nyfletoné arrived on Cavanon with a few ships worth of equipment and supplies asked for by the King. With him, he brought his best and brightest technicians to setup the time machine as they had before. This time, with a few more brains amongst them, together they would work to isolate the protocol within the machine and isolate other systems with the same machines. The skies were clear and unobstructed, so they had no worry of rain or other moisture that might possibly affect operations.

To the right of the time machine, thousands of Cavanonian warriors aided in the construction of new domiciles for humans that the king assumed would be arriving. Many had assumed the new arrivals would be so out of sorts both physically and mentally that they might not make it and have severe trouble adjusting, if they could adjust at all. Zérnoda, Kayla, and Sarah were there to assist with the introductions and the indoctrination. But first, other warriors would stand guard around the time machine, forming a perimeter just in case something dangerous came through during the operation. After all, a few had witnessed that before the last time the machine operated and now was not the time to bring trouble to the homeland.

Out on the plains, the Srotaderp participating in the upcoming battle were saying their farewells to their brethren. Those remaining behind wished them well and happy hunting. Elsewhere, other Cavanonians were loading up ships with the equipment and supplies. The reprogramming of the Nogzakh machines took some doing. The programmers discovered that the machines did possess a mind of their own as the King had warned them, but taking out all but the manual controls and radio equipment did the trick.

Adoné sat with Xashsa, Zérnoda, Laura, and the baby prince, giving them their last minute instructions before the time for departure came. The feelings emanating from the two daughters reached the parents hearts and told them how they really felt. This was a sad moment, although it was not meant to be. They did not like the idea of their parents being gone, not to mention on the most dangerous and hazardous undertaking yet.

"You have to think positive, you two," Adoné said calmly. "Its not like we are saying goodbye, we're just giving you the rundown of what to do while we are away."

"Dad," Zérnoda sighed, "I know you've done some dangerous things in the past, but this is different."

"This is *way* different than the past," Laura added. "I've seen you tackle some real bad guys before, but this one will top them all. From what I've heard, you won't stand a chance."

"And Mom is going, too?" Zérnoda butted in.

"Look, girls," Xashsa started in, "this is something we *have* to do, its not that we want to, ha, I'd rather stay here at home and live peacefully. However, if we do not do this, if we do not go and try to stop the evil from returning then all will be lost."

"Think of it this way," Adoné chimed in immediately, "you enjoy the peace and tranquility of this present life, all the things you have, and the blessings we've received since our return. True, it has been a hard life, but that has made us stronger and more determined. Remember what it was like when we first arrived, how scared and helpless we felt? Remember when we escaped the black fortress and ran for our lives because of fear? Imagine having to do that all over again in this present life? *That* is what we have to fight to avoid."

"If we don't, we will all lose." Xashsa went and hugged them both, tenderly, trying to alleviate their fears and worries. "You two will not be alone here. You will have at least two hundred warriors on guard outside the mountain to make absolutely sure nothing happens to you, nothing like what happened the last time."

"The reason why that won't happen," Adoné said, "is because all of the bad guys will be in one place for the same reason. You will be safe here and you two must look after the prince while we are away."

"Okay, Dad, Mom, we understand," Zérnoda smiled while tears of hope wept from her eyes. "Just promise us you will return safe and sound."

"Hey," Adoné chuckled, "we will go, fight the bad guys, kick the evil lords' ass, and return before you know it. Now, your mother and I must go up top and make a call, we'll not be very long."

The two daughters nodded positively and walked them to the balcony. There, the King and Queen ascended to the peak of the mountain to a flat spot, spacious enough for the two of them, and more. Adoné and Xashsa glanced around and surveyed all the lands around them, as if taking in one last sight before the plunge into certain doom.

Adoné knelt down facing the western sun; Xashsa did similar. As they bowed there heads, the wind began to pick up slightly, blowing there hair about wildly, fluffing up their clothes. As the royal couple concentrated, the light around them dimmed, faded, and changed to an almost negative version of the current picture. Swirling energies blew up from all sides in waves, cascading upward, lightly touching the faces of royalty. Darkened clouds formed circles above them in whirlpool like fashion, causing a gentle tornado of mist to descend and encircle the couple. Lifting upward, Adoné and Xashsa left their bodies in their current frozen stance and spiritually rose up through the mist, above the cloud cover, and into the vastness of space. There, above the planet, as if walking on the clouds themselves, Aurora, Ariel, Jasmine, and the other servants came to them and kneeled, briefly. The royal couple seemed mystified by this, wondering why they did not hearing the voices of the ancestors. Instead, Aurora had this to say:

"Your calling was inevitable, my Lord. The Great Ancestors know why you have placed this call and have sent us to answer. They are well aware of the tribulations you will face and what it will mean to the Cavanonian race should you fail. They have foreseen your request and have already provided us with the answers you seek. Ask and I will answer you in kind."

"Aurora," Adoné started, "the Ancestors know we are to embark on the most dangerous task ever to visit this era and I do have a request of them. I seek their wisdom, their greatness, and their aid as well."

"Father," Ariel replied, "you already have that which you need to be successful in this great task that stands before you. There is no more aid that can be given to assist you against what you will face."

"You have all that is required to defeat the evil that comes in the night," Jasmine said.

"And you possess more than you know," Sharizar added.

"Only the true King can put the evil to rest," Leila stated, "and there is a great secret yet to be revealed when the time is right."

"Your Son has the answer," Aurora said, "although, you know it not."

"Our Son?" Xashsa said, surprised.

"Yes, Mother, and after the King holds the baby near to him, he will receive all the help he will ever need. Be not discouraged by this news, for what will be, will happen for a reason…as with all things."

"When the time is right, you will know the truth of what we speak," Ariel said, smiling at them both.

"If we simply told you the truth of the matter, it would detract from your state of preparedness," Aurora said. "However, knowing that you are the pride of Cavanon, graced by divine light, and gifted above all others, the Ancestors know you will do everything in your power to destroy the evil and save all."

"I am thankful that the Ancestors have such confidence in us," Adoné said, "and you must thank them for me for answering my call. We will fight for the glory of Cavanon and to honor the Ancestors."

The spirits all bowed to each other; Aurora and the other servants faded away as easily as they appeared, Adoné and Xashsa returned to their bodies and descended one last time to their home. Inside, Adoné did as Aurora told him and held his son one last time. The heartfelt embrace and told those around him how much he loves his little prince. However, the King did not see or realize the slight breath of air that entered into his system, something passed from the son to the father and then became hidden. Adoné would know later what had transpired in that momentary hug, but now it was time to leave.

As Adoné handed the prince back to Laura, the baby began to cry, probably for the first time ever. All the women were surprised to see such a reaction from the littlest one and they glanced at Adoné in wonder. Adoné perceived that the baby had read his mind and somehow felt the dangers of battle emanate from his pores. Adoné stood back, changed his aura from its normal status to the battle ready warrior inside. Adoné's clothes changed into a flowing black robe from his neck down to his feet, with large sleeves and a large collar. His long white hair fell over the robe and swayed effortlessly in the wind. The color content of the robe shimmered and flowed within a cloud of grayish-black flames that rose up from below his feet, up over his height. After sensing a change in the father, the baby calmed his crying and became peaceful, grinning, and giggling, as if knowing his fathers true Kingly aura.

"Time to go, Love," he said, holding out his hand to her. "You girls behave!"

"Damn," Zérnoda mumbled, "I thought he would have forgotten that phrase."

The royal couple ascended to the skies and met up with the captured enemy ship as it passed overhead. Jumping in through a lowered ramp, the royal couple entered in and take off commenced. Shortly before disappearing into the heavens, Sestanon relayed word from the King to the Kostejaanians to commence startup of the time machine and begin importation procedures. Nyfletoné and the others with him knew what to do and carried out the request in full; hundreds of Cavanonians were present to provide overwatch and security, just in case.

The captured enemy ship, dubbed Krylis, now headed straight for Tnemucodas, with hundreds of other Cavanonian ships bringing up the rear. The friendly force now had two days time to get there, before the ritual began.

Chapter 25

Good vs. Evil

At the temple on Tnemucoda, Federoth finally arrived, exited his ship, and made his way through the myriad of forces all gathering in the area surrounding the great sight. Dominion ships emptied out their contents and remained grounded for the time being. Since they did not assume anything or anyone would even attempt to disturb the scene, the alert status of all Dominion forces lessened to a great degree. Nogzakh machines placed themselves along the outer perimeter of the Nosrévis hellions, Xhenutian warriors, and Nomaseri warriors all eagerly prepared for battle, but without the possibility of an enemy, their guard had lowered significantly.

Inside the temple, Nosrévis and Othragon finished preparing the site. With everything in place, all there was to do now was to wait until Cinodas came into alignment. Both creatures smiled at the other, knowing that they were only hours away from the emergence of their ultimate God, their evil creator, and malevolent king.

Federoth entered into the chambers and became somewhat nervous from the scene. He had his own intentions and agenda different from the expectations of the other two. He carefully hid his feelings and thoughts in the back of his mind, knowing that if his own plan were revealed, he might not make it out of here alive against the likes of Othragon, and if Ellononis emerged, Federoth would be finished.

While Federoth entered into the temple and proceeded down into the grand hall, on the far side of the northern mountain range, Adoné and his forces secretly landed and began to unload the thousands of Cavanonian warriors. The stolen white Nogzakh machines remained on board to be taken to the south side of the temple after last minute instructions were given to all the visiting team. Once orders were double-checked, everyone moved into position. The Krylis lifted off and skimmed over the surface of the planet, taking a westerly route around the temple. Once a landing position had been spotted, the ship descended behind two other Dominion ships and began unloaded the friendly machines. Slowly and without challenge, the friendly forces secretly moved into position around the outside of the temple and waited.

While peaking over the northern mountain range, in their red vision, Adoné and Xashsa watched as the cloaked Cavanonian warriors encircled the great enemy forces and held their positions until the signal was given. With the rising anticipation, all friendly forces prepared to engage the enemy as the cloaked ships flew over head and fired on a few the Dominion ships, except for the Krylis. This caused the enemy force to react in extreme surprise and wonder, that was when the Cavanonians engaged their fury. Around the temple, the friendly Nogzakh machines began firing into the backs of the myriad of warriors; a wave of invisible energy began to make its way through the outer perimeter towards the center through the thousands of enemy machines and troops.

Stan, Zach, and other selected Cavanonians swiftly entered into the enemy ships and began their own attack on the unsuspecting enemy; hacking away in their secret shield of invisibility, firing their beefed up swords at key compartmented locations of guidance and fire control systems on board.

Outside, Adoné, Xashsa, Tanazakh, Nivlac, and Maillewvan all flew off towards the temple. From above, the scene below erupted in chaos and turmoil. Enemy body parts flew all over the place, blood misting through the air, and machines firing in all directions not really knowing from which direction the enemy came from. Landing on the slopes of the temple, Adoné found an entrance through a large hole in the ceiling, spacious enough for even Nivlac and Maillewvan to enter through.

"What the hell is going on out there?" Federoth shouted.

"It's an attack you fool," Othragon shouted.

"Federoth," Nosrévis said, "see what it is, the time for my concentration is coming and I mustn't be disturbed."

Federoth took a look outside and saw the chaotic random blasting of the machines and warriors fighting, flying through the air as if an unseen body struck his warriors. Federoth didn't know what to make of it, until he changed his vision to red.

"*SHIT!*" he shouted, "the Cavanonians are here; they are attacking our forces!"

"Engage all forces; have them subdue the enemy, immediately, keep them away from the temple!" Othragon shouted to his Xhenutian warriors, Nosrévis' hellions followed suit and swiftly raced outside to join in the battle.

"Now, Federoth," Nosrévis said, "if you will be so kind as to give me the Sword of Fire, so that I may aid out creator during his emergence."

"Oh, come now," said Federoth as he began to sweat, "What makes you think I have the Firesword?"

"Do not insult my intelligence, Federoth," Nosrévis sneered. "You may have created me, but in a few moments you will not be the lord of my being any more. Our true creator, Ellononis, shall emerge and you shall pay for your deception and treachery."

"I have committed no such acts of treason."

"It is in your thoughts, even now as we speak, you harbor ill-will and great deceit." Nosrévis summoned his great mind powers and seized Federoth's body, forcing him to walk towards his creation. "You think you are formidable, but you are just a foolish imbecile in your thoughts of domination."

"You are not in a position to judge me, Nosrévis."

"No? Then perhaps Othragon will judge you as your thoughts of his attempted assassination are revealed from your inner most mind."

"So," Othragon slammed his foot down onto the stone flooring, "you did bring the Cavanonian enemy to my chambers on Muidiri in order to kill me. Perhaps you two were in league with each other; one to subdue me whilst the other slay me."

"I had no idea the Cavanonian was there," Federoth scoffed, "I did not know."

Nosrévis held his hand up to Federoth and summoned the firesword out of him. Both Nosrévis and Othragon gazed at the splendor of the sword, its mystical aura, and brightly burning flames. As Nosrévis held it in his hand, he motioned for Federoth to kneel before him, and Federoth could do nothing else as his creation still had control over the commanders' body.

"You are even more stupid than I thought, Federoth," Nosrévis hissed as he studied the sword in great detail. "This isn't even the real sword!"

"What? Of course it is," he snarled back.

"It's a fake, you idiot! Can't you see that? There are no markings on it; the real sword has the symbols of the Gods engraved in it by from their own fingernails.

And look at this," Nosrévis spit on the sword, and the fire went out, "the fire of the true crown does not extinguish, ever! What we have here is a clever copy."

"I swear that is the crown, I found it in a ship engulfed in flames. The body of the one who stole it burnt up from the swords energy."

"You have been deceived, Federoth," Nosrévis snarled back. "If this were the true crown, then I would be writhing in flames right now. The King still lives and he is the only one that can wield it, that is, until the ritual begins."

Federoth cursed himself for falling into this trap and exposing himself to these beings who now stood menacingly over him.

"So," his evil creation said, "since you believe this is the sword, and then you shall die by it."

Suddenly, from above Adoné and his party dropped down through the hole and soared to the temple floor, each taking up a position inside.

"Far be it from me to stop you from killing one of my enemies," Adoné said, burning in his own aura of black flames, "why don't you kill yourselves and save me the trouble?"

"*YOU!*" shouted Othragon, "I shall slay you for plaguing this sacred place with your presence."

"Damn, Adoné," Tanazakh exclaimed, "he's a big one!"

"Yeah, you'll have fun with that one," he remarked.

"Ah, I see the Queen has decided to return for another go round," Nosrévis sinisterly smiled. "You should have stayed in the grave where you belong, bitch of a ruler." Nosrévis attempted to perform the same mind control trick on her as he did previously when he murdered her long ago. Adoné sensed this and knew that the only way to counter this was to take Nosrévis' mind off her and onto something else more important.

"I suggest you not waste your time on my Queen," the King said, revealing the true Crown to all, "its time we end this, once and for all."

Gazing at the sword with only one goal in mind, Nosrévis nodded to his opponent.

"I couldn't agree more."

As the evil creation drew his own sword out, he began to strike down at the king and a battle of swords ensued. This took Nosrévis' attention off Federoth, who was now free to do his own battle, choosing the Queen as his opponent. Without giving Othragon a chance to intervene, Tanazakh lunged at him with his exposed battle-axe and began hacking away at the great beast. Nivlac and Maillewvan turned round in time to begin defending themselves against the Xhenutian warriors and hellions entering into the temple area.

Outside the battle raged on, machines on machines, Nomaseri warriors swinging their weapons furiously in the air around them, hoping to strike at the invisible forces wreaking havoc on their forces. In the Dominion ships, Cavanonian warriors had entered and began sabotage operations, decimating the equipment and crew before they had a chance to react. Racing through the halls and passageways, Stan and Zach were having a field day blasting enemy Nogzakhs with their newly designed swords. Smoke filled their way as they continued through the ship. They came to the detention level and began a search for possible other beings wanting in on the action. They opened up a cell and stood in amazement at the sight of Eñala.

"Whoa," Zach remarked, "who is that?"

"Man, she's hot!" Stan commented, almost drooling.

"*Where is he?*" Eñala forcefully screamed, "where is that bastard, Federoth!"

"He's probably in the temple," Zach said.

"That bastard's going to pay for locking me up!" she scorned as she raced through the halls to find a way out.

"Hey wait, let me help you," Stan screamed.

From the Krylis ship, Sestanon released Slagis and instructed him to go to the temple and seek out his master. Slagis—although thought to be himself again—was not himself at all. Inside he had a different purpose in mind and raced off to the temple with his goal impregnated in his soul.

Inside the temple, Adoné fought viciously against Nosrévis, swinging their swords, punching, jabbing, ducking, and attempting to outdo the other in combat. Tanazakh continually struck at Othragon with his battle-axe, jumping, crouching, and thrusting at the hideous beast as he smacked away Tanazakh's futile attempts to meet his flesh with steel. Xashsa took up her stance against Federoth. It was high time he paid for all he had inflicted on the Cavanonian Queen and she would not let him forget his sins.

"We meet again, deceitful traitor," she scorned.

"Xashsa," he replied, "I should have killed you when I captured you long ago, then I wouldn't have to deal with your persistent nagging again."

"Who said anything about dealing with my nagging? I'm going to slit your throat as you did to Aurora!"

"You can try, foul wench, but I am much too powerful for you," Federoth bragged.

"I think not." At that time, Xashsa heard the speech given by Adoné back on Cavanon, the one that said to unleash the inner demon and all its capabilities. She then began transforming, twisting, turning, and morphing into her own towering hideous beast, complete with drooling elongated fangs, menacing red eyes, claws that could tear kindling to shreds, and a will Federoth could not penetrate with his powers.

In a roaring voice, Xashsa howled at him with her mouth agape, spitting up the vile contents of her stomach into his face. Federoth wrenched the residue away from his eyes, and swung his sword at her, but she blocked it with her own blade and repeated his action against him. All inside the temple fought with determination and fervor, vehemently striking at their opponents with all of their inner strength and will to overpower the enemy.

Outside, the battle continued to rage out of control. Aerial flyers swooped down on the Cavanonian forces, friendly white machines threw blasts of energy at the flyers, striking them with precision shots causing the flyers to spiral out of control and onto other enemy machines. Explosions shot up all around, blaster energy shooting in all directions; the scene was filled with genuine pandemonium, a breathtaking sight to behold.

Unbeknownst to them all, inside, and outside the temple, Cinodas had already breached the path of alignment and was within seconds of becoming directly inline with Elaveshan and Tnemucoda.

Inside the temple, Adoné and Nosrévis fought violently against each other, not stopping for a minute to catch a breath or give the other the chance to do so. Simultaneously, as Othragon battled Tanazakh, the great beast fell back and inadvertently bumped Adoné with a hard knock, causing the Sword of Fire to fly out of the King's grip. Slow motion began to fill the enclave as the sword flew through the air, spinning, spiraling, and flickering flames in all directions. Just then, as Nosrévis seized the sword from the air, the alignment of the planets had taken place. All in the temple threw their glances at the engraved region of the doorway to oblivion as the energy within the circle blasted away to reveal what had not been seen in five thousand years. An enormous howling sound filled the enclave and sent hearts beating wildly, blood racing, and caused adrenaline to kick into overdrive. Nosrévis stood at the edge of the opened doorway, holding the Sword of Fire in his left hand. He gazed for a second at his raised arm and felt a tremendous pain rising up through his bones. The left arm bubbled and cracked from something rising up through him. In that few moments of time, another hand came up through the middle of the exposed left arm and split the skin of Nosrévis, grabbing the sword in a new grip of blood-drenched flesh. The rest of Nosrévis' body began to shake and convulse, and at the last second, his body split in half and Ellononis had emerged from within the evil creation, swallowing up the head of his servant as it rose up. A crashing chomp of his massive teeth lined jaws crunched the bones and splattered Nosrévis brains on all in front of him.

Adoné was shocked and astounded for two reasons. One, his worst nightmare had come true and the beast now loomed over him. Two, the worst imaginable enemy now held the crown in his grasp. Ellononis slammed his massive blood-stained feet on both sides of the king, the great evil howled at Adoné from a looming stance over his victim.

While Ellononis walked towards his prey, Slagis had entered into the enclave and had begun to quiver and shake profusely, violent convulsions seized his body, uncontrollably, and he lost his stance, falling to the floor.

"Foul visionary," Ellononis shouted to Adoné, "you've failed to stop my return, you're pitiful highness. I shall take pleasure in devouring your soul and consuming your meager forces. Your reign of rebellion against me is over and I shall once again rule the galaxy without the likes of the filthy line of my brother. Prepare to meet oblivion, King of Cavanon!"

Ellononis brought the Firesword down towards the King and in a flash, Adoné saw his life flicker before his eyes. However, before he had the chance to dwell a second longer on that thought, another sword blocked the downward thrust of the crown, stopping it inches away from Adoné's head.

"I don't think so, *Brother*!" said a new voice, a great voice, one not heard in several millenniums.

All in the temple gasped, their mouths agape, and in shock as Xashsa shouted the name of the new arrival.

"Cavanon!"

"What?" Federoth shouted back, turning to see the great sight of the two original created Sons of the Gods facing off against one another. "Oh, shit!" he exclaimed, "this can't be happening."

"Oh, it's happening, *asshole*!" Eñala shouted as she emerged from behind Xashsa.

Now he had to face two of the women he scorned and mistreated. Instantly he began to feel symptoms of regret and immediately sought to escape from this situation gone terribly bad.

"It seems you've now two to tangle with, Federoth," Xashsa's demon shouted.

"Ah, ladies, can' we talk about this?"

"I'm afraid not," Eñala scoffed, smacking him with a mallet she picked up on her way in. the battle between them raged on, again. The massive force of her blast knocked him through the doorway she had entered, but the actions inside caused them to hesitate to follow their hated scorner.

"Cavanon," hissed Ellononis, "you are too late to stop me, I am already here."

"Who said anything about stopping you?" he swung is own sword at him but his blade met with the firesword. Sparks of fire flew in all directions as the two brothers now engaged in mortal combat.

Adoné rose up and assisted his Anadonian friend in combating Othragon. Othragon whisked his tail around and knocked Adoné over to the left side of the doorway, simultaneously as Cavanon clipped the crown gripping hand off Ellononis left arm. The sword flew high above the doorway, right when Cavanon was about to do in his brother, Othragon spun around, and lunged his own menacing blade through Cavanon's back.

"*NO!*" screamed the King.

Without a moment to lose, Adoné flew through the air, grabbed the crown, and lunged the sword of fire through the head of Ellononis, driving the blade all the way through his neck, piercing his heart. The sudden trauma of the blades power consumed his body inside and caused him to stagger here and there. Adoné clung to the wall above the doorway and remained out of the way trying to grasp the sword from the great beast before he fell into the doorway.

Once the energy of the sword crossed over the threshold of the door, a massive build of up of energy caused a reversal in the doorways continuum. Instantly, winds picked up, flashes of light blinded all inside, and a gripping wave began pulling inward, grabbing the body of Ellononis and sending it inward to meet its new home. The force of the pulling winds sucked everything and every evil being towards the doorway.

Adoné screamed at his friends and wife, "up here, get above it, *NOW!*"

With their remaining strength, the raced to both sides and began furiously climbing upward. Adoné grabbed Cavanon's tremendously weakened body as it began to enter in the doorway, pulling him up and holding him against his body. Xashsa grabbed Eñala and saved her from plunging to her doom. Tanazakh and Nivlac, surrounded by Maillewvan's wings, held on to each other for dear life, but the force of the doorways inward suction was much greater than all could know. At the last second, as their bodies began to slide downward towards the doorway, Stan emerged from the far side of the enclave.

"Whoa! What the fuck?" he exclaimed.

"Stan," Adoné shouted, "dislodge the rock there in the middle, hurry!"

"You got it!" he shouted back.

Using his newly designed sword, Stan blasted the base of the rock with enough energy to cause the rock to vibrate and shake. Within seconds, the rock and Stan flew towards the doorway as all above and around it used their remaining strength to roll out of the way, as the rock crashed into place, sealing up the entrance. The release of pressure was enough to cause all to fall to the ground.

"Whew," Tanazakh blew out the air in his lungs; that was close!"

"Yeah," Adoné said, "good thing Stan was here to save us."

"Hey, check that out, Stan, you're a hero!" Zach patted him on the back.

But the door to oblivion was impatient. The pressure of the inward force began to shake the rock that obstructed the way and at once all knew what had to be done.

"Lets get out of here, now!" Adoné shouted.

Racing out of the temple, the battle outside raged on. Adoné sent a telepathic cry to all Cavanonians to both board the Krylis, or another ship and get off the planet. Without warning or knowledge to the Nogzakh and Nomaseri forces, the battle ceased faster than it began, and they all turned in fright awaiting another strike that would not come. Sestanon already commenced lift off as Cavanonians abandoned the white machines, all of the friendly forces raced to a nearby ship and entered into the hangar bays. As the ship rose up to the clouds, Adoné, and all with him entered in and screamed for the bridge through the radio intercom.

"Sestanon, destroy the planet, NOW!"

"You got it, Sir!"

With the press of a button, the undercarriage of the Krylis opened up and spread outward, revealing the sinister super weapon once used against Cavanon and Earth. In a staggering display of payback, the Krylis fired on the planet and engulfed the surface in flames. The energy of the Krylis penetrated deep into the planet, cracking the surface, mantle, and crust layers, reaching all the way to the core itself. The Krylis sped away through space in time to witness the awesome destruction of the planet as the combined energy of both the Krylis blast and the Doorway of Oblivion married and disintegrated the system, completely.

Afterwards, before anyone had the chance to cheer in, Adoné ordered Sestanon to notify the Kostejaanians to initiate the last stage of the battle.

On Cavanon, Nyfletoné received the word and immediately had his technicians reverse the polarity on the time machine. They had successfully imported over two hundred thousand humans and other aliens out of the clutches of Dominion control and when he received the signal, it had been awhile since anything else had come through.

With Laura, Zérnoda, Kayla, and Sarah all positioned round the machine, their combined concentration and direction of the energy Laura summoned up from Cavanon's planet core, they all threw huge chunks of the crystals into the time machine. The crystals immediately disappeared and a build up of reverse energy began to light up the area.

Waiting until the last second, Laura shouted, "*CUT THE CABLE!*"

Nyfletoné severed the power lines and the machine instantly shutdown.

Out in the time space dimension, the racing, pulsating positive energy of the Crystals clashed with other negative forces and sent the massive thrusts of build up to the waiting time machines still operating as normal.

On Celceloris, the glowing light pierced through the chambers of the importation center and instantly exploded with magnificent force. The power of the energy, mixed with the distortions of intruding time caused an explosive force that ripped through the planets surface, splitting the planet in half. One part blew away and flew out in to space, the other, headed straight for the unsuspecting neighbor planet of Nomaseri. The might of the blast knocked the system out of orbit, sending it twisting and turning out of control on a lone voyage through the galaxy.

On Elaveshan, the might of the combined energy and time caused the system to implode on itself, pulling in the nearby other six planets. With the crashing force of the systems collision, the blast wave of immense proportions sent fragments of the nebulous systems out into space.

The Cinodas surface erupted with explosions of its own as the build up of energy and time distortion cut the planet in half, massively wiping out all life forms on the system.

In a rage of happiness, all creatures on the ships headed for home cheered and shouted, shaking their fists, clapping their hands, patting each other on the back, and hugging their victorious brethren. All engaged in cries of joy and shouts of praise at the miracle of their victory…all except a few in an spacious upper room.

After all had made sure they were without injury, Adoné and Xashsa remained in the room and cared for Cavanon, whose condition worsened greatly. The sadness in Adoné's face told Cavanon many things, but he would have to ease the Kings despair and reassure him.

"Do not be sad for me, my Son," Cavanon said softly, "you could not have prevented destiny from reaching even my hands."

"But, Cavanon, it doesn't seem fair to lose you so soon after coming back," Adoné said sadly.

"What's fair about destiny? Once it is set in motion, there is no way to stop it from advancing to its target. You cannot stop fate. Everything happens for a reason, remember?"

"We may have won the battle against evil, but I've lost the crown, the symbol that has survived ever since it was first given to you." Adoné lowered his head, "How could I have been so reckless as to lose an object that originated from the divine hands of the Gods?"

"Ha!" Cavanon chuckled, "you didn't lose the crown...you just lost a flaming sword of fire."

"What?" Xashsa gasped.

"Excuse me?" Adoné said, with all seriousness coming out in his expression.

"The Sword of Fire was not the crown, my Son; it was a great tool of deception ever since it was given to me."

"Uh, your going to have to explain this," Adoné said, confused, "I mean, everyone wanted it, everyone wanted it for its power, its ability to grant the ruling Cavanonian unlimited power and authority. How can you say it is not what we thought it to be?"

"That is very easy," Cavanon whispered. "When the two fathers made the sword, they gave it to me right in front of Ellononis, letting him know who had authority over who. No one ever said it was the crown of authority, my brother assumed it so. Secretly, and behind the back of the one great father who favored Ellononis, the other father placed another sword into my being, to be absorbed into me. Subliminally, he instructed me to keep it secret and not to reveal its true nature to anyone, not even the most trusted, nearest or dearest to my person would ever know of what I was told. Throughout the ages, each king after me has sworn to uphold and defend the crown, to secret its true identity and bar the truth from others. Without ever knowing the truth, every creature assumed the Sword of Fire to be the true crown because of the enormous power it did contain. When Xashsa had been sent away from Cavanon, the crown went with her, although she knew it not. When she met you, she unknowingly handed the crown of Cavanon to you and gave it to you as a mere gift. There is no fault in her for this, and actually, she should is to be praised for unknowingly keeping the crown safe. It became a part of you from the moment you touched it. When it came into your being, the crown instantly recognized you as the future ruler of my empire, my race. From then on, the crown has been with you, a part of you, and safe."

Adoné squinted his eyes and thought hard about what he said. There was no way he already had the crown, how could he? At that moment, he looked at Cavanon, then Xashsa, and pulled out his secreted blade. There in front of all three of them, the black blade glistened and shimmered in its own black and gray flames, magnificent and awe inspiring. Cavanon slowly raised his hand and grasped the crown along with the King, and together, the blade recognized the two great leaders both of the beginning, and the present.

"You are now the pride of the Ancestors, an example to the Ancients, and a living legend to all who come after you. I have fought many battles, and have had many kings after me who have exemplified my race with grace and majesty, but *you*...you have surpassed the best of them. You were human once and because of your willful change you have graced this galaxy and time with another species of the highest caliber."

Cavanon's voice began to fade, and Adoné rose up Cavanon's head slightly.

"No, please, stay with me, don't go yet."

"I'm sorry, my Son, but I cannot stay with you." Cavanon's light began to fade as well and with one last breath, he imparted this knowledge on this ruling King.

"Your place is set in the heavens, alongside of mine. I shall wait for you, my Son, because you will not arrive for sometime. Pass on my blessings to the race; I will see you again...*farewell*." The whispered voice drifted off into silence.

"No, No!" Adoné cried, but the life force of the father had already departed. With fervent tears and sadness, Adoné lowered his head onto the fathers' chest and grieved. Xashsa tearfully staggered over to the door and opened it. Her immediate look to those in the hallway signified what had transpired, and slowly but surely, the message made its way through the intercom system over the ship.

"Attention on board, attention!" Tanazakh said, choking a bit from the sadness he felt within. "The Great Lord Cavanon has passed on."

He held the intercom button a minute longer, the ear splitting silence pierced through every part of the ship and all remained quiet. Tanazakh was about to say something else, but his emotions got the better of him, and he let go of the intercom switch. All Cavanonians bowed in respect and lowered their heads at the passing of their ultimate King. With the personal blessings of Cavanon himself, Adoné became the new light of the Cavanonian race. They were all blessed with the fact that they participated in the one single battle that not only defeated the great evil and their entire forces, but had also brought about the reemergence of Cavanon himself, a miracle foretold but slightly conjectured on purpose. If they all had known he would reemerge as well, then they all might not have fought so valiantly, so desperately, or willing. They went the full length of the distance and won the day over their tormentors and potential enemies to come.

A day later, after arriving at home, a great ceremony was held to honor Cavanon. At the peak of the Royal Mountain, the King had carved out a glorious grave and placed the Father delicately inside. The mountain peak itself the headstone, and the mountain itself the marker, and all would bask under the glory of the first created Cavanonian.

Standing outside of the main entrance to the Royal palace, Adoné graced all in a wondrous ceremony, praising them for their undying efforts, their trust, and will to defend the race against all enemies. The other creatures in their midst were praised for their aid and assistance and were honored as well. By keeping the crown a secret, all assumed now that Adoné himself was the new symbol of unlimited authority, bestowed on him by the father as a final blessing before he passed away.

Afterwards, a glorious celebration commenced for all on the planet, each and every creature participated and joined in on the festivities. It was a festival to surpass all others. On the throne of Cavanon—Adoné, Xashsa his Queen, the baby prince Solisynas, Zérnoda, and the one little Laura—shined in their majesty as the new realm of the Cavanonians commenced. The day of their freedom from oppression and extinction had finally arrived, and they would enjoy this Royal life for centuries to come.

Epilogue

With Cavanon secure and the enemy defeated, it was safe for all to begin a life free of worry or fear of any sort of retaliation. The two hundred thousand humans rescued from the clutches were successfully sent back to their own time, plus or minus a few years, so that they could once again resume their own lives in their own dimension. If they ever told anyone the real truth of where they had disappeared to, they might be locked up. However it worked out, at least they were safely back in their own time and the worry of being sucked through time again…erased.

On Cavanon, all assumed a normal lifestyle, gathering around their dinner tables, parties, or regular gatherings telling tales of the great battle that would make them legendary as time went on. Enthusiasm swarmed over the surface of the planet in a state never before seen since the first creation of the planet itself, in the days before the great evil made its presence known. The fact that the enemy had been wiped out gave them all a sense of pride and greatness that their race had once again attained the level of fear and formidability that would cause any would be race to think twice before ever coming up against them…again.

In the heavens, high above Cavanon, up over the domain of the Ancients, farther than the heavens themselves, two great Gods sat in wonder and amazement—one happy, the other somewhat happy, but a little flustered. Both peered downward through space and time, enjoying the happiness that abounded in the descendants of their first Son.

"It seems they are more persistent then you gave them credit for," said the first omnipotent being.

"So it seems," replied the other. "Perhaps this would not have happened had it not been for this new species, these...*humans*, as they are called. Without the determination and will of this...*Adoné*, I do not think they would have come this far."

"I am in agreement with your thoughts. Nevertheless, they have earned their place in the universe and will live on peacefully."

"We shall become bored," the second omnipotent being stated, "what say you to a new task for them, one befitting their ingenuity and perseverance?"

"They would think us mad or insane, without purpose." The first being wondered and smiled. "Let us give them a decade or so of peace, then, you may initiate your plan and I shall intercede in my own way."

"It is already in the works," said the great second being, pointing off to a system in the distance of space, a familiar system, one forgotten.

Irol sat his throne room, saddened and very gloomy from the loss of so great a being as Ellononis, his deity. The despair was much too great for Irol to bear and the grief struck at his heart more than he wished. Inside, a whirling torment of anger and frustration arose and sat there in his mind, stagnant and without direction. Now, in their present state, there were no remaining forces except for a few hundred Nogzakh creatures and some hardware. A couple of fighter aircraft remained for force protection, but nothing significant at all. Left alone and isolated in the galaxy, Irol surmised that they would have time to rebuild, since time was all they had now.

"This is most unfortunate," Irol said, "to have lost the most precious of our Gods to oblivion. I will weep for centuries, knowing that never again will I ever have the chance of seeing Ellononis alive."

"Not for another five thousand years, at least," said a voice from the doorway of Irol's illuminated chambers. "I shouldn't expect that you would live that long either, Irol."

"Nor you either, Federoth," he replied. "It seems you have attained the true status of Ruler over this small remaining force of Dominion territory and beings. What shall we do now?"

"We will rebuild, repopulate with other species in the universe more sinister and evil than before. We *must* rebuild," said Federoth, displaying a sinister look of anger in his face, "there is no other choice."

After his making his comments to Irol, Federoth wandered through the subterranean halls of Samajap. His thoughts of failure loomed over his soul and hardened his heart to anything and everything. Torment raced through his heart and he sought to extinguish the pain in one way or another.

In another room, busy with Nogzakh bio-grogs and technicians. Federoth picked up an arm of a recently killed arrival. Carrying the dead arm, which dripped of fresh blood, Federoth stood outside the glass room and watched as the only remaining time machine continue to operate. The time machine survived since it had been shut off before the overload to the time space dimension. Federoth watched as it operated at full swing, slowly but surely importing other creatures as well as humans into this era. Federoth raised the arm up to his mouth, and wrenched off a chunk of the fresh meat, chewing away at the cartilage and fleshy tissues of some male human. His sinister glance glared through the glass and passed the machine, passed all time and space, and in his mind he had thoughts, thoughts worse than before.

"They thought Ellononis was bad," he hissed, "they haven't seen anything...*yet*!"

978-0-595-39958-1
0-595-39958-4

Printed in the United States
52293LVS00003B/202-222